Stage

MIDNIGHT STAGE

Cover Design: Artscandare
Editing: Fox Proof Editing
Formatting: Sheridan Anne

CONTENT WARNING

Midnight Stage is a Dark Rockstar Romance and is not suitable for readers under eighteen years of age. The storyline is not typical of common dark romance themes and can be considered tame. However, it does explore quite graphic scenes that could be uncomfortable for some readers.

Your mental health is important to me so please carefully consider these triggers in determining if this book is right for you.

MIDNIGHT STAGE
CONTAINS

Family death
Grief
Drug use
Homelessness
Explicit sexual content
Graphic violence
Rape (of minor - 16 years old)
Rape (of adult)
Murder
Loss of control

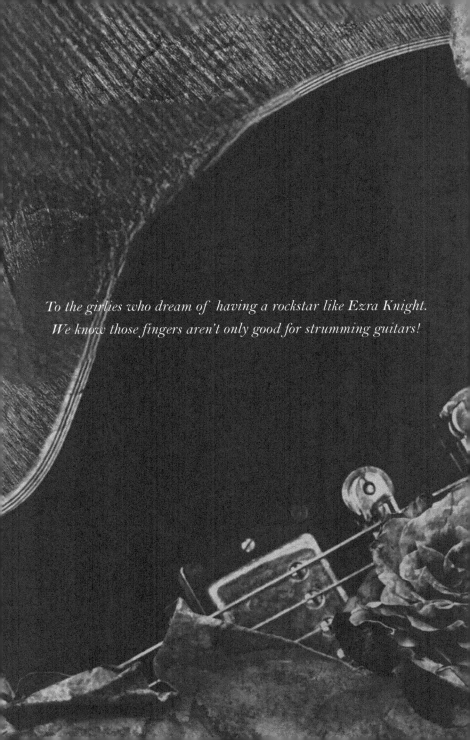

To the girlies who dream of having a rockstar like Ezra Knight.
We know those fingers aren't only good for strumming guitars!

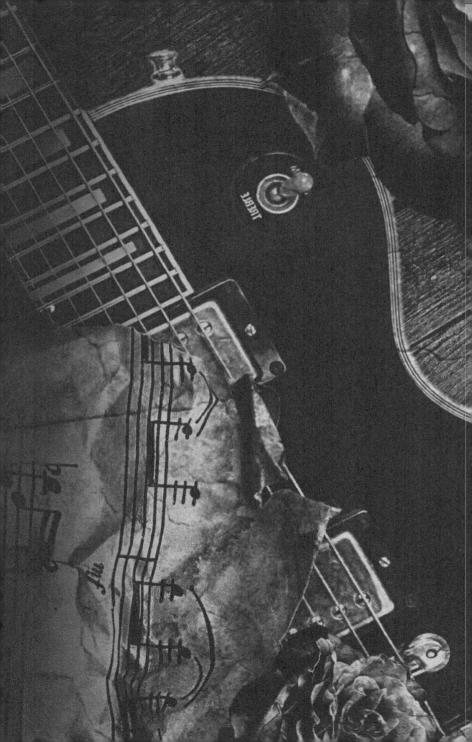

CHAPTER 1

Raleigh

How the hell does one sibling shoot out of the uterus fanny pack and turn into a literal rockstar with millions of screaming fans, while the next kid sludges out of the hoo-ha of life and turns out like me?

Someone make it make sense, 'cause the math ain't mathing. Like, please? I'm not above begging. Just give me some kind of explanation as to how my brother was awarded all the good DNA, and I was left with the scraps. Like, come on! There are a good three years between us, so surely the incubator chamber had plenty of time to cook up some of that good DNA, and yet, it decided to pop out a dud instead.

My brother, Axel Stone—the best friend I've ever had—is quite literally one of the biggest rockstars in the world. He and his best friend—*He Who Shall Not Be Named*—started a band as teenagers, and now Demon's Curse is the number one reason for panties dropping all over the globe.

Axel is out dominating the world with the devil spawn and their bandmates while I'm out here failing every college class I signed up for. Okay, that might be an exaggeration. I'm not failing all of them, but the dean has one hell of a good excuse to kick my ass out of here if the mood strikes, but she won't because her phone wallpaper is a photograph of my brother in his tighty-whities for his big Calvin Klein campaign. Don't ask me how I know that. It was an awkward encounter for both of us. I'm just glad she didn't come at me with a printout and ask me to get it signed like my high school biology teacher did.

On the other hand, I don't have a single talented bone in my body. That was obvious the day Axel handed me his guitar with the grand idea to turn me into a little rockette. Or rock chick. Or . . . Wait. What do they call a girl version of a rockstar? You know what? Who fucking cares? All that matters is that Axel isn't a quitter. He pushes himself until his every dream is in the palm of his hand. That much is clear by his successful career, and yet, the asshole took one look at me scrambling to hold his guitar and gave up within two minutes. He's only a quitter when it comes to me.

Okay, that's not fair. I suppose I'm a little sour. Don't get me wrong, I'm not jealous of my brother, I really couldn't be prouder of him. He has everything he's ever wanted, and he worked his ass off. Me, Axel, and Devil Spawn sat around our tiny little coffee table back home in Michigan and hand made flyers for their very first gig, and now those stupid little flyers are billboards in Times Square that lead to sold-out arenas across the globe.

It's insane.

I just wish he took me with him.

Fuck, I miss that asshole.

Life back home . . . Well, there's a reason I worked my ass off to get into the farthest college from my hometown. Being away from that place was the only dream I've ever had, and now that I've achieved that, I have no idea what I'm supposed to do with myself.

The grand plan is to make it to New York or Los Angeles and go from there. I want to be in the music industry, working behind the scenes on tour prep. I always loved that when I was helping the boys. I excelled at it, and even though I was three years younger than them, I was the one running the show. That's where I was in my element, and while I know Axel will pull all the strings in the world to make it happen, it'd be cool if I could somehow do it on my own. I want to know that I earned it, and I wasn't just handed success as a favor to my big brother.

Letting out a heavy sigh, I push back from the table and tear my gaze away from my laptop screen. I can't look at my shitty grade for another moment. My communications class was my strongest class last semester, and in the space of a few months, I've crashed and burned.

It's depressing. What big label is going to want to hire me on my own merit like this? I'll be the laughingstock of the music industry. Just what I wanted!

"How'd you do?" my best friend Madds asks as we spend our Thursday afternoon sprawled across our cramped apartment.

"I did just about as well as you did on your business exam last week."

"Shit," she says, sucking in a breath and cringing. "That bad, huh?"

An unladylike groan rumbles through my chest, and I drop my forehead to the hard table, instantly regretting it as pain shoots through my brain. "I'm a mess," I tell her, talking directly into the table, my lips smooshed against the wood.

"You're not a mess," she tells me. "You just need a little retail therapy."

I lift my head and stare at Madds as I resist rolling my eyes. By retail therapy, she means candles. She always means candles. It's a sick obsession. They're everywhere and take up every available surface, but there's no denying our home smells like a fortress of magical wonder. But after tripping over a box of them for three months, I had to put my foot down, and now she tries—and fails—to keep them within the confines of her bedroom, but who am I to tell her she can't live her best life?

Getting up from the table, I go to find my bag, knowing that once retail therapy has been mentioned, there's simply no avoiding it. "And to think, I could be on a world tour right now."

Madds scoffs. "Stop trying to kid yourself," she says. "You and I both know you were never going on that tour."

This time there's no resisting the eye roll. She has a very valid point.

Demon's Curse is currently making their way around the globe for their third world tour, and as long as He Who Shall Not Be Named is the front man, I've made a point to stay away. Hell, I know Axel is hurt by the fact I won't listen to their music anymore, but he understands why and forces himself to be okay with it.

Their first tour was huge. They were already experiencing international stardom once their first album dropped, but by the time they wrapped the first tour, they were household names. I was only sixteen and there was no way Axel was going to let me drop out of high school just to go on tour with them, but by the time the tour had wrapped, it didn't matter anyway because everything had already changed.

Ezra Knight. The lead singer of Demon's Curse, A.K.A. Devil Spawn, and Axel's best friend. Also often referred to as He Who Shall Not Be Named, but I suppose I ruined that now. Maybe it should be He Who Shall Not Be Named Out Loud.

He may or may not be the man I've been desperately in love with since I was thirteen years old, the one I still can't seem to shake all these years later. He was sixteen when he first came around, and every time I looked at him, I knew that he would be someone special.

He was everything to me—the other half of my soul. We were the sweetest symphony, so perfectly in sync, but we were too young. *I was too young.*

Ezra is the textbook definition of *right man, wrong time.*

By the time I was sixteen, we were inseparable. He captured me in a way that would ruin me forever, but he was always careful not to completely cross that line. He kept the distance I needed to be respectful of my age, and while sometimes I hated it, I'm grateful for that now. We knew there would come a time when those limitations didn't seem so bad, and I held on to that hope tighter than I've ever held on to anything in my life.

Everybody knew it. We were soul mates. The perfect couple that nobody else could even attempt to compare to. I was so lucky to have him, to have experienced him in his rawest form. To know him and to be the woman . . . or the girl he loved.

Not knowing him anymore hurts.

Hearing the songs I know are about me . . . hurts.

But knowing that the epic, all-consuming love we once had will never exist again in this lifetime . . . Well, that fucking kills me.

Maybe I was wrong to assume that Axel is the only lucky one in the family. Maybe we're all allotted a certain amount of luck in a lifetime, and while Axel is out there using his in the best way possible, I used up all of mine on a man who would disappear in the blink of an eye.

That first tour should have been the best moment of our lives, but the second they packed their bags and walked out the door, the woman I could have been disappeared with them.

Everything changed, and almost in an instant, Ezra Knight became a stranger. He was no longer mine. *He was theirs.*

The boys were gone, and I was left alone . . . *with him.* Every day was a fight to survive, and I'll never forgive them for leaving me behind. It wasn't their fault. They couldn't have known what was going to happen, nor did I ever whisper a word about it. I know it's irrational to blame them for leaving me behind to endure that, but I still do.

If they never left . . . Fuck.

After their first tour, they made LA their home and got straight to work on their second album. Axel came home to check on me every now and then, but Devil Spawn never did. It's been six years since I've seen him in the flesh. But when it comes to Ezra Knight, there is no avoiding him. He's everywhere I go. Every time I turn on the radio. In my Spotify recommendations. News articles. Magazine covers. There's no escaping the magnitude of Ezra Knight.

He was like a ghost that had whisked through my life and then left me in shambles. Maybe I was a stupid kid for assuming he'd come home to me after experiencing the crazy whirlwind of a tour. All the fans. The drugs. The parties. I'm sure all the guys were screwing their way across the globe, and yet I held out hope that he might have still been mine.

God, I was a fool for giving him my heart. He didn't even have the decency to give it back. He just collected it like another one of his many guitars—something to be played with but never cherished.

"Your car or mine?" Madds asks, pulling me out of my internal spiral. She knows what mentioning the tour does to me.

"Uhhh, you drove last time. Let's take mine."

"Oh, thank fuck," she says with a heavy sigh. "Mine's on empty, and I really don't have the cash this week for gas."

I can't help but laugh. "But you have cash for retail therapy?"

"Candles are a necessity. They're a way of life," she throws back at me, having the audacity to appear offended. "Gas isn't."

"You're an idiot. You know that, right?"

"That may be true, but I'm an idiot with amazing candles."

Ten minutes later, we're flying down the road with the windows down and the music blasting from the speakers. My long, auburn hair whips around my face as we scream the lyrics, and a sense of peace settles in my chest. Thoughts of stupid rockstars and failed exams fall from my mind. Instead, I focus on our retail therapy.

I'm not exactly swimming in money. Don't get me wrong, Axel has given me a credit card and insists that I use it for whatever I want or need, but I don't. Using the money he worked hard to earn doesn't sit right with me. I don't like the thought of taking advantage of his success, so instead, I work for everything I've got. Mostly.

Okay, fine. When Axel insisted he pay for my college tuition and rent, I couldn't resist. And not just because it sounded like every girl's dream, but because the thought of getting out of my hometown was simply too good to refuse. Staying there wasn't an option, and if he'd offered to pay for me to live in a cardboard box on the street, I would have accepted that too, assuming the cardboard box was anywhere but my hometown. The day I go back there will be a cold day in hell.

We creep closer to the mall, and as the music fades and a new song begins, the familiar chords played by my brother have my back stiffening. My heart begins to race as an immediate sweat begins taking over my body.

Oh no.

I have all of three seconds before *his* sweet words blare through my speakers—lyrics he wrote while sitting at the foot of my bed after dreaming about the life we could have had together. I was only fifteen, but the memory is etched into the fabric of my soul and will live there until my dying days.

"Shit. Shit. Shit," Madds rushes out in a panic, wildly slamming her hand against the skip button on my dash, only to slip and smash her fists against the button for the hazard lights. "Oh fuck."

The song skips to the next, and as another Demon's Curse song fills the air, the panic becomes a fucking mockery. "Shit. I'm sorry," Madds says, her brain short-circuiting as her hand dances between the skip button and the hazard lights, not sure which situation to fix first.

I go to help, reaching for the hazards, but our hands bump together, prolonging the whole situation, and as my panic turns into blind terror, I prepare myself for what I know is coming in *three . . . two . . .*

A call cuts through my Bluetooth, and I have no choice but to pull over and give myself just a moment to ease my racing heart. "Holy fuck," I breathe, trying to get myself back on track, only to notice the call is from Axel.

Now don't get me wrong, I absolutely adore my brother. He's my best friend and the greatest person I've ever known, but when I'm around Madds, I go to extraordinary lengths to try and avoid him. While she is incredible in every possible way, her only downfall is her inability to mask her super-fan tendencies.

Demon's Curse is her go-to for everything. She loves them, just like every other soul on the planet, and I really can't fault her for it. They're that good, fucking excellent actually. But I love her for trying to downplay her obsession while she's around me.

Not entirely recovered, I let the call ring out and wait a few moments to feel somewhat human again. I'm not always thrown off course when their music smacks me in the face, but every now and then, I'm caught off guard, and on a day like today, my fragile little heart simply can't take it.

"You know," she muses as I finally pull back out onto the road. "You really shouldn't leave Axel hanging like that. He worries about you. You should definitely call him back."

I give her a blank stare, knowing there are so many things on the tip of her tongue. "Really? That's what you want to say right now?"

Her eyes all but bulge out of her head. "Hell no," she blurts. "That song, 'Hypothetically Yours' is about you, but you know that, right? Like that's insane! I wish I had some sex god who wrote songs like that about me. So fucking dreamy. And to think he was only eighteen when he wrote it."

Madds lets out a heavy sigh and melts back into her seat. "Okay," she says after a moment. "I think I got it out of my system."

I eye her warily. I've been fooled by that one before, only to end up listening to her Demon's Curse word vomit for three hours straight. "You sure?" I ask, arching a brow.

"Positive."

I nod in relief and focus on the road. 'Hypothetically Yours' is strictly a song I don't talk about because it's so much more than just a song. It's my whole heart in words—words forged out of a soul-crushing, intense kind of love that only comes around once every few lifetimes. I've never told her about the day he wrote it, never even whispered a word about it because, while the song is out there for the world to scream at the top of their lungs, the story behind it belongs exclusively to me and Ezra.

"So, you're really just going to leave your brother hanging like that?" Madds asks a moment later. "You know how Axel worries."

I side-eye her again, knowing she's right, but like I said, I specifically go out of my way to avoid Axel while in her presence. I cringe, weighing up my options. "Can you be cool?"

Her mouth pops open, feigning offense. "Say what?! Me? Of course I can."

"Really? Because last time you admitted to stealing clothes out of his suitcase and sleeping in them for three weeks straight after he visited me."

"Can you blame me? It's Axel freaking Stone."

"No, it's not. It's my brother."

"Yeah, who is also Axel Stone."

I groan and press his name on my car screen before I get a chance to regret it. The call barely gets a chance to ring a whole time when Axel's deep tone rumbles through my car speakers. "Sup turd."

I let out a heavy sigh. "I'm twenty-two. You can't call me that anymore."

"You're my sister. I'll be calling you a turd until the day I die."

I roll my eyes and can't help but notice the way Madds practically shakes with excitement beside me. "Just so you know, you're on speakerphone so don't say anything incriminating."

"Let me guess," he says, instantly turning on the rockstar charm.

"Madds?"

Her eyes light up like Christmas morning. "How'd you know?" she gushes, her cheeks turning beet red.

"I can always tell when there's a beautiful woman around," he says, making me want to gag. "Call it a gift."

"Oh my god! You're so funny," she says. "How's the tour going? Wait. Where are you? Australia?"

"Nah. Australia is up next. We just wrapped our last show in Singapore."

"Wait, like . . . just now?" she asks, getting all ditzy.

"Few hours ago."

My brows furrow, and I glance down at the time. It's already late afternoon here, so that must mean . . . "Shit, Axel. What time is it over there?" I demand. "Your shows always end around midnight, and if it's been a few hours . . . Why aren't you back in your hotel room sleeping?"

An amused laugh sounds through the car speakers. "I'll give you one guess."

My face falls, realizing he's been spending his night indulging in the rockstar lifestyle. Alcohol, drugs, and easy women. And if that's how he spent his night, then I can guarantee that He Who Shall Not Be Named Out Loud has too. Wonderful.

"Gross," I mutter, hoping we can get this call back on track. "Why are you calling me so late then? Is everything okay?"

"Yeah, everything's sweet," he says. "I was just checking up on you. You said you were getting your exam results back today. How'd that go?"

"We're almost at the mall," Madds offers.

"Ahhh, fuck. It didn't go well? Retail therapy?"

"Yup," I say, popping the *p*.

"Candles?"

"You know it," Madds sings.

Axel sucks in a breath, the sound hissing between his teeth, and I can imagine the way he would have awkwardly grasped the back of his neck. "Shit. Okay, umm . . . You wanna talk about it?"

"Nah, I'm good—"

I hear a noise in the background, something kind of like a door opening. "Shit. Didn't realize you were in here," a familiar voice says, penetrating right through my soul. There's a slight pause, giving me just a second to remind myself to breathe before it comes again. "Fuck . . . that her?"

Axel lets out a heavy sigh. "Shit. Yeah, man. Just . . . just give me a minute, alright?"

I hear the door close, and while it's a subtle thud that fills the car, to me, it feels like a bullet right through the chest. "I'm sorry," Axel says. "You good?"

I plaster a fake smile across my face as the heaviness weighs me down. "Yeah, I'm good," I lie as Madds reaches across the center console and grabs my hand, giving it a tight squeeze. She's capable of reading me so easily.

"Sure?"

"Yeah, listen, we're just pulling into the mall parking complex," I say, lying right through my teeth again. "The call will probably drop, but I'll check in with you tomorrow before your flight to Australia."

"Okay, yeah," he says, his tone shifting with a shallow heaviness, making it clear he knows I'm lying but not being able to do anything about it. "I'll talk to you later. Be safe, okay? And Madds?"

"Yeah?" she says, perking up.

"Look after my sister."

"You know it!"

Ending the call before it somehow gets harder, I let out a heavy breath. "You really okay?" Madds asks, a deep skepticism in her tone as my eyes begin filling with tears.

"No," I admit, needing to pull over again. "Just need a second."

"Okay. Take your time."

I blow out a heavy breath, my cheeks inflating like balloons, and in a flash, I hit the gas and whip the car back around. "Woah," Madds says, gripping the door. "Where are we going?"

"Home."

"But . . . but candles."

"Fuck the candles, Madds," I say, pressing a little harder on the gas. "We're getting drunk."

CHAPTER 2

Ezra

Rain pours over us, sticking my black button-down to my open chest, as the eager crowd roars, and I step back from the microphone before breaking into the guitar solo of our final song. It's been a wild night. Hell, a wild fucking week, and now the rain only makes it better. There's nothing I love more than a rain show, and the fact that we're in Australia is the fucking cherry on top. These Aussies know how to go off. They're always our loudest crowd, and performing for them always leaves me on a fucking high.

It's the best type of chaos.

Tonight is our final show for the Australian leg of the tour, and while I live for this shit, I'm more than looking forward to the next two weeks of rest before we hit up Europe. Nobody ever warns you how exhausting these world tours are. Night after night, performing in a different city. Getting sick is not an option, and if we're unlucky enough to fall victim to the common cold—tough luck—the show must go on.

The fans come first. That's been our mentality right from the start, and fuck they're loyal because of it.

Most of them have been with us from the moment our first single 'Hypothetically Yours' was released. It's been a fucking whirlwind since then with our fanbase growing day by day. Our label saw the hype building around us, fast-tracked our album release, and within two months, we were told we were going on tour. And fuck, that tour was a mess. We were barely nineteen, most of us had never even left our hometown, and there we were performing for sold-out stadiums.

We had instant stardom, and honestly, most of us didn't know how to handle it.

The girls. Partying. Drugs. Alcohol. Anything that was thrust in our faces, we took. Our faces were splashed across every magazine, our cell numbers were leaked by the press, our personal lives were exploited for entertainment, and once the fans figured out our home addresses, it was hell on Earth. For a while at least. It didn't take long for us to put together a proper team we could trust, and after that, it was smooth sailing.

We lived it up like fucking gods, and by the time we were wrapping our first tour, not one of us recognized ourselves. But this tour is our third rotation around the globe, and we've learned from our mistakes . . . sort of.

Management caters to our needs and doesn't allow us to run rampant like we did in our early days, and on top of that, we've learned how to say no. No to the media. No to management. No to assholes who use us for their own gain. It was a learning curve, but you don't get to where we are by letting others walk all over you.

It's a balancing act, and for the most part, it works. Though come tonight, I can guarantee that balancing act is going to be sent flying off course because I don't intend to fly back to the U.S. without partying it up one last time with these wild Aussies.

Two and a half more minutes, and we'll be done.

My fingers work madly over the strings as the sound of my solo breaks the fucking sound barrier. Okay, not really, but I like to think it does, and judging by the way the crowd screams for more, I like to think they think so too.

My solo ends, and not needing my electric guitar for the rest of the song, I whip it around to my back and toss my pick toward the crowd before grabbing the microphone and leaning into it.

The lyrics fall from my mouth like second nature, and I watch as girls scramble in the crowd, fighting over the pick I just tossed down to them. I can't help but smirk. It's the same everywhere we go. Any scrap of us they can get their hands on, they'll fucking try.

Me on lead vocals and rhythm guitar, Axel on lead guitar and backup vocals, Dylan Pope is our bass man, and of course Rock Huxley on the drums. The four of us make up Demon's Curse, and as of six months ago, we became the top-selling band of the century. Not going to lie, hearing that news right before leaving on a world tour might have been the highlight of my career.

I'm just entering the final chorus of the song when a woman sitting on her man's shoulders rips her tank up, letting her big ol' titties fly free, and just like every time we get flashed, a stupid grin tears across my face. It happens every show without fail, and yet every damn time, I turn to Axel and watch as he struggles to keep his composure.

What can I say? The man is addicted to tits. He's like a kid in a candy store, and if he could, he'd crowd surf off the stage and motorboat her. But the moment his gaze lifts to mine, it's fucking over for us.

We giggle like teenagers who've skipped out on third-period history, hiding behind the science building and looking at porn because someone said something about a rusty trombone, and you just had to figure out what the fuck they were talking about.

I try to remember that I'm supposed to be a professional, but I barely get the last few words of the chorus out. Anyone would think this shit would bounce off me by now, but apparently, no amount of years as a fucking rockstar and having girls throw themselves at me is going to keep me from laughing at a pair of jiggly tits.

Who would have known?

The show comes to an end, and after bidding farewell to our incredible audience, we finally put an end to the Australian leg of the tour.

It was amazing. Such a fucking rush.

Performing like this for sold-out stadiums across the world is more than just a dream come true. There's only a small handful of people who get to say they can do this for a living, and it's the best feeling in the world.

The guys and I stumble our way backstage. I can't speak for them, but the rush of the show has left me feeling alive. It's like inhaling a line of coke without having to deal with the comedown that follows. Though to be fair, coming off weeks of back-to-back shows always leaves me feeling hungover, which is exactly why these next two weeks of rest couldn't come sooner.

My downtime is writing time, and with the tour wrapping in a few months, we'll be heading back into the studio to work on a new album. When that happens, I need to be prepared.

I'm the only one in the band who writes. The others dabble from time to time, but they've never felt confident enough to put their words forward. So far, it seems to be working for us, and to be honest, I don't think I'd be comfortable singing someone else's words. When I write, it means something. They're not just words on paper. Every song we've put out comes directly from my soul, and it's the only way I'm able to find peace within myself.

I'm a fucking wreck. Have been since the day I packed my bag and left Michigan behind.

For me, writing lyrics and putting them into songs is my diary. Eventually, every thought and emotion that's torn through me becomes part of a song. It's my coping mechanism, and so far, it's the only one I've found that works. The only issue is, there's only one person who creates such a stir within me and is capable of bringing out those words, and the longer I go without seeing her, the harder the songs become.

It's been six years, but there's no turning back now. She needs a better man than me, someone who can give her more than just a headline in a bullshit magazine. There was a time I thought I could be that for her, but the realities of my life and how I deal with it made it clear that this isn't what she deserves.

She should have so much more than a life on the road, being reduced to a tabloid story, being mistaken for a groupie, and missing out on normal school and college experiences. Rae has the potential to conquer the whole damn world, and I wasn't about to subject her to a life of following me from city to city, being nothing more than my girl.

Crashing through to our small dressing room backstage, I go to grab my shit, more than ready to get out of here, when the rush of thoughts from back home has me reaching for my notepad. "Yo, wait up," I tell the guys, searching every corner of the dressing room for a pen.

As if reading my mind, Axel pulls a pen from a bag and shoves it into my hand, knowing I won't be able to relax until every word is scribbled into my notepad. It'll be a mess of words tonight, but on the flight back to LA tomorrow, I'll turn that mess into art, and by spring, every household across the globe will be singing these words.

Getting to work, I flip to a new page and scrawl the words across the paper while Axel peers over my shoulder, reading the jumbled mess. "Fucking hell," he mutters, reading the overly sexualized lyrics. "This better not be about my sister."

A grin tears across my lips. The poor fucker. He's spent years performing my songs, and while there are a handful that are very clearly about Raleigh, like "Hypothetically Yours," the rest he has no clue about.

I tell him stories, let him think they're nothing more than random scenes that play out in my head. But joke's on him because the truth of the matter is, every last song I have ever written is about her.

It's always her.

Our first single off our current album, *Bleed for Me*, is our opening song for the tour. I told the guys that it was inspired by a wild night with a French woman, but in reality, it's about physically needing someone so bad that you crumble because you can't have her. It's about not being able to breathe without her, desperately needing to hear her soft moans, her touch on your skin, her lips on yours. It's about raw, passionate sex, and every word that comes out of my mouth when I first hit that stage comes from those lonely nights when I fantasize about having Raleigh in my bed.

Ha. The fact that it's one of Axel's favorites only makes it funnier. If only he knew he was singing backup vocals to a song about nailing his little sister. Not that we ever had the chance . . .

Rock moves in on my other side and glances over the lyrics before laughing at Axel. "Dude, that's fucked up," he says before crashing on the couch and kicking his feet up. "I don't know how you do it, man. If this bastard was writing songs like that about my little sister . . ."

My grin widens as he lets his words trail off, and as I finish off the thoughts tumbling around inside my head, I do my best to zone out as the guys rave about how epic that show was. We're all fucking exhausted, but that's not going to stop us from heading out to the rooftop bar that looks out over the Sydney Harbour and making the most of our last night in this beautiful country. Just as soon as we get back to the hotel and have a chance to get out of our rain-soaked clothes, that is.

Content that I've gotten everything down, I grab my notebook and shove it into my bag, not trusting it with anyone. I take this notebook everywhere because I never know when the inspiration might hit, but having it everywhere often means leaving it everywhere. There have been multiple occasions when I've left it behind in a restaurant, a dressing room, a train, hell, even at a fucking urinal. But even those times when I've left it in another city, nothing has stopped me from going back and getting it. These words are liquid gold, and if it were just my career riding on it, I probably wouldn't be so pedantic about it, but it's all of ours. If I don't write good shit, the boys will suffer for it, and we're not even close to being done yet.

Leaving the arena, we make our way back to the hotel, and within twenty minutes, we're ready to hit up the VIP party at the rooftop bar.

There are fans spilled out onto the road while security works overtime trying to keep them contained, and as our SUV pulls to a stop outside the venue, each of us plasters on our fake smiles. "Showtime, boys," Dylan announces, being the first out the door.

The crowd roars for him, and I watch his performance as he strides toward the door. He's the best at turning it on for the fans. We could have walked through hell and back, and he would still have the energy to engage with his fans.

Rock scoots out of the SUV next, followed by Axel, and then

finally, it's my turn.

It's a short walk from the SUV to the venue entrance, but that short walk seems to take a lifetime. Girls weep as I try to engage with as many fans as possible. I sign autographs and instinctively lean in when people shove smartphones in my face.

Women hang off me, refusing to let go after they've had their photo, and when one woman screams directly into my ear, I call it quits and continue to the door where the boys are waiting for me.

We ride the elevator right to the top, and the moment we step out into the VIP party, the place goes off. The DJ welcomes us over the microphone, and the eager partiers lose their shit.

Dylan fucking loves it, putting his hands up and striding through the roaring crowd as our manager beelines for the bar, hopefully to tell them our drink preferences with clear instructions to keep them coming.

The music is loud, and I'm grateful the DJ steers clear of our songs. There have been far too many times that we've walked into a party, hoping to relax, only for the DJ to play our songs. I understand it, of course. Plus, the fans love that shit, but when I'm out at a party, I'm done performing.

We're ushered into a private area that looks out over the incredible city, and Rock immediately flops down on the couch. "Fuck me," he says with a heavy sigh, bracing his hand behind his head as he gazes out at the eager partiers. "I'm wrecked."

I couldn't agree more.

I drop down beside him as Axel and Dylan hover by the balcony that overlooks the city. They gaze out at the sight, and I can't lie, it's fucking beautiful. We've been in Sydney a handful of times, seen all the sights, and done all the wildlife experiences, but there's nothing quite like the city lights at night.

When our drinks arrive, the boys waste no time diving in.

Dylan remains by the balcony but turns to take in the two girls dancing by us, and judging by the desire in his eyes and the way they look back at him, there's no denying that he'll be taking both of them to bed tonight. A smirk lingers on his lips. "What are the chances they're down to get fucked up?"

Rock groans. "Just keep it private," he says. "We don't need pictures of you snorting coke splashed across the internet first thing in the morning."

"Since when am I not discreet?" he questions, already moving toward them. "Don't worry about me, boys. I always keep it classy."

I roll my eyes and drop my head forward, and even over the sound of the raging music, I can still hear their giggles as Dylan approaches.

Management ushers a few women into our space, and while they immediately drop down beside me, it's Rock who gives them the attention they want. "You wanna have a little fun?" the girl beside me whispers in my ear as she drapes half of her body across me.

I glance up at her, and the look in her eye suggests she's not talking about a quick fuck. "What do you have?"

"Molly. Coke."

Damn. It's fucking tempting, but with so many witnesses here, I won't risk it. Like Dylan said, we keep it classy. Most of the time. While in private at home or in the studio, that's different. Usually coke is my go-to, ecstasy's never sat well with me, and with that long-ass flight tomorrow, I don't want to be dealing with the fallout that comes from that.

"Nah, baby. I'm good."

"You know, if you're not down for that kind of fun, I'm sure I could please you in other ways."

"I'm sure you could."

Her tongue rolls over her bottom lip, and for a split moment, I consider taking her into the bathroom and seeing what those lips look like closed around my cock. Only Rock's arm flings out in front of my face, pulling my attention from the girl beside me, and leaving the thoughts of her mouth on my cock to fade from existence.

"The fuck are you doing, bro?" Rock questions.

My brows furrow, following his outstretched hand toward Axel on the balcony to find the fucker with his phone out, snapping photo after photo of the view below. A fond smile pulls at my lips. We're not the kind of guys who need to take photos like this, so I understand Rock's tone, but I also know exactly why Axel's doing it.

"She always wanted to see the Opera House at night," I respond before Axel has the chance.

The woman beside me looks my way, and I suddenly feel so fucking dirty for having her this close. "Who's she?"

I don't entertain her question. It's none of her business, but it needs no clarification for Rock. The boys know exactly who I'm referring to, and I'm sure anyone who's truly listened to my lyrics and followed the stories from our beginning would have been able to put the pieces together.

Getting up, I join Axel on the balcony and look out at the stunning view. It truly is beautiful.

"She would love this," Axel mutters, a clear heaviness weighing him down.

"How's she doing?"

He shrugs his shoulders. "Honestly, I don't know. She doesn't really open up to me much anymore. She's hurting, but she puts on a show."

"Always trying to be brave."

"You know it." He's quiet for a moment before letting out a heavy sigh. "I know those first few years were hard on her after we left, but I thought at some point she'd settle into a new routine and find her purpose. And honestly, I'm really not sure she did. I think she feels lost, and I think she still hates me for leaving her behind."

"If she hates anyone for leaving, it's me," I say bluntly, repeating the words that have circled my head for six long years. Raleigh Stone, the other half of my soul, fucking despises me. "But you're wrong. She doesn't hate you. You're her big brother, and she always looked at you as though you were larger than life. As for feeling lost . . . don't we all?"

"I don't know, man," he says, sipping his drink. "This . . . It's different. She hasn't been the same since we left. We abandoned her, and it broke something in her soul."

I nod, knowing it all too well, but I repeat the same old excuses because they're the only things that help me get by. "She would have been miserable following us from city to city. This wasn't the life for her. She needs to finish high school and college, and then she's going to forge her own path."

"Yeah, I hope so."

"She's always been strong, Ax. She'll pull through."

His gaze shifts back to the view, and our conversation falls silent, leaving me struggling to breathe. I've always told myself that we left her behind for good reason, but Ax is right. We abandoned her. There's no other way to put it.

I abandoned the girl I always thought I'd spend the rest of my life with.

Fucking hell.

The realization is like a shot straight through the chest, and before I can even get a good conscious thought through my head, I turn on my heel and stalk back to the chick on the couch. "Yo," I say, watching her head snap up. "You still wanna get fucked up?"

She nods and gets to her feet, and not a moment later, my hand is pressed against her lower back, leading her into a private room. My manager steps into the room, guarding the door, and just like that, she slips her hand into her bra and pulls out a small bag of white powder.

"You sure?" she asks. "You didn't seem so down before."

I nod, feeling the desperation gnawing at my chest.

I abandoned her.

"Just do it," I tell her. "Rack me up."

CHAPTER 3

Raleigh

My knee bounces as I wait for my communications class to end. I've been a wreck ever since I emailed my professor after my last exam, requesting a chance for some extra credit or a re-do of the exam to try and claw my way out of the hole I seem to be digging. He emailed me back saying he'd like a chance to review my work over the past year to see if my failing results are a lack of understanding or a lack of asserting myself.

He said he'd have an answer for me in a week's time, and over the past week, all I've been able to focus on is the fact he suggested I'm just not trying hard enough. Because let's be honest, it's not that I don't understand the coursework. I know what I'm doing, and I understand the work. Hell, I'm spending every waking hour studying as well, yet when it comes time to sit down for these exams, I just . . . can't.

I bomb every time. It's like there's some kind of mental wall that slams down and prevents me from going any further along this journey. It's as though I'm doomed to remain as this nothingness I've become, no matter how hard I work to claw my way out.

This is my only hope to save myself. I have no choice but to pass this class. Giving up and returning home isn't an option. I'm in this for the long haul.

The class ends, and I watch as the students around me begin packing up. There are a million of them, and it seems to take forever before they've cleared out enough to offer me some sort of privacy to talk with the professor.

Getting up from my small space in the amphitheater, I make my way down to the professor, my whole body shaking with nerves. I clutch my bag tightly, each step bringing me closer and closer to doom.

By the time I reach the bottom step, the room is completely cleared out, and as I somehow manage to hold my composure, I approach his desk. "Excuse me, Professor," I say, inching toward him. "My name is Raleigh Stone. I emailed you last week in regard to the recent exam. I was wondering if you—"

"Had the chance to review your work?" he finishes for me, not looking very pleased to see me standing here as he pushes his glasses up his nose. "Yes, Miss Stone, I have, and let me tell you, I am not impressed."

I swallow hard. "I'm sorry?" I mutter, not having expected him to be quite so bold.

SHERIDAN ANNE

"I have been considering your request all week, and I am honestly dumbfounded," he says. "Where on this green Earth do you get off thinking it's acceptable to request a re-do of an exam? You are one of three hundred students, and I don't know if it's because you believe you are superior to the other students taking my course who are actually putting in the work, but in no way, shape, or form, would it be fair for me to allow you to re-take this exam. It was designed to test your current knowledge and understanding of the course work, and a re-do would be nothing but a slap in the face to those who are actually putting in the effort to pass this course."

"I . . . that's not at all what—"

"Being the sister of a rockstar does not give you advantages. This isn't high school. This is the real world, Miss Stone, and unfortunately, it's time for you to adjust your expectations. You won't sail through riding on the coattails of your brother's success. If you wish to succeed, put the effort in just like everyone else."

"With all due respect, Sir. You are making an unfair assumption about me," I tell him. "It was not my intention to suggest I get advantages over the other students. I've worked hard to ensure that doesn't happen, and I see now how foolish it was to ask for a re-do of an exam. I didn't look at it in that light. However, I don't believe it's an unfair request for extra credit. I'm sure if you look back, you will see that I am a good student. I work hard, and I believe I have a fair understanding of your course. I really want to pass this class, Sir. I need to pass."

The professor sits back in his seat, his gaze locked on me as the silence in the room becomes unbearable. "Okay, Miss Stone," he finally says. "I will allow you one final chance to prove that you belong here. Let me down, and you'll leave me with no choice but to fail you. Is that clear?"

"Yes, Sir," I say with a heavy sigh of relief. "I won't let you down."

"See that you don't."

I scram, all but racing out of there before he gets a chance to change his mind. It wasn't exactly how I imagined that conversation to go, and I'm not going to lie, the assumption that I would try to use my brother's fame as a free ride through college is offensive. But what matters is that he's willing to give me a chance.

All hope has not been lost.

Assuming the professor will email my extra credit work, I make my way back home after quickly stopping for a late lunch.

It's been a day, and after being blindsided by the pictures splashed all over social media of Demon's Curse partying it up in Sydney after wrapping the Australian leg of the tour, I'm so ready to call it a day. It's bad enough seeing pictures of your brother snorting coke off a hooker's tits, but to see just how fucked up Devil Spawn was . . . Well, those are the pictures that always kill me.

Ezra is far from being the incredible man I fell in love with. The man who would sit at the end of my bed and scrawl lyrics while I talked shit. The man who held me after my mother died. I don't think the real Ezra Knight even exists anymore, and nothing is more gut-wrenching than that.

Getting home, I make my way into my bedroom and drop my

bag onto my bed before pulling out all of my books. If I'm going to pass this damn class, then I'm going to have to get my shit together and learn how to block out the world around me. I can't allow myself to fall to pieces every time someone captures Ezra in a compromising position, otherwise, I'll never live a normal life.

Hell, it's been six years. Why can't I seem to move past this already? He's nothing but a figment of my imagination.

I start cramming as though I were preparing for a test and going over everything I've ever learned in my comms class, even the stuff I feel I already know better than my own black heart. I won't fail this class. Like I said, it's not an option. Not just because I owe it to Axel after he so generously paid my tuition fees, but because going back to that house in Michigan is something I will never do.

It's just after five when I hear Madds come in, and as I track her footsteps through our small apartment, I lift my gaze, sensing her right outside my door. She kicks it open a moment later with a huge candle in her hand and her nose shoved into it. She inhales deeply. "Holy shit, girl. You have to smell this. It's Fireball."

I arch a brow and stare at her as she hurries around my bed and shoves her brand-new candle in my face. I take a whiff, and a stupid smirk stretches across my face. "Those of us who aren't alcoholics refer to that as cinnamon."

She rolls her eyes. "Those of us who make a point to enjoy the smaller things in life would disagree," she tells me.

My jaw drops. "I do enjoy the smaller things in life."

"Says the girl currently sprawled across her bed on a Monday afternoon, buried under a pile of textbooks." I stare blankly, and she puts the candle down on my bedside table before sweeping the books off my bed to make space for her ass. "Is this because of your comms class?"

I nod as a heavy sigh tears from deep inside of me. "Yep. He's giving me one last shot to pull my shit together, otherwise, he's failing me."

"What? That's bullshit."

"No, bullshit was when he suggested I was a freeloader who thought she was going to sail through college on her brother's fame."

"No," she gasps. "Tell me you're lying."

"I wish I were," I say. "So now on top of needing to raise my grade, I also have to prove I'm actually good enough to be here, and that my admission wasn't just accepted because I'm Axel Stone's little sister."

Her face scrunches with distaste before her eyes light up. "You know what you need?" she asks, watching me a little too closely. "Dick. You need a lot of dick. Like a big, thick dick that'll take you to pound town."

"I do not need a dick."

"The girls who say they don't need a dick are the ones who need it the most. Just a wham, bam, thank you, ma'am. It'll be done and dusted in twenty minutes, and assuming he knows how to use his equipment, you'll be left feeling like a whole new woman."

"I don't think so."

"You know, it's scientifically proven that releasing all that pent-up frustration is great for the mind. Once you come and throw him out, you can get back to your textbooks and your mind will be like a little sponge soaking up all the communications drivel that nobody actually cares about."

I give her a blank stare. "You made that up."

Madds shrugs her shoulders. "It could be true."

I roll my eyes, but before I get a chance to tell her how ridiculous she is, she pulls her phone out. "Listen, I wasn't going to tell you this, but I ran into this guy yesterday who said that he saw us together last week and wanted to know if you were single, and of course I told him you were available. He's really cute and seems super down to Earth, and I think you should go to dinner with him tonight and see where it goes."

"Absolutely not."

"Don't be a bore. We're twenty-two years old. This is our time to fuck around and have a good time. Before we know it, college will be over, and we'll be out there in the real world, and when you look back on these days, it won't be with fondness. You'll be bummed that you wasted your youth holed up in a stinky bedroom, reading over textbooks you already know back to front."

My shoulders sag as I gaze up at her. I haven't been with anyone since starting college, to the point I'm becoming quite fond of the cobwebs growing in my vagina. Fucking around with random guys isn't really my style. He Who Shall Not Be Named Out Loud ruined me for that, but the idea of being touched by a man . . .

Shit. I have mixed feelings. I have a whole closet of trauma that

I refuse to look at, but at what point am I supposed to claim my life back? My years with Ezra were amazing, but after they left me alone with *him* . . . It destroyed me in every way.

Physically. Emotionally. Mentally.

I have more scars than any woman should ever have to deal with, and they're all packaged up inside of me. But every day, I feel the seals of that package begin to weaken, like little tendrils of a rope, slowly breaking fiber by fiber, and eventually, it's going to tear wide open, and I'm terrified of the day that happens.

I'm not coping. I can feel myself falling to pieces, but maybe Madds is right. Maybe holding out on myself isn't the key. Maybe it's time to let go and try to enjoy the smaller things in life. Who knows, maybe this guy is the one who's going to light a match inside of me and ignite the fire that Ezra burned out.

"Alright," I finally tell her, feeling the small amount of hope I just mustered up already fading fast. "Give me his number."

Madds gapes at me. "Wait. What?" she stutters. "For real? I was just talking shit. There's no way I thought you'd actually agree. I was already thinking about ordering Thai food."

"Do you want me to go or not?"

"Yes!" she screeches, flying up from my bed. "Oh my god, yes! We need to figure out something for you to wear. Holy shit." Madds pauses and looks at me, tears forming in her big blue eyes. "My girl is finally going to get laid."

Well, shit. What could possibly go wrong?

Two hours later, I walk into the only fancy restaurant in town, and by fancy, I mean it's the only one that offers napkins and clean cutlery. Apart from this, our options were McDonald's or the college bar. At least here I could maybe get a decent steak.

Making my way to the hostess, I offer her a small smile. "Hi, I'm meeting someone. I'm not sure what he looks like."

"Do you have a name?"

I cringe. Shit. Why'd she have to hit me with the hard questions? "Uhhh . . . Brad. I think?"

The hostess looks over her booking sheet, trailing her fingers through the names. "Ah, yes. Brad. We have you right here. It doesn't look as though he's arrived yet. Can I offer you a seat at the bar while you wait, or would you like to go straight to your table?"

"The table will be fine, thank you."

"Sure thing."

The hostess leads me through the restaurant and shows me to my table, and as she scurries off, I take my seat and gaze over the menu.

The waitress comes by, and I order a glass of water while I wait. As the time passes, I stop watching the door with anticipation and stare into my empty glass.

By the thirty minute mark, any remaining hope I had for tonight plummets out of existence. The waitress brings me a fresh water, and I let out a sigh as she places it down in front of me. "I'm embarrassing myself, aren't I?" I ask. "I should leave and save my dignity."

"Girl, I would have left twenty minutes ago. Any man who makes you wait thirty minutes on a first date is not a man worth waiting for."

"Yeah, you're right," I say, getting up. "Sorry for wasting your time.

You could have been waiting on a decent table instead of watching me sulk for half an hour."

"It's fine, honey."

She gives me a pitying smile before disappearing. Trying to save what's left of my night, I make my way toward the exit of the restaurant when the door opens and a tall beast of a man strides in. His gaze shifts around the restaurant, quickly scanning the faces before finally landing directly on mine.

A forced smile cracks across his face as he approaches me. "Hey, Raleigh, right?"

My gaze shifts up and down his tall frame. There's no denying that he's hot. Almost perfect, actually, but I'm not impressed. "I take it you're Brad?"

"Yeah. Shit. How long have you been here?" he questions, not giving me a chance to bail before stepping into me and bustling me back toward the table I just vacated.

"Long enough," I tell him. "I'm out."

"Don't be stupid. Sit down. Have a drink," he says, leaning back as though he's got this in the bag. "Relax."

Getting the feeling he's the type to cause an embarrassing scene, I drop my ass back to the seat and swallow my pride. Who knows, maybe he might have some redeeming qualities buried in there somewhere. It's unlikely, but would I be the kind-hearted person I've always claimed to be if I didn't at least give him a chance? Perhaps he got a flat on the way. Maybe he spilled water down his pants and had to head home to change so he didn't look like he'd pissed himself. There could be any number of excuses for why he's late.

Brad clicks his fingers at the waitress. "Yo, baby. Hit me with a menu."

The fuck? Is this guy for real?

The waitress comes back over and hands Brad a menu before turning her body to face me. She meets my eye and pulls a face, and I do what I can to swallow my laughter.

Brad scans over the menu, looking less than impressed with the options as he makes an attempt at small talk. "So, you're Raleigh Stone, huh?" he asks, glancing up to show me the deceit in his eyes. "Is that any relation to Axel Stone from Demon's Curse?"

Well, fuck. I should have known.

How could a man possibly be interested in me when he could use me to get to my brother instead?

"The one and only," I say blandly, realizing within an instant that Madds was so off the mark with this one. There will be no dick tonight, no solid pounding up against the wall, no Earth-shattering orgasm to clear out the cobwebs.

This guy is a fucking joke.

"Oh, cool. So like, they just wrapped up their Australian tour, right? So that means they're heading back to the States."

"Yeah. Sure, I suppose."

"So, I guess you see your brother a lot, then?" he questions, his brow raised. "Will he come see you now that he's got a few weeks off? Like surely you're his first stop on his way back to LA?"

I shrug my shoulders, and as I watch him closer, it occurs to me that this asshole is trying to figure out if he fucks me for the next few days, what his chances are at meeting Axel.

Holy fucking shit. "You know what, he doesn't usually come out to see me mid-tour."

"Oh."

His whole face falls, and he does what he can to mask his disappointment by looking back down at the menu. The discomfort at the table is almost comical, and as I look around, I catch the eye of the waitress. She gives me a thumbs up before flipping it upside down, silently asking me how it's going, and I don't hesitate to return her thumbs down.

"Fuck, this place is shit," Brad says, stealing my attention from the waitress. "Glad I just stopped for a burger on the way."

My eyes practically burst out of my head. "Excuse me?"

"No big deal, baby. Just grabbed something to eat," he says before winking. "Figured we wouldn't be here long."

"You left me waiting here for you for thirty minutes while you stopped to get yourself a burger?" I question, trying to wrap my head around this. "Holy fuck. You're a piece of shit."

"What?"

I stand and grab my purse. "I see men like you all the time. You think you can fuck your way into meeting my brother, but the joke's on you because after finding out that you left me waiting for thirty minutes while you stopped to feed your arrogant ass, he wouldn't even give you the time of day. And for what it's worth, meeting the fucking waitress was more thrilling than sitting opposite you. I honestly pity the poor woman you end up with."

With that, I hightail it out of there, and as I pass the hostess, she holds her hand out for a high five, and I don't fucking miss. Only the second I get back into my car and the silence surrounds me, all I feel is empty.

I used to have it all, and now this is what I'm subjected to.

How the hell have I fallen so low?

I'm pathetic. Nothing more than someone else's meal ticket to my brother . . . or Ezra. The number of girls who've asked me if I can give them Ezra's number is just insane.

Tears roll down my cheeks as I pull out of my parking space, and by the time I'm halfway back to my apartment, there are enough tears to fill the Nile, and I have no choice but to pull over and wait for it to run its course.

The tears just keep coming, and before I know it, heavy sobs tear through my chest. I'm fucking pathetic. I'm failing my classes, I'm a joke to those around me, and on top of that, I've lost my happiness. Every day is a struggle, and I feel myself breaking. Hell, I think I'm already there.

My phone rings, cutting through the Bluetooth in my car, and instead of rejecting the call until I find just a semblance of composure, a wave of anger infects me. Before I know it, I'm answering Axel's call.

"Hey Turd—"

"It's all your fault," I rush out between my heavy sobs, barely able to catch my breath. "Do you have any idea what life is like for me? As long as you're my brother, I don't stand a chance of having a normal life."

"Rae—"

"No. Don't *Rae*, me," I cry. "You have no idea what kind of hell I had to endure after you left. You were my only protection, both of you were, and then you were just gone. Do you have any idea how that feels? What he did to me? What it's like to have to go through that night after night? How could you leave me to endure that?"

"What?" he says, a shift in his tone that sends searing hot panic through my chest.

Fuck.

I wasn't supposed to say that. I've gone six agonizing years without saying a word, and in one fell swoop, I've word vomited it all out onto the pavement. My heart races as horror leaves me absolutely speechless.

"What the fuck did you just say, Raleigh? What are you talking about? Did someone touch you?"

"I . . . I . . . It's nothing. Just forget I said anything," I tell him, my whole body shaking with unease.

If he knew. If they knew.

I've gone out of my way not to breathe a word of my past to Axel because the moment he discovers the truth, his career is over. He would be back in Michigan within an instant, undoing everything he's worked for. And the guilt . . . It would cripple him.

"Rae. I'm not fucking around. What are you talking about?"

"Really, I'm fine," I tell him, wiping my tears on the back of my arm. "I'm just having a really shitty day. Madds talked me into going on a blind date, and after making me wait for over half an hour, turns out all he wanted was to fuck me in the hopes of getting an in with you."

"The fuck?"

"Welcome to my life," I say with a heavy sigh.

"Shit. It's happened before?"

"Not that specific situation," I tell him, feeling my heart begin to ease. "But as a whole. Yes. All the time. Just today my communications professor accused me of being a freeloader who thinks she can get a pass through college because I'm Axel Stone's little sister simply for asking for an extra credit assignment. This is just my life, Ax. I don't get to be normal."

"Fuck, Rae. I'm sorry," he murmurs. "Do you want me to put in a call with the dean and see if I can help?"

An unladylike scoff tears out of me. "Hell no," I tell him. "Are you trying to make everything worse?"

"No, I just—"

"It's fine, Axel. I know you mean well, and I swear, I didn't mean to worry you. It's just been a rough week, and you just happened to call right at the worst time. I just need the night to feel sorry for myself, and I'll be good as new tomorrow."

There's a slight pause before a slow "Mm-hmm" comes through the speakers.

"You're on your way home, right?" I ask, trying to act as though everything is right in the world. "You get two weeks off to relax."

"Yeah, we're on the jet now," he says with a slight hesitation in his tone.

I force a ridiculous smile across my face. "After partying it up in

Australia with hookers and coke?" I ask, trying to be supportive of his night, despite how the idea of Ezra being involved seems to eat me alive.

"Fuck," he mutters, and I can all but hear the cringe ripping across his face. "You saw that, huh?"

"More like who didn't see it? It was splashed across every news page in the country. You and Devil Spawn practically broke the internet."

"Devil Spawn?"

"He Who Shall Not Be Named."

"Right."

"Yeah . . ."

An awkward silence seems to settle between us and, not being able to handle it, I quickly wrap up this nightmare. "Listen, it's starting to rain, and it looks like it'll be a nasty storm, so I better go before I get stuck driving in it."

"Okay, sure. I'll ummm . . . drive safe, alright? Text me when you get home so I know you're okay."

"Sure thing, Ax. Love you."

"Love you, too, Turd."

My thumb sweeps over the hang-up button on my steering wheel and as the car falls into a heavy silence, I feel another piece of my soul crumble. Then after looking up at the crystal clear sky, I finally dry my face and get my ass back home where I can spend the rest of my night wishing that my life could have been different.

Wishing that Axel never left.

Wishing that Ezra never broke me to pieces.

And wishing that *he* never even looked my way.

CHAPTER 4

Ezra

The flight from Australia to the U.S. has never been my favorite, even in our private jet. But add the torture of being scolded by management for two straight hours while nursing the worst fucking hangover, and it's practically hell. Not to mention Rock's inability to quit drumming against the table, but after so many years, it's a noise one must become accustomed to.

It's almost a fourteen-hour flight, and we're barely past the halfway mark. If it weren't for the knowledge that Axel is currently on the phone with Raleigh while sitting directly opposite me, I probably would have crashed by now.

Something is wrong.

The moment she accepted his call and he started twisting his ring around his finger, I knew it.

His whole tone changed, and he was on high alert, but the questions spewing out of his mouth were the worst. *"What the fuck did you just say, Raleigh? What are you talking about? Did someone touch you?"*

I swear to whatever greater power exists, if some motherfucker put his hands on that girl, I'll tear him to shreds. Just the image has me fucked up. My fingers curl into tight fists, and my nails cut into my palms, but it only lasts a moment before Axel relaxes enough for me to realize that whatever she said to him, he'd taken it the wrong way.

Raleigh is fine. At least, physically. Just because she hasn't been hurt doesn't mean she's doing well, and by the way Axel slouches in his seat, it's pretty damn clear we're thinking the same thing. She's hurting, and there's not a damn thing we can do about it.

He gets up to pace the length of the jet as he chats to Raleigh, and as I do my best to ignore him and the too-soft mumble of her voice coming through the silence, I scrawl meaningless words in my notebook, hoping that one of these days, the pain might subside for just a moment to feel normal.

"Devil Spawn?" he questions, pausing his pacing. A subtle smirk flitters across his lips as his gaze lands on me. "Right."

Great. Suppose I have a new nickname now. It's fitting though. I can see why she'd refer to me as the devil spawn. It's not as though I've left her with anything good, only heartbreak, longing, and anger.

The moment Axel wraps up his call with Raleigh, I'm finally able to concentrate on the words before me, and after writing "Devil Spawn" at the top of the page, I start stringing the words into lyrics.

Axel sits in broody silence opposite me. He doesn't say a word, simply stares at his hands as waves of tension roll off him. I consider asking him about the conversation, but where Raleigh is concerned, I purposefully keep out of it. It's a touchy subject between us. He was always down with us being together . . . kind of. We were never officially together, but no matter how I look at it, she was mine, and I was hers. He saw that she was happy, and that's all he ever wanted for her, but our decision to leave . . . fuck. I know we made the decision as a group, but he hates that my leaving tore her to shreds. Fuck, I hate it too.

"I think I need to go see her," he finally says.

I lift my gaze, my brows furrowed. Don't get me wrong, he loves his little sister. She's the sun in his sky, but he goes out of his way not to visit her, especially during tour because all it does is fuck with everyone involved. "After the tour, you mean?"

He shakes his head, a heaviness clear in his eyes, and I fear the words teetering on the edge of his lips. "Nah. The second we land, I'm taking off. She's not coping right now. College is kicking her ass, and her professor just accused her of trying to get a free ride because she's my sister. She was bawling her fucking eyes out. You know her, man. That's not her. Something bigger is going on, and whatever it is, she's keeping it from me. As long as I'm away, I'll never get to the bottom of it. I just need . . . a week, maybe."

My eyes widen in horror as my stare collides with Axel's. "The fuck?"

Raleigh Stone doesn't cry. The girl I knew would sooner die than let anyone see her fall apart, and for her to break like that over a simple phone call . . . Axel is right. Something's going on.

"Yeah," he says in agreement. "I think she's just having a rough time. At least, I hope that's all it is. All I know is that whatever she's holding back, it's fucking with her head, and I can't stand it. I need to get to the bottom of it. I won't be able to focus on the rest of the tour if I don't sort this shit out. She's my world, man. She's all I've got, and if she's not doing okay . . . I can't worry about her like that when we're on tour. I need to know she's alright. I mean, fuck, man. What if something happens and I'm across the fucking globe?"

"Yeah, alright," I mutter, hating every moment of this. The last thing I ever wanted was for Rae to be unhappy, and if Axel is right, and there really is something going on, then he needs to be there to make it okay. "Apart from college and her bullshit professor, how's she doing?"

Axel lifts his gaze as his brow arches. "You know, she'll never admit it, but she misses you. I think that's part of whatever this is. Maybe she's all up in her feelings," he suggests, his gaze falling out the window and falling into a deep silence for the quickest moment. "You should come with me."

I scoff, the idea of me showing up uninvited in her dorm room almost comical. "Yeah, right. That'll go down well. Besides, if she's having a hard time, the last thing she needs is me coming and making things worse."

"Yeah, maybe you're right," he says, letting out a heavy breath. He reclines his seat, his head tilted back against the headrest, staring up at the ceiling of the cabin, and it's clear that whatever is going through his head is deep enough to bring him down.

A minute of silence turns into ten before he sits back up again, his elbows braced against his knees, a somber expression on his face. "I think we fucked up leaving her behind. She needs you."

Fuck. Why did that gut me so violently?

I shake my head, trying to shake off the uneasiness coursing through my veins. He couldn't be more wrong. I'm everything she *doesn't* need. "No, she might think she needs me, but she doesn't. I'm not the guy she's missing anymore. I haven't been in years. This life isn't for her," I tell him. We may be living the dream, but the double-edged sword of fame cuts deeply, and the last thing I'd ever want is for her to see me this way. "She's going to finish college with her fancy degree and make something of herself, not get caught up in this bullshit. Besides, I'm a fucking mess. Nobody needs this."

A cocky grin creeps across his face, and without a doubt, I know there's a sharp retort sitting right on the end of his tongue. It's a miracle he's able to swallow it before managing to put a proper response together. "Well, maybe she doesn't need you, but you sure as fuck need her."

Shit. Just when I thought I was off the hook, I'm right back in the deep end.

I clench my jaw, refusing to respond because fuck knows he's right. The second I got on a flight and left Michigan behind, my world spiraled, and it hasn't stopped since.

Raleigh is my compass, and without her, I'm fucking lost, but like I said, she deserves better than this life, better than anything I could ever give her.

"So, I've been upgraded to Devil Spawn, huh?" I ask, swiftly changing the topic but doing anything in my power to keep talking about her. It's rare he unloads about her like this. He keeps it to himself to keep me from falling to pieces, but I need to hear it more than I need my next breath.

Axel shrugs his shoulders, his lips quirking into a small smile. "It's better than when she referred to you as The Epic Mistake."

I cringe. That one still stings, but it did create a bestseller. "You're not wrong!"

"I'm never wrong."

I roll my eyes and settle in for the next seven hours of the flight, assuming the conversation is over, only when he volunteers more, I listen up like a starved animal begging for scraps. "When I called her, she'd just walked out on a date."

"A date?" I ask, my heart pounding erratically in my chest. We've spoken on every topic under the sun when it comes to Raleigh Stone over these past six years, but never about her dating.

For the most part, I had assumed she wasn't interested, that a part of her was still mine, and that the thought of being with another man made her as sick as I feel now.

How fucking conceited could I be?

Of course she's not waiting around for me. She's fucking beautiful and has so much to offer someone. I'm sure she probably goes out of her way to avoid it, but I know she's aware of the lifestyle I lead, and if I'm sinking into a different woman every night, why shouldn't she be with any man she wants?

Fuck. Maybe I'm stuck in the past, but a part of me had always thought I'd be her first.

"Mm-hmm," Axel responds as his hand curls into a tight fist. "The fucker treated her like shit. Kept her waiting half the night and then assumed he could fuck her for a chance at getting closer to me."

Shit. There's that nausea rolling up on me again.

The vivid images of Raleigh in bed with some asshole hits me like a fucking freight train, and as my stomach rolls with unease, I realize this is so much more than the aftershock of my wild night in Sydney. I'm actually going to be sick.

Lunging from my seat, I barrel down the length of the jet to the small bathroom, and the second my knees hit the ground, the contents of my stomach erupt in violent waves.

Hanging my head over the toilet bowl, I desperately try to get it all up, and I'm suddenly all too aware of Axel hovering in the doorway.

"One mention of Rae dating, and you're puking your guts up," he comments as though I hadn't quite noticed my current predicament. He crosses his arms over his chest, leaning against the doorframe. "Interesting."

Getting back to my feet, I clean myself up before bracing my hands against the sink and staring at him through the small mirror.

"You're still in love with her."

And without a moment of hesitation, I nod, feeling the weight of my heart burning to ashes inside my chest. "I never fucking stopped."

CHAPTER 5

Raleigh

13 YEARS OLD

The cool Michigan air rushes through the kitchen window, blowing my homework across the table as I frantically scramble after it. "No, no, no," I panic, throwing myself from the old barstool behind the small island table.

Mom laughs, wiping her flour-covered hands on her apron before hurrying across the kitchen and warring with the old window as it gets jammed. This house is falling apart, but it's ours, and I wouldn't have it any other way.

Well, kinda. If someone offered me a McMansion in Beverly Hills, living it up like royalty, I'm not going to say no, but this is home.

My papers continue flying across the room, and just as I pin one under my foot, Mom finally wins the battle and unjams the window, pulling it down into place. "My goodness," she laughs, pressing her hand to her chest when something catches her attention outside. Her brows furrow. "Oh, looks like Axel's bringing home strays again."

"Huh?"

I cross the kitchen and step into Mom's side before peering out the window to see Axel striding down the footpath with a dark-haired boy beside him, but he doesn't seem boyish in the same way Axel does. He seems like . . . more.

My gaze narrows, he's too far to really make out the features of his face, but there's something there, something alluring that demands every bit of my attention.

His hair is floppy, almost covering his eyes, and the black sleeveless tank that shows off defined arms has something clenching in my stomach. He's kinda gorgeous. But add that guitar slung over his shoulder and suddenly there's not a single thought inside my head.

Axel is sixteen and thinks he's going to be a big deal, and I love that for him. You know, I think it's great he's so happy to live in delusion. On the other hand, I'm hoping to make it to the big leagues. Any of the big colleges would do, I'm not picky, but that's about where my plan stops. I have no idea what I want to do with my life, but I know I want to make it count.

I want to help people. I want to do good; I just don't know how.

I watch Axel and his new friend as they reach the top of our driveway and make their way toward the front door, and with every step they take, my heart races just a little bit faster.

What the hell is this?

"Did you want to stop drooling before they come through the door?" Mom teases. "Or should I let you keep gaping out the window like a love-sick puppy?"

My eyes widen in horror, realizing way too late just how obvious I'm being. "I'm not—I don't . . ."

Mom laughs at my display but when the door opens and Axel and his new friend stride into the kitchen, every last stuttered word falls away.

His gaze quickly sweeps the kitchen, taking in his new surroundings, and the moment those dark, exotic eyes land on mine, I'm ruined.

I suck in a breath as the strangest booming takes over my chest. I've never felt anything like it. My pulse starts to race, and my hands become sweaty, and all I can do is stand here and stare back at him.

My god. He's beautiful.

"Yo, Mom," Axel says, pausing in the entrance of the kitchen. "We're starting a band together. We're gonna clear out the garage for practice space."

Axel turns on his heel, already stalking toward the internal garage door when Mom calls out behind him. "Get your ass back here Axel Stone," she says, crossing her arms over her chest as my gaze greedily sails over the gorgeous, tanned stranger in my kitchen. He's so tall. I always thought Axel was tall, but this guy has got to have at least three inches on Ax.

Axel groans and turns back, giving Mom a blank stare. "Yes?"

"Were you going to introduce us to your new friend, or were you planning on waltzing perfect strangers right through the door?"

Axel glances at his friend as if only just realizing where he went wrong. "Oh. He's the new guy. Just started at school today. Said he liked to play guitar so figured we'd hang out."

"Okay," Mom says slowly. "And does the *new guy* have a name?"

New Guy laughs to himself before stepping forward and holding his hand out to my mother. "Ezra," he says as Mom takes his hand and gently shakes it. "Ezra Knight. It's a pleasure to meet you, ma'am. I hope it's not a bother that we play in the garage. We can find somewhere else if you'd prefer."

"Not at all," Mom says. "Are you hungry? Rae and I were just about to bake chocolate chip cookies."

Ezra's gaze shifts back to mine, a deep curiosity in his eyes. "Sure," he says slowly before turning his head toward Axel without taking his stare off mine. "Uhhhh, dude. Your sister is staring at me."

My brother scoffs. "Yeah, she does that. You'll get used to it," he says. "She's trying to work out if you're going to be worth her time or if she's going to make it a living hell for you every time you walk through the door."

Ezra arches a brow, and while Axel would usually be right, this one time, I'm not thinking a damn thing. I can't. It's as though nothing exists but the halo that seems to surround Ezra Knight.

"Rae, is it?"

"Raleigh," I manage to croak out, not sure why my hands seem to be shaking so much.

"What's it going to be, Raleigh?" he asks as a smirk lifts the corner of his lips, showing off a row of perfectly straight teeth. "You gonna make my life hell, or what? Because I think it'd be more fun to be friends, especially considering your mom is cool enough to let me play guitar in your garage."

I cross my arms over my chest, immediately deciding I like this new boy, and not wanting to chase him off just yet. "Okay, I'll give you a trial run," I tell him, wishing my voice didn't sound so shaky. "I'll play nice, but if you two sound like a bunch of screeching cats in that garage, the deal is off. There's only so much I'll tolerate."

Ezra extends his hand toward me. "You've got yourself a deal, Raleigh Stone."

My gaze falls to his outstretched hand and a wave of panic sweeps through me. There's no way in hell I can shake his hand while mine are clammy with nervous sweat. So instead, I keep my arms crossed and fix my perfect bratty-sister expression across my face. "I'm not shaking that hand," I tell him. "Who knows where that's been. Besides, this deal is not official until after I'm sure you don't sound like a dying cat."

"It was a screeching cat," he confirms as his eyes sparkle with silent laughter that has my knees threatening to buckle beneath me.

Holy cow.

Am I in love? Is this what it feels like? I've had more than my fair share of stupid boy crushes, but it's never felt like this, so strong and instantaneous. It's as though a piece of me already belongs to him, but that's insane, right? He's Axel's friend, and I only just met him. He's probably sixteen. Maybe seventeen, and I'm just some stupid kid.

"Alright, go on," Mom says, ushering the boys out of her kitchen.

"Go convert the garage into a band space, but if you break any of my things, you'll have me to deal with. Understood?"

"Yes, Mom," Axel says, turning away and stalking back to the garage door.

Erza follows him, but just before he disappears out of sight, he glances back over his shoulder, his gaze colliding with mine like a sonic boom, and just like that, I know my life will never be the same.

"What the hell was that?" Mom asks once the boys are locked away in the garage. She moves around the kitchen, plucking my sheet of homework off the ground and fixing it on the island table.

"What was what?" I throw back at her, feigning disinterest.

"You can't fool me, Raleigh Stone. I was a thirteen-year-old girl once," she reminds me. "And that . . . Well, let's just put it out there that Ezra Knight is way too old for you. I always knew there'd come a day when you'd start crushing on your brother's friends, but I'd hoped that wouldn't happen until you were at least eighteen. Just know, that one right there, the one with the floppy dark hair and charming words, he's trouble."

A stupid grin cuts across my face, and within seconds, I'm beaming from ear to ear, unable to even attempt to hide the overwhelming rush of emotions coursing through my veins. "You saw that smile, right?" I ask. "And the arms?"

"Oh, hush," she laughs, rolling her eyes as she settles back in front of the cookie batter. "You have homework to do. There will be plenty of time to dream about silly boys when you're older, but for now, you need to focus on geography."

I groan and roll my eyes before settling back at the kitchen island, but the knowledge of having the most gorgeous dark-haired boy currently moving old furniture around in my garage makes it almost impossible to concentrate.

For every word I manage to scrawl on my homework sheet, there are two loud thumps coming from the garage, and after thirty minutes of forcing myself to focus, the loud thumps morph into guitar riffs.

"Oh," Mom says, arching her brows as she slides the cookies into the oven. "They're not bad."

I won't lie, she's right. The boys sound good together. I can immediately tell the difference between Axel's and Ezra's playing. I've been forced to listen to enough hours of Axel practicing to recognize his style on the guitar. He plays sharp and to the point like he's reading sheet music and refuses to mess it up. He's incredible, but Ezra's style seems more relaxed. Wild and reckless somehow. It's as though the sheet music just flew out the window, and he's putting his own spin on it. It's hypnotic, and while they each sound amazing on their own, together it's mesmerizing.

God, what I wouldn't give to go peek into the garage and get just a little glimpse of Ezra working that guitar.

My homework is quickly replaced by endless minutes of daydreaming about dark-haired boys wearing muscle tanks and hypnotizing smirks, wondering just what it'd feel like to be the object of their attention.

The front door opens, and the sound of Dad's clattering keys pulls me from my daydream. "Why does my garage look like a scene out of a teen movie?" Dad asks, striding into the kitchen and placing a hand on Mom's lower back, making her stiffen. He leans in and drops a swift kiss to her lips before hastily pulling away.

Mom laughs, but there's an odd strain to her tone. "Axel's serious about this whole wanting to be a rockstar thing," she explains. "He met a new friend at school, and the two of them wanted to turn the garage into a practice space."

"And I suppose I should just start parking on the curb? How about across the lawn? Hell, maybe I could just drive straight through the front window and park in the dining room instead."

Mom smirks as she drops her gaze to the table, keeping her hands busy. "Oh, relax. I'll tell the boys to pack it up just before dinner and then you can reclaim the garage. Besides, we've been talking about cleaning out the garage for months, and now the boys have done it for us. It's a win, Michael. You've gotta take them as they come."

Dad groans and leans back against the kitchen counter, crossing his foot over the other before swiftly glancing toward the oven. "Your cookies are burning."

"What?" Mom's eyes widen in horror. Her pottery is her career, but baking is her passion. She darts around Dad, scooping the oven mitts off the bench and flying toward the oven. She pulls them out, and as always, her cookies are absolutely mouthwatering perfection.

She glares at my father, and all he can do is laugh as he traipses past me, all but ignoring me here before taking off to do whatever it is that fathers like to do with their evenings.

Mom leaves the cookies to cool, and I can't help but steal one as

I finish off what's left of my homework. Just as I start packing my books back into my school bag, Mom comes to me with a plate piled high with chocolate chip cookies. "Here," she says. "You should take these in for the boys. They've been practicing non-stop. They need a moment of silence for their brains to stop shaking inside their skulls."

A wave of nervousness comes over me, but I can't help but jump at the opportunity. After grabbing the plate of cookies, I hurry to the garage door and find myself hovering, my hands shaking at just the thought of walking in there and seeing Ezra again.

That's ridiculous, right? I only just met the guy, not to mention, our interaction lasted less than two minutes. I shouldn't be so infatuated with him like this, but I can't help it. I suppose I really can't be blamed. It's human nature.

Gathering what little courage I have, I open the door and stride into the garage with my head held high. The boys are in the middle of a set, and as they play, Ezra looks up and smiles at me, knocking the breath right out of my lungs.

Okay, I thought he was hot before, but seeing him play . . . Woah. Someone pinch me.

My heart races in my chest and suddenly my mouth is crazy dry.

My hands shake, and I do what I can to seem cool, but it's a well-known fact that little sisters of big brothers are never perceived as cool. We're traditionally known for being brats. At least that's the stereotype. Personally, I like to think that I'm the coolest little sister any brother could want. Axel has always been great to me. We're close for siblings. At least, I consider us to be compared to how my friends are with their older siblings. Their brothers never seem to have time for them, but Axel always makes sure to give me the time of day, even when it's clear he thinks I'm being annoying.

He never yells at me, never tells me to get lost, and sometimes, he even values my opinion. None of my friends can say their brothers are like that.

Putting the plate down on a stool, the boys wrap up whatever it is they were working on, and before I can even form a sentence, they're already shoveling the cookies down their throats. "Shit. These are good," Ezra says, glancing at me. "You make these?"

I shake my head. "I wish I were that good at baking," I murmur. "This is all Mom."

"Jesus," he says, putting his guitar down and collapsing onto a chair. "You guys don't know how good you've got it. My mom would have flipped out if I came home and told her I was going to convert the garage into a practice space, and she sure as hell wouldn't have made us cookies."

"Yeah," Axel laughs. "Mom's pretty cool."

Ezra nods and turns his attention to me. "So, what's it gonna be?" he asks, a teasing smile lighting up his face and making everything crumble inside of me. "Are we as terrible as you were hoping we'd be?"

I can't keep the smirk off my face. "It's worse," I joke. "I don't know how your hearing is, maybe it's all frazzled by the constant ringing from your guitar, but from in the kitchen, it definitely sounded like some kind of massacre was happening in here."

He doesn't take his stare off mine, and every passing second with his full attention has something solidifying between us, yet I have no idea what it is. There's something here, something that simply can't be denied. A bond? A friendship? It's too soon to say.

"You're lying," he says. "We fucking rock."

"Okay, whatever," I admit, rolling my eyes as I make my way back to the door, despite how desperately I want to stay right here and watch him play for the rest of my life. "You might be alright."

Ezra laughs. "Alright enough to make it to the top?"

I pause by the door. "Maybe, but you're going to need a kickass manager," I tell them, holding up a finger at Axel before he has a chance to cut me off. "And before you even attempt to tell me no, it's too late. The spot has been filled. It's official."

"Deal," Ezra says with a cheesy grin as Axel rolls his eyes.

I go to reach for the door when he calls out again. "Wait. Do you know how to hold a beat?"

I whip around to face him, my face twisted with concern. A beat is certainly not something I am capable of holding. "Uhhhhh . . . No."

"Come on," he says, getting up from the chair and carrying it into the center of the practice space. He puts it down before grabbing an old tub and flipping it upside down. "Don't worry, it's not hard. I'll teach you."

"I'm really not good with music."

"Yeah, she's really not," Axel agrees.

"Well, until we can find a drummer, she's all we've got," Ezra says, waving me over. "Plus, you know if we had a backing beat, it'd be easier to stay in sync."

Axel scoffs, his lips quirking with a cheesy grin. "Maybe for you."

Ezra gapes at him, and I roll my eyes, more than used to my brother's stupid humor. "Okay, fine. Teach me what I have to do," I say, striding toward him and sitting down in front of the makeshift drum, dreading whatever's about to happen. Axel has tried to teach me before, but after realizing I had no hope, he quickly gave up. But the only difference here is that I'm more than happy to fail in front of my brother. As for Ezra, I want to be good.

"Okay. We're gonna start with a count of four," Ezra says, crouching down beside me as he lays both of his hands on top of the tub. "With your right hand, just tap. One. Two. Three. Four."

He demonstrates, and as he starts a second count of four, I join in.

"Good," he says. "Now, keeping the same tempo, we're going to go double time. So, for every count, you tap twice."

He demonstrates again, still keeping the same slow count, but tapping his hand a little faster. "One, and two, and three, and four."

Eight taps. Four counts. I can manage this.

I try it with him, tapping my right hand on the drum. "One, and two, and three, and four. And—"

"Good. Now, your left hand," he says, not stopping the rhythm on the drum. "Every time I say two and four, you tap your left hand."

My eyes widen, and I watch as he shows me. Continuing with his right hand and then adding the left on the even counts. "One and *two*, and three, and *four*. One and *two*, and—"

"Huh. Okay."

Adding my left hand to the drum, I count inside my head, trying to perfect the rhythm and after only a second, I quickly master it. "Yes!" Ezra calls, standing back up. "That's it. Just like that. Keep going."

A stupid beaming grin stretches across my face as I hold a beat for the first time in my life, and without even a moment of hesitation, the boys reach for their guitars, hooking the straps over their shoulders. They meet each other's stares across the practice space and without saying a damn word, they pick up where they left off, somehow sounding even better.

My hands tap the drum like I'm a warrior princess and with every strum of Ezra's skilled fingers across the strings, I realize that I don't ever want this to end. If this could be my life, I would die a happy woman. To have his attention would be everything. He smiles at me as he plays, and I almost lose my beat, and judging by the smirk that cuts across his face, he knows.

Ezra Knight is more than aware of the effect he's having on me, and maybe I'm crazy. Maybe I'm just as delusional as Axel's dreams of being a rockstar, but I think there might just be something here. Maybe he feels just a fraction of what I'm feeling.

That's crazy, though. He couldn't possibly feel any sort of way toward me. I'm just some dumb kid.

The boys wrap up the song, and as I stop tapping my makeshift drum, Axel grins at Ezra. "We're good, man," he says. "Like really fucking good."

Ezra nods as though something has just occurred to him, something I can't quite figure out.

"We need a full band," Ezra says. "Drummer and bassist."

"And a singer," I add, trying to be helpful.

A sheepish grin pulls at the corners of Ezra's lips. "Well, I uhhh . . . I kinda sing."

"No shit," Axel says, his brow arching with curiosity. "Well, go on then. Let's see what you've got."

Ezra glances toward me as I wait on bated breath, and there's no denying the flash of nervousness in his eyes. I can't blame him, the thought of standing in front of my class and having to deliver a speech sends me into a blind panic. I can only imagine that singing in front of people you've only just met might feel something like that.

I give him a small nod of encouragement, and he indicates to my makeshift drum, silently asking me to pick up the beat again, and I do just that. "Little slower," he asks.

I slow my pace and keep my eyes on him until he nods, letting me know I've got it right, and with that, he grips his guitar and slowly strums it. A moment passes as he plays the intro into the song, and the second the first few words sail out of his mouth, my hands pause on the drums, unable to continue.

I quickly recognize the song as "Never Tear Us Apart" by INXS, and as my chest rises and falls with heavy breaths, listening as his deep, raspy tone fills the garage, I become intoxicated by everything that he is. There's no longer a single doubt in my mind that with Ezra by Axel's side, their dream of dominating the world with their music isn't as out of reach as I thought.

Everything they want is right there for the taking.

Axel is just as mesmerized, and when Ezra sings the final notes of the song, he starts to clap. "Holy fuck," Axel breathes, shaking his head in disbelief. "That was fucking amazing."

"Yeah?" Ezra asks before glancing at me, but all I can do is stare at him with my mouth hanging open.

"No question about it, you're our front man," Axel says, still shaking his head. He grips the back of his neck. "Fuck me. That was . . . shit. Okay, so it's settled. You're lead singer and guitar. I'll be lead guitar and backup vocals. Rae wants to be manager, and so we just need a drummer and a bassist."

Their conversation pulls me out of my head, and I snap into action. "Ummm, Maxton Huxley at school has an older brother who plays the drums. I think his name is Rock, but he goes to the private school just outside of town."

"Yeah, alright," Axel says. "Have you got Maxton's number?"

I shrug my shoulders. "No, but I can get it."

"Okay, do that. As for a bass guy, I think I know someone. Dylan Pope. He's the grade under us, a bit quiet, but I think he's good."

"So, it's settled?" Ezra questions. "We're doing this?"

A wide grin stretches across Axel's face. "We're fucking doing this."

CHAPTER 6

Raleigh

The door flies open and Madds barges into my bedroom with tears streaking down her face. "Rae," she cries, flipping on the light and blinding me before racing to my bedside.

"Mmmmm. What the hell, Madds?" I groan, positive that it's got to be at least two or three in the morning. I rub my hand over my eyes and peer up at her to find tears streaming down her face, her phone clutched in her hand as her whole body shakes.

"I . . . I . . . I—"

"Madds," I rush out, sitting up with her as a strange unease fills my veins. "What's going on? What's wrong?"

She visibly swallows, but the longer she looks at me, the harder her tears flow, and within seconds, she's uncontrollably sobbing.

"Madds, I swear—"

She holds her phone out to me, and the pity and sadness in her eyes destroy me. "I'm . . . I'm so sorry," she's finally able to croak out.

Sorry? What the hell? Why's she sorry?

My brows furrow, and I avert my gaze to her outstretched hand where her phone lingers between us, and as I take it from her, the unease morphs into dread. It's the boys. It has to be. Why else would she be handing me her phone?

Dropping my gaze to the phone, I swipe my thumb across the screen, unlocking it to find it already open to a video of a news anchor. I immediately recognize her face. She's one of the main anchors on the biggest news outlet across the country—the one everyone watches to confirm if the bullshit story they've just heard on social media is actually true.

The words BREAKING NEWS are across the bottom, and as I play the video, my hands begin to shake.

The woman—Samantha Hartley—looks directly at the camera, and I put the volume up to hear over the heavy sobbing that Madds can't seem to get under control. "Wait—" Samantha says, pressing her fingers to the small device in her ear as horror dances across her face. "Are . . . Are you sure?"

There's a slight commotion off screen and her eyes shine with unshed tears. "I'm sorry," she says, doing what she can to try and regain her professionalism. "We have breaking news coming in—devastating news for fans of Demon's Curse."

The screen splits, showing both Samantha in the studio and

a picture of Demon's Curse, the four boys—Ezra, Axel, Rock, and Dylan—at the close of their Australian show.

"Details are only just coming in. However, it has been confirmed that one of the members of the rock sensation, Demon's Curse, has died."

My heart stops. Time stops.

My whole fucking world stops.

This can't be right. This has to be some kind of sick joke.

"As of yet, we have no details to confirm which member has perished or the details surrounding the death. Reports state that during the night, the band arrived safely back in the States after the Australian leg of their world tour. As you can imagine, this is shocking news, and fans everywhere will feel this heavy loss," Samantha continues, desperately trying to keep her composure. "We will keep you posted as news comes in."

The video cuts to a montage of the band, and as my hands shake so violently, the phone falls from my fingers and crashes onto my bedsheet. "No," I whisper, shaking my head. "No. This isn't happening. It's a joke, some bullshit social media prank. I would know," I tell Madds. "I would know if something happened to one of them."

"Rae," she whispers, reaching for my arm, but I spring away, grabbing my phone.

"I WOULD KNOW."

The deepest pity flashes in her eyes as the overwhelming grief infects me like a deadly illness. Surely I would know. If something happened to Ezra or Axel, I would feel it right in the center of my chest. I wouldn't be able to breathe. My soul would be shattered on the floor.

If something had happened to either of them, surely I would be dead too because I couldn't possibly survive in a world where they're not here.

No. This isn't right.

If Axel was dead, my phone would be ringing non-stop. I wouldn't be able to keep up with the notifications. The police should be calling, fans flooding my social media accounts demanding to know what I know, my friends, the record label . . . Ezra. If this were true, he would have called, but there's nothing but silence.

But what if it's him? What if Ezra was the one who . . . fuck. I can't even bring myself to think the words.

"Rae," Madds tries again.

"No," I say, shaking my head. "I can't lose them. Either of them."

Tears stream down my face like waterfalls, and I unlock my phone, determined to prove them wrong. I know it's the middle of the night, and Axel is probably tucked in bed, but all I need is to call him. He'll set the record straight, but as my screen comes to life, I finally see it.

Over a hundred missed calls.

Thousands of Instagram DMs.

Threads. TikTok. Facebook. Whatsapp. Even my emails are flooded. My phone simply can't keep up with the demand. While it's shocking and heartbreaking, it's also more than enough to prove that this is so much more than some bullshit social media story.

This is as real as it gets.

One of them is gone.

I instantly curse myself. I'd gotten home from my bullshit date and thrown myself into my studies. I'd put my phone on Do Not Disturb and thumbed through the endless pages of my textbooks until I couldn't keep my eyes open a moment longer. If I'd just left my phone alone—

Oh God. My last conversation with Axel, I was so short with him. What if that was our very last conversation? What if I never get a chance to tell him how much I love him? How his happiness means the world to me. How I'm so damn proud of him?

Throwing myself from my bed, I pace my room as I madly start trying numbers.

Axel. Dylan. Rock. The label. The boys' manager. Their fucking producer and sound technician. But nothing. Every one of their phones are off.

The panic and emptiness within me feel like nothing I've ever known, and as the hopelessness weighs down on me, I crumble to the ground. The pain is agonizing, like a vise closing around my chest and refusing me just a moment of peace, but what does it matter? If it's Ezra or Axel, peace is something I'll never find again.

My face falls into my hands as the gut-wrenching sobs tear from the back of my throat, and not a moment later, Madds is right there with me, her knees crashing against the cheap carpet as she pulls me into her arms. "It's going to be okay," she vows, struggling to get the words out. "I'm going to be right here every step of the way. We'll get through this."

I shake my head. "How is it ever going to be okay?" I ask. "If it's Ax or Ezra . . . Am I a monster for hoping it's Rock or Dylan?"

A new wave of heavy sobs comes on, and I crumble right into Madds as she struggles to hold me up. Rock and Dylan are just as much my family as Axel and Ezra are. They were there through my awkward teen years and stood by and teased me about being head over heels in love with Ezra. They're the only ones who truly know what it was like between us. They knew how rare our bond was. They're like brothers to me. To lose any of them would be devastating, but Axel and Ezra . . . They're my whole entire world.

"You're not a monster," Madds soothes, trying to get to her feet and pulling me up. "Come on, let's get you back to bed. Someone is going to call you soon, and you'll get the answers you need."

I nod, letting her pull me up, and a moment later, I'm snuggled in my bed, holding my pillow to my chest as the tears continue rolling down my cheeks. Madds sits up beside me, silently crying as she goes through my phone and disables all my notifications, even going as far as to tell the random asshole from the press who knocks on our door to fuck off.

The long, drawn-out minutes turn into hours as I stare at my bedroom window, watching the pitch-black sky morph into a frosty orange sunrise. There hasn't been a single update online or on the news, no calls from anyone who could give me insight, no texts, no sliding into my DMs. Just agonizing silence.

I can't take it a moment longer.

The tears never dried up, and after three hours of constant crying, my swollen, red eyes feel like sandpaper, but true to her word, Madds hasn't left me for even a moment, and it somehow makes everything just that bit easier.

I've started to convince myself that no news is good news. If it were Rock or Dylan who had passed, there wouldn't be a call. At least, not yet. Their family would need to be notified first and then maybe at a decent time in the morning, Axel would call to let me know the details. But if it were Axel or Ezra, surely the phone should have rung by now. I know things are weird between me and Ezra, but if it were Axel, he'd call. He wouldn't allow anyone else to do it. He'd pick up the phone and call the one number he's avoided for so long, knowing that it needed to be him.

"Can I get you a coffee?" she asks, knowing it's useless to suggest I try and get some sleep.

"No, I—"

The sound of my phone ringing cuts through the room, and my response turns to silence as our gazes drop to the small device in the middle of my messed-up bedsheets. It's a private number, but somehow, I just know. This is the call I've been waiting for.

My heart races, beating right out of my chest as fear grips me in a chokehold.

My hands shake, too terrified to even reach for the phone, but I know if I miss it, it could be hours before it rings again.

The tears grow fatter in my eyes, and a weight drops against my chest, making it almost impossible to breathe. I stare at the phone like it's a bomb about to detonate, and as I curl my fingers around the cool metal, it feels heavier than it ever has before.

My gaze flitters to Madds, and as she holds my stare, she grabs my other hand and squeezes it tight. "I'm right here," she whispers, and with that, I swipe my thumb across the screen and lift my phone to my ear.

"Hello," I croak, my voice wavering and cracking with pain.

"Rae."

And there it is, right there in that one heartbroken, breathy syllable from a voice I've spent years trying to forget. I don't need anything more, not an explanation, not even a name, because everything I need to know is right there in his tone, his actions, his silence.

My brother, my best friend in the whole world, is dead.

CHAPTER 7

Raleigh

Thousands of screaming fans linger in the street, causing hell for the security team as my driver slowly tries to make his way through the masses. People throw themselves against the car window, desperate to peer in and see who's inside, and realizing that I'm not one of the three remaining members of the band, they pull away in disappointment.

It takes almost an hour to get from the top of the street to the front of the church, and the whole time, I can barely manage to hold myself together.

Today, I say goodbye to my brother.

It's been a week since his passing, and I still can't believe it's real. It's as though someone is playing a cruel joke on me and, at any moment, he's going to jump out at me, call me a turd, and laugh about how clever he thinks he is. But I'm starting to realize that the only cruel joke going on is my life.

My driver pulls to a stop, finally making it through the weeping fans to the front of the church. There's a sectioned-off area for attendees to get from their cars to the front doors, which allows them not to get mobbed, but unfortunately, that means there's plenty of space for the press.

They're all lined up and snapping shots of the guests like this is the red carpet for the Met Gala, and I've never been so uncomfortable. Obviously I know they have no interest in me. They're waiting for the band and all the famous friends Axel met along the way, but just the thought that this will be splashed across every news outlet before the funeral has even begun makes me sick.

A man in a suit steps up to my door and opens it for me before offering me his hand, which I graciously ignore. "Thank you," I mutter, my voice not feeling like my own. Hell, nothing has felt like my own this past week.

As I stand out on the street, a heaviness weighs down on me, and I lift my gaze to the church, taking it all in. It's huge. Don't get me wrong, it's an architectural piece of art, but it's not what I would have pictured for Axel. None of it is. He would have preferred his privacy, maybe something back in our hometown where he could be buried next to our mom.

My feet feel glued to the ground, but the longer I stand here, the sharper the ache in my chest becomes, and if I don't get my ass inside,

I fear I'll never get my chance to say goodbye. I take a shaky breath and as my driver slips away behind me, I'm left with no choice but to get a move on.

Keeping my head down, I make my way to the church doors, ignoring the press as they scream out, asking me who I am and what relation I have to Axel Stone. Their cameras go off nonetheless, flash after arrogant flash, blinding me as I stumble across the entryway.

Stepping into the foyer of the big church, the insane noise from outside is somewhat blocked out, and I'm greeted by a woman with a clipboard. "Welcome," she says, handing me a small program. "Name?"

"Oh, ummm," I say, not having expected there to be an exclusive guest list at the door. "Raleigh Stone. I am . . . was Axel's—"

"Sister," a burly man finishes for me as he steps closer, his eyes lingering on mine. He immediately scoops my hand into his big ones, holding it like he'll never let go. "Raleigh, it's a pleasure to finally meet you. So terrible that it's happened under these circumstances. Your brother was such a light in this world."

I nod, and he continues. "My name is Lenny Davidson. I'm the head of—"

"Louder Records," I say, noticing a bunch of suited men just behind him staring at me. This is the label, the men Axel worked his ass off to impress, and time and time again, he would succeed. Hell, I can't even begin to imagine how much money the band must have made for these assholes.

"That's correct," he says. "Now, I understand that you grew up with the band, so we've made the arrangements for you to be seated with them. I hope that's okay."

"No," I rush out, a sheer panic gripping me. "I'd prefer not to. I'll be fine finding my own seat."

"Oh, umm . . . okay. As you wish," he says, probably not used to a young woman going out of her way to avoid the band. "We do have your father on our guest list. Would you prefer to be seated with him?"

Oh, hell no.

"He's . . . he's coming?" I ask, feeling my whole body begin to cramp up with fear. "Is he here?"

"I, uhhh . . . I don't believe he has arrived," Lenny says, glancing toward the woman with the clipboard to confirm. "He was invited, of course. However, I don't believe we ever received a formal RSVP."

I let out a shaky breath, doing what I can to keep a lid on my trauma. Saying goodbye to my best friend in the world while having to see Ezra for the first time in six years will be hard enough without seeing my father as well . . . no. I can't. It's too much.

"Right, okay. Ummmm . . . If it's okay, I'd really prefer to sit on my own."

"Of course," he says with a nod. "Just let me know if there's anything we can do for you."

I force a smile and clutch my program as I step around him and make my way deeper into the church.

There are a lot of people here already, a sea of black suits and designer dresses, and as I start down the aisle and to the front of the church, I feel all their judgmental gazes on me, wondering who I am, why I'm so important to be able to walk all the way to the front in my cheap dress and heels, why the label went out of their way to talk to me.

Almost at the front, I lift my gaze and come to an abrupt stop.

The casket.

Holy shit.

There he is.

Tears well in my eyes, and as my hands tremble, I force myself to keep going until I'm standing right before it. I lay my shaky hand on top as the tears track down my face. The casket is closed. Apparently, his body was too messed up for easy recognition. I wouldn't know. I wasn't allowed the chance to see him, but a part of me is grateful. I don't think I would have wanted to see him like that.

There's a lot about Axel's death I don't know.

How it happened.

Where it happened.

Why it happened.

I've spent the past week desperate to get ahold of someone with answers, but after being hung up on and having my number blocked by multiple people assuming I was just a fan using my name to try and get unreleased information, I had no choice but to give up. A part of me has started to wonder if I'm ever going to get the answers I'm looking for, or if I'm just doomed to walk through life as a lost little girl.

Taking a heavy breath, I stare down at the closed casket. "I'm so sorry, Axel," I whisper, feeling my voice begin to break. "I love you so much, and I know I didn't tell you nearly enough, but you were my best friend, and even though you were far away, I always knew I could count on you to make everything better. I don't know how to miss you, Ax."

Needing to step back before I crumble right here at the front of the church in front of everyone who means something in the music industry, I let my hand fall away before inching back.

I turn to face the church, taking it all in, and as I gaze upon the many faces staring back at me, it becomes all too clear just how much Ax would have hated this. He wouldn't have wanted some big fancy funeral in LA where the people he loved from back home would have had to dip into their savings just to afford the flight out here. He wouldn't have wanted all the bullshit flowers and the big fancy church. He wouldn't have wanted the screaming fans lingering outside.

He would have wanted the park where we used to go on family camping trips by the lake at sunset. He would have wanted his close friends and the guys in the band. Not the label and management. Not these familiar faces he only saw at award shows. Not the fucking press.

Unable to take it any longer, I creep away from the casket and find the furthest seat in the front row, opposite of the boys' empty seats. The ceremony isn't set to start for another fifteen minutes, and I'm grateful for the small window by my seat that allows me something to focus on other than the casket only a few feet away.

I watch as the eager fans scream and chant with every approaching car, but when the screaming becomes so loud that I feel it vibrating through the ground, I realize *they're* here.

Demon's Curse.

Ezra Knight.

Fuck me. I could really use Madds right now, but no matter how hard I tried, an invitation was never granted, and I was left to face all of this on my own.

I can't help but keep my gaze trained on the approaching SUV as it slowly makes its way through the overcrowded street, and with every passing second, my heart races just a little bit faster.

It's been six long years since I've seen any of their faces in person.

The crowd outside is deafening, and I can't help noticing the people in the church looking around and trying to peer out the windows, desperate to lay their eyes on the most famous men in the world.

The SUV comes to a stop and, not a moment later, the same man who opened my door and offered me his hand is standing right there, opening the rear door of the SUV. A moment passes before I see Rock step out, only the blinding flashes from the paparazzi make it almost impossible to see him.

Dylan comes next, stepping out and fixing his suit as he presents a mask of indifference. He's always been the best at putting on a show and masking the wild emotions inside. The cameras flash again as the screaming fans desperately try to push past security to get just a bit closer.

Both Dylan and Rock disappear inside the foyer of the church, and I find myself scoffing at the realization that they won't have to stop to have their name marked off. They'd just walk right through like they own the place.

A moment passes, and I keep my gaze locked on the back of the SUV when finally, the front man of Demon's Curse steps out into the daylight and my chest sinks.

There he is. The very man who offered me the world, only to let it burn right there in my fingertips, and then had the audacity to sing about it as though he's the one all broken up inside.

Ezra fucking Knight.

CHAPTER 8

Raleigh

He's gorgeous, just as he's always been. He was nineteen when I last saw him, but he's so much bigger now. His arms have filled out, and even beneath his suit jacket, I can tell how strong he is. His dark, floppy hair is still the same but edgier. It's like he's finally figured out how to tame it.

A sharp, masculine jaw dances below light stubble, and as my heart races out of control, I feel all the coldness within me begin to warm. Even as a teenager, he had this effect on me. He could simply walk into a room, and suddenly I'd see the world in vibrant colors. Judging by the way their fans scream for him, he does the same for them too.

He's not mine anymore, he's theirs.

The paparazzi do their thing, and even from inside, I can hear the press throwing questions at him, and for the first time since leaving six years ago, I feel sorry for him. While this is the life he signed up for, I'm sure he never expected it to be this unforgiving.

The guests within the church begin to stir, and I can't help but look back up the aisle and watch as Rock and Dylan stride in. They nod to people, shake hands, and management welcomes them. As they make their way down the aisle, their gazes come to mine, and they come right over.

"Rae, it's been way too long," Dylan says as I get to my feet. He doesn't allow me even a chance to smile before he pulls me into his strong arms. "I'm so sorry. Ax was . . . He was the best friend I've ever known."

He presses a kiss to my cheek and squeezes me a little tighter before finally releasing me, only for Rock to step in and take his place. "Hey Rae," he murmurs as his hand gently roams up and down my back. "How're you doing?"

"From the looks of it, about as well as you are," I tell him, noticing the red rims around his tired eyes.

Rock pulls back, releasing me, but he grips my hand and gently squeezes. "I know just how hard this is going to be," he tells me. "I don't want you to be alone. Why don't you come sit with us? You know you're always welcome."

"Thanks," I say with a small smile, wondering if Lenny from the label put him up to this before immediately dismissing the thought. Rock is just a nice guy, and clearly that hasn't worn off. "I just . . . I don't think it's a good idea."

"You sure?" he asks, just as an even louder stir comes, telling me that Ezra has just walked in.

"Oh yeah," I say, giving him a knowing look. "I'm sure."

"Alright," he says, knowing not to push me on this as he releases my hand. "Well, we're right here if you change your mind. And that doesn't just count for today. I know we haven't been back home in a while, but you're family, Rae. Always will be."

I nod, not able to form a proper response as the words get caught up in my throat, and before I turn into an emotional wreck, I sit back down and watch Rock and Dylan make their way up to Axel's casket to say goodbye.

The tears are heavy in my eyes, and I quickly wipe them away when I *feel* his presence. It's electrifying, like the other half of my soul that's been missing for so long is floating nearby, begging me to reach out and grab it.

I can't help but discreetly glance over my shoulder and watch as he walks down the aisle, but the moment my eyes reach his face, his gaze shifts and collides with mine. Then just like the very first day I met him, I become locked in his orbit.

It's impossible to look away, and with every step he takes down the aisle, the tension between us becomes unbearable. I've never felt anything like it. So many unsaid words, so many emotions. Pain. Regret. Heartache. Each one of them lingers between us, crippling me in a way I know I'll never recover from.

I struggle to take a breath, and as if knowing just how hard this is for me, he cuts away, dropping his gaze and breaking the vicious intensity.

Ezra joins Rock and Dylan at the casket, and the whole congregation falls silent as if trying to hear what's being said, and I take a moment to trail my gaze over him. I always knew he went all out with tattoos the same way Axel did. They're peeking out from beneath his suit, just enough to leave me wanting to explore, to see what pieces meant so much to him that he had to have them put on to his skin. Then a sick thought occurs that if I were really that desperate to know, I could just Google it, because the internet now knows him in a way I never have.

The boys begin to shift away from the casket, and as if on cue, the blinding flashes from the paparazzi invade the church.

People gasp, desperately searching for where it's coming from before finding them with their cameras shoved up against the church windows. The boys hastily move away and find their seats, but tomorrow's headlines have already been solidified, and there's not a damn thing they can do about it.

Security tackles the paparazzi, and when the church finally finds just a shred of privacy, Axel's funeral service finally begins.

His favorite songs play softly behind a montage of images and achievements, and every story told is more heartbreaking than the last. When the sound of his most treasured guitar solo fills the church, my tears begin cascading down my cheeks.

Twenty minutes in, I hear my name, and I quickly wipe my face before digging into my purse and pulling out the folded paper that I've written and rewritten a million times over the past week. No matter what I wrote down, it never seemed to be enough. Nothing seemed right.

Making my way up front, I take my position behind the dais and look out over the crowd, doing everything I can to avoid the one set of eyes I want to drown in.

As I unfold my paper, a slight panic hits me that my father could be in the crowd somewhere, but I push my trauma aside and do what I can to pull myself together.

I clear my throat and glance up again, my hands shaking as I try not to see the flood of celebrities, but simply the faces of those who cared about him just as much as I always have.

"I never thought I'd have to eulogize my brother," I start, already going off script. "Many of you have known him in recent years. His band took off six years ago, and since then, he's been the apple of everyone's eyes, but not many of you got to experience Axel in his younger years."

I take a breath, already feeling my voice begin to waver. "Axel was three when I was born, and my childhood years with him were the happiest times of my life, though I don't think he ever knew that. He was always patient with me, always kind, caring, and larger than life. He never pushed me away, was never irritated by his little sister always being around, never berated or shamed me. He was my biggest champion, right up until the day he was taken from this life."

"He—" my voice cracks, and the lump in my throat is too much to bear. Tears flow over and cascade down my face, and every remaining piece of me crumbles. My gaze shifts toward the casket, wishing there were some way it would just open up and he'd walk right out, but he's never coming back.

"He was—" I try again, but the words refuse to come, and as I look back toward the crowd, my gaze lands on Ezra's. There's a brokenness there, and I know he's feeling every ounce of my pain. He goes to get up, to help me through the final words of my eulogy, but Dylan beats him to it, already stepping into my side.

He captures my hand behind the dais and gives a gentle squeeze. "I've got you, Rae," Dylan says before scanning my messy speech and picking up right where I left off.

It seems to last forever, when in reality it's only a few minutes before I finally get to step down and make my way back to my seat, only as I pass by Ezra's row, his hand sneaks out and captures mine. I pause, glancing down and meeting his heavy stare as a million messages pass between us.

My skin burns where he touches me, and for just a moment, I'm rooted to the spot, unable to move. I can't look away, and as he squeezes my hand, I want nothing more than to fall into his strong arms and feel the way he holds me, feel the way he brings me home, but remembering the agony he left me in all those years ago, I drop my gaze to where he holds me, distantly noticing a familiar ring on his finger—Axel's ring—and I pull my hand free before finally turning my back.

I can't take it today. I can't handle seeing him, feeling him. I need to get out of here.

My heart races as I make my way back to my seat, and as Ezra is called up after me, my knee bounces, counting down the minutes until

I can race out of the church and take a deep breath.

The pain is too great. It hurts too much. How am I ever supposed to go on without Axel?

Ezra makes his way to the front, and the eager crowd seems much more thrilled about hearing his speech than mine. He clears his throat, and just like that, the Ezra show has been turned on. "Axel was my best friend and the reason I am who I am today, not that I'm exactly someone to be proud of, and yet he was. No matter what shit I got myself into, he was always right there. He had my back, just as I had his, and I'm proud to say that right up until the day he died, he was able to achieve everything he wanted, every dream, no matter how big or small."

Ezra pauses, taking a slight breath. "He had three great loves in his life—his mom, his beautiful sister, Raleigh, and performing for our fans night after night, which was his greatest dream of all—a dream he pulled me into before I even had a chance to question it." The congregation laughs and Ezra has no choice but to wait so he can be heard. "The day I first met him," he continues, his hypnotic gaze shifting to me. "It was easily the best day of my life. My father had moved us to Michigan for work, and there in our new small hometown, my life changed. My first day of school, I met Axel, and within ten minutes of meeting, he was already demanding that I come home with him to start a band. At that point, I'd never heard him play, but there was something so compelling about him that I agreed. That afternoon, Demon's Curse was born, and everything in my life somehow became so much brighter. I found my purpose, and for the first time, I felt a true love for not only music, but for these new people in my life."

He goes on to explain their time together and how it shaped him to be the man he is today—someone who's nothing but a stranger to me now.

His words are calming, and as his deep tone fills the church, I'm able to breathe easy for the first time since Madds pried me awake in tears.

When Ezra finally wraps up his speech and heads to his seat, another video of my brother plays. Axel's goofy smile fills the screen, and the sound of his carefree laugh hypnotizes me. The grainy backstage footage was from someone's phone, and the thrill in his eyes breaks my heart all over again, knowing this might be the very last time I ever see this side of my brother.

He was everything. The light in every room. The fire in everyone's hearts, and now there's nothing but emptiness.

The funeral comes to an end, and as I sit here listening to the people pouring out of the church, I'm forced to face the fact that it's all over. I have no choice but to say goodbye to the one man who's always been there for me, the one who never gave up, and the only man in my life who didn't break me.

Grief bubbles up viciously, and as I cry into my hands, I try to find a way to make this any easier, but there's no use, nothing will ever make this okay.

"Rae," that familiar tone says, standing way too close for comfort.

My head snaps up to find Ezra standing over me, so close that I can see the agony in his dark eyes, smell that familiar scent, and see the hint of his tattoos creeping out beneath the neckline of his dress shirt.

He creeps closer, his hand reaching toward me, and I spring out of my seat, grabbing my purse as I quickly back away from his touch. "No. Don't," I panic, already having to deal with too much of this man for one day.

"Rae, please."

He steps toward me again, but this time, I know better, and I turn my back and race for the exit with tears streaming down my face. "Raleigh, come on. Don't leave like this."

Ezra hurries after me, and just as I reach the massive open doors in the foyer, his warm hand curls around my elbow, pulling me to a stop. "Come on, Rae. You can't leave. Just give me a second to—"

"To what?" I cry while pulling my arm free, all too aware of the people around me and the hundreds of paparazzi just a few feet away, pointing their fancy cameras at us in the doorway. "To finally give me the answers I've been begging for all week? To apologize for letting me find out through social media? To admit that this was all your fault?"

"What?" he says as his brows furrow. "My fault?"

"He was strung out on drugs and alcohol, right?" I demand, having heard the exact same news report that everyone else had—that the toxicology report stated that at the time of death, there were large amounts of cocaine in his system. "You know he was never into that shit before you. If it weren't for you—if you never took him away—"

He reaches for me. "Don't you dare finish that sentence."

I pull out of his reach. "You don't get to touch me," I growl, the tears rolling down my cheeks in waves. I take a breath, willing myself to find just a little more strength. "Tell me what happened."

Ezra just stares at me, refusing to respond, but the heartache in his eyes tells me exactly what I need to know—that I was right. That this world is what killed him. Whether it be drugs or alcohol, it was only a matter of time before the bullshit caught up to him, and now that bullshit has left me more alone than ever.

Heat rises inside of me like burning lava, and I find myself creeping in closer, wanting everyone else to hurt just as much as I do. "When you left, I knew everything was going to change, but I begged you for one thing. I begged you to keep him safe," I remind him, that day so clear in my mind. "You failed him, Ezra. You failed me."

I see the very moment everything crumbles inside of him, and he reaches for me again. "Rae."

"No," I whimper, my bottom lip quivering. "I'm done. I've waited six years for you, but I'm done. Just go back to pretending I don't exist. It's better for everyone that way."

I turn away, crossing my arms over my chest, but not being brave enough to face the press just yet, I simply hover nearby as Ezra stares at me, the pain rolling off him in waves.

It's only a moment before Rock and Dylan crowd around us, and as Rock steps into me and pulls me into his arms, I try to force a comforting smile across my face. "We're going to have a little party in Axel's honor, celebrate everything that he achieved, you know, stuff like that. Do you want to come?"

I shake my head and squeeze his hand. "No, but thank you. I just want to get home so I can crawl into a hole and remain there until the end of time."

"Fair call," he says. "But you know where to find us if you change your mind."

Rock leans in and presses a kiss to my cheek, and not a second later, he's replaced by Dylan, wrapping his arms around us. "Don't be such a stranger, okay?"

"I'll try," I tell him, squeezing him right back. "And thanks. I wouldn't have been able to get through that eulogy without you."

"No problem, Rae. You know you're like a sister to me."

I give him a tight smile, and just like that, their security ushers the boys out of the church, and all I can do is watch Ezra stride past me, the agony in his eyes like nothing I've ever seen. It takes only a moment before the boys disappear into the crowd, and before I know it, Ezra is gone from my life once again.

"I hope everything was to your liking," a gruff voice says beside me.

I glance up to find Lenny Davidson, the head of the boys' label and presumably the man behind this big, outrageous funeral. "That's a joke, right? Did you even know Axel at all? He would have hated every moment of this. It's not at all what he would have wanted, but as usual, you're too focused on the money it could have brought in and appeasing the millions of fans instead of giving him the send-off he truly would have wanted," I say, having heard Axel's complaints on more than one occasion. "Not to mention, your team couldn't answer a single one of my phone calls to give me answers on how this actually happened, to the point my number was blocked. I had to learn everything online, and on top of that, when I emailed to request an invitation for a friend to accompany me so I didn't have to face this alone, it was ignored. So no, not a single bit of this has been to my liking. Where are the people Ax and I grew up with? Where are our aunts and uncles, our cousins? Where's the small hometown funeral by the lake? Where is the mention of him being buried with my mother?"

The tears come in faster, but I force myself to get these last few words out. "My brother is dead, and all I'm left with is a mountain of questions about how such a successful label could have failed him so badly. Where were his minders? Who was responsible for supplying his cocaine? Axel deserved so much better from his label," I tell him. "Do better . . . because the way those boys are going, it'll be one of them you're burying next."

And with that, I stride out of the church and walk away.

CHAPTER 9

Ezra

2 YEARS LATER

A deep scowl settles across my face as I stare at Lenny Davidson and the rest of the label executives across the massive table. They're fucking kidding themselves if they think I'm going back on tour. When Axel died, so did every ounce of my passion for my music.

It means nothing without him.

Lenny stares back at me, doing everything he can to exert his power over me, and while it's definitely worked in the past, I'm no longer down to play his bullshit games. "Enough is enough, Ezra," he growls, his tone making both Rock and Dylan clamp up on either side of me. They're sticklers for the rules . . . within reason, of course. "Now, you've made it more than clear how you feel about completing the tour, but the time for fucking around is over. I've given you the time to grieve, to seek therapy, and get yourself in the right mind frame. You're completing the tour whether you like it or not."

I get to my feet, slamming my fists against the massive table. "That's fucking bullshit, and you know it."

"What's bullshit is that tickets for the remainder of the tour were sold over three years ago. You have millions of fans out there, and while we've held them off with the promise of postponing the tour, there's only so long we can push it. They're becoming restless, Ezra. Your time is up."

"FUCK!"

I whip around, pacing up and down the length of the boardroom as I blow my cheeks out, willing myself to find just a fraction of control. My hands pulse into fists at my sides as I close my eyes, not daring to slow my pace.

"Come on, man," Rock says. "Just hear them out. You know we were always best when we were out on tour."

"Without Ax?" I demand, turning my glare on him. "You're fucking kidding me, right? You want to do this knowing that they're going to replace him, knowing that every time you look across the fucking stage, there's some imposter standing where he used to be?"

Rock stands, returning my glare tenfold. "And you want to have a fucking tantrum and let down all of our fans, knowing that this is what Ax would have wanted?"

I clench my jaw, hating it when he uses reason with me. I know completing this tour is the right thing to do, and sure, I plan on doing it at some point, but I don't think there's ever going to be a time when it feels right.

Letting out a heavy breath, I turn to Dylan, already knowing what his answer will be. "And you?"

"You know how I feel," he tells me. "I just want to get the rest of the tour over and done with, and then after that . . . I don't know. We can enter a new era. Maybe we can look at some new music that won't feel so fucking wrong to perform without him."

I shake my head. "You know I'm not writing anything new," I remind him. The day Axel died, so did any connection to Rae. She was my muse, and the day she stood in the foyer of that church and told me I'd failed Axel with nothing but pure hatred in her eyes, it was finally over.

I hurt her when I left, and in one fell swoop, she took all the pain she felt over those years, bundled it up, and let it storm down over me like acid rain. She left me crippled, and since that moment, I've done nothing but spiral. Hell, I haven't even started to grieve for my best friend. I haven't been able to even feel the agony of his death because that day, Rae left me empty.

"I know. But this might just be what you need to kickstart the process," he says. "Bottom line is, we have to complete this tour. Canceling it is not an option, and postponing again is only going to cause an avalanche of bullshit to land on our fucking doorstep. It's time, Ezra."

Fuck.

I feel the familiar vise closing around my chest, squeezing me too fucking tight—a feeling I've become all too accustomed to over the past two years. "I'm not writing. If you fuckers want new music, then come to the fucking party for a change. I'm done pouring my life into my words, only for them to be exploited by assholes like this," I say, waving a hand toward the executives sitting before me.

"Okay, we'll deal with that when the time comes," Rock says. "If your muse is gone, that's fine. We'll figure something out. For now, let's just focus on wrapping the tour. After that, we'll see where our heads are and figure out our next steps."

I nod, not liking it one fucking bit.

There's no doubt about it, next to losing Axel and letting Rae officially walk out of my life, this will be the hardest thing I will ever do.

The fight leaves me, and I turn my broken stare on Lenny. "Every show has a dedication to Ax."

"Of course."

I nod, trying to mentally go over everything before making any official agreement. "We have final say over Axel's replacement. Talent alone isn't going to cut it. If he's a piece of shit, he's out. He needs to understand he's nothing but a stand-in."

Lenny nods. "Consider it done."

I drop back down into my seat, dragging my hands over my face. "How much time?"

"Two months and you'll be commencing the European leg of the tour."

"Two months?" I ask, whipping my head up. Two months is

nothing. We haven't rehearsed since Axel died. I haven't even picked up my fucking guitar. My throat is wrecked, and I can barely make it through the day without taking a hit of something. "That's bullshit. We need at least six."

"No. You get two, so I suggest you get your asses in the studio and get your shit together," Lenny says. "The dancers are ready to go and have been working on choreography. They've put everything together based on the current setlist. However, they'd be able to switch things up if you need to swap out a few songs."

"Wait. Dancers?" Rock asks. "We've never had dancers."

"After making your fans wait two years for this show, you not only have dancers, you have pyrotechnics, full stage LED screens, props, costumes, and we've upped the arena lighting display. Gone are the days of rocking out on the stage. You're putting on a fucking show, and your fans are going to eat it up."

Dylan shakes his head. "No. Nobody said shit about costumes."

"Nothing dramatic, just a set wardrobe which will be approved by each of you."

"You're mixing us up with a fucking boy band. That ain't our style," I say. "Never has been. Our fans aren't coming to see us prance around stage like a bunch of fucking morons. They come to watch us perform our songs."

"*Perform* being the operative word," Lenny snaps. "If you get out on that stage looking like the dried up, ungrateful piece of shit you've shown up as today, everything we've all worked for will be gone. Everything Axel achieved will be for nothing."

I throw myself to my feet again. "Don't you use his name against me."

Lenny shakes his head, looking at me like I'm a fucking disaster, and he'd be right. I haven't had my head straight since the day Axel died. Hell, if Ax were still here, he'd probably argue that I haven't been right since leaving Rae behind. And again, he'd probably be right. He was always right where she was concerned.

"You're circling the drain, Ezra," Lenny says. "I've been patient with you out of respect for Axel. The band has enough popularity that you could still pull through this and get your name back on the top of the charts, but it's time to carry your weight. There's only so much we can do before you become irrelevant, and trust me, if you're done, that's fine. There are a thousand other bands waiting to step into your shadows. So get your shit together, pick up your fucking guitar, and get back to work. Hell, maybe even pick up that old pen of yours, dust it off, and write some lyrics. Nobody gives a fuck what it's about, as long as it's new music."

The anger bubbles up inside of me, and as my hands ball into fists, I push away from the table and storm out of the boardroom with Rock's muttered tone falling behind me. "Well, that went well."

This is fucking bullshit.

Not only am I being forced back on tour, but now our show is about to turn into a fucking spectacle. All I can hope is that Rock and Dylan have been working with the label behind the scenes to make sure our tour isn't about to be turned into a fucking circus.

Pyrotechnics and dancers? Fuck me.

Being too on edge to drive, I stop in the artists' lounge and help myself to a drink to clear my head. Before I can even wrap my head around everything that just went down in there, I hear Rock and Dylan talking in the hallway, clearly assuming I hightailed it outta here.

"You really think we're making the right move?" Dylan asks him. "You saw him in there. He's not ready."

"We've got no choice, man," Rock says. "Lenny's right. Our fans have been patient with us, but there's only so long we can postpone this before their patience turns into anger. Besides, he's spiraling. He can't see it now, and I don't know if he's hesitant because he doesn't want to get on that stage without Ax, or if he's just too fucking scared to face the pain that will come with it, but being on tour is where he's at home. He needs that stage more than he knows. If we don't do something to help him, he's going to end up buried right beside Ax."

"Fuck."

Their words feel like a fucking weight against my chest, making it almost impossible to breathe, and honestly, I don't know why. It's nothing I haven't heard them say a million times over the past two years, but those were always conversations spoken directly to my face. Hearing the agony in their voices now somehow makes it real.

Do they really think I'm spiraling too far, that there's no coming back for me?

"Yeah," Rock murmurs. "I just wish there was some way we could help him. None of the usual tricks are working. Hookers, drugs, alcohol. I've thrown it all at him trying to pull him out of this. I'm fucking close to throwing his ass inside a therapist's office and not letting him out until he's dealt with his shit."

"I know what you're saying. I thought he just needed time and space, but all that's done is force a wedge between us. I know he was closest to Ax, but at some point, I thought he'd come to us. At least, I hoped. And I know this is going to sound bad, but with Ax gone, the show can at least go on. There are other guys who can play guitar, and while I know it will never be the same, at least we could still get through the tour and maybe even have a shot at making another album. But without Ezra . . . I don't know. He's our frontman. If he goes down, the whole fucking ship sinks with him."

There's silence for a while before Dylan speaks up again, but there's a fierce reluctance in his tone that puts me on edge. "Look, I've got an idea," he tells Rock. "I don't know how it'll play out. It could either make or break him, and if it breaks him, I don't think anything will ever be the same."

"Fuck." Rock lets out a heavy breath, and even from within the lounge, I can hear it. "What have we got to lose?"

Dylan scoffs. "Oh, I don't know. Only everything we've ever worked for."

Rock laughs, and I can imagine the way he would drag his hands down his face. "Alright then," he says. "Any idea of yours, even a shitty one, is better than doing nothing."

"Okay," Dylan says. "Let me do some digging, and if I think it's actually manageable, I'll put it forward. But beware, Ezra's gonna be pissed."

"Shit," Rock mutters. "I'll take pissed Ezra a million times over watching him waste his life away. At least it gives him something to fight about."

"True."

"Alright, I'm out," Rock says. "I've got some shit to do, and then I'm spending the night looking over Lenny's suggestions for new guitarists. The sooner we get someone in, the quicker we'll know if they're a good match."

"Yeah, alright," Dylan says. "I'll talk to Ezra and make sure he's sober enough to start rehearsals tomorrow. Knowing him, it's bound to be a fucked-up night after that meeting."

"Okay. Keep his ass out of the media. The last thing we need is another fucking scandal right before announcing the commencement of the tour."

"I've got it, man."

And with that, their voices fade away, leaving me here with nothing but my internal torture, desperately wishing there was some way to make it all . . . disappear.

CHAPTER 10

Raleigh

14 YEARS OLD

The band plays as I sit cross-legged on the couch that Axel and Ezra picked up off the side of the street. I was hesitant to sit on it for the first six months. The couch is old and falling apart, and it came with a pungent stink to it, but after Mom got sick of staring at the stains every time she walked into the garage, she finally hit it with the carpet shampooer and suddenly it was good as new. That didn't stop me from laying a sheet over it first.

My laptop rests against my knees as I do my thing, working on the design of the guys' first flyer for their upcoming gig. It's nothing astronomical, just a forty-five-minute set at one of our local bars that offer live music, but it's their first real stepping stone, and since the moment we heard the news, it's been guns blazing around here.

Every spare moment, the guys practice. If they're not at school, they're right here, and I'm not going to lie, I don't hate it. I know technically I'm not in the band, but I might as well be. I've been right here since day one. I know their songs just as well as they do, know all the ins and outs, know all the drama that's going on behind the scenes, and honestly, the drama isn't that great. They really need to work on that if they intend to be rockstars.

Axel is too focused on the band to worry about having a girlfriend. Rock and Dylan are the manwhores of the group. They tend to have random girls show up during practice who think they're about to become the apple of the boys' eyes. As for Ezra ... Well, he's somewhat focused on me.

God, just the thought of it makes my cheeks flame.

Since day one, Ezra has been at the very front of my brain. I'm so aware of him it's ridiculous. When he walks into a room, I don't just see it, I *feel* it. When he brushes past me, my skin burns from his touch. When he looks at me, my heart explodes into a million tiny Ezra-shaped pieces. Sometimes when it's just the two of us, he will drape his arm over my shoulder and gently press a kiss to my temple, and I swear I could fly.

I'm in love.

Scratch that. I'm not just in love. I'm head over heels, unbearably falling for a boy who I'm not sure is even okay for me to want. He's seventeen now, and no matter the age difference, I always feel like some dumb kid in comparison. Yet, when he looks at me, I swear he feels something too.

Maybe I'm insane. He's the most gorgeous boy I've ever met. Girls are always falling at his feet, and that's before they've heard him sing. He could have anyone he wants, yet whenever I'm in the room, it's my stare he seeks out.

Don't get me wrong, he's never actually said that I'm anything more than just his best friend's little sister. He's never touched me or kissed me for real. He's never done anything that warrants me believing there could be something between us, but I *feel* it.

When he looks at me, it's not just a passing gaze, it's a deep, longing stare that has a million messages passing between us, and it's everything to me. The second our gazes collide, there's a connection that's unlike anything I've ever felt, and I don't ever want to let it go. When he's not here, I feel cold, and when his mom insists on family weekends out of town, my soul physically aches, and while I've never found the guts to tell him that, I think he knows.

Who am I kidding? He's Ezra Knight, of course he knows.

Trying to keep my attention focused on the flyer, I put on the finishing details, adding the location and time of their gig before holding my laptop out and looking at it from a distance. The boys plan to print at least five hundred of these and basically throw them from the top of the stairwell at their school like a scene out of a teen movie.

Truth be told, I think it's overkill. The bar isn't that big. There's no way they're going to fit more than a hundred people in there, but if they're able to pull a crowd, which I have no doubt they will, they'll be invited back again. It's a no-brainer that the guys want to go all out on this.

After deciding the flyer is as perfectly brilliant as it's ever going to be, I rest back against the couch and wait for the boys to finish their song while getting lost in the sound of Ezra's voice. It's my favorite thing to do. Every day I sit right here to do my homework. It's unofficially become my spot, plus it has the best vantage spot to watch Ezra without it being completely obvious. Yet, every time I look at him, his gaze automatically comes to mine as if he feels my stare the way I feel his.

And right now, it's no different.

The boys play together like a well-oiled machine. They never miss.

The four of them together are a force to be reckoned with, and it's clear to every single one of us that this is going somewhere big. Even Mom and Dad have finally come around to the idea of it. Hell, sometimes I even catch Mom singing their songs while she bakes in the afternoons.

All of the guys like to write lyrics, but Ezra is the only one who's had the guts to turn them into songs, and so far, every song he's ever written has been incredible. In some of the songs, he talks about a girl who's so far away, he'll never be able to have her, and when I first heard the lyrics, it gutted me. I thought maybe there was someone else, another girl he had his heart set on before he moved here, but now, I'm not so sure.

Deciphering Ezra's lyrics has officially become my full-time job.

The song is just coming to a close when Ezra turns and meets my stare, and as he sings the rest of the lyrics, he doesn't dare look away. With every passing second, my cheeks flush, heating up until they're burning hot. His dark eyes sparkle as they soften, and for just a moment, I'm lost within the dark depths of his stare.

My heart races as I fall even more in love with this mystical man, and as the song comes to a close and the room falls silent, a cocky grin stretches across his full lips.

God, what I wouldn't give to kiss those lips.

"Dude," Axel grunts, breaking through the heavy silence and snapping us out of our stare. "How many times do I have to tell you to quit serenading my sister? You know she goes all stupid and loopy every time you do it."

Ezra smirks as a laugh bubbles up his throat and catches on the microphone, letting the sound reverberate through the garage as Rock and Dylan roll their eyes. This isn't exactly a new conversation. It's been like this since the very beginning, and while anyone looking in would think the connection Ezra and I share is somewhat inappropriate considering he's three years older than me, everyone in this very room . . . they get it. Even Axel.

Whatever this is between me and Ezra, there's nothing wrong about it. There's nothing sexual or violating. It's simply an emotional connection that's never been pushed. Hell, had it gone anywhere, or if Ezra had pressured me in any way, Axel would have beat the shit out of him.

"Sorry," Ezra mutters to Ax despite every single person in this room knowing he doesn't mean it. A moment later, he looks back at me, and his whole face lights up like Christmas morning.

My smile widens, and I beam back at him as everything inside of me clenches. I know he's made a point not to press anything physical between us, but would it really be terrible if he did?

Letting out a breath and not wanting my traitorous thoughts to become too obvious, I grip the laptop and spin it around, showing the guys the flyer. "What do you think?" I ask, watching the four of them creep in to get a better look at my laptop.

"Fuck yeah, Rae. That's amazing," Ezra says with his guitar flung over his shoulder, his gaze lingering on mine opposed to the actual flyer.

"Just needs a band name, and it'll be done."

"Ugh," Rock groans. "Not this again."

"We need a fucking name," Axel says, discreetly shoving Ezra a step away from me. "It's been a year, and we still can't agree on anything."

A smirk cuts across my face. "I mean, I still think Satan's Asshole is a clear winner."

Axel rolls his eyes. "Our band is not being named after the devil's forbidden backdoor."

"I don't know," I tease. "I think it suits you."

"What about Sinkhole?" Dylan suggests, waving his hands out as if imagining the name in lights, but let's be honest, while it certainly has some kind of merit, it's not right.

Rock shakes his head, a smirk lingering on his lips. "Nah, I'm still down for—"

"If the next words out of your mouth are Dirty Areola," I warn,

"I'm going to use your head as a bass drum."

Rock laughs, knowing exactly how to get a rise out of me. It's a name that came up the very first day the guys got together, and it's been a running joke ever since.

I feel Ezra's stare on me, and as I glance up, I find a strange look in his eyes, as if he's thinking too hard that his brain is about to explode. "What about . . . okay, hear me out," he says, as if somewhat nervous. He pauses, his lips pressing into a hard line as he waits for all the guys to look his way. "What about Demon's Curse?"

"Hmm," Axel says, his brows furrowed. "That's actually not too bad."

"Demon's Curse," Rock says, trying the words out for himself, slowly nodding. "I like it."

"Yeah?" Ezra says, his gaze nervously flicking between me and the guys, making me wonder if there's maybe something a little deeper there, something that clearly none of us have figured out.

"I'm in," Dylan says. "It's a shit load better than Rusty Trombone or Dirty Areolas."

I roll my eyes and feel my face flush. There are some things these guys simply shouldn't talk about when I'm around, and for the most part, they're pretty good, but every now and then, they forget, and the most horrendous things fly out of their ridiculous mouths. Trust me, I was horrified when I sat in my room and consulted my good friend Google about what a rusty trombone and a Viennese oyster are. I couldn't look the boys in the eyes for days.

"So, it's settled?" I ask, turning my laptop back around and starting to type their new band name in. "You're Demon's Curse?"

"Settled," Ax says as we hear the familiar sound of Dad's car pulling into the driveway. There are a few loud noises coming from outside, sounding as though Dad might have taken a little stumble on the front porch, but just as I go to get up to see if he needs any help, I hear him walk through the front door.

"Yo," Rock says, turning toward Ax as I start to wonder where the hell Mom is. She's always home before Dad gets home, and more times than not, she's home before I get home from school. "Your dad good?"

Axel shrugs his shoulders, and as he goes to respond, the internal garage door opens. Dad wobbles in the doorway, his eyes glassy and red. He's always been a respectable, well-dressed man, but right now, he looks as though someone just scraped him off the floor of some shitty dive bar.

"Woah, Dad. Are you drunk?" Axel says as I watch my father all but fall into the garage with his shirt untucked, buttons missing, and what looks like hot sauce smeared across his chest. "Wait. Did you just drive home like this?"

"OUT," he roars, striding to the garage fridge and pulling out a beer. "All of you little fuckers out."

What the hell?

Ezra discreetly steps in front of me, blocking my view of my father, and I put my laptop down on the couch beside me before getting to my feet. I peer around Ezra to gaze at my father, confusion blasting through my veins. I've never seen him like this. "Is everything okay?" I ask, unease gripping me in a chokehold. "Where's Mom? She hasn't come home yet."

Dad fumbles toward me, his lips twisting into a scowl, and I don't miss the way Ezra grabs me and shuffles me aside. He moves toward the couch, shoving Rock out of his way as Axel barely manages to escape a nasty push. "Your mother is never coming home," he spits, just before crashing down onto the couch and snapping my laptop in half. "She's dead."

"What?" I breathe, my voice barely audible as the pulse in my ears thumps so loudly that it threatens to deafen me. Surely I misheard him.

Dad cracks the lid of his beer as I feel my world closing in on me. My knees give out as I struggle to keep myself upright. Ezra clutches onto my side, and my nails dig into his forearm.

"I SAID GET OUT!"

Axel rips the beer out of Dad's hand and launches it across the garage, making me jump as it smashes against the drywall. "What the fuck is wrong with you? Why the hell would you say that?"

Dad launches to his feet and stumbles into Axel. "You good for nothing piece of shit," he roars, trying to hit Axel but missing as he falls back against the couch, his weight breaking the old springs inside.

He sits there for a moment as I simply stare at him, too afraid to push any further, too terrified to hear those words come out of his mouth again, but I have to try. I have to know if it's true. "Dad," I whisper, the single word like a crack of lightning striking right through my chest.

The fight leaves him, and he stares ahead, his bloodshot eyes incapable of focusing on a single thing in the garage as he silently begins to weep. "Some asshole ran her off the road," he cried, falling to pieces right there on the couch. "She's gone, Rae. Dead on impact."

I crumble, and not even Ezra's strong arms are capable of keeping me on my feet. My knees crash against the cold concrete as he holds me to his chest, but all I can do is look up at my brother, his stare just as lost as mine as he tries to process everything our father said.

Our mother is gone.

Dead on impact.

Axel stumbles back as though the weight of our father's words physically stuck him, and Dylan reaches out for him as my world blurs behind tear-filled eyes.

Ezra murmurs something into my ear, but I don't hear his soothing words over my father's torturous ones—*Dead on impact.*

Dead on impact.

Dead. On. Impact.

They repeat over and over, sending me into a whirlpool of unbearable agony. My mom is gone. I'm never going to see her again. Never going to feel her arms wrap around me when I walk through the door after a long day at school. Never going to hear her sing the boys' songs as she bakes cookies in the afternoon.

She won't be here when I come in from my first date. She won't be there for my first heartbreak or to make everything better when my world is falling apart. She won't get to see me walk down the aisle or hold my hand through pregnancy.

She won't ever get to grow old.

This can't be real.

Everything around me fades from existence, and time warps as though I'm no longer living in the same universe. All I know is that one minute, I'm crumbling on the dirty garage floor, and the next, I'm silently crying in bed with my face smashed against the pillow.

I don't know what time it is, only that there's not a single star in the dark sky tonight.

I've never felt despair like this before. The grief is overwhelming, and I can't make it stop. I don't know how. When my world is falling apart, Mom is the one I run to. She's the one who knows how to calm me, how to ease my pain, but without her, I'm lost—just an empty soul floating out at sea with no lighthouse to guide me home.

A soft knock sounds and my gaze shifts to the door, barely able to see it through my tears, and when I see Ezra standing awkwardly in my doorway, my brows furrow with confusion. He stays over all the time, especially nights when the guys have been working on turning his lyrics into melodies, but he's never knocked on my door before.

I push up onto my elbow as I awkwardly watch him and try to wipe the tears from my eyes, but it's no use, more replace them quicker than I can wipe them away. "I ummm . . . I wanted to check on you," he murmurs, keeping his tone low. "I wasn't sure if you'd be able to sleep."

I shake my head. "I can't make it stop hurting."

"I know."

I crumble back to my tear-soaked pillow as he awkwardly stands in the doorway, slowly creeping closer. "Fuck. I . . . I know I'm probably crossing some kind of invisible line by just being in here, but I can't walk away knowing you're hurting like this. Tell me to leave, Rae."

I shake my head again. "Don't go," I whimper, terrified of being alone and falling back into the dark abyss of agony. "Please, I . . . I won't tell Ax. I just—"

I don't get a chance to finish my sentence before Ezra gently nudges the door closed with his foot and strides across my room. His tall frame collapses onto my bed, keeping on top of the sheets, and within seconds, I'm in his arms, my body curled against him as I rest my head on his chest.

"I'm sorry, Rae," he whispers as his warm lips brush against my temple. "I'm so fucking sorry."

Ezra's hands wrap around me, one against my arm and the other holding my waist as his thumb trails back and forth. He doesn't dare move, doesn't make a peep, just simply lays there with me as the grief tears through my chest, shredding it to pieces with its vicious talons.

I listen to the steady beat of his breaking heart—the only sound that could offer me just a scrap of solace in this cruel world—until finally, exhaustion claims me, and I fall into a broken, cold sleep, dreaming of the woman who promised to always be right by my side.

But that's the tricky thing about promises—they give you a false sense of security. In reality, things like time can't be promised because how long we get to walk this Earth isn't a choice. At any given moment, all of it can be ripped away and broken, promises be damned.

CHAPTER 11

Raleigh

This is officially rock bottom.

Who would have known, two years after dropping out of college and being forced back to the hometown I always vowed never to return to, I'd be nothing more than a wreck, living out of the back of my car.

Fucking pathetic.

Happy birthday to me, I suppose. Twenty-four has never looked so good.

These past two years have been insufferable. I've been angry, and every day I find a reason to blame Axel for all the shit in my life, for all the hell I've had to suffer through, despite knowing he did nothing but chase a dream. And that realization only sends me spiraling further.

Life has a way of kicking you when you're down, and in the past, I've had people around me who've been there to help pick me up, but now . . . I'm all alone.

I tried. I really did, but after Axel's funeral, I just . . . couldn't. Getting out of bed was impossible, and it didn't take long before I was called in to meet with the dean. She offered to give me time, to put my studies on pause and come back to it next semester after I'd had time to grieve, but the idea of spending another day in this place that was supposed to offer me freedom suddenly left me feeling more caged than ever. I walked out of that office and waved goodbye to everything I'd worked my ass off for.

My college degree had already begun slipping out of my hands, and I suppose I helped it on its way down. Axel had been paying my rent up until then, and while Madds did everything she could to try and make it easier for me, I couldn't put her under that kind of financial strain, especially so close to finals.

The desperation, grief, and fear of the unknown were too much, and despite everything, I packed my bags and found my way back to the town I vowed to never see again. The town where I experienced the best and worst times of my life. The town that holds the greatest memories of my mother and the darkest ones of my father I've never dared to speak out loud. It was the town I first fell in love, the town where I had my heart torn to shreds, and the town that forced me to spread my wings and take flight. It was almost ironic how the cruel world left me as a crippled bird with no choice but to return to its viper-filled nest.

I had more than my fair share of fears when I realized there was nowhere else for me to go, but all I needed was a few weeks to get back on my feet. I thought if I had just a little bit of familiarity, just long enough to find a job and save some cash, I'd be able to get out of there with most of my sanity intact. I should have known better, but desperation makes us do crazy things and make foolish choices.

That town never felt like home after the boys left.

Then after watching my father leave for work, I ransacked the home that left me broken, grabbed what little cash and supplies I could find, and since then, I've been struggling just to survive.

I've worked day shifts as a waitress and then raced across the street to start my second shift for the day in the only dive bar willing to hire me. The tips were shit, but at least I was able to eat. Showering and laundry? Well, that's a different story.

Most nights, I crash in the back of my car, and on the odd occasion where the tips are somewhat decent, I splurge and get myself a room in the shitty motel across town. The beds are hard and lumpy, and I can't always guarantee that the sheets have been washed, but I get a decent shower and a chance to relax in a way I can't do from the backseat of my car.

It's nothing special, nothing to be proud of, but it beats going back to that house, and I'd take the struggle a million times over submitting to the devil.

Every few months, I move around and find a new town, never able to find somewhere to settle. Ever since I lost Axel, I've felt like a hopeless soul, destined to wander without a purpose, and damn it, it makes me so angry. Before him, before Ezra and the band, I wanted to be something. I wanted to do good in the world, but I'm broken beyond repair, and I don't know how to claw my way out of the darkness. I'm barely surviving, and all I want to do is scream.

Don't get me wrong, every now and then I find the courage to laugh and smile again. It never lasts long, but it's always enough to give me what I need to keep going, to see the light at the end of the tunnel, no matter how dim that light might be.

Today, the dim light is the ice cream cake I'm going to splurge on. It'll probably leave my lactose intolerant body hunched over a toilet later as a big fuck you, but it'll be worth it. I hope.

I stand in the bathroom mirror of the shitty motel I found late last night. The bed is just as terrible as I expected it to be, but at least the door offered a dead bolt, and the TV had more than one channel to occupy my lonely night.

Most of the time, I do what I can to avoid social media. I have my phone, and while it's nothing special, it allows me to keep in contact with Madds and check up on Dylan and Rock every now and then. Truth be told, I haven't responded to many of their texts lately. They don't tell me how Ezra's doing, and I don't dare ask, but I'd be lying to myself if I didn't admit that I'd wondered on more than a few occasions.

Losing Ax would have hit him just as hard as it hit me, and while a part of me hates myself for what I said to him at the funeral, I can't bring myself to regret it.

The words I said to him repeat in my head a million times a day, and while it kills me every time, nothing guts me more than remembering the haunted emptiness in his eyes before his security team escorted him out. Axel's death killed him, but my ruthless rejection burned him to ashes.

I needed him to feel my pain. I needed him to hurt, and hell, I think I still do.

I have too much anger, too much to blame them for, but since Axel's not here to take the brunt of my wrath, I have no choice but to let it eat me from the inside out.

This pent-up anger is slowly killing me, and I hate that I'm not capable of letting it go.

I'm wasting my life away, and when I think of everything my mom and Axel would have wanted for me, all I can do is laugh before it turns into a broken, gut-wrenching sob.

My phone rings from the small bedside table in my motel room, and I step back from the mirror and make a show of forcing a smile across my face and hating how fake it looks. It's showtime.

Hurrying out of the bathroom, I quickly scoop up my phone and accept the call from Madds. She checks in almost every day, and honestly, I'm so glad she's so easily swayed and never thinks to dig deeper than the surface. Otherwise, she would have seen through my lies years ago. "Oh my god! Happy birthday," she squeals into the phone before I have a chance to even say hello. "I feel like it was only yesterday I was calling on your last birthday. It's insane how quickly these past twelve months have gone."

"Right," I say, despite not being able to agree with her even a little bit. It's crazy how long the days feel when you work two jobs and spend the nights sleeping with a knife you stole from a restaurant just so you can feel safe enough to close your eyes. "How are you doing? How's work? Is that boss of yours still giving you a hard time?"

"Ugh, yes," she says. "She's such a cow."

Madds instantly dives into a rant while giving me more than enough corporate gossip than I can handle for the day, and as she chats away, I grab my small makeup collection and head back into the bathroom.

I start getting ready for my first shift in this new town that I didn't bother to learn the name of, and when she turns the conversation back on me, I start to sweat. "So, how's everything going for you? You've gotta tell me all about this guy you're dating. Oh, scrap that! How did it go with that promotion? Did you get it?"

I cringe, more than thrilled that Madds didn't feel the need to video chat today. If she had, she surely would have seen the look on my face and known that everything I've said to her over the past two years has been nothing but lies, but what choice do I have? If she knew how I was living and what kind of hell I've been suffering through, she'd take the weight of that right on her shoulders, and these burdens are only mine to bear.

As far as Madds is aware, I'm working some lowly marketing job back in Michigan, living in a cheap apartment that's walking distance from my fake job. I also made up a fake boyfriend, Jason, who may or may not be a little kinky. She thinks I'm living the life I always set out to achieve . . . more or less, and while my lies make me feel like an even bigger piece of shit, it puts a smile on her face, and that's all that matters to me.

As I'm about to explain my non-existent promotion, my phone beeps in my ear, and I pull it back to find an unknown number flashing across the screen. "Shit, someone's trying to call me," I tell Madds, hoping like fuck it's not someone from my new job canceling on me before I've even had the chance to start. "This could be important. I'll give you a call back in a minute."

"Kay, love you," she says before ending the call.

There's a split second of silence before I accept the call, and I let out a heavy breath, already expecting the worst. "Hello."

"Hello, is this Raleigh Stone?"

"Yep, that's me."

"My god, you're a hard woman to get a hold of, but nonetheless, it's an absolute pleasure to speak with you again," the too-formal voice says in a tone that nudges at a memory I can't quite place. "It's Lenny Davidson from Louder Records. How are you doing, sweetheart? It's been far too long."

My jaw drops, and I struggle to form words into sentences. This is some kind of joke, right? Some old fan of Axel's has found my number and is now pranking me. There is literally no possible reason under the sun for why the CEO of Louder Records would call me. "Umm . . . Hi," I say. I haven't heard from the man since Axel's funeral when I all but threatened to ruin him if he let anything bad happen to any of the guys. "I've been . . . I don't know, fine I guess."

"Wonderful news," he says, clearly not picking up on my tone. "Listen, I know this is a little out of left field, however, I have a proposal for you."

My face scrunches with unease. "What kind of proposal?"

"A job offer."

I scoff. "I don't know what kind of job offer you could possibly have for me, but the answer is no. I'm not some struggling artist hoping to make it big time, and I'm not some fancy producer. There's literally nothing I could possibly offer Louder Records that would be beneficial for anyone involved."

"Ahhh, I disagree," he says, way too chipper for a man currently speaking to a woman who holds him somewhat responsible for her brother's death. "Your brother, may he rest in peace, always spoke so highly of you. You were such an important factor in his life, and he would always tell me that one day, you would be marketing director for Demon's Curse and would be running circles around those boys."

His words are like a direct strike against my chest, and I have to force myself to sit so that I don't crumble to the ground. Axel was always so proud of me, no matter how much I screwed up. He always believed I could do anything I set my mind to, just as he did, so when I first told him as an awkward teenager that I wanted to be the marketing director for Demon's Curse, he took it as a challenge. For him, it was a done deal, but for me, things were different.

"Yeah, well, that was a long time ago," I say, trying to keep the positivity in my tone.

"Look, I understand that working for Demon's Curse was always a dream of yours, and while I can't quite offer you that, I can, however, offer you a stepping stone."

My brows furrow, too curious to deny him right away. "What kind of stepping stone?"

"A new band," he says. "They're going on their first tour, and when my team came to me and said that they're in need of a marketing genius to help kickstart this tour, you were the first name that came to mind."

"I—"

"Don't say no just yet," he says. "I understand that working for the same company that your brother spent so many wonderful years with isn't going to be easy, but this is what he always wanted for you. I'm not sure what direction your life has taken over the past few years, but if you want to take a leap and make a change, the opportunity is right here."

"Thank you," I say, unsure of where all the tears on my face are coming from. "I really appreciate it. I do, but I'm not the person you're looking for. After Axel died, so did any chance I had of becoming something. I dropped out of college, and I'm sure a company like Louder Records isn't looking for some college dropout to run the marketing team for the launch of a new band that I'm sure is some kind of replacement for Demon's Curse."

"You're not wrong. Louder Records isn't searching for some college dropout to run the launch of this band's tour, but Axel had faith in you," he tells me. "Your brother believed that you were born to do this. He even had me write it into a contract before he passed. He was an incredible musician but an even better man who was a great judge of character. He knew what he wanted and how to get it, and he knew when something was right, and you Raleigh, he knew you would be right for this. So, I'm choosing to have faith in him again. If Axel Stone believed that you would be the right fit for this, then who the hell am I to question it?"

I let out a breath, my knee bouncing as I consider it. It's not as though I have much to lose. "What exactly does this position entail?" I question, realizing that working for Louder Records puts me right in the Ezra Knight danger zone.

"There are too many components of this position to list over the phone. However, it will be expected that you travel with the band on tour."

My brows rise, starting to get a little intrigued. "And what band is it, exactly?"

"Unfortunately, I can't disclose that information until an NDA is signed and secured. However, I must stress that this is not an opportunity that is going to wait around. If you don't scoop it up, someone else will."

"Even without my degree?"

"That's correct, Raleigh."

"Shit. It's a lot to think about."

"Indeed it is," he agrees. "Listen, why don't you fly out to LA? I can have a private jet waiting for you at any airport of your desire within the hour. Come check out the studio, meet the band, hear them play, and we'll go from there. If you're feeling it, we'll sit down and talk terms, and you can give me a decision then. Otherwise, I'll leave you to get on with your life."

"Fly to LA?" I ask. "Just drop everything and get on a jet."

"I will be sure to make this worth your while," Lenny says. "Any sister of Axel's is considered family to Louder Records, and we take care of our own. You will be more than fairly compensated for your work and time."

"Shit."

"What have you got to lose, Raleigh?" he questions like a sleazy car salesman, and he's right, what the hell do I have to lose? Not a damn thing.

"Okay," I finally tell him. "I can be at O'Hare International Airport in forty minutes."

"Is that Chicago?"

"Yes."

"Alright," he says slowly, as though writing something down. "You should be touching down in LA a little after lunch. We'll put you up in a hotel, give you a chance to get yourself together, and then we can arrange to meet in the studio . . . say, around three. Does that work for you?"

"Three is fine," I tell him as my head begins to spin. Am I seriously considering this? Surely this is insane, right? Or perhaps this is Axel's way of looking out for me.

"Perfect. I look forward to it, Raleigh." And with that, he ends the call, and not a moment later, I'm scrambling through my shitty motel room, collecting all my things, and getting my ass out the door. Apparently, I have one hell of a flight to catch.

CHAPTER 12

Raleigh

The private jet touches down in LA, and as I step onto the tarmac, I have to remind myself to breathe. This is insane. Is this really how Axel was living for those last six years of his life? Getting the royal treatment everywhere he went?

The jet was mind-blowing. It's luxury on a new scale, not to mention, it's the only plane I've ever been on that's offered free Wi-Fi and champagne just for existing.

If Lenny's plan is to dazzle me with the good life so I have to accept his offer, it's already working. Sure, I'd be on tour with a band I don't know, but I'd be doing the work I spent all those years cramming for, and while I never completed college and officially got my degree, it would be a shame to waste all of that knowledge. Besides, I'd be put up in fancy hotels night after night with security and a constant paycheck at the end of every week. I could eat like a normal person and actually enjoy life.

It sure beats living out of my car and having to sleep with a knife to make sure I don't get raped in the middle of the night. It's a no-brainer. And on the plus side, if I'm careful with my paycheck, by the end of the tour, I might even have enough saved for a place of my own. You know, assuming Lenny meant it when he said they take care of their own. I mean, I sure as hell don't feel like family to Louder Records, but if he insists, who am I to say no?

Assuming all goes well, this is an opportunity that could open doors. If the label likes my work and we have a successful tour, there's every chance they could offer me another tour, maybe regular work in a proper office where I get to do what I love every day of the week, not just during tour.

The warm LA sun shines down on me, already beginning to thaw my cold heart, and without even trying, I sense peace pulsing through my veins. Maybe this is why Axel loved LA so much and made this place his home. I never had a chance to visit him here, never got to see his home or the world he'd built for himself, but I can only assume it was everything he ever wanted.

A driver waits for me, and I try not to get giddy at the sight of the limo. "Miss Stone," he says, opening the back door and waving me in.

"Thank you," I say, but the second my ass hits the expensive leather seat, I can't hold on to the giddiness for another moment. A stupid grin rips across my face, and within seconds, I have my phone against my ear.

It rings twice before Madds whispers into the phone. "Girl, you know I'm working." I hear the sound of her heels clicking down a hallway, probably after making some excuse about needing to pee so she could take the call. "Is everything okay?"

"Break out the fucking candles, Madds. You'll never believe where I am right now."

"I'm assuming your ass is at work where it's supposed to be."

"Nope," I say, popping the *p*. "That call I had this morning, it was Lenny Davidson from Louder Records."

"Wait. What?" she breathes. "That's the label Demon's Curse is under, right?"

"Yeah."

"Shit," she says with a heavy sigh. "Are you okay? Did he want to talk with you about Axel? I know it's been two years, but I know how that shit tears you to pieces."

"I mean, yeah. He brought up Axel a few too many times for comfort, but he was actually calling to offer me a job."

"What?"

"That's what I said, but apparently Ax was already putting things in motion before he died and had mentioned me enough that when they started to put a team together for a new band, my name was at the top of his list."

"Holy fucking shit."

"Yeah," I say with disbelief. "That's pretty much how I responded too."

"So, it's a marketing gig, then?"

"As far as I'm aware," I say. "I have a meeting with him today to discuss all the ins and outs of the contract and hopefully have a chance to meet the band to see if I mesh well with them. Then assuming everything is as good as I think it will be, I'll be going on tour with this band."

There's stunned silence on the other end of the phone, and by the time a slow smirk finally spreads across my face, Madds pulls herself together enough to respond. "That's incredible," she breathes. "Holy fuck. I'm struggling to wrap my head around everything. Okay, ummm . . . What about your current job?"

"It's a piece of shit entry-level job that I'll never really find growth in considering my lack of degree," I lie, immediately feeling like a piece of shit for it. "It's a no-brainer. And besides, if this doesn't work out how I'm hoping, I'll just head back home, claim I needed the day for a stomach virus, and be back at work first thing tomorrow."

"Wait. Hold up," she says. "What do you mean *head back home?* Where the hell are you?"

"Oh, haven't I told you that part yet?" I ask with a laugh as the excitement begins to infect me, but hell, it's the first time I've felt any kind of excitement in two long years. After college, Madds took a job in LA, and she's been killing it ever since, so of course I'm going to find her while I'm here. But even if this job doesn't work out for me, I needed this excitement more than I realized. I've only ever been in LA one time before, and that was for Axel's show-stopping funeral, but this time, it's for me. Maybe I could even visit his home and delve into the life he had here. Hell, I know Madds wouldn't say no to accompanying me to the former home of Axel Stone. Hopefully it was left just as he always had it. Actually, I wonder what happened to all of his things. His home, cars, and expensive guitar collection. He had so many things he was so proud of, and now, they're probably just sitting in some shitty Demon's Curse memorial hall collecting dust.

"Uhhh no. Are you not in Michigan right now?"

"Not even close," I say. "The label sent a private jet to come get me, and I've spent the last four hours sipping champagne and being waited on while I made the journey to LA!"

"L—FREAKING—A?" Madds squeals, probably way too loudly for her office building. "Holy fucking shit. Girl, why didn't you start with that? We have to do something. How long are you going to be here?"

"I have no idea. If everything goes well with this meeting, I could be here indefinitely . . . I think. But if it doesn't, then probably just the night."

"Okay, well, for what it's worth, I know you're going to kill it at this meeting today. This is the most exciting thing ever, and you might even get to see Rock and Dylan and—" she cuts herself off before the name slips out of her mouth, and I'm grateful that she doesn't linger on the almost slip. "Anyway, I think we should meet up tonight, you know, just in case walking in there is too much and you need time to chill afterward."

"Absolutely."

"What hotel are you staying at?"

"Is it bad I never actually asked?" I laugh. "Lenny said private jet, and I got in my car without a second thought."

"Okay. Well text me when you know, and I can meet you there after work," she says. "And Rae? You really are gonna kill this. You're the best choice, and Lenny freaking Davidson would be a fool not to hire you on the spot."

"Thanks, Madds."

"Yeah, yeah," she says, and I can practically hear the way she rolls her eyes. "I have to get back to work before you get my ass fired. I'll see you tonight, okay? Love you."

"Love you too," and with that, the line goes dead.

It's a short twenty-minute drive from LAX to the hotel, and when the driver pulls up out front, all I can do is gape at the massive building. I've never seen anything like it. It's the picture of luxury, exclusive to only the highest caliber people—the one percenters, billionaires, socialites, and celebrities. People like Ezra Knight.

The door opens for me, and someone else moves to grab my bags from the back. I'm almost embarrassed by my shitty canvas bag bought from the mall nearly ten years ago. I'm sure these guys are used to handling designer suitcases that cost more than I've made over the past two years, but nonetheless, I hold my head up high and allow the door opener to usher me inside the exclusive hotel.

Checking in takes all of two seconds, and before I know it, I'm escorted up to one of the executive suites. It's not quite the penthouse, but it's high enough that the man escorting me needs a special access card just to activate the elevator.

Getting into the room that's bigger than my family home back in Michigan, I make my way right over to the floor-to-ceiling windows and stare out at the incredible view. The city below is gorgeous, and with the afternoon sun glistening off the other building, I find myself completely mesmerized.

A specially prepared meal is waiting for me on the table, and since I haven't had the chance to eat like this since the last time I was with Axel, I don't hesitate to dig in.

I have an hour before I'm due to meet with Lenny, so I take advantage of the time to pamper myself with an everything shower, using the expensive shampoo and conditioner as opposed to the cheap two-in-one shit I've been reduced to over the years.

Basking in the endless hot water, I finally have the motivation to shave, but it's not for Lenny's benefit of course. Looking my best means feeling my best, and as I stand in the bathroom wrapped in the expensive lush robe provided, I spend a few extra minutes hacking away at my brows.

I feel better than I have in so long, and it's more refreshing than I could have known. As I pull on the best clean outfit from my bag, I feel as though I'm ready to conquer the world. My eyes hesitate in the mirror before leaving the bathroom, and even though I don't have the wardrobe for this type of interview, I could walk in there wearing a garbage bag and still bring every bit of confidence. After all, isn't that what they say? Confidence is key.

There's a light knock at the door before a voice calls out. "Miss Stone, pardon the interruption, however, it is time to leave."

Oooh. I wasn't expecting such detailed service, but I'm down for it. "Coming," I call back, grabbing my shitty little purse before thinking better of it and just taking my phone instead. I slip it into the back of my jeans, really wishing I had something nicer to wear, but it's not as though there was time to go on some grand shopping spree with a credit card that doesn't exist.

Fifteen minutes later, my driver pulls into a gated community, and my eyes widen as he pulls through the streets. "Holy shit," I murmur to myself, taking in all the incredible mansions around me. It's like a scene out of a movie and definitely not somewhere a girl like me should be. I thought the hotel was my "Not in Kansas anymore" moment, but I couldn't have been more wrong.

"Is something the matter, Miss Stone?" my driver asks.

"No. Not at all," I say. "I just assumed I was meeting Lenny at the studio or the office, not a private residence."

"Yes, that was the original plan," he confirms. "However, one of the band members has a studio space built into their home, and with the band currently rehearsing every waking hour of the day, they prefer not to travel to a stuffy studio."

"Oh, of course."

"Yes, plus I believe Mr. Davidson thought it was prudent you meet with the band and see what you'll be working with to ensure you can make the most informed decision moving forward."

"And he will be there?" I ask. "Lenny, that is."

"Of course, Miss Stone."

I nod, and as I gaze out the window at the impressive properties, a thought occurs. "You, uhhh . . . wouldn't happen to know where my brother lived? Axel Stone."

"Yes, actually. I drove for him quite a bit. Such a shame what happened," he says. "He actually lived in this neighborhood. I would be happy to show you after you're done with your meeting if you wish."

"Yeah, actually," I say, a smile lingering on my lips, though I can't tell if it's because I'm in the presence of someone who knew my brother on a personal level, or just the thought of being so close to the place he called home. "I'd actually really like that. I never got the chance to visit him out here."

"Oh, I know," he says. "Your brother was quite fond of you. He would tell me about you all the time. Last I spoke to him, he was hoping to surprise you with a mid-tour visit."

My smile lingers, and for once, it's nice to think about Ax without the searing hot pain slicing me open. "I would have really liked that," I murmur before letting out a heavy breath and trying to push the thoughts away. I need to keep focused, and I can't do that if I'm lost in my grief.

The driver pulls up to a huge home that's surrounded by large gates and hedges to offer the owner as much privacy as possible, though to be completely honest, something isn't exactly lining up here. I thought Lenny said this band was still quite new. How are they able to afford properties like this? Unless Mommy and Daddy's money bought them this property and their way into the label. After all, money talks, right? But I suppose it's not my place to speculate. That's not the job I'm here to do.

The driver pulls up to the gate and enters a code into the keypad, and I watch in awe as the massive iron gates inch open to reveal the incredible home within. It's amazing, and my jaw pops open. Am I seriously about to spend time within this mansion? This is crazy. Even if I don't get the job and everything goes to hell, at least just getting to experience this would make it all worth it. Happy birthday to me. All I need is a glass of champagne and a chance to dip into the hot tub . . . you know, assuming there is one. Who am I kidding? Of course there is.

My driver takes us right to the top of the circular driveway, bypassing the array of parked cars lingering out front, letting me know just how many bigwigs I'm probably about to meet. Then snapping out of my pampering mindset and into a business one, I open my own door, plant my feet on the ground, and keep my chin raised. Don't get me wrong, I'll allow this fancy world to continue pampering me after the meeting, but for now, I'm a boss bitch, and I've got shit to accomplish, just as Axel always said I could.

Making my way up the grand entrance, I situate myself right in front of the door, and just as I go to knock, someone opens it from within. A beautiful woman stares back at me with a beaming smile, wearing the most stunning pantsuit I've ever seen in my life. "You must be Raleigh," she says, offering me her hand. "My name is Marley, I'm Lenny's assistant. It's a pleasure to meet you."

"Thank you," I say, feeling more underdressed than ever before. "You too."

"Come on in."

Marley ushers me into the mega-mansion and sets off at a pace that has me breaking into a small jog just to keep up with her long legs. "Lenny is stuck on a conference call, but he should be wrapping it up shortly. In the meantime, would you like to check in with the band to get a feel for their music and see if this might be a good match for you?"

"Oh yeah. Of course. I would love to," I tell her as she leads me through the exquisite mansion. "But also, in regard to Lenny's call, please don't let him rush on account of me. I have nowhere else to be."

"Sure thing," she says. "As you're probably aware, the boys are in the middle of rehearsals, but judging from the lack of sound, they must be taking a quick break. I'm sure they'll be back at it any moment now."

Marley reaches the stairs and begins sailing down them like a beautiful swan while I'm left to grapple at the railing, trying not to trip over my own feet.

We reach the bottom step just as her phone begins to ring, and she glances down before sucking in a breath. "Oh shoot. I have to get this," she rushes out. "Just head down the hall and to the right. They're expecting you."

"Okay, thanks," I say with a smile as Marley quickly answers her call.

She scurries away with the phone to her ear, and before I know it, I'm left alone to meet the newest additions to Louder Records.

Making my way down the hall, I quickly find the studio, only as I walk into it, I come up short. The place is deserted, but it's clear they were just in here . . . or have been at some point during the day. There are cups and take-out containers spread across the studio and hoodies thrown over the back of a couch. For just a moment, I feel like a teenager again, walking into the garage to see the boys fucking around as they practiced. That garage was their home just as Ezra's arms were mine. Hell, it even smells the same in here. Or maybe that's just the stench that comes along with boy bands.

A fondness rustles through my chest as I take a quick look around. There's nothing in here that gives anything away about the new band. So, I walk deeper into the room to find the bass drum that would usually have the band's name across the front, but the soft sound of laughter from deeper in the studio pulls my attention elsewhere.

Today is not the day to linger on thoughts of the past. Today, I get to move forward.

I follow the murmured voices across the studio to a private room. The door is open, but from where I'm standing, I can't see in, and I'm assuming by the continued laughter inside, whoever is in there hasn't noticed me yet.

Then, stepping right into the open doorway, I lift my hand to knock, only to come face-to-face with Ezra fucking Knight.

My heart stops, horror blasting through my system and leaving me momentarily paralyzed. He sits on a small couch with two women hovering over him. His shirt is nowhere to be seen, showing off a full chest of tattoos and three pendants hanging from loose chains around his neck that have me desperate to look closer, but I wouldn't dare. The button of his jeans is undone as though he were just about to spend the rest of his day sinking into these two women . . . or maybe he already has. They look like dancers, but it's not even the half-naked women breaking my heart, it's the white powder he's too busy snorting to even notice me here.

I've seen it in all the tabloids, splashed over the internet as though it were a personal attack, but to see him like this in the flesh . . . I've never felt so disgusted in my life. Is this really what he gave everything up for? He broke me so thoroughly just so he could be some fucking joke, living up the rockstar lifestyle and snorting coke in the basement of his fucking mansion with a bunch of half-naked women?

It becomes all too obvious that this magnificent home I'm in is his, and this job offer was nothing more than a scam just to get me through the door. But surely if he knew I was coming, this isn't the way he'd greet me. No, this asshole doesn't know a damn thing. He's spiraling, and his label is making one final attempt to pull him out of the darkness, and they think they're going to use me to do it. Well fuck that. I'm nobody's pawn.

Happy fucking birthday to me. I knew it was too good to be real.

I suck in a gasp, and the girl draped over the lap that used to be mine glances up. "Oh, sorry," she says, climbing off Ezra's lap. "I didn't see you there. You must be the new marketing chick."

Ezra lazily lifts his gaze, starting at my feet and slowly working up my body. He's indifferent, not giving a shit about the random woman standing before him. It's as if he no longer cares about his career or the people on his team. As that dark, familiar gaze lifts to my face, his indifference morphs into nothing but pure horror.

His chest rises and falls, and he stares at me like a deer in headlights. "Rae," he breathes, starting to get to his feet, but it's too fucking late, I've seen more than enough. I turn on my heel and make a break for it. Sprinting out of the studio, I catch Dylan out of the corner of my eye.

"FUCK! Rae," Dylan calls out after me.

I hear the telltale sounds of someone chasing after me, but I don't dare look back as I break free from the studio and fly up the stairs, taking them two at a time.

What a fucking joke.

I should have known better.

Tears begin streaking down my face as I reach the front door, and before I know it, I'm hurrying down the stairs and toward the back door of the limo I only just stepped out of. It's almost comical how confident I felt when I first walked up to that damn door. I thought my life was about to change. I thought I could actually make something of myself. Yet Ezra Knight is always right there to knock me back down.

A strong hand curls around my elbow, yanking me back, and I fall into a chest that's somehow so familiar and yet completely unfamiliar at the same time. "Don't you fucking run from me," Ezra growls, not daring to release his grasp on my elbow. I have no choice but to shove my hands against his chest just to put a shred of space between us.

"Let go of me," I demand, spitting the words through a clenched jaw.

"What the hell are you doing here?"

"Ask your fucking label," I growl, not owing him any kind of explanation. "They're the ones coming up with the bullshit lies to get me here."

"What are you talking about?"

I yank my arm free and back up a step, hating how every piece of me crumbles under his stare. All I can do is scoff with disgust, noticing how he's too fucking strung out to stand straight. "Look at you," I say, shaking my head as I truly take him in. Remnants of the powder linger on his nose, and his cheeks look hollowed out as though he's not eating properly. His eyes used to be so full of life, but now . . . They're so empty now. "I thought I was the joke."

"Rae, I . . . I didn't know you were going to be here. Otherwise, I never would have—"

"Never would have what?" I challenge, backing up even more as I notice Lenny, Rock, and Dylan at the top of the stairs, hastily making their way toward us. "Turned into a man that not even you recognize anymore?"

"That's not fair," he demands as his chains move around on his exposed chest, all but demanding the attention I won't give. "I lost everything."

"AND I DIDN'T?" I throw back at him, hating how my traitorous body urges me to wrap my arms around him and hold him until all the pain is gone, but I don't dare. He's not mine anymore, and despite the way my soul so easily recognizes its other half right here in front of me, I focus on the hurt, more determined than ever to hate him.

"Woah, okay," Lenny says as Dylan subtly moves between me and Ezra before taking my hand and giving it a gentle squeeze. "Raleigh, I'm sorry. Why don't you come inside, and we can talk everything through?"

"You're kidding, right?" I say to the man who I should have known better than to trust. "You lied to me. You told me there was an opportunity here for me, one that could change everything for me, and you used Axel's name to do it. So no, I'm not—"

"You did what?" Ezra demands, turning on Lenny.

"Get him out of here," Lenny says to Rock before turning back to Ezra. "I'll deal with you later. In the meantime, it's in your best interest to sober up."

Rock hesitantly steps into Ezra, grabbing his arm and pulling him away, but he fights it with every step, his broken gaze locked on mine, and the way he stares at me, it's as though he's looking at a ghost—someone he thought he was never going to see again.

Left with Dylan and Lenny, I focus my attention on them, not even knowing where to start, but damn it, I have a lot to say. "Just . . . hear us out," Dylan says, cutting me off before I get a chance to let loose on them both. "Yes, lying to get you here was a shitty thing to do, and I take full responsibility for that. But Ezra . . . He's drowning Rae."

I shake my head. "He left me behind eight years ago and never looked back. He's not my problem anymore."

"Look, it doesn't change the facts," Lenny says. "Have as little or as much to do with Ezra as you're comfortable with, it means nothing to me. I brought you here under the guise of a job in marketing for the boys' upcoming tour, and when I told you that Axel believed in you to do this, I meant every word of it. He told me every chance he got that his little sister, Raleigh Stone, was going to work for me one day, and despite how this afternoon has played out, that offer still stands."

"You told me this was for a new band," I press.

"I know," Lenny says, having the audacity to look ashamed of himself. "I had to get you here first. If I told you this was for Demon's Curse, you never would have stepped onto that jet."

"Exactly."

Dylan creeps a little closer. "He needs you."

"Don't—"

"I'm sorry, Rae, but I have no choice," Dylan says. "If there were another way, I'd do it, but everyone knows you're his backbone. He's so fucking lost, he doesn't know how to pull himself out. He needs you, Rae. Just . . . Please, for mine, Rock's, and Axel's sake. Just consider it. We're losing him, and while I know the two of you have gone to great lengths to avoid one another, I don't think he can do this without you anymore. He's slowly dying, and he doesn't even see it."

I shake my head. "I . . . I'm not his backbone," I whisper, feeling the heaviness of his words. "I might have been once, but I'm not anymore."

"You are, Rae. You always have been."

My gaze falls away, but Dylan steps right into me, curling his strength around me and holding me the same way Axel used to. "We love you, Rae. You're like a sister to us, and we don't want to force you to do anything you're not willing to do, but Ezra is also a brother to us, just like Axel was, and I can't bear to see him like this anymore. Just tell me you'll consider it."

I swallow over the lump in my throat, and as Dylan releases me, I meet his haunted stare. "Is it really that bad?"

He nods, and I see the heaviness in his eyes. "It's worse."

"Okay," I finally say. "I'll think about it."

CHAPTER 13

Ezra

My hands drag down my face as I pace through my home studio. I expected a lot of things to come from today, but having Raleigh Stone walk through the door right as I snorted a line of coke sure as fuck wasn't one of them. When I bought this house, I always dreamed she'd share it with me one day, but this wasn't the homecoming I imagined.

"WHAT THE FUCK WERE YOU THINKING BRINGING HER HERE?" I demand as Dylan and Lenny stride back into the studio.

"You need her," Dylan says. "Deny it all you fucking want, but you need her."

"He's right," Lenny says. "It's already been two months of

rehearsals, and you're not even close to pulling your shit together. She's your fucking ace, Ezra, and you'd be a fool to send her packing."

I shake my head, the anger welling up in me like a fucking tornado. "She shouldn't be here. I never wanted her to see me like this."

"Well, now she has, and it's too fucking late to do anything about it," Lenny says. "The ball's in your court, Ezra, and your back is against the wall. From where I'm sitting, you have two options."

"Oh please," I scoff. "Share with the fucking class."

"You can either continue going the way you're going and pre-purchase the gravesite beside Axel's, or you can step the fuck up, admit that you need her, and hope like hell that she's willing to come on this tour with you. If she's capable of settling at least one of those demons inside your head, then she might just be the reason you live through this tour."

His words are like a shot straight through the chest, and as I glance across the studio to Rock, all he can do is nod in agreement. "You two really think this is a good idea?"

"We know it is," Dylan says. "Remember back in the day when we were doing bullshit gigs in bars and clubs? Rae was always right there, and when you sang to her, the whole fucking room could feel the chemistry. You're killing yourself by forcing this distance between the two of you. You need her to breathe, man, and it seems everyone but you can see it."

I clench my jaw, my control quickly slipping. "She didn't sign up for this."

"But she did," Rock says. "She always wanted this. She begged us to take her with us, and you said she needed to finish school first. She did it, Ezra. She went to college and did the work, and every step of it led her right back here. Making it in Demon's Curse was always our dream, but it was hers too, and now we have this shot to bring her home. Besides, you know how good she is. We've worked with the very best this industry has to offer, and they've never compared to how it was with Rae. She's our family, Ezra. No matter how hard that is for you, she belongs with us, just as Axel always wanted."

I crash down against the stage, bracing my elbows on my knees as my face falls into my hands. "I don't know how to be around her," I admit. "She blames me for Axel's death, and she's fucking right. How the hell am I supposed to face her every day?"

"Axel's death is not on you."

"Isn't it?" I challenge. "No matter how you look at it, it always comes back to the fact that she asked me to look out for him and I failed."

"If that's the case, then we all fucking failed," Dylan throws back at me. "Have you even talked to her about it? Does she even know how it happened?"

I shake my head. "She doesn't need to know," I tell them. "It'll only eat her up inside. She's better off believing the media about a drug overdose. Knowing the truth . . . It'll fucking kill her."

The boys nod, and without needing to press them on it, I know they'll keep their mouths shut. They might be assholes who constantly overstep my boundaries, but when it comes to Rae, they've always had her best interests at heart.

"What's it going to be?" Lenny asks a moment later, reminding me he's still here.

"What does she want?"

"She doesn't know," Dylan says. "We gave her the night to think about it. She thought she was coming here to meet a new band and to work on their tour marketing, so she's a little . . . thrown. Plus, I can't imagine walking in to see you snorting a line with Jessica and Stacey was really on her bingo card for the day."

The day.

Fuck.

I let out a breath and bury my face in my hands again. "It's her birthday."

"Shit," Rock says as both he and Dylan automatically reach for their things, more than ready to go after her and somehow turn her day around. Though after seeing me in that room with the dancers, I'm not sure anything could fix that. But neither Rock nor Dylan has ever shied away from a challenge, and if anyone could put a smile on her face, it's them.

The boys walk out of the studio, and a piece of my soul goes with them. I'd give anything to spend the night celebrating her twenty-fourth birthday. Fuck, I'd spend the rest of my life celebrating her if I could, every fucking night, over and over again, but that's a warped reality that's never going to happen. It's something that used to be in reach, something we could have held onto and created a life together with, but I let go, and the reality of that dream slowly drowned until there was nothing left to grab hold of.

Cutting across the studio, I grab a Demon's Curse muscle tee and pull it over my head before clutching the three pendants hanging around my neck—the guitar chain my mother gave to me as a kid, Axel's ring, and a simple R that's been with me since the day I left. They're my lifelines, a reminder of where I came from and the things I've had to leave behind.

Jett, the newest member of Demon's Curse, walks out of the bathroom after missing the whole fucking showdown since he took his damn time backing one out. He stares after Dylan and Rock as they disappear around the corner. "Yo, where the fuck are they going?" he questions, oblivious to the tension in the room.

All I can do is stare at him.

I can't stand the fucker, and every time he steps up onto my studio stage and stands in the same place Axel used to stand, I want to rip his teeth out with my bare hands. I know I'm not being fair to him. He's an alright guy and an incredible musician, and if I'd met him under different circumstances, we might have even been friends, and yet I can't help but hate him. Dylan and Rock think he's our best option, and while he vibes well with all of us on the stage, I can't seem to allow him in.

No one answers him, but it doesn't faze him as he wanders back across the studio and picks up his guitar. Jett is a whiz on that guitar and has easily picked up all of our music. In fact, he plays it flawlessly, but we've been playing these songs for years. I could play them in my sleep, and until Jett is as natural as we are, he'll be spending every waking hour perfecting the sets.

"So," Jett says as he strums his fingers across the strings for the opening chords of "Hypothetically Yours." "Has that new marketing chick been by yet? I wanted to see if she'd be an easy screw since the dancers have been all over you."

Irritation burns through me, but I manage to keep a lid on it. It's not the first time I've had to deal with people talking about Raleigh. She's fucking gorgeous, and given I was only a teenager then, I had to learn quickly that not only could she handle herself, but I couldn't go around beating the shit out of every guy who appreciated her beauty. Though, there were a handful of those who all but begged me to, and I was more than happy to rise to the occasion.

Jett has no clue the depth of what he just said, but assuming Rae is coming on tour with us, I'll let her teach him that lesson the hard way.

"Don't think I haven't noticed that you haven't given me a firm answer yet," Lenny goes on as though Jett isn't busily practicing behind me. "What's it going to be? Are you continuing down this destructive path, or are you going to give this a real shot and hope like fuck that Rae is able to spark some kind of fire under your ass and bring you back?"

The question isn't if she's capable of bringing me back, I know she can. The question is if I deserve it or not.

"Yeah, all right. I'm on board," I finally tell him. "But at the end of the day, the call is hers. If she's willing to head on tour with us, then so be it. But if she's not . . . I'm not going to beg for her to change her mind."

"Okay, then we'll wait for her answer," he tells me with a curt nod.

He turns on his heel to stalk out of the studio when I call after him. "Lenny?" He turns back, his brow arched in question. "If you ever go behind my back again, lie to my fucking girl, or use Axel's name as a bargaining chip, I'll gut you where you stand. Do you understand me?"

Lenny holds my stare, and I know he's seeing the conviction in my eyes. I mean every fucking word, and he knows it.

"Okay, Ezra. I hear you," he finally says. "It won't happen again." And with that, he walks out of the studio, and for the first time in over two long years, I pick up my notepad and start scrawling the words that have haunted me for far too long.

CHAPTER 14

Raleigh

One tequila. Two tequila. Three tequila. More.

"Hit me again," I say, pushing my little shot glass back toward the bartender who's been keeping me company for the better half of an hour.

The poor guy stares at me, his brows furrowing with concern. "You sure, sweetheart?"

"Oh yeah," I say. "If I'm still able to remember my name by the end of the night, then we didn't do it properly."

"Bad day, huh?" he asks, scooping up the shot glass and quickly filling it before sliding it back toward me.

I grab the saltshaker and pour it out on top of my hand. "More like a bad decade," I inform him before picking up my shot and lifting it to my lips, only at the very last second, it's stolen out of my hand, and I watch Madds pour it down her throat. She grunts through the burn and licks the salt off my hand before reaching across me and completely violating what's left of my little slice of lime.

"Hey," I whine.

"You snooze, you lose," she says, dropping onto the stool beside me and coiling her arm tightly around my shoulders. She drops a kiss to my cheek, and before she gets a chance to pull away, I snake my arms around her and hold her tight.

"You have no idea how much I've missed you."

"Right back at ya," she says, refusing to let go.

She's not home, but she's the closest thing I have to it, and as she continues to hold me, I feel my eyes begin to well with tears. "Hey," she says, pulling back and holding my stare. "There are no tears on your birthday. We're celebrating your epic new job."

I shake my head. "It's not an epic new job."

"Huh? What do you mean? A tour working under Louder Records for their new band."

I glance toward the bartender, and without a word, he nods, takes my empty shot glass, and replaces it with two new ones filled to the brim. "There was no new band," I tell her. "The whole thing was a ruse to get me to LA to straighten out Ezra."

Her eyes widen. "Get fucked! Tell me you're lying."

"I really wish I could."

"Shit," she says, as we take our new shots and throw them back. She chokes on it as it goes down, but I'm well past that stage. It's basically water to me now. "So, there's no awesome job offer? You're just going back to Michigan?"

"Oh, there's a job offer all right."

"Why don't you sound thrilled about it?"

"Because the official title for it is marketing manager for Demon's Curse. I'd have to go on tour with them for who knows how long with absolutely no way to avoid Ezra. I'll be doomed to have to watch him drown himself in his bullshit rockstar lifestyle night after stupid night."

"Ohhhhh," she says, trying to sound as though this is the worst thing that could ever happen, but the undeniable excitement in her eyes is telling one hell of a different story. "That's so terrible. Poor little sad girl has to go on tour with the most epic band in the whole fucking world that she practically founded with her even epic-er big brother."

I give her a blank stare. "I hate you."

"No, you really don't," she says, scanning over the drinks menu and ordering us frozen margaritas. Apparently, my troubles are not fitting with her birthday celebration vibes. "I'm struggling to see this as a bad thing," Madds continues. "Yes, it'll be hard being in Axel's world without him there. You're going to feel his lack of presence more than ever, but at the same time, you'll be with the people you consider family, and maybe it might allow you a chance to reconnect with Ezra. I know you said you still felt that pull toward him at Axel's funeral. Maybe there's something still there."

"I don't know," I tell her. "Not after what I saw today. He was a mess. I've never seen him so low. He couldn't even walk straight, plus he was angry. Like a deep, profound kind of anger, not just pissed that

I walked in and disturbed his peace. He's broken."

"And so are you," she reminds me as though that thought hadn't already occurred to me.

"Yeah, well, two broken halves don't make a whole. It just makes an even bigger mess."

"Cheers to that," she says before noticing a candle at the end of the bar. Her brow arches and she rises from her seat like a magician and moves across the bar. She picks it up, holds it to her face, and sniffs for all she's worth. "Ohhhh. It's a good kind."

I roll my eyes and watch as she steals the candle and brings it over to me before shoving it in my face. "Smell."

"Ughhhh. You know, I haven't missed your messed-up candle addiction," I tell her, sniffing the damn thing because I know better than to resist.

"Don't be silly. Of course you have," she says, settling it between us and turning our birthday drinks into a romantic night for two with our new mood lighting. "Anyway, so because you're not stupid and you're obviously taking this job, I'm assuming this thing you have going with this dude will be coming to an end?"

I cringe, needing another shot. "Yeah . . . about that."

"I FUCKING KNEW IT!" she says before I even get to tell her what's up. "There is no guy. You made him up so I wouldn't be worried about you. And as for that job promotion, there wasn't one."

My eyes widen. "How the fuck did you know that?"

"Because I know you, Raleigh Stone. I know when you're actually excited about something, and I know when you're just trying to placate me because you feel like your life is falling apart."

"Why the hell didn't you say anything?"

"Because you were too far away for me to push you on it and be there to get you blind drunk when you finally admitted it and then turned into a sobbing wreck, but now that you're sitting right in front of me, those reservations no longer exist. You should have been honest with me since the beginning."

"I know," I say with a heavy sigh. "I'm sorry. I just didn't want you to know how far I'd fallen. I've been so embarrassed about my situation. I'm barely hanging on, but I'm not your problem to try to fix anymore, and you and I both know you would have been worried sick if I'd told you the truth."

Her shoulders sink. "Just how bad is it?"

"Trust me," I whisper, taking her hand and giving it a squeeze. "It's really best you don't know. But if I accept this job with Louder Records, maybe everything will turn around for me. And even if it doesn't, at least I would have had a chance to see—"

A noise at the door catches my attention, and I glance up in time to see Dylan and Rock striding into the hotel bar, looking more than ready to cause the best kind of havoc.

"To see who?"

"Those two," I mutter, nodding behind her shoulder.

Madds glances back, and her eyes practically fall out of her head as she notices the boys striding toward her, and I can just imagine the scene playing out in her mind. This is her ultimate dream, only I'm sure there are a few key differences, say like in her dream, I'm not here, the bar is a bed, and everybody is naked.

"Be cool," I warn her, knowing not a damn thing has changed with her unhealthy obsession with Demon's Curse. "They're just here to have a good time."

"I am so cool," she mutters, already swaying from the few shots of tequila.

The boys reach us, and within seconds, Rock is dragging me off my stool and pulling me into the warmth of his strong arms. "HAPPY BIRTHDAY!" he cheers, and without a doubt, I know it was Ezra who reminded them that today was my birthday, and while he hasn't said happy birthday to me over the past eight years, I know it's him who's responsible for the texts I get every year from the guys. Axel was always terrible with remembering special dates.

I pull out of Rock's arms and try to balance on my feet, but Dylan is right there, pulling me into his wide chest. "Happy birthday, Rae."

"You're on my shit list," I remind him just in case it slipped his mind.

"I know, but I'm hoping we can get you drunk enough that you don't remember what an asshole I am," he says as Rock starts listing off drinks for the bartender to get working on while also taking a moment to let Madds fangirl over him.

"There's not enough alcohol on the planet that could make me forget that," I tell him as a wicked grin stretches across my face. "But I might consider forgiving you if you strip naked and do the chicken dance up and down the street."

Dylan's face falls. "You're not serious."

"I hope you're up to date on your manscaping."

"Fuck, Rae. Can I at least keep one hand covering the junk?"

"Oooh, I'll give you one hand over the junk, but in return, I require you to move slow enough so that at least five people on the street have enough time to capture your full ass on their shitty camera phones, and they better be able to get all the angles."

"And then you'll forgive me?" he questions.

"Pinky promise."

I hold my pinky out to him, and after a moment, he hooks his pinky around mine and we shake on our deal. "Shit, I better start drinking."

I can't help but laugh, but as Dylan releases my pinky and reaches for a drink, he smirks back at me. "Joke's on you," he tells me. "I would have done it just because it's your birthday."

I scoff. "More like joke's on you, I was gonna cave and let you keep your little tighty-whities on, but you had to go and push for a hand covering the junk."

"Ahh fuck."

Two hours later, we stand out on the street, both Madds and I tucked under Rock's arms as Dylan flies up the street, whipping his shirt around like a helicopter as he clutches his dick. I have to give it to him, he's kept in amazing shape. He was always the one to get naked at parties as a teen, and I'm more than happy to report that his delectable ass is just as yummy as it's always been, but it's not the ass that always had my attention.

"Holy shit," Madds laughs as Dylan races back toward us, and without warning, she scoops his jeans off the ground and makes a break for it, running as fast as she can as tears of laughter streak down her face. Though she doesn't get far before Dylan is on her, using her body as a human shield as he tries to get his clothes back.

We all head back into the bar, and I have to admit, despite the way my birthday started, it's the best one I've had in years.

The bar closed to the public a while ago, but the boys paid to keep the lights on just for us, turning it into a private party, which is the best present anyone could have gotten me. Being with these guys is incredible, but I can't help but feel a longing for those who aren't here.

"Fuck me," Dylan sighs, dropping down in the booth beside Madds once he's finally got his clothes back on. He slings one arm over her shoulder, and her cheeks flame, absolutely living her greatest dreams right now.

I scoop up a few more drinks and make my way over to the booth, setting them down on the table and watching everyone dive in.

"So, what's it gonna be, Rae?" Dylan pushes as I wobble on my feet, almost certain I'm going to be tasting all the tequila again in the morning. "Now that you've officially forgiven me, are you going to join us on tour?"

"I want to," I admit. "But I don't think Ezra wants me there."

"Oh, he wants you there," Rock says as Dylan nods in agreement.

"I've never even met the dude, and even I know he wants you there," Madds says. "You've heard his songs, right? And I don't just mean the ones from the first album. I mean the ones after he started missing you. They are deep."

I cringe. "I uhhhh . . . actually haven't."

"WHAT?" Dylan screeches, his eyes bulging out of his head in shock. "You're fucking lying. You haven't heard our songs? What the fuck, Rae? Do you live under a rock? I don't know if you know this, but we're kind of a big deal. Our music is literally everywhere. I can't even escape it."

I scoff. "I don't live under a fucking rock," I throw back at him. I just live out of the back of my car and am oddly specific about what music I allow myself to be around. You know, in case of any unwanted mental breakdowns. A girl can only be too careful.

"Songs aside," Dylan says, clearly over his horror. "I meant what I said this afternoon. You're his backbone, but more than that, you're the glue that's going to keep us together. It's not just Ezra who needs you. We need you too. Before Ax . . . you know, we felt like a family. Every time we stepped out on that stage, we were united, and now without him, we don't feel like a family unit anymore. We're scrambling to keep our heads above water, and I think you're the missing puzzle piece that can bring us back together."

"I'm not the missing puzzle piece," I murmur, a heaviness weighing me down. "Ax is. And having me there isn't going to magically save you from missing him. I'm not a replacement for Axel."

"No, we've got one of them already, and he's a fucking idiot," Rock mutters under his breath.

"Look, I just . . . I'm happy to try, and clearly we all know that I'm trying to play it cool at the moment, but it's literally my dream job. I just think you're all hoping that I can press a button and fix him, but I don't think I can anymore. We're both different people now. We've been through shit and have our own trauma to deal with."

Madds reaches across the table and takes my hand, gently squeezing. "Don't you think it's worth a try, though?" she asks. "Bottom line is you get to go on tour with an amazing band and be with your family again while doing a job you love. If there's progress between you and Ezra, and you're able to see just a sliver of the guy you remember, then consider it a bonus. Besides, you know Lenny's going to hit you with that big baller money."

I roll my eyes, but there's no denying the wide grin that stretches across my face. "Okay, fine," I finally say. "I'll do it."

"Yeah?" Dylan asks, his eyes widening for the millionth time tonight as his phone starts exploding with notifications as his ass goes viral.

"Yeah."

"FUCK YES! I'll drink to that."

After countless drinks between the four of us, we are blind drunk and having the time of our lives. "Here," Dylan says a moment later, holding his phone out to me. "It's Lenny. Do you want to tell him the good news, or should I?"

A beaming grin rips across my face as I pluck his phone out of his hand and hold it to my ear. "Hello?"

"Raleigh," Lenny says. "I trust you're enjoying your birthday."

"Sure am," I tell him. "But you know what would make it even better?"

"What's that?"

"If you take that contract that's sitting on your desk with my name on it, and add an extra zero to the end, because if I'm expected to deal with Ezra Knight and keep a smile on my face, then Sir, you better make it worth my while."

Lenny laughs. "Okay, Raleigh. Consider it done. Are there any other negotiations you'd like to make?"

"My hotel room while on tour. I want the good rooms with the pretty city views and food packages. Like, I wanna eat well on your dime. Actually, I wanna eat well on Ezra's dime," I amend, feeling all too proud of myself. Take that Ezra! "Oh, and those skanky dancers, they have to wear more clothes around the boys. This is a professional setting, after all."

Rock groans beside me, clearly enjoying the way the dancers like to keep their tits hanging out. Hell, I know Ezra did. "Anything else, Miss Stone?"

"Uhhhhh . . . drugs."

"You want drugs?" he questions, clearly confused.

"No. The opposite. I want no drugs. But if you want me to somehow snap your lead singer into gear, then he needs to have no drugs. The occasional drink is fine, and maybe something to help him relax every now and then. But he's not falling down the addict rabbit hole on my watch."

"Understood," he says. "Does this mean you're in?"

"I'm in," I say. "Consider me your new favorite marketing exec."

"Sure thing," he laughs. "Be ready to leave for Europe in two days."

"Wait. What?"

My eyes widen, not having realized just how soon the start of the tour is, but before I can ask anything else, Lenny ends the call, and I'm left with a chorus of deafening cheers around me. As I hand the phone back to Dylan, I grin at the boys. "You want the good news or the bad news?"

"Hit me with the good news first," Rock says.

"I'm basically going to be like . . . one of your bosses," I tell them.

Dylan laughs and shakes his head. "That's really not how it works, but it's your birthday, so I'm gonna let you have it," he says. "But go on, give us the bad news."

I stand from the booth with a laugh and scoop up one last shot of tequila, throw it back, and slam it down on the table, grinning at the boys. "You two assholes are officially in charge of breaking the news to Ezra."

"Fuck."

CHAPTER 15

Raleigh

15 YEARS OLD

The soft sounds of Ezra's guitar fill the house as I make my way into the kitchen to find him sitting up on the island bench, softly strumming a sweet acoustic melody. "Is that new?" I ask, opening the fridge and pulling out a soda, unable to keep from glancing back over my shoulder and taking in the way his shirt gapes open, showing off the defined pecs beneath.

"Mm-hmm," he murmurs, tracking my every step across the kitchen with eyes so dark they hold me captive every time I look his way. "I think I've almost finished the melody, but I haven't worked out the lyrics yet."

My brows furrow. Usually, he works the other way around and

fits the music to the lyrics he'd already spent hours slaving over. "Everything good?" I ask, cracking my soda and dropping a straw in the top before taking a sip.

I lean back against the counter, my eyes greedily raking over him. He's eighteen now, far from the boy I first met two years ago, and while he's still exactly the same, he's also so different. He was tall then, but now he towers over me, and when he pulls me into his warm arms, I've never felt so protected. His jaw is sharper and his voice even deeper, but the stubble that grows across his jaw brings me to my knees. He's simply gorgeous.

Ezra Knight is my whole world, and it only gets better every day. However, now that the band is starting to get a little more traction, they're getting fans, and they're not just the kind of people who sit back and listen to their music while nodding along. They're screaming girls who desperately try to throw themselves at the boys, and my patience is wearing thin . . . as well as my self-esteem.

The girls are always gorgeous, model-like beauties who are naturally older than me, more developed than me, more experienced, and definitely more suitable for Ezra than his best friend's fifteen-year-old sister. It's bullshit. I hate it and for the most part, I think I do a pretty good job at hiding my insecurities, but I know he knows. He knows everything about me. It's as though he can read the thoughts entering my mind before I've even had a chance to decipher them for myself, and despite those girls and their frantic attempts to get his attention, his eyes are always on me.

Ezra tilts his head, silently asking me to come closer, and I push off the counter before striding across the kitchen. I move toward him, and he reaches out for me with his leg, drawing me even closer until I hover between his strong thighs.

"I've been wanting to ask you something," he murmurs as his guitar rests between us, forcing us to keep a respectable distance . . . mostly.

My eyes bug out of my head, my heart kickstarting as though it just received a potent shot of adrenaline. I've been waiting for this day for two long years. Twenty-four agonizing months. But realizing what he said and how I've very clearly interpreted it, he quickly rushes in. "Woah, Rae. Chill. I'm not talking about that," he says. "I know I tend to toe the line every now and then, but I really don't feel like having your brother beat the shit out of me today."

"What about tomorrow?" I tease, my gaze dropping to the guitar pendant that hangs around his neck. He's had it since before I knew him, a gift from his mother that he's always cherished.

Ezra rolls his eyes and grabs the neck of his acoustic guitar before lifting it off his lap and placing it on the table behind him. "I wanted to ask you about a song," he clarifies.

My whole body sags, the disappointment clear across my face. "Oh."

"Well, shit. I didn't realize asking you about my songs was such a boring topic for you."

"Compared to what I thought you were going to do, uhhhh yeah. It kinda is. But go on then. I suppose I have a spare minute to unload my infinite wisdom on you," I say, trying my hardest to keep a straight face before pulling out my best southern accent. "What seems to be the problem officer?"

Ezra waits a minute as if really considering the way he wants to approach this, and his lips twist with unease, which instantly puts me on edge. "Hypothetically, there was a girl," he starts while sending my heart falling straight out of my chest and splattering into a million pieces on the floor between us. "And I've maybe been wanting to write a song about her, but wasn't sure how you'd feel about that."

I pull back just an inch, feeling my first true heartbreak coming on. I've been preparing for it these past few months. I know it's been coming; I just never knew when, but surely there would come a time when Ezra realized I'm just some stupid kid. And I guess that day just came.

My jaw clenches, not wanting to fall to pieces right in front of him. I've always seen him as mine, as the other half of my soul, but technically, he never has been. Nothing has ever happened between us. He's never touched me, never kissed me, never done any of the things I hear Rock, Dylan, and Axel brag about doing with the girls who come to watch them perform.

"A girl, huh?" I ask, my voice wavering, on the verge of tears.

"Hypothetically," he reminds me, watching me a little too closely as I inch back again, only for him to pull me right back in.

"Well, *hypothetically*, who is she?"

He thinks on it for a moment. "She's someone I maybe want but can't have."

God. Why can't he just be straight with me? The more he dances around the answer, the harder it gets to keep my composure. "Why not?" I mutter, more than aware of the fire in my tone.

"Because she's far too beautiful for an asshole like me," he says as his fingers dance across my face, pushing my hair back behind my ear. "She's got this thick auburn hair with eyes that somehow penetrate right through to my soul. Since the day I met her, everything that I am has belonged to her, but it doesn't change that the one thing I want most in this world is the one thing I can't have."

Ezra holds my gaze as my heart races for a whole new reason.

How stupid could I have been? *I'm the girl.*

I swallow over the lump in my throat, not knowing how to respond, when his hand circles around the back of my neck and he pulls me in just enough to drop a kiss to my temple. "I wanna write her a song," he continues. "But hypothetically, if I did, I'd want to know that she's okay with me putting it out there."

"I see," I mutter, purposefully taking a long sip from my soda just to give me a moment to rearrange the wild thoughts racing through my head. "I think if you *hypothetically* really liked this girl with the soul-penetrating eyes enough to write a song about her, then you should have the guts to tell her what you're really feeling instead of dancing around the topic. But I also think that if you were to write a song for her, that would be really sweet."

"Yeah?"

"Yeah," I say, "Though, I don't know why all of a sudden this song has you feeling like you need to start asking questions. It's not as though this hypothetical girl doesn't already know that every song you've ever put forward to the guys has been about her. *Hypothetically,* of course."

"Fuck. She already knows that, huh?"

I nod. "She does."

His eyes glisten with silent laughter. "Even Scarlett Rose?" he asks, questioning the one song that's a clear metaphor for all the nasty thoughts he's ever had about me.

My cheeks flush, and I have no choice but to glance away, unable to take the heat in his eyes. "Even Scarlett Rose."

"Shit."

"Yeah . . ."

I can't help but laugh, but as his fingers brush a searing trail down the length of my arm, a seriousness falls over us. "I wish it could be different, Rae," he murmurs as those dark eyes stare so deeply into mine.

"Are you sure?" I whisper, airing my insecurities for the first time. "There are so many girls out there who throw themselves at you, and they're beautiful . . . and older than me. You could be with them without having to fear Axel wanting to kick your ass. Not to mention, you wouldn't have to wait. It would be okay."

"Okay for who? Okay for you?"

I shake my head. "You know it would crush me."

"Do you know the difference between you and those girls?" he asks me. "I don't even see them, don't even notice when they walk into a room, but you? Just knowing I'm under the same roof as you makes everything feel as though it's going to be okay. When the guys talk shit and use those girls, I couldn't care less, but the thought of anybody even thinking about touching you drives me insane with rage. I'm yours, Rae. Always have been since the day I first walked in here and you stood right here in this kitchen gaping at me."

I push up onto my tippy toes, my lips barely a breath away from his, though I know he'll never cross that line, never risk it. "All mine, huh?"

A stupid smirk stretches across his lips. "Hypothetically, of course."

I roll my eyes and groan, and as I pull out of his arms, he jumps down from the counter and steps into me again, his eyes dancing with silent laughter. "You were jealous though, huh? When you thought I was talking about some other girl."

I scoff. "I don't get jealous."

"That right there, Raleigh Stone, was the biggest lie you've ever told."

I shake my head. "Nope. The biggest lie I ever told was when you were going out to that gig across town, the one with the cranky bar manager, and you asked me if I liked your shirt. I didn't. It was hideous. I hate that shirt, but I told you I liked it because it was already too late for you to change."

His jaw drops. "Holy fucking shit. Raleigh Stone is a stone-cold liar."

"I know. Isn't it thrilling?" I say, grinning. "You better watch yourself, 'cause you never know when I might strike next."

His gaze narrows. "What other lies have you told me?"

I chew the inside of my cheek, trying to figure out just how honest

I'm willing to be. "That it doesn't bother me if you were to become some big-time rockstar and go on tour," I admit. "I know we always talk about it happening, and I want that for you, I really do, but I see how good you are, and if I can see it, then so can some big-time record label. It won't be long before that happens, and I guess . . . I'm scared it's going to happen too soon."

"Too soon?"

"You're eighteen, Ezra. I'm fifteen. If you get a record deal tomorrow and go on tour, you'd have no choice but to leave me behind, despite how much of a fight I put up about it. You're going to leave me behind."

He shakes his head. "That's never going to happen," he tells me. "I'm not leaving this place without you. I promise."

A heaviness settles into my chest like a dead weight, refusing to budge. "Don't make promises you can't keep."

"Have I ever broken a promise before?"

"I ummm . . . I don't think you've ever promised me anything before, so how am I supposed to know?" I challenge. "You could be a terrible promise keeper."

"Actually," he says. "I think you're right. I'm kinda shit with promises. Secrets too. Don't tell me shit. I've got a big mouth. But when it comes to you, Raleigh Stone, I'm not breaking anything. We're going to make it big one day, and when we are performing in sold-out stadiums across the world, you're going to be right there with me, and this time, there's nothing hypothetical about that."

A stupid smile stretches across my face, and everything inside of me begins to melt as Ezra reaches for his guitar. He takes my hand and pulls me toward the garage just as the familiar sound of Dad coming home fills the kitchen, and suddenly, the warmth in the house fades away. It's been a year since Mom passed, and I hate to admit it, but I think Dad has been drunk every single one of those days, and what's worse, he's a nasty, mean drunk.

For the most part, he leaves us alone, but every now and then, he turns his sights on me, and when he does, I always spend the rest of my day in tears. I think it's because I look so much like Mom. He struggles to even look at me, struggles to have any kind of relationship with me, and I hate it. This home was always my sanctuary, but that's starting to shift now, and when the boys aren't here, leaving me alone with Dad, my sanctuary morphs into a prison.

"Come on," Ezra murmurs, keeping his voice down. "I wanna take you somewhere."

My brows furrow, and I let him lead me along, stopping by the garage to put his guitar away before slipping out the garage door to avoid an awkward run-in with my father. Before I know it, we're in his car, flying down the street.

He pulls to a stop outside a tattoo parlor, and I stare out the window, gaping at the shop. "We're going in there?" I ask, wondering just how sanitary it is.

"Uh-huh," he says. "How am I supposed to be some famous rockstar without a single tattoo?"

My face scrunches, not too sure about the whole tattoo thing. Axel got one a few months ago—a tribute to our mom—and it was a nightmare. Pretty sure he almost ended up with an infection that had him sulking on the couch like a little baby for nearly two weeks. I don't want to see the same thing happen to Ezra.

"Come on. It'll be fine," he says, knowing exactly where my head has gone.

I groan and get out of his car before letting him drag me into the tattoo parlor and over the space of the next thirty minutes, I watch with hearts in my eyes as he gets the words *Hypothetically Yours* tattooed across his chest, a permanent gesture to remind me that no matter where he is in the world or how many screaming fans are calling his name, his heart will always belong right here, entwined with mine.

As he gets up off the table and wanders across the tattoo parlor toward the full-length mirror, his hand slips into mine, pulling me along with him. He stands in the mirror, and I can't help but stare at the beautiful cursive words written across his chest.

He pulls me into him, my back against his chest as he winds his arms around my waist, the two of us staring at one another through the big mirror, his new ink still visible just over my shoulder, and when he drops his head and presses a kiss to my cheek, it's everything I've ever needed. "Yours, Rae."

"Yours," I repeat.

Four hours later, way after we spent a good portion of the night having to explain where we were to Axel and what the hell "Hypothetically Yours" is supposed to mean, I lay sprawled across my mattress with my head hanging over the edge as I watch Ezra get lost in his music. He strums his guitar, repeating the same melody I'd heard earlier over and over as he jots down lyrics in his notepad.

I can't help but notice the words *Hypothetically Yours* scrawled across the top of the page in his messy handwriting. He works on it for an hour at most, the words falling from his brain onto the paper with ease, and as he finally starts matching those lyrics to the melody, I realize that one day, this song is going to kickstart the boys' careers, and when that happens, he won't hypothetically be mine anymore, he'll belong to the world.

CHAPTER 16

Ezra

My fingers strum against the strings, and just as I step up to the microphone, Dylan and Rock finally decide to grace us with their presence, still wearing yesterday's clothes of course.

"Where the fuck have you been?" I demand, hating how fucking jealous I've been of their wild night. The videos of Dylan's bare ass running up and down the street have more than made the rounds, but the fact that I could make out Rae in the background, laughing in a way she used to, makes everything clench inside my gut. I fucking miss hearing that laugh so goddamn much. "If I can make it here on time, then so the fuck should you."

Dylan rubs his temples, clearly trying to zone me out. "Why so loud?" he whines. "We're only twenty minutes late. Besides, you live here. If you couldn't get here on time, I'd be concerned."

"Twenty minutes is still twenty minutes," I argue, knowing damn well that I've been way more than twenty minutes late in the past and nobody has ever blinked an eye, but suddenly Rae is involved, and I can't manage to get a grip on my emotions.

"Chill out," Rock says. "We were celebrating Rae's birthday, and besides, she needed it. We weren't stopping until she passed out cold."

I let out a heavy sigh. "And did she?"

Dylan laughs. "Oh yeah. It'll be a miracle if she drags her ass in here today."

My brow arches. "So, I take it she accepted the job?"

"She didn't just accept it," Rock says with a smirk as he throws his hoodie down and climbs up the stage, making his way to his drums. "She put Lenny through his paces. Negotiated a deal better than any of us would have been able to get while also managing to stick it to your stupid ass at the same time."

"Huh?"

Dylan and Rock share a glance, and I hate that I'm not already in on whatever inside joke they have. "She requested particular luxuries during the tour, negotiated her pay, and insisted that all meals be included, which should all come out of your cut."

I stare at Dylan. Surely he's lying. She didn't do that. Everything I have is all for her anyway, and I would have done it without asking, but her boldness has me stumped. This was supposed to be a way to get back at me, not that I don't deserve it, but it's clear that she intends to make this tour as painful for me as possible. She wants to hurt me like I hurt her. She wants me to feel her pain, and I'll take it any day of the week.

As if on cue, Raleigh strides into the studio, and just like yesterday, everything stops.

She's so fucking beautiful. The last time I saw her in the flesh was Axel's funeral, and before that, she was sixteen years old. Now, at twenty-four, she's more radiant than ever. She keeps her gaze down, refusing to meet my stare, because she knows exactly what she'll find there, but even with her head down, there's no mistaking her sharper features. Her carefree youthful face is gone, replaced by the features of a grown woman, and damn, it fucking suits her.

Don't get me wrong, I more than noticed yesterday, but I was too busy reeling in the shock of seeing her again that I didn't get a chance to truly take her in, but now, just like that very first day, she holds every ounce of my attention.

Rock makes a low whistle as Rae walks across the studio. "Well hey there, gorgeous," he says in a stupid tone that only the people close enough would recognize as teasing. "Not gonna lie, I'm not used to seeing the woman I spent the night with the next morning."

Fuck. I could kill him.

Rae continues walking, not skipping a beat, and sure as fuck not lifting her gaze toward us. "You fucking wish, Rock," she says, holding her hand up and giving him the bird. "Keep your manwhore tendencies to yourself."

Rock laughs as Dylan steps in beside me. "Don't stress, man," he says, keeping his tone low so that Rae doesn't hear him across the studio. "He's just fucking with her. Nothing happened."

"Yeah, no shit," I say, knowing both Rock and Rae well enough to know they would never cross that line, doesn't grate on my nerves any less though.

"As for her friend," Dylan says with a cringe. "I don't think I can say the same. I think I fucked her, but I can't be sure. I was so fucking drunk I don't even remember going to bed. All I know is that I woke up in Rae's hotel room next to her friend and the word 'MINE' was written across my chest in black Sharpie."

My head whips toward him. "What?"

He shrugs his shoulders as if having no idea himself, but grips the bottom of his shirt and tears it up, showing me the faded word where he's clearly spent ages trying to scrub it off. "I don't fucking know, man."

I let out a breath, my cheeks blowing out. "She's gonna kill you."

"Shit."

Rae slows her pace, her brows furrowed as she reaches for her phone, and I watch as she swipes her thumb across the screen. Her gaze narrows, and in an instant, her slow pace comes to a dead stop as she looks over something—a text, maybe.

Her head snaps up, her feral stare locking onto Dylan's.

"YOU DIDN'T!"

"Oh fuck," he mutters beside me.

"Run," I say, knowing that look all too well. "Fucking run, bro."

Dylan shoves his guitar at me, and I barely manage to catch it before he takes off at a sprint. "I'm sorry," he throws over his shoulder as Rae bolts after him.

His killer hangover slows him down, and in seconds, she has him pinned on the couch, sitting on his chest, and using her thighs to keep his arms locked at his side. "How many times . . ." she says, grabbing a cushion and whacking him with it. "Do I have to tell you," whack, "that my friends are off limits?" She thumps him again before shoving the cushion against his face and trying to suffocate him. "I swear, you assholes never fucking change."

Rock laughs as Jett watches, clearly having no idea what's going on, but all I feel is intense jealousy. I'd give anything to have that carefree nature with Rae again. It used to be me she tried to suffocate with cushions, but that was another life, one so far away that I don't think I can ever get back.

Remembering that Rae is tiny, Dylan grabs her, and in the space of a second, he has her pinned on the couch. "Don't make me fart on you, Raleigh Stone," Dylan warns.

"You wouldn't," she shrieks.

"I thought last night would have been a clear indicator that I never matured anywhere past the age of nineteen," Dylan says, and honestly, I've never heard a truer statement come from his mouth. "You know damn well that I'll do it."

"Okay, fine," she says. "Let me up."

Dylan relents and allows her the chance to get up, and when they're both back on their feet, she meets his stare. "I hate you."

"You love me," he says, hooking his arm over her shoulder and yanking her into his side. "How are you feeling this morning? Bet you're regretting that last shot of tequila right about now."

Rae scoffs. "I'm regretting the last five shots of tequila."

A throat clears across the room, and I glance toward the door to see Lenny and Marley making their way into the studio. "Are we spending the day fucking around or are we actually going to do some work today?" Lenny demands. "Last day of rehearsals before we jet off to Europe, and I need to know that you all have this shit down."

"We've had it down since we were sixteen," Rock says.

Lenny shakes his head, clearly not in the mood this morning, and he focuses his attention on Rae. "Raleigh, you're with me," he snaps before striding into the attached office with Marley hastily chasing behind.

Rae glances at Dylan and gives him a knowing look. "Showtime."

"You're gonna kill it," he tells her, and with that, Rae traipses after Lenny, walking into the office and closing the door behind her.

"Woah," Jett says, gaping after her. "Who the fuck was that? Is she the new marketing chick?"

"Sure is," Rock says proudly.

Jett whistles low in appreciation. "Fuck me. I call dibs. Bet I can have her bent over that desk by the end of the day," he says with a cocky laugh that has my teeth grinding. "She looks like a wild one. Bet she's a screamer."

Fucking silence.

Eyes become shifty. Dylan looks at me. I look at Rock. They look at each other and back to me again. Dylan subtly shakes his head, warning me not to do anything, but Rock is nodding, warning me that if I don't put this fucker in his place now, then he will. And while I was happy to let it slide yesterday, today he's taken it way too far.

As if knowing he's lost this one, Dylan sighs and makes his way back toward the stage as I turn toward Jett and put Dylan's guitar down. I take two purposeful strides toward him, and just as his brows furrow, I grip his shoulder with one hand and use the other to sucker punch him right in the gut.

He goes down like a sack of shit. "What the fuck was that for?" Jett roars, clutching his stomach in agony.

"Do you have any idea who the fuck that was?" I demand as his eyes water with pain, looking up at me from the ground. He shakes his head, and I don't waste a second filling him in. "Raleigh Stone. Axel's little sister, and the woman that every fucking song I've ever written has been about, so watch your fucking mouth when you speak about her."

His eyes widen, realizing the severity of the situation. He didn't just fuck up. He almost ended his career before it even began.

"Fuck, man," he grunts, still clutching his stomach as he tries to get back to his feet. "I'm sorry. I didn't realize."

"Let me make myself clear," I growl, not giving a shit that Rae could turn around at any moment and see exactly what's going on out here. "You don't touch her. You don't breathe near her. You don't even fucking talk to her unless she talks to your first. Raleigh is mine. Always has been."

He visibly swallows and quickly nods as real fear flashes in his eyes. "Yeah, I mean, I wasn't serious. I was just . . . I wasn't going to touch her."

I hold his stare for a long moment before finally turning away, more than ready to get this rehearsal underway. There's a lot to go through today. The dancers should be here in the next hour with the pyrotechnics team to confirm the final arrangements, the wardrobe team will want final confirmations as well as the sound and lighting team, despite all of this having been sorted out weeks ago.

Grabbing the neck of my guitar, I settle in front of the microphone. "Let's take it from the very beginning," I tell the guys, knowing they have the set list memorized, and with that, Rock counts us in.

The moment we start playing, Marley excuses herself from the office, leaving Lenny and Rae to talk, and as I sing the very words I wrote for her, I watch their conversation quickly morph into a heated argument, but from where I'm standing, it looks as though Rae is the one with the upper hand.

Hands fly while Lenny paces back and forth, and when Rae turns around in anger and goes to storm for the door, Lenny dives after her, begging her to come back. I watch as Rae lets out a heavy sigh and clearly accepts whatever Lenny is saying, but the subtle smirk on her lips tells me she just played him and got whatever it is she was hoping for.

They talk for another twenty minutes before Lenny strides out of the office, leaving Rae to do whatever it is she needs to do, and as I continue playing, I watch her stride around my office, making the desk her own. From her new position at the desk, she now has the perfect view of the studio, and I know without a doubt, it's her stubborn nature that has her refusing to look up.

Marley comes back in a moment later, holding a brand-new laptop still in its box and delivers it to Rae, who doesn't waste a moment diving in and getting herself set up. As she works, I can't help but be thrown back in time to the days we would practice while she worked on her laptop, doing homework, putting together the flyers for our gigs, and pushing us on every social media account she created for the band—accounts we still use to this day. Only now we have a whole team responsible for posting, and we don't have to lift a finger.

The day quickly begins to pass with Rae lost in her work as we perfect our sets. When the dancers show up, she barely even notices, even after catching them all over me yesterday. Before Rae stormed through here, I was more than happy to allow Stacey and Jessica to distract me with their bodies and provocative dance moves, but today, I couldn't care less.

As we take a break, I jump down from the stage and walk across the studio to get a drink, and with every step I take, I feel Rae's stare tracking me. I almost want to look up, just to catch her in the act, but I won't dare. Being here in my space is just as hard for her as it is for me. This isn't just my studio, it's my home, and there was a time I thought that it would someday be ours, that we would raise a family here.

After taking a drink, I glance up to notice Dylan has followed me, and after grabbing a drink for himself, he steps in beside me and nods toward Rae. "You think she's okay in there?"

"Yeah," I say as a small smile pulls at the corners of my lips. "Look at her. We should have brought her on the second she graduated college. She's in her element. She hasn't stopped all morning. Not to mention, you saw the way she played Lenny. I don't think I've met anyone who's ever been able to do that apart from Axel."

"Yeah, kinda badass," he says. "But you know she never graduated, right? She was talking about it last night after the whole naked street run. She said that after the funeral, she spiraled, kinda the same way we all did, but she couldn't pull herself out of the darkness and everything just . . . sucked for her. She never completed her degree, never got to graduate, and eventually moved back home to Michigan."

"Fuck."

"Yeah. Wasn't all she said last night though," he says with a sharp edge in his tone.

"What are you talking about?" I ask, watching one of the label's assistants pause at the door of Rae's new temporary office, knocks, and then walks in with lunch. Rae thanks him, and as he walks back out, he pulls against the door to close it, only it doesn't quite seal.

"She hasn't heard any of our newer music," he tells me, his gaze locked on the cracked door just as mine swivels around to meet his stare.

"The fuck?"

"Yeah, that's what I said," he tells me. "She's avoided every album since the first tour. She doesn't even know the titles."

I shake my head, unable to process what the hell he's trying to tell me. "But all those songs, I wrote them for her—"

"Yeah, she's never heard them," he confirms as my head spins.

There's no fucking way.

She used to lay on her bed reading while I wrote. My lyrics were so entwined with her, they could have easily come from her brain instead of mine, and to know she hasn't even heard these songs that have been out for years is almost absurd.

A wave of anger takes over me, and for a moment, I consider storming in there and demanding answers, but it quickly morphs into a strange mix of sadness and regret. All those years, knowing I couldn't reach out to her, I thought I could communicate through my lyrics. I would imagine her begging Axel for early copies of our new albums and sitting in her bed pouring over the lyrics, knowing that I was speaking directly to her. But to know she never even attempted to hear them guts me in a way I wasn't prepared for.

"Come on," I say. "We've got shit to do."

Dylan and I make our way back to the stage, and as I reach for my guitar and hook the strap over my shoulder, I look to Rock. "We're doing 'Cold Hearted Bitch.' "

"Huh?" he says as he reaches for his drumsticks. "That's not on the setlist."

"Oh, he knows," Dylan mumbles under his breath.

"Fuck," Rock grunts, the two guys knowing clear as day that this is a message for Rae. If she thinks she can get through this without hearing our songs and taking in the lyrics I slaved over for her, she's got another thing coming.

Keeping my gaze locked on Rae through the office window, I prepare myself for the start of the song. Rock slams against the drums for the killer intro of "Cold Hearted Bitch" and Rae jumps in surprise, her head snapping up as the crack in the door makes her little soundproof office not so peaceful anymore.

She stands, probably to close the door properly, but as she crosses the office and reaches for the door, the lyrics come in, and I sing them with every raw, pain-filled emotion coursing through my veins.

Her gaze snaps to mine, and I don't dare look away as she becomes my captive, mesmerized by my words, my voice, or maybe it's the raw anger in my tone. I don't know what's drawing her in, but for as long as I have her attention, I'll continue to sing.

This song was written at a low point in my life. I was missing her, and after realizing the wedge I'd forced between us was destroying both of us, I was angry. Hell, I've been angry for a long fucking time, and after hearing from Ax that she didn't want anything to do with me, I took my pen and wrote down the ugliness of the excruciating emotions that plagued me.

She didn't deserve this song, and after it had already been recorded and released, I'd started to regret ever writing it. But right now, I can't help but feel that same hurt. Feel the agony of the realization that she's no longer mine and hasn't been for years.

That girl who laid across her bed and stared over my shoulder as I wrote down every last emotion that coursed through my body no longer exists. I broke her. I made her cold and closed off, and in leaving her behind, in abandoning her back in Michigan, I abandoned myself.

As the words flow out of me, Rae continues to watch, and as a single tear rolls down her cheek, my anger only deepens, but not because of her. Because of me. I had this chance to do something real, to dive deep and sing something that actually holds weight, something that has the power to heal both of us, and instead, I chose to be a fucking petty, butthurt asshole.

Great move on my part.

The song comes to an end, and as the boys start moving around and putting their guitars down, Rae and I remain locked in position, her gaze singeing me from the inside out. A million messages pass between us as that old connection flickers back to life, only it's not the same.

We always had a connection, an invisible string that tied us together, and whenever she was in the room, I felt it pulse to life, glowing the most radiant golden hues. Even a million miles apart, it was still there, lying dormant, waiting for her to bring it back to life. Even after all these years, it was never severed, but now, it no longer pulses with golden light and love. It's cold and hard, flickering with profound darkness, and it fucking kills me.

The heaviness of her pain weighs down on me, and giving her just a fraction of respite, I finally lower my gaze, releasing her from my hold. She doesn't skip a beat, grabbing her new laptop and taking off, and all I can do is watch as the other half of my soul turns her back and walks away.

CHAPTER 17

Raleigh

Ezra fucking Knight can go and fuck himself for all I care. 'Cold Hearted Bitch.' Is he for real? More like 'Cold Hearted Asshole.' I'm not the one who walked away. I'm not the one who left me behind. I'm not the one who tore his heart into a million little pieces then trampled all over them while living up the rockstar lifestyle.

He's an ass. There's no other way to put it.

He purposefully set out to hurt me today, and I've never wanted to nut-punch him harder. But I get it, he's going through the motions. Seeing me again and suddenly having me on his tour . . . There's a lot for him to process. Not to mention, having me around is an almost certain reminder of Axel, and I'm sure that can't be easy. But it's not easy for me either, and he sure as fuck doesn't need to be going out of his way to try and make it harder.

I'm not here for him, despite how everybody was trying to sell me on it. I'm here for me.

I'm here because returning to Michigan isn't an option.

I'm here because I was drowning in my old life.

I'm here because I deserve this, and this job is everything I worked all those years for.

I'm here because despite how much pain I feel inside my soul, I need my family more than I ever have before, and as much as I hate it, Ezra is part of that family. Hell, he's my whole damn home.

Fuck. Just thinking about it gets me all worked up.

After taking off from the studio, I made my way through Ezra's home. I didn't want to leave in case Lenny wanted to look over the work I'd done, and after looking over their current marketing plan for this tour, it seems there is a lot more work for me to do than I anticipated, but I'm more than up for the job.

I spent at least twenty minutes snooping around his ridiculously massive home before pushing through a door, only to find myself in his bedroom, and while I knew it was risky being in there, I could smell him all around me, and the strangest peace settled into my chest.

Call me unprofessional if you must, but I sat on his bed, pulled my new laptop onto my knees, and got stuck into my work. Minutes turned into hours, and before I knew it, it was already after eight and my stomach was pissed.

I called my driver and took off. I'd already been in there long enough, and the last thing I needed was Ezra to walk in and find me in his bed. I'm sure that would have gone down well. We leave for Europe first thing in the morning, and I'm sure he's going to want an early night after spending all day finalizing everything for the tour, which I can already tell is going to be amazing.

Don't get me wrong, I've made a point not to see them perform on tour, and while a part of me is terrified by what I'll hear in Ezra's lyrics, there's no denying that it's going to be the biggest rush I'll ever experience. I just hate that I was too stubborn to have pulled myself together long enough to see Axel perform on tour. It's always been one of my greatest regrets, but I'm sure wherever he is in his afterlife, he always knew how much I supported him and wanted him to achieve everything he set his mind to.

After returning to the hotel, the guy running the valet opens my door, and I climb out. I still have so much to do. I haven't packed, not that I have very many clothes here with me. I honestly didn't expect my life to change so drastically the moment I stepped foot in LA. I packed what I needed for a quick trip and left everything else in my car—a car that I'm sure has probably been towed by now. But the moment that first check comes in, I'll be able to buy myself a new wardrobe, and the fact that it'll be clothes bought in Europe just makes it seem even better . . . even if those clothes are bargain bin finds.

I'll take advantage of the yummy goodness offered on the room service menu, and after that, I'll be right back on my laptop. Hell, I'll probably spend the whole flight working on it too. I doubt I'll have a chance to get much sleep, but there's just so much to do.

Times have changed, even over the last two years, and the

marketing plan the label put in place at the very start of the tour, before Axel passed, was incredible, but now that he's gone and everything is different, following that current plan would be a mistake.

Lenny gave me the day to put a plan together, and after spending the morning arguing with him about his cheap-ass budget and getting it boosted to a level the boys are worthy of, I was finally able to start putting my proposal in place. Sure, the tour starts tomorrow, but assuming Lenny approves what I come to him with, we can start implementing these changes over the coming weeks.

Exhaustion ripples through me as I make my way up to my incredible room, and while I can't wait to get to Europe and finally discover what I've been missing all these years, a part of me never wants to leave this hotel. If I could live here with a bar downstairs, room service, and a pool, I'd be happy every day of my life.

Reaching my door, I swipe my access card against the scanner and make my way into my room. My brain is fried, but as long as I can keep my eyes open, I'll keep working.

The suite is dark with nothing but the city lights pouring through the window, and as I make my way in, I pause, finding a familiar silhouette staring out at the beautiful view.

I suck in a gasp. I can't deal with this right now.

"You shouldn't be here," I murmur, my heart racing a million miles an hour. It's the first time we've truly been alone in over eight years, and the way my body sings with electricity is too much for me to handle. I can deal with seeing him in the studio and being stuck on a private jet with him for hours at a time, but a dark hotel room with just the two of us? It's too much.

Ezra doesn't move or turn to face me.

"No, Rae. You shouldn't be here," he says in that deep tone that's spent so many nights haunting my dreams.

His words are like a knife right through the chest, but I know he's been thinking them. His little performance of "Cold Hearted Bitch" was a message, and despite hearing his meaning loud and clear, I know he doesn't really want me to leave.

Creeping through the luxury suite, I slide the laptop onto the edge of the table before continuing toward him, not stopping until I stand right at his back, barely a breath between us. My heart thunders in my chest, the same way I know his must be, and I can't help but reach out, allowing my fingers to slip up the back of his loose tank. The moment my fingertips brush against his warm skin, I'm physically burned, but I can't pull away. Instead, I continue sliding my hand up his strong back, feeling the familiar curves of his spine.

He sucks in a breath, his body tightening, but he doesn't dare pull away, and as the tension boils between us, I close my eyes, having needed his touch more than I've needed air.

"Rae," he breathes, a deep pain in his tone.

"I'm not leaving," I tell him, my voice threatening to break over the lump in my throat. "I'm not going anywhere."

"You need to go home," he rumbles without an ounce of conviction in his tone. "It's better that way. Easier."

I scoff. If only he knew the hell I endured at that house after they left me, he would never suggest such a thing. "Easier for who?" I ask.

"Easier for you? My life has not been easy. It's been one heartbreak after another that I've barely survived, but that place I'm supposed to call home . . . That's the worst of it all. I will never go back there."

Ezra turns, his confused gaze locking onto mine in an instant as my hand now hovers at his chest. I go to drop it away, but he catches it, refusing to release me. My fingers flatten against his skin, feeling the rapid beat of a heart I used to call my own. "What the fuck are you talking about?" he demands as I get lost in a sea of darkness. "Your home . . . Michigan. That's the only home we've ever had."

I shake my head, not daring to tell him the real reason why I've run as far from that place as humanly possible. "Not to me. Not after you left."

His hand tightens around mine as the fabric of his shirt tangles between his fingers, pulling it aside just enough for me to see the familiar tattoo branded across his chest. Now, he's covered in them, head to toe, just as Axel was, but I always assumed that his very first one would have eventually been covered up.

"You still have it," I whisper, my gaze reading over the words *Hypothetically Yours* as everything crumbles inside of me. "I thought you would have had it covered by now."

There's a desperation in his eyes, and with every passing second, it grows more out of control. He's dying inside, and it has everything to do with me being here in his world, but he has no choice but to find peace with it because I'm not going anywhere.

Ezra clenches his jaw, a hardness creeping into his eyes as he releases my hand, only in doing so, he pushes mine away, and it drops carelessly back to my side as my palm stings from the electricity burning between us. "You never listened to our songs," he says, the words hitting me like a devastating accusation.

A scoff tears from the back of my throat, and I back up a step as I fix him with a hard glare. "That's what your little performance was about today?" I demand. "You did that all because the guys told you I've never listened to your songs?"

His gaze narrows, refusing to admit that I'm right, but something tells me his reasoning isn't what's important here. "Why?" he pushes, stepping closer and eating up the distance I'd only just created. "Why the fuck not? Every one of those songs, they're—"

"For me?" I question, cutting him off. "That's the whole point, Ezra. I know you. I know you on a level that I don't think you've ever allowed anyone else to know you, not even Ax, but those words in those songs . . . I didn't listen to them because I knew exactly what they were going to say, and I knew just how much it would destroy me to hear them."

He simply stares at me, waiting for more of an explanation, and I let out a heavy breath, more than ready to get real with him. "Back in Michigan, before everything went to hell, every song you ever wrote was for me in one way or another. Whether it was a direct message or just something you were feeling at the time, no matter what, it always came back to you and me. And after you left, I couldn't bear it. And when that first album came out, it made me sick thinking of the words that would have been in there. I knew you were hurting just as much as I was, and I couldn't bring myself to listen to it because I knew what it would do to me, but as the years passed, I feared the day they stopped being about me, and I'd be forced to listen as you fell in love with someone else. I couldn't do it to myself."

A heavy silence fills the air as my words sink in, and taking a breath, I take a hesitant step, closing the distance and feeling the warmth radiating off his body. "You'd already hurt me enough, Ezra," I whisper as my fingers latch onto the bottom of his shirt. "I wasn't going to allow you to do it again."

He shakes his head. "You don't know what the fuck you're talking about."

My hand immediately releases his shirt, falling back down. "Don't I?" He clenches his jaw again, trying to find just a shred of control, but I push him further. "Tell me I'm wrong. Tell me those songs aren't written about any other woman, and I'll spend all fucking night listening to them."

He just stares, but the anger in his eyes tells me I'm right. "I knew it," I say with a scoff, shaking my head as I turn and walk away, only he grabs my wrist and pulls me back to him before pressing me against the wall.

His whole body moves against mine, and my brain turns to mush as the endorphins race through my system. My hand braces against his chest as it rapidly rises and falls, his heart booming just as fast as mine.

His lips are only a breath away, and all it would take is the slightest lift of my chin and they would be right there, moving against mine like I've always dreamed they would. "You really fucking think I was out here falling in love with someone else?"

"What was I supposed to think?" I demand. "Your pictures were splashed over every magazine. Night after night, living up the rockstar lifestyle. Drugs. Alcohol. Women. You refused to come home. No calls. No texts. Nothing. I was a ghost to you. I could have died in Axel's place, and you wouldn't have even blinked an eye. You wouldn't have even known."

His hands grip my waist, squeezing tight as though he still can't grasp the fact that I'm standing right here in front of him. "FUCK!" he roars, tearing away from me and leaving me colder than ever. He paces in front of me. "You don't know a damn thing about what I was going through. The kind of pressure that comes with being me."

"Oh no. Poor little rockstar," I scoff. "That's really the card you want to play right now? Because you will lose every fucking time. You have no idea what you left me behind to deal with. Both you and Axel. I loved you. Every piece of me was yours, but you walked away. The two of you packed your shit and left me, and I will never forgive you. I loved you, Ezra. Since the day I met you at thirteen years old, I have loved you, but fuck. For the last eight years, I have done nothing but hate you."

He pulls back, clearly not having expected the venom in my tone. "You hate me?" he questions, his tone wavering as those dark eyes lock onto mine with the kind of intensity no woman could ever be prepared for.

"I do," I tell him, holding my chin up and refusing to cry. "But what does it even matter? I don't even know who you are anymore."

He visibly swallows, and the tension in the room is like nothing

I've ever felt. "No," he finally says, his tone cold and dark. "You don't."

And with that, he turns on his heel and walks away, leaving me as a crumpled mess, falling to my knees and crying for the man he used to be.

CHAPTER 18

Raleigh

16 YEARS OLD

I race down the sidewalk, all too aware that I'm going to be late. Tonight is a big deal. No, it's a huge deal, and if I miss even a second of it, the boys are never going to forgive me.

Their first gig was such a success that they were invited back to play again the following week, even despite the ridiculous handmade flyers we had to make after my laptop was broken. And from there, it's become a standing booking, but along with their standing booking comes the insane number of fans and their smartphones, each one of them uploading videos to social media which has gone crazy viral. The boys haven't even officially put music out, and they're already known across the country.

It's insane. It wasn't long until the call we had all been waiting for finally came in. A record deal. Well, almost. We hope at least. But tonight is the night. Some big scout from Louder Records is coming out to see them, and if all goes well, which I know it will, everything they've worked for could become a reality.

My boys are going to be rockstars.

And I'm going to fucking miss it.

Ughhhhhh. They're going to kill me.

I've spent all afternoon locked in the school library working on a group project, and as much as I love to spend every waking minute slaving over a project where I seem to be the only one actually putting in any work, I couldn't take it a second longer. Everybody was too busy flirting with each other to bother contributing to the project, leaving me to scramble to pull it all together in the hopes I'd still get out of there on time. Had I not been so anxious to get out of there, I might have even taken a moment to tell them to pull their shit together and pull their own weight, but I was on a time crunch, and wasting precious moments on their bullshit wasn't going to cut it.

I have all of twenty minutes to get myself showered, dressed, and ready, and I'm not going to lie, I don't think I'm capable. I'm a strict thirty-minute-shower girl. That's my thinking time, and I don't like to rush, but tonight is special, and I'm going to have to make an exception.

Ezra and I . . . We're becoming something more.

Well, I suppose we've been something right since the start, but I'm not a kid anymore. I'm sixteen, and I'm ready to cross that line.

I'm sick of having him so close and wondering what it would feel like to have him close the distance and kiss me. I want to feel his hands all over my body, his lips on my neck, and the rush when he slowly draws my panties down my thighs. I want to truly be his in every meaning of the word, and I need it to happen tonight. I can't possibly wait another second.

Racing through my front door, I ignore my father as he takes up space in our living room, drunk as usual and not worth a moment of my time. I used to miss the old dad, the one who'd come home and joke around with us. The one who'd mess up my hair and tell me how beautiful I was. But now, I just want him gone.

Straight up, he's an asshole and a nasty drunk. I don't know how many times he's called me a whore over the past few months simply for spending my time with the guys, no different to how I've always done. But apparently that's a thing now.

I've never told the boys, Ezra and Axel especially. They've been butting heads with him a lot lately, and it's not a fire I particularly want to add fuel to. But it doesn't matter because soon enough, the boys are going to be big-time rockstars, and we'll all be free of this place. My father will be nothing but a distant memory.

Hurrying up the stairs, I crash into the bathroom and tear my clothes off, tossing them around the room before diving into the shower and scrubbing every inch of my body. I want to be perfect for Ezra. I want him to look at me and be so overcome by raw desire that he can't help but touch me, I want him at his knees, begging me to let him have me, and then I want—

A knock sounds at the door, breaking me out of my thoughts. "Hurry up, Turd," Axel calls. "We're leaving in ten. You're gonna be late."

Shit.

After quickly trailing the razor over my legs and everywhere else that matters, I finish in the shower and go to grab my towel before realizing it's not there and scolding myself for not stopping to grab my clothes first.

"Crap."

I'm not exactly a stranger to doing the quick nudie run from the bathroom, but I don't exactly feel great about it knowing that Axel was just walking around out here. Not to mention, my father being home.

Not having the time to waste, I suck in a breath, open the door, and peek out, checking the coast is clear. Not seeing anyone, I make a break for it, racing across the hall to my room, only to hear a horrified gasp of disgust come from behind me. "What the fu—"

I slam my bedroom door, cutting off my brother's revulsion as my face flushes with humiliation, knowing that Axel is going to hit me with all the jokes about needing to claw out his eyeballs. Now, I know I wanted one of the members of Demon's Curse to see me naked tonight, but that was definitely not the one.

Diving through my closet, I quickly dry up and find an outfit—a mini skirt with a cute, cropped tank that shows off just enough of my waist, and I pair it with the brand-new underwear I'd gone shopping for earlier in the week, underwear I specifically picked out just for Ezra.

After getting dressed, I let my hair out, feeling the ends of my long auburn hair brush against my lower back. I tame the natural waves, adding a bit of mousse and spray to style it just the way Ezra likes it, and then to finish off, I add just a touch of makeup to accentuate everything I've already got.

I hear Axel passing outside my room, making his way to the stairs, and I wait a few extra seconds, not quite ready to deal with the fallout from my nudie run. Once he's at the bottom, I open the door and make my way down to the kitchen, going the long way around to avoid my father in the living room, only as I turn the corner into the kitchen, I come face-to-face with the asshole holding a fresh beer in his hand.

"Well," he scoffs, taking one look at me. "If it isn't my whore of a daughter."

I clench my jaw and keep quiet, knowing that the times I fight back usually end up worse for me.

"Cat got your tongue, princess?" he questions, stumbling closer toward me as his gaze drops down my body, lingering on my tits and waist. His tongue slips out, rolling over his bottom lip. "If you really insist on dressing like a whore, I have no problem treating you like one."

My stomach rolls with unease, and I back up, unable to keep my mouth shut. Surely he doesn't mean what I think he means . . .

"Mom would despise you," I say with disgust, keeping my voice low so not to alert the boys in the garage. Their night is too big to ruin with something like this. If they heard what he had just said, tonight wouldn't be about a record deal, it'd be about blood.

Dad lunges toward me, gripping my chin in his tight grasp. "Yeah, well what's she going to do about it?" he demands as I feel my jaw on the brink of snapping. "The fucking bitch is dead."

Anger booms through my system, and without a single thought, I bring my knee up in a devastating blow, slamming it right between his legs, and as he crumbles to the ground, groaning in agony, I sprint to the garage.

I throw the door open and run right into Ezra. "Woah," he says, catching me by the shoulders. "You alright? You look—"

"Yeah," I say, trying to shake it off as I reach back and pull the garage door closed behind me, hoping he doesn't hear my father's pained cries coming from the kitchen. "I thought we were late. I didn't want to keep you waiting."

"Yeah, I was just coming to get you," he says before pulling back and really taking me in. His brow arches as his dark eyes deepen with hunger, and whatever fear my father had instilled in me is replaced with nothing but pure lust. "Fuck, Rae. You look good enough to eat."

"Do I just?"

"Mm-hmm," he murmurs, pulling me in and hooking his arm over my shoulder as he leads me out of the garage and to his car. His head tilts down, more than aware that my brother is two feet away. "Fuck the label. All I want is to concentrate on you."

A wide grin stretches across my face as I tilt my chin up to meet his stare. "You know, I was thinking—"

"YOU!" Axel's voice booms, the raw anger in his tone making Ezra and I spring apart from each other as though we'd just got caught with our fingers in the cookie jar. At least, that's where I hope to catch his fingers after his gig.

My eyes widen as I whip around and take in my big brother as he lunges toward me, and I panic, trying to remember the exact words Ezra just said to me and what he might have overheard.

"What?" I rush out.

"You and I need to have a little conversation about the appropriate exit and entry strategy from the bathroom. Nudie runs were funny when you were a kid, but I don't need to be seeing that shit now that you're all . . . You know."

"Now that I'm all what?" I push as a wicked grin stretches across my face, loving how awkward he is about this. "You mean now that I'm all grown up and have tits?"

"Ewwww. You're my sister. That word isn't supposed to come out of your mouth," he groans as Ezra and the boys break into snickers.

"Wait. Which word?" I ask, playing dumb. "You mean tits? You know, every girl has them. They come in all shapes and sizes. Big tits. Small tits. Voluptuous, bouncy tits."

"Oh, don't forget the *Dirty Areola* tits," Dylan adds.

"STOP. Stop," Axel cries, bracing his hands against his ears like a child refusing to listen to his mother. "For the love of all that's holy, please fucking stop."

I shrug my shoulders and stride toward him, pressing up onto my tippy toes and dropping a kiss to his cheek. "Just trying to have an educational conversation with you, big brother," I say, sugary sweet. "But if titties freak you out so much, you better not go diving between a woman's legs. You'll be horrified to find what they have hiding in there."

Axel glares at me before lifting his gaze to the boys. "Can we get going before she starts drawing diagrams?"

Ezra laughs and slips his hand into mine, pulling me along. "Come on," he says. "You're riding with me."

The ride to the old bar is quick, and before I know it, the boys are busy hauling drums and sound equipment out of the back of Rock's van, and not wanting to get in the way, I make myself comfortable at the bar.

In most cases, I wouldn't even be allowed through the door of this place, but after putting up a fight the first night, the bar staff have become more than familiar with me and allow me to chill here where they can keep an eye on me.

I don't get a chance to speak with Ezra before they start their set, but it doesn't matter because I know afterward, he's going to want to celebrate, and when he does, I'll drop it on him then. Maybe we could go somewhere private, just the two of us. A motel or down to the lake. It's not a cold night, and with the moonlight glistening off the water, it would be beautiful. I might get a mosquito bite to the ass, but it'll be more than worth it.

The boys are in the middle of their second song, performing for the crowded bar of screaming women, when three men in business suits stride through the door. People don't wear business suits around here, so there's no doubt in my mind that these are the men from the label. The chorus of "Hypothetically Yours" fills the bar, and as the men take a seat to my left, Ezra's eyes come to mine, a silent question lingering within them, wondering if I think these are the men they've been waiting for.

I nod and his face lights up like Christmas morning, and when he glances to Ax and nods, they both grin like idiots.

I watch the suits as they watch the band, and there's no denying they're impressed with what they see. Though, how could they not be? They're incredible, and anyone with a single brain cell would be able to see it. They're not the run-of-the-mill garage band. They have that spark that everyone looks for, the fire and drive to go the whole way, and what's more, the moment they finish their set, the crowd is always begging for more.

By the time they're halfway through their setlist, there's a line outside the door waiting to get in, and girls are pressed up against the windows, peering in for just the chance at laying their eyes on Demon's Curse.

The bar staff looks busier than ever, and the owner comes over to me, offering me complimentary drinks and fries to keep me happy. After all, he learned quickly that as long as I was happy and allowed to sit here to watch the boys, then they'll continue to come back.

By the time the boys are wrapping their final song, I've never been more excited or anxious. Don't get me wrong, I could sit here for the rest of my life and listen to Ezra sing, and I'd be the happiest girl who ever lived, but the thought of what we're going to do tonight has me more than ready to get out of here.

I can't resist him another moment. I know he's been biding his time, trying to wait until I was older and our age gap didn't seem so daunting, but I'm sixteen now. I'm a woman, and I'm sick of just trying to tell him with words how much he means to me. I want to show him. I want to feel him, and more than that, I want him to feel me.

The adoring fans scream for the boys, and I try not to let it affect me. There's no denying that every bone in my body was infused with copious amounts of jealousy and a sick sense of possession the day Ezra Knight came waltzing through my front door. And despite the way he keeps his dark gaze on me, I can't help but despise the beautiful women screaming his name.

The boys leave the stage and make their way through the rowdy crowd toward me, but the three men in suits intercept them, and when they offer the band to join them at their booth, I can't help but watch with a stupid grin as they talk and shake hands.

It seems to last forever, but when they all stand and say their goodbyes, Ezra's gaze shoots to me, and without a damn word spoken between us, I know exactly what just went down.

The suits make their way out of the bar, and the boys desperately try to maintain their professionalism, but the second the door closes behind them, the cheering begins. Axel throws himself onto the table, roaring with excitement as Ezra races to me, scoops me off my barstool, and spins me around. The atmosphere in the bar ramps up, and suddenly all these people we don't know are celebrating with us.

"What'd they say?" I ask as he balances me back on my feet, his hands so warm at my waist.

"They want to see us again, but it looks like they're going to sign us," he tells me. "They want to talk between themselves, let it sit for a few days, and then they're going to bring us an offer."

"Holy shit," I breathe. "That's amazing."

"No, Rae," he says, his eyes dancing with undeniable happiness. "You're fucking amazing."

Ezra leans down and drops his lips to mine in a swift kiss that takes me by surprise. He's done it only a handful of times, and while every single one has been incredible and cherished dearly, they're not the type of kisses I've been holding out for, and he damn well knows it.

He pulls me into him, his arms tightening around my waist as he buries his face into the curve of my neck, breathing me in as though needing just a moment to center himself. He gently kisses my neck, and even over the sound of the busy bar, I hear his words clear as day. "I love you, Rae."

"I know," I murmur, pushing up onto my toes, needing to get even closer.

Slipping his hand into mine, Ezra drags me back over to the guys, and I cling to his side for the next hour as we celebrate their massive win.

Then before I know it, the bar starts clearing out, and the guys make their way over to the stage. They begin pulling everything apart as I try my best to be helpful, but aside from carrying the small things out to the van, that's about as much help as I can be. Even after years of being involved with the band, I still can't work out how a drum set is supposed to go together.

I stand out back with the boys as Ezra and Rock load the last of the drum set into the van, and as I watch him, that strange feeling of excitement and anxiousness increases, only now it's definitely tipping toward the anxious side.

This is it. He's about to say goodbye to the guys, hook his arm over my shoulder, and take me back to his car, and it's there I'll suggest we go somewhere private.

I love gig nights. We always get to hang out afterward. Sometimes we go to parties or the lake while the guys throw back a few drinks, and other times we chill in my room, just the two of us. But tonight, it's all going to change.

Tonight, I'm truly going to make him mine.

I'm done waiting, and I think he knows. Besides, when you're this in love with someone, why should you be made to wait? Why should he have to hold back all the time when we both know how right it really is?

The sliding van door closes, and I stand up a little taller, watching the guys pile into the old van. Ezra turns and flashes a brilliant smile, and as butterflies explode in my stomach, he makes his way over to me. His arm raises, and I prepare myself for how it will drop over my shoulder, only it falls lower, hooking around my waist and pulling me against him instead.

He doesn't try to walk back to his car. We just stand there in the middle of the bar's loading area. "Sooo," he starts, his tone laced with hesitation as he drops a kiss to my temple. "The guys kinda wanna go to this dive bar across town to keep celebrating. Apparently, there are some girls there that Rock knows, and he's been wanting to meet up with them."

"Oh," I say, pulling out of his arms and feeling all of my hopes for tonight catch fire and burn to ashes at my feet. I try to force a smile across my face, not wanting him to feel guilted to spend the night with me if he'd rather celebrate with the guys, something he should absolutely do. But his tone is clear, it's not something I'll be invited to. I'm too young, and unlike these guys who can somehow walk into any bar or club without even a hint of being asked for ID, I don't seem to have the same advantages. "You wanna go?"

"Yeah, I mean, nights like this don't just happen every day."

"Okay yeah, I'm kinda tired anyway," I tell him, struggling to hold the smile on my face as I feel my eyes beginning to prick with tears.

"Alright, cool," he says, digging his hand into his pocket and grabbing his car keys. He hands them to me with a stupid wink that almost has me wanting to forgive him. "Don't wreck her."

My brow arches as I stare at the keys in my hand. He knows damn well I'm not supposed to drive without a supervising adult yet. After all, he and Axel are the ones who've been teaching me, but I suppose Ezra's never really been the type to follow the rules. I mean, falling in love with his best friend's little sister and writing songs about all the things he wants to do to her is definitely breaking a few. "And if I get pulled over?"

Ezra grins as he starts walking backward to the van. "Then drive it like you stole it, baby."

And with that, he disappears into the back of the van, but before I can even say goodbye, Rock hits the gas, taking off like a bat out of hell and leaving me alone in the empty loading area, desperately wishing for the millionth time that things could have been different.

Then because going home to spend the night alone in my house with my father is no longer an option, I slide into Ezra's car and take off, not stopping until I pull up at the secluded lake where I pictured us spending the night together. As the moonlight glimmers against the still water, I allow the tears to roll down my face, hating the way my heart shatters.

CHAPTER 19

Ezra

Our opening act wraps their set to a full house in Paris, and the roar of the crowd sends mixed feelings coursing through my veins. I'm pumped for the show. There's only ever been two places I've truly felt at home, and that was on a stage or with Raleigh wrapped in my arms. But I never imagined that I'd be performing without Axel.

I've had two years to process that he's gone, and I knew this day was going to come, but it still feels so fucking wrong. How am I supposed to look across the stage and see Jett instead of Ax? Don't get me wrong, I'll still put on the best show for the Parisians, but the whole time, there will be something . . . someone missing.

On the other hand, watching Rae dominate backstage just like she used to for our early gigs has me ready to throw her up against a wall for a whole new reason. The other night in her hotel room, I was a wreck. The day had been too much. I thought I could handle it, but being that close to her and feeling as though she were a stranger didn't sit right with me.

I sense a darkness in her. Something has made her cold, and it's more than just me and Ax abandoning her in Michigan. Something else left scars on her heart, and it kills me, but I'm not in a position to ask. Maybe this is what Axel had been sensing in those weeks before his death.

He had planned to visit her at college, though judging by the way he was talking, it was more of an intervention than a visit. He was going to find out what had her all messed up, make it better, and then return so we could complete this part of the tour. But that trip to visit her at college never happened.

The thought makes my hand shoot up to clasp Axel's ring that's hanging from a chain and resting over my heart. A wave of agonizing guilt rocks through me as I grip the cool metal.

That day fucking destroyed me, and now I somehow have to walk onto that stage as though everything is right in the world.

Fuck this. I was never supposed to do this without him.

Needing just a shred of normalcy, I watch Rae move around, ordering people into positions and making sure everything runs smoothly. It's not her job, we have specific people to do this, but clearly she's doing a hell of a better job at it than they ever have. She's punctual and precise and not afraid to tell people to get fucked when they're in the wrong, especially me.

This version of Rae reminds me of the girl I used to adore, the one who would barge into schools she didn't attend and throw flyers down the stairwell, the girl who would so bravely call record labels and tell them they're idiots for not having signed us already, the girl who would champion for us at every fucking turn. But that girl had her heart broken, and I don't think she'll ever be the same.

She hates me.

She looked me dead in the fucking eyes and told me that despite how much she's loved me all of these years, she hates me, and those words crippled me in a way I'll never be able to come back from.

She fucking hates me.

The agony of it all cascades over me, plunging me into a world of darkness, and as Rae makes her way over to Rock and Dylan, checking to see how they're doing, all I can do is turn away.

There are fifteen minutes until we're due on stage, and I weave my way through the backstage area until I find our dressing room. I barge through and crash down onto the small couch, hating that I see my reflection in the shitty mirror directly across from me.

Who the fuck places a mirror right there? I'm trying to avoid myself, not be forced to come face-to-face with it.

I'm a fucking joke. A fraud.

I look the part. Ripped black jeans with a barely buttoned shirt. Tattoos on display. Chains and rings and my signature messy hair. I'm the exact picture of what that roaring crowd out there has come to expect, but inside, everything is crumbling. Every day, I lose another piece of myself, and I'm not sure how much longer I can do this.

If Ax were here, he'd know how to make it right. Hell, if Ax were here, I wouldn't be in this position. The tour would be over. We would have already released another album and already be hammering out the details of another world tour.

A knock sounds at the door before a woman with a headset barges in. "Five minutes," she says.

I nod and let out a heavy breath, crashing back against the couch cushion as she hastily disappears, leaving me to endure the loneliness of my pity party. There's only one thing, one person, capable of making this pain recede in my chest, but despite being only a few feet away, she's so out of reach that I'll never be able to catch her.

Another knock. "Two minutes, Ezra."

Fuck.

Getting up, I make my way back out, feeling as though that moment of solitude did nothing but make everything worse. I'm a fucking wreck, and now I somehow have to get out there and perform for fifty thousand people.

I'm not ready. No amount of rehearsals or training is going to prepare me for having to face this without Axel.

"Woah," Dylan says, clapping his hand on my back and looking me right in my eyes, forcing me to focus on him. "You good?"

"I can't do it without him," I say, feeling the world crumbling from under my feet. I'm sinking. I can't do it.

"Snap the fuck out of it," Dylan says, his fingers tightening on my shoulder. "You can do it and you will. There's no time for this self-doubting spiraling bullshit. You have fifty thousand people out there screaming your fucking name."

"You don't think I know that?" I hiss.

He pulls away, bracing his hands at his temples. "FUCK."

He paces for a second before looking back at Rock and Rae, but before he even gets a chance to call them over, Stacey and Jessica make themselves known. "What's wrong? We're still going on, right?"

"Yeah," Dylan says, trying to sound as though he's got this under control, as he eyes the execs from the label, trying to keep this from reaching them. "He just needs a second to relax is all."

"Oh, ummm . . . " Jessica says, lowering her tone as she cautiously looks around. "Call it unprofessional if you will, but sometimes I struggle with the same thing. I get really worked up before a big performance and need a little something to relax."

"Keep talking," Dylan says.

She pulls out a small bag of powder from within her costume, and I look at it longingly. That'll more than do the trick.

"Fucking hell," Dylan mutters, but knowing we have no choice, he nods. "Line him up, but be fucking discreet about it."

"Okay," she nods.

"I swear, Jessica," Dylan warns. "If this gets out, I'll protect my boy a million times over you. I'll say you coerced him into doing it and you'll be fired before you even get a chance to say I allowed it."

"Yeah, okay," she says, gripping my arm and starting to pull me away. "I've got it."

I let her pull me away, and as she moves to the side of the stage, covered by a big, thick curtain, she pours the powder on the back of her hand. It's not exactly the easiest line up, but she makes do with what little we have.

"Here," she says, lifting her hand toward my face.

I go to lean in when a ray of fucking delight storms into us, shoving Jessica's hand away from my face. "The fuck do you think you're doing?" Rae demands, staring up at me with such anger and disappointment in those beautiful big eyes, it kills me.

"Don't fucking start with me, Rae. I need this."

"Like hell you do," she spits, shoving Jessica right out of her way to get in my face. "You might be willing to go out there and ruin the legacy Axel left behind, but it'll be a cold day in hell before I ever allow you to do it. Pull your shit together, Ezra."

"You don't fucking get it," I tell her, feeling myself slipping. "I can't go out there without him."

"Yes," she says with the kind of confidence that pulls me up short. "You can. I know you, Ezra. You can do this."

I shake my head. "You might think you know me, but you don't. Not anymore," I remind her just as Rock, Jett, and Dylan's cue to take the stage comes through our inner ear speakers.

"That's bullshit and you know it. No amount of time or distance can change the fact that I know you on a level that nobody else ever has or ever will, not even Axel," she argues, stepping into me and gripping my arms as desperation flashes in those beautiful eyes. "You don't need that shit. You never have, and despite how I feel about you right now, I am yours and you are mine, and all you've ever needed is me."

The crowd roars for the boys. Their screaming is deafening, but nothing will keep me from hearing the words of this sweet angel before me.

"Ezra," the stage manager warns, needing me in place, but I don't move a fucking muscle, knowing she's not nearly through with me yet.

The intro starts, the speaker physically shaking the stage as the vibrations rock through my chest, and along with it comes the screams of fifty thousand people, every single one of them waiting for me to give them the performance of a lifetime.

Her hand moves further up my arm, over my shoulder, and doesn't stop until she's gripping the back of my neck. Her other hand clutches my wrist. "You can do this, Ezra. I know you can," she tells me, creeping in so close that I feel the warmth of her body against my skin. "If you feel yourself start to spiral, just look at me. I'll be there the whole time. I've got you."

"EZRA!" The stage manager calls, knowing I'm dangerously close to missing my cue. "NOW!"

I go to pull away, but Rae closes the gap, crushing her lips to mine, and I feel everything I've ever wanted right there in my grasp. Her body is stiff as though she can't believe what she's doing, and as she goes to make a hasty escape, my arms lock around her, pulling her right back in.

I've waited eleven fucking years to feel her lips against mine, and there's no chance in hell I'm about to let her pull away from me just yet.

Her lips are so fucking warm, just as I knew they would be, and as I kiss her back, her body finally relaxes against mine. She opens her mouth just a little wider, and I take everything she's willing to give as my world finally comes back into focus.

She was right. All I've ever needed was her.

She pulls back, her chest heaving, but I don't dare release her. "Ezra," she murmurs, clutching me tighter than ever before. "You need to go."

I nod, knowing she's right, but the idea of stepping away to do this show and not being able to touch her physically pains me. But there's still tonight. I'll get this done and then tonight . . . we talk. Or maybe we don't, and I just spend the rest of my life drowning in her lips.

Reluctantly, I release my hold around her waist and allow her to back up, and as I listen to the intro coming to a close, I grab her hand and drag her to the side of the stage. "Stay right here," I tell her.

She nods, and I move back into her, holding her stare as I clutch her wrist, unable to be so close without physically touching her. "After."

"After," Rae confirms. "Now go."

Fuck.

I turn on my heel and sprint, racing down a ramp and through the scaffolding beneath the stage as I desperately try to reach my mark. Then just as I hear Rock's tempo increase on the drums, starting my intro, I launch myself onto the base just in time for it to catapult me high up into the center of the stage.

The crowd is fucking insane, screaming in a way I've never heard before. The light show goes off with the pyrotechnics, and I can't lie, it's the best introduction I've ever had. Maybe Lenny was on to something.

Jett leads into the opening song, and I take the microphone, glance back at Dylan and Rock to let them know I'm good, and then without skipping a beat, I give my all to the eager Parisians, knowing that as long as Rae remains right there at the side of the stage, I've got everything I need.

A wide fucking grin stretches across my face, and despite not having Axel here, I feel more at home than I ever have in the past eight years, and it has everything to do with having Raleigh's eyes on me.

I can't help but glance toward her and take in the awe on her face. She's never seen anything like this, at least, not with Demon's Curse. I don't know if she's been to other concerts over the years and what her experience was like, but judging by how wide her eyes are, I'd dare say this is a first.

She watches me as though she's never met me before, as though she didn't just have her lips on mine less than a minute ago, and the wonder in her eyes is something I'll hold on to for the rest of my life. I'm not performing for the crowd tonight; this is all for her.

As I near the final chorus of the first song, I hear a slight muffle in my inner ear speaker, and I glance across at Dylan who shrugs, clearly having heard it too. It's not a big deal and has no effect on the show, and just as I go to shrug it off, I hear it again.

I look back to the side of the stage, trying to figure out what it was when I see the two dancers, Jessica and Stacey, lingering too close to Rae for my liking. They'll be coming out during the second song, but judging by the look on Rae's face as they speak to her, they won't be coming out anywhere if I find out they're being less than welcoming.

Rae and I might not have any idea where we stand with each other right now, but that doesn't make me any less protective over her. Especially now that Axel is gone, she's mine to protect, and if these girls are causing her trouble, they'll be replaced within seconds.

When the first song comes to an end, I face my eager audience and hold my hands out wide, welcoming the onslaught of praise from the crowd. "How are you tonight?" I call into the microphone, listening as my voice fills the stadium. They scream, and I pull out my inner earpiece and take a moment to truly take it all in.

"Welcome to the *Bleed for Me* tour. We are Demon's Curse, and it's a pleasure to spend the night with you." I walk back, and as Rock hits us with the intro of our second song, I scoop my electric guitar off the stand and hook the strap over my shoulder.

The dancers come out and do their thing, and as they move into me, one on each side, I turn away from the microphone and let them have it. "Let's get one thing straight," I tell them. "If you two even breathe near Raleigh again, you'll be out. Got it?"

Jessica scoffs while maintaining her smile for the eager crowd. "Come on, Ezra. Keep it real. She's just some girl. We have a whole tour to get through. Forget about her, and I promise, Stacey and I can make this the best tour you've ever been on. You don't want to be shacked up with that bitch when you could be having fun with us. Besides, she's nothing, a nobody."

"Don't push me," I warn her. "I will choose her every fucking day. You hear me?"

The girls spin away before Jessica has a chance to respond, but I know she hears me loud and clear, and if she values her job, she'll treat Raleigh with the respect she deserves.

Getting stuck into the second song, I relax deeper into the set, and as the familiar lyrics pour out of me, I turn back and meet Raleigh's stare. This is the first time she's truly going to hear all of these lyrics, and I realize that I've been presented with an opportunity.

She might have refused to hear me through my lyrics over the years, but now, standing at the side of my stage, night after night, I'm going to force her to hear me.

CHAPTER 20

Raleigh

Ezra is hypnotic on the stage. I've never seen anything like it, even back in Michigan when the boys would have their gigs in all the old bars and clubs around town, it was never like this. He was always confident on the stage, always knew how to command a crowd, but this is like nothing I've ever experienced.

The bass drum rattles my chest as the sound of Jett's guitar makes the hair on my arms stand up. But it's nothing compared to the way Ezra sings into that microphone, and judging by the fifty thousand people in the stadium who can't seem to take their eyes off him, they're feeling it too.

He has a stage presence that rivals incredible artists like Michael Jackson or Queen, so alluring and capable of commanding the whole stadium. I always knew he could, but witnessing him like this is different, and as he gets further through the set list, I'm reminded of just how much I love him. Put all the pain and hurt aside, and it's still right there, beating stronger than ever before, and as my gaze shifts to Dylan and Rock, getting to see them on the big stage for the first time, I realize just how proud I am of all of them, Axel included.

They worked their asses off to get here, and they deserve every bit of their success, and despite how happy I am in this moment, I'm also devastated that I could never put my pain aside for one single night to witness Axel perform like this. It would have made him so happy to see me standing in the crowd. God, the smile on his face would have split his stupid head in two, but it would have been worth it.

I'm not going to lie, being in his world like this has been crippling. Seeing someone else on the stage where he should have been guts me, and hearing the solos he created has tears welling in my eyes. But I stick it out for Ezra, knowing he's feeling it just as deeply as I am.

I can't believe I kissed him. I've waited eleven long years to feel the way his lips would move over mine, and it was everything I always thought and more. The way I melted into him, the way his arm snaked around my waist. It was like two broken halves finally finding one another and molding back together. In reality, that's not at all what happened. We're still just as broken as we always were, and despite how incredible that kiss was, it's not enough to erase the pain he caused.

And standing here, listening to song after song, really isn't helping.

His lyrics are deep. Some are ice cold, while others are warm and inviting, but no matter how they sound or the intention behind them, every single one feels like a knife to an artery.

The boys slow it down, and Ezra switches out his electric guitar for his acoustic before taking a seat on a tall wooden stool. The lights in the stadium fade out, and all I see is a single spotlight on Ezra as he strums his fingers across the strings.

My heart sings, reminded of the way he used to sit at the foot of my bed and strum his guitar as he worked out new melodies and tried to figure out how to fit the lyrics into them. I recognize the tune to one of the melodies Axel wrote right at the very beginning—before they'd even started doing gigs. This song was never released on the album, the boys wanted to keep it just for themselves, but when the massive LED screen lights up with a montage of my big brother, I understand why they did it.

Tears fill my eyes as I listen to the soothing sounds of Ezra's voice while watching my brother smile at the camera. There are clips of him on stage from the beginning of the *Bleed for Me* tour, and then some from their earlier tours. As the song goes on, Ezra's voice begins to crack, and I realize he's about to break. It's too much for him, and I silently will him to look at me, and then as if reading the very thoughts in my mind, his gaze shifts and lands right on me, and with his stare locked firmly on mine, he sings out the rest of the song.

When it comes to an end, he gets off the stool and makes his way across the stage, walking right over to me. He hands his acoustic guitar to his stage manager and takes the water offered. He tips the bottle to drink, but with every passing second, he doesn't take his eyes off me.

"Rae," he breathes, dropping the empty bottle and stepping into me, wiping the tears off my face.

"I'm good," I tell him, capturing his hand and lowering it. "Just go. I'll be okay."

With that, he nods, and as he makes his way back to the stage, I realize just how unfair I've been to him. I've been so angry about the way they abandoned me and how they left me there at the hands of my father. I've blamed him for things out of his control, especially when it came to Axel. I begged him before he left to watch out for him, to keep him safe, and I realize now that I never should have done that. They were only nineteen when they left to chase their dreams, only kids, and Ezra was already dealing with the guilt of having to leave me behind. I never should have put that pressure on his shoulders, and afterward, at the funeral, I never should have told him he was at fault.

He couldn't have seen it coming.

I never knew just how much the boys were dealing with until standing here in this stadium, never knew the kind of pressure they were under. In my young mind, they were just a group of idiots playing for their fans, but it's so much more than that. They have the whole world waiting for them to fail, and when they do, the media is right there to splash it across every news outlet across the globe.

There's no escaping it, and I haven't made it any easier.

I've blamed him for things he never even knew were happening, and there's nothing fair about that.

Guilt resides heavily on my chest as Ezra collects his electric guitar once again. He strikes the chords to their next song and turns to face me. My brows furrow, noticing the way Rock and Dylan both glance nervously at one another. This definitely wasn't in the script, but as long as Ezra continues to play, so will the rest of the band.

Lyrics pour out of him about a girl he'd lost, one he broke into a million shattered pieces, but one that he vows to catch.

He tells me how one day, he will make up for the time they lost, how one day he'll swim across every ocean to get to her, how one day he's going to be able to love her the way she deserves, and it occurs to me that he's taking his chance to make me truly hear him. To hear the way he's longed for me, to hear the way he hurts, to hear how no matter what obstacles stand in our way, he will make this right.

And as he sings his sweet words to a packed stadium, he can't take his eyes off me. Tears roll down my cheeks, replacing the ones he'd only just wiped away, and as I hold his dark gaze, I see the agony deep within his eyes, and I know that he means every last word with his whole heart.

"One Day" comes to an end, and as his attention falls back to his screaming fans, the music hitches up and turns into something a little more sexual, and as the dancers make their way back on the stage, a hardback iron chair is put out.

Ezra sits, lounging back with his legs casually stretched out, and as the lights fade out, I hear Ezra's voice come over the speaker. This song is about pure, unadulterated lust. Wanting something so bad, it hurts, and as he sings in that deep tone I've loved since I was a girl, the dancers move up on him.

They roll their hips as Ezra moves his hand over their curves, one walking around behind him as the other drops down in front. She takes his knees and forces them apart before rolling toward him, her full tits rubbing against his groin. It's the epitome of sex expressed in dance, and every part of me despises it.

Ezra doesn't dare look this way, and as the crowd roars with excitement, whoops, and wolf-whistles, it spurs the dancers on.

They grind against him, taking liberties I've never had, and as Jessica looks this way and grins, I want nothing more than to gouge her eyes out of her fake-tanned face. She might be able to dance all over him for the world to see, but she'll never have him, not like I do.

There's no denying she's a fucking bitch.

At the start of the show, she stood next to me and declared that my undying desperation for Ezra was too obvious, and I was embarrassing myself, and while that might be true on some level, she wasn't the one kissing him right before the show.

She insisted that he could do better, which again, I'm sure is true, but when she told me that he'll never want me the way he wants her, it became startlingly obvious that she truly has no idea who the hell I am. One quick Google search and she'll know all about our history, and I'm sure she'll be left feeling like an idiot. But her bullshit isn't something I'm interested in, and all I could do was scowl as she sashayed to the stage.

Fucking bitch.

I have always prided myself on being a woman who supports other women, but then people like Jessica come along, and there's nothing I want more than to bitch-slap her right across her fake titties. All I know is that the song he's singing perfectly lays out everything he's wondered about me over the years. The way I'd feel. The way I'd taste. It's just another part of our story—the part we never got to explore—and right now, he's allowing some skank to rub herself all over him while he sings about me, and I am not okay with it.

Call me a jealous bitch if you must. Actually, I know damn well that I'm a jealous bitch. I've been one since the second it occurred to me as a kid that I was too young for him and that there were so many other beautiful women out there who could give him exactly what he wanted without it seeming like a terrible scandal.

Yep. Even knowing he would never choose her over me, every bone in my body is full of jealousy, through and through.

Fuck this.

What am I even doing standing here and watching this? I know I'm a sucker for punishment, but this is too much. It's not just making me jealous, it's infuriating me. How can he sit there and let this happen knowing I'm standing right here? How could he have known about this during rehearsals and not even mentioned it in passing? Why would he try to blindside me like this?

I get it's just a show, and it doesn't mean a damn thing, but fuck. I hate this.

Feeling someone's stare upon me, I shift my gaze to Dylan to find a sadness in his eyes. "You okay?" he mouths as he plays for his adoring fans.

I shake my head and hook my thumb around toward the exit. "I'm gonna go."

Dylan nods. "Sorry."

I give him a tight smile, hoping to convey that I'm okay, but he knows I'm not. There's no hiding from these guys. I'm just as close to them as I was with Axel. They're the only real family I have, which is exactly how I know that his apology isn't just a sorry for having to see this. It's a sorry that I didn't warn you, sorry this is happening, sorry you're hurting, sorry there's nothing I can do to take away the pain.

Not wanting to linger on it, I turn my gaze back to Ezra and watch Jessica look my way again, her tongue rolling over her bottom lip as she tilts her head back and gasps, all while Stacey slides her hand up his strong thigh.

I can't do it. I can't stand here and watch as they tag-team my man.

Without a second thought, I turn on my heel and disappear, not willing to hear the rest of the song. Hell, not wanting to hear the rest of the show.

I weave my way through the backstage area, and with everyone already so focused on the show and being where they need to be, not a single person questions where the hell I'm going.

Making my way out into the cool Paris night, I start walking. If I were smart, I'd order an Uber, but like I said, I'm a sucker for punishment. The air is refreshing and helps to somewhat clear my head, and by the time I walk twenty minutes back to the hotel, all I want to do is forget.

Making my way to the elevator, I get in and reach for the button for my floor, when my gaze settles on the word heated pool. My brow arches, and having nothing else to do with the rest of my night, I press the corresponding button.

The elevator arrives in no time, and as I step out, I find a luxurious heated pool that looks out over Paris. Parts of the pool are indoors while the rest is outside. The lights are out, and as I gaze over the signage on the wall, I realize the pool closed a few hours ago, but my access card gives me and the boys full, all-hours access to every facility available in the hotel at any time we desire. I guess it pays to be rolling with the VIPs.

Calling down to the lobby, I order a bottle of champagne and strip out of my clothes. It would have been nice if I'd brought a bikini with me, but apparently, girls who live out of the back of their car simply can't afford the luxury of owning swimwear.

Leaving my jeans and top on the bench, I roll my hair up into a bun and step into the heated pool in nothing but my black bra and thong. The city lights illuminate the pool, and as I wade through the water and out into the open air, my gaze lingers on the steam rolling off the top of the water.

This is perfect. Just what I need.

I make my way right over to the edge and prop my arms on the side as I gaze out at the beautiful Paris views. It's insane to think this is where I am right now. Only three days ago, I was locked in a shitty motel room with the TV stand barricading the door, just in case anyone decided to pay me an unexpected visit. And now, I'm in a heated pool overlooking the beautiful Parisian city views. I can barely wrap my head around it.

And yet, a piece of me feels more pathetic than ever.

I was the girl he walked away from. The girl he never crossed the line with. The loser who waited years for him to come back to her. And now I'm here as his marketing manager, chasing him around the world like a lost puppy desperate for affection.

He never kissed me, not in the way I wanted to be kissed. Never touched me how I needed to be touched, and then he was gone. Just being here is a slap in the face, and yet, not a single piece of me could ever be convinced to go back home.

I'd rather be Ezra's emotional punching bag than go back to living out of my car or being my father's pawn to use and abuse.

The sound of people approaching has me stiffening, and as I glance back over my shoulder, I immediately relax, finding two of the hotel employees. One carries a bottle of champagne and a glass, while the other holds a perfectly folded towel.

"Miss Stone," the champagne wielder says in a thick French accent. He bows his head, and I gingerly make my way to the side of the pool, watching him pop the top of the champagne and begin filling the glass.

He hands it to me, and I don't hesitate to take a sip. "Shall I leave the bottle?" he asks as the other guy places the towel down on the bench next to my discarded clothes.

"Please do," I say with a fond smile, more than able to get used to this level of luxury, but I suppose I shouldn't become too accustomed to it. After all, the tour will be complete in four months, and after that, I'll be back on my own. Though, I'll have the funds to purchase my own home and make a decent start for myself. Unless Lenny decides I'm irreplaceable and sends me on the next tour with a band that won't make me relive my agony every second I see their faces.

The man places the bottle of champagne in a bucket of ice by the side of the pool, and not a moment later, the two men scurry off, leaving me to my peace. With my glass in hand, I drift back through the warm water, sipping my champagne and taking in the night sky. Despite the pain from watching Ezra on stage, I think this might be the happiest I've been in the past eight years.

My champagne goes down like a treat, and before I know it, my glass is empty. As I turn around to go refill my glass, a wave of goosebumps rises on my skin. I lift my gaze, and there he is, sitting right there next to my clothes with his elbows braced against his knees and his heart hanging out on his sleeve for the world to see.

Ezra fucking Knight.

CHAPTER 21

Raleigh

My whole body stiffens as I take him in. He doesn't lift his head, but I know he senses that I've seen him. He could always tell wherever I was in a room, but when my eyes were on him, it was as though something inside him came alive.

My heart races wildly, and I put my empty champagne glass down beside the ice bucket, sensing that whatever happens next, I'm going to want to avoid having something in my hand that could potentially be thrown at his stupidly gorgeous face.

"You left," his deep voice rumbles through the big room, and the sound is still capable of affecting me in every physical way.

I scoff, wishing he could have chosen to fight with me about this tomorrow after I was done indulging in this amazing pool. "What did you expect? That I'd hang around to watch skank one and skank two try to figure out the size of your dick with their fake asses?"

He lifts his head and looks at me, the fire in his eyes physically branding me and keeping me pinned. "That's what this is about?" he demands, getting to his feet. "You're jealous of them? Surely after everything, you know they mean nothing to me. They're props for the show."

"Oh, I see how it is. I should submit myself to having to watch that bullshit just because you needed me there. Okay, sure," I scoff, letting him hear the thick sarcasm in my tone as I nod along. "But what about what I need? Because that sure as fuck wasn't it. You didn't even warn me, not a single mention about it because all you've wanted to do since I got here was hurt me. Well congratulations, you did it. Again, and again, and again."

Suddenly I don't think I'm referring to the past couple of days anymore, and I know he senses that, but as he stares back at me, he doesn't pull me up on it. Instead, he stands and starts unbuttoning his shirt.

"You were jealous," he repeats.

Oh no. This isn't good.

His eyes don't leave mine, and not a moment later, his shirt is on the ground.

"Of those two? No."

His shoes come off, and he slowly strides to the edge of the pool, stepping down into it and letting the water soak through his ripped black jeans. A small smile lingers on his lips, and suddenly all I can think about is that kiss that ended way too soon. "Some things never change," he says fondly, only those words are like a shot straight to the chest.

"What the hell is that supposed to mean?" I demand, the tension thickening in the pool with every step he takes toward me. Tears burn the backs of my eyes, and I feel the very second I lose control. "Everything changes. Everything did change. I was in love with you, and then you left, and Axel died. And I . . . fuck."

I reach for the neck of the bottle. Fuck the glass. I need the whole thing.

I lift it to my lips and take a deep drink, only as I lower the bottle, I realize how much closer he's gotten. "Was?" he questions with agony in his eyes. "Past tense."

I swallow over the lump in my throat as he steals the bottle out of my hand and drinks, needing it just as much. If I open my mouth now, I'm terrified the truth might spill out—that no matter how hard I've tried, I've never been able to stop loving him. I have been wholeheartedly his since the very day I met him, and nothing has ever changed.

He creeps closer as he reaches past me, putting the bottle back on the edge of the pool, but the movement brings him way too close for comfort. "Don't," I warn him, knowing neither of us will be able to resist if that gap closes.

"Why the hell not?" he challenges.

I scoff, gaping at him as though I'm staring at a complete stranger. "Are you kidding me? How could this possibly be a good idea? No amount of history between us changes the facts. You killed me, Ezra. You left me behind and destroyed everything good that was in me, and then after Axel . . . Don't think for one second that I'm not blatantly aware of the fact that you still haven't given me the answers I deserve."

A coldness comes over him, and suddenly I feel as though I'm standing in an ice bath, not a heated pool. "There's nothing to say," he snaps.

"That's fucking bullshit, and you know it," I throw back at him, shoving my hand against the water so it splashes up over him. "Tell me. It's been two years, Ezra. I deserve to know exactly how my brother died. Hell, there are a lot of things regarding Axel's death I deserved that I never got."

"Like what?" he demands.

I gape at him. "Oh, you really want to get into it? I deserved to know before the fucking media. I deserved to not have to find out by my best friend barging into my room in the middle of the night. I deserved to not have my number blocked by your whole fucking team when I was begging for answers. I deserved to at least have a say in how he was buried, and where. I deser—"

"Okay, shit, Rae. I get it," he says, firing back at me, just as worked up as I am. "I fucked up. Every chance I've ever had with both you and Axel, I have fucked it up, and you punish me for it every fucking chance you get. You've made it crystal clear that I've let you down." He takes a breath, running his hand through his thick, dark hair. "Do you have any idea what it's like to have to live with that guilt every fucking day? To live with the fact that the only person I've ever wanted despises me for living my dream."

I simply stare at him. "That's what you think?" I scoff.

He opens his arms out wide. "What the fuck am I supposed to think, Rae? You're not exactly known for being honest anymore."

"Pray tell," I groan, getting more frustrated with him by the second. "I'm an open book, Ezra. I've been up-front with you since the moment I got here. What the hell have I lied about?"

He steps closer, his eyes brimming with fire. "Why are you so fucking sick at the idea of going back home?"

His words are like a slap to the face, and I hastily back away from him, my heart racing with fear at just the mention of home. "Don't," I say, grabbing the bottle and turning away, desperate to conceal the fear in my eyes, knowing he will sense it without even trying.

I wade through the water until I'm back outside, needing the air, and I hear him moving through the water behind me without missing a beat.

"Rae," he murmurs.

"No," I whisper, moving right to the edge and staring out at the view that doesn't quite seem so incredible anymore. "We're not doing this."

I feel him move in behind me, his body so close and yet not an inch of his skin brushes mine, not until I feel his fingers at the top of my spine. His touch is like a shot of electricity pulsing right through my skin. "What the hell is this?" he murmurs, tracing the lines of my tattoo that I'd so foolishly forgotten about.

Fuck.

"It's nothing."

I close my eyes as his fingers continue moving across the petals of the finely lined rose tattooed at the very top of my spine. A chill sweeps through me as he follows the stem lower to the words that read, "Hypothetically Yours."

"When?" he murmurs, inching closer until his other hand grasps my waist.

"I was sixteen," I tell him, feeling the weight of that particular day like a bullet right through the heart. "I got it as a surprise. I was planning on showing you, but . . . you broke my heart instead."

"Rae."

"Don't," I whisper, trying to shrug him off, feeling my body trembling under his touch.

I go to lift the bottle to my lips, but he reaches around me, takes it from my hands, and places it back on the edge of the pool. When his hand returns to my waist, he slowly turns me until those dark eyes are locked on mine.

He holds my stare as his fingers tighten on my waist, both of us breathing heavily as the tension around us becomes unbearable. "Ezra," I whisper, as the pendants around his neck catch in the soft moonlight, illuminating the 'R' that rests right by his chest and making my heart long for something it shouldn't want.

My gaze drops to his mouth with anticipation, and just as I suck in a deep breath, his lips crash down on mine.

A million fireworks go off in my head as I instantly sink into his kiss. My lips furiously move against his with a longing that's been building for far too long. Our kiss from earlier at the show was barely a taste, but this is hunger. This is fire, lust, and desperation, and it's everything I've needed.

His arm locks around my waist, pulling me hard against his warm body as he presses me against the edge of the pool, my back flattening against the tiles. My hand scoops around the back of his neck, holding him to me as his tongue dips into my mouth, exploring what's always been his, what we never should have waited to do.

He grabs my ass, lifting me into his arms, and my legs instantly lock around his waist as the hunger grows more intense within me. His lips drop to my neck, working their way to the sensitive spot below my ear, and I tip my head back in ecstasy as the pleasure rocks through my body.

"God, Ezra," I groan, clinging onto him as my fingers knot into his hair, but as I feel him grind against me and feel his sheer size hidden within his wet jeans, the desperation morphs into pure animalistic need.

I have to have him, and I have to have him now. I've waited too long. I need to have his hands on my body, his lips on mine as I feel the way he pushes that thick cock inside of me. I need to feel the way he works me, the way he stretches me, and fuck, I need to feel the way I come alive beneath his skilled touch.

Lowering my legs from his waist, I reach for the front of his pants, and he pauses, pulling back just an inch. "Are you sure, Rae? I can stop—"

I release the button of his jeans and pull him back in. "If you even think about stopping, I'll kill you," I warn as his lips crash back to mine. "I've waited too long for this."

A new determination creeps in, and our kisses become a reckless, needy surrender to every desire we've stifled through the years.

His hands roam over my bare skin, learning the way my body has changed, committing every new curve to memory, and when his hand trails high on my thigh, I suck in a breath, more than ready.

Instead of hesitating like he would have when we were younger, he gives me exactly what I want. His hand closes over my pussy, grinding his palm against my clit as a low groan rumbles through my chest.

I get his wet jeans undone, and I don't waste a moment, reaching in and curling my hand around his sheer size. My fingers barely close, and as my hand trails up and down his long length, feeling the piercing at the top, he shudders and drops his forehead to my shoulder. "Fuck, Rae," he grumbles, shifting his hand until it slips inside my thong, his fingers finally against my bare skin.

I explore every inch of him, learning his body just as he does to me, and when my desperation becomes all too much, I start pulling at my thong, desperate to get it off.

Ezra helps me so that I don't have to release him, and the moment it's gone and discarded at the bottom of the pool, his fingers are right back at it. He finds my clit, rolling tight circles with his thumb as his fingers explore further. He pushes one inside of me, and as I tremble, he adds another.

His lips brush across the rim of my ear, and it sends a shiver shooting down my spine. "You like that, Rae?"

"Mmmm, God, yes," I groan, rolling my thumb over his tip

before making my way back down to his base and committing him to memory—every angry vein, the feel of his piercing beneath my thumb, and his sheer size.

There's no way he'll fit, but I'm not walking away from this until we're done. There's no stopping us now. We've waited too long.

Ezra works my cunt, curving his fingers and pushing back inside of me. His fingers split massaging deep inside of me until my hips are jolting with undeniable pleasure. "More," I breathe as his other hand moves behind me, unclasping my wet bra and letting it fall away.

"Fuck, Rae," he murmurs as his gaze sails over my naked body. He reaches up and cups my breast, brushing his thumb over my pebbled nipple and sending hot pulses shooting right to my core. "You're so fucking gorgeous."

"Don't stop," I beg.

His thumb keeps moving over my nipple and my whole body shudders, never having realized just how sensitive they were. "Never."

The more he touches me, the more worked up I become, and as he continues working my clit, I feel the familiar pull from inside me, something I've only ever been able to achieve on my own. "Oh God," I gasp, tightening my grasp on his thick cock. "I need to have you."

"You sure, baby?" he asks, and there is a deep pain in his voice at the thought of having to stop. "If you're not ready—"

"Fucking hell, Ezra," I mutter, barely able to string a full sentence together. I pull him closer, and without skipping a beat, I lock my legs around his waist again, feeling his velvety cock pressed right up against my core. The move forces both of our hands out of the way, but I don't care because I'll take what's coming next a million times over. "Don't make me beg for it. I've wanted you like this since I was sixteen. Don't make me wait any longer."

He groans, and as though my desperate pleas are music to his ears, he reaches between us, takes his thick cock, and guides it to my entrance. Then just as I feel his piercing against me, he leans in and captures my lips in his.

As he kisses me slowly, I feel him start to push, instantly stretching me.

We both tremble, but he doesn't dare stop, taking me inch by inch. "Fuck, Rae," he groans against my lips.

"Don't stop," I whisper, closing my eyes as the undeniable pleasure courses through my veins.

My walls stretch and contract around him as I'm thrown into a world of pure bliss, and once he's fully seated inside of me, his fingers tighten on my skin, both of us just as affected as the other.

"Baby, I need to move," he says.

"Do it," I gasp. "Fuck me, Ezra."

Not needing to be told twice, he draws back, and this time when he thrusts into me, there's no hesitation. He doesn't take it slow, and he sure as fuck doesn't hold back. He gives me everything, his cock slamming deep inside of me as the water crashes around us.

My arm hooks around the back of his neck, holding on as I get used to the feel of him inside of me, and it's like nothing I've ever felt before. It's everything. Intoxicating. Hypnotic. Incredible.

I've never felt so alive.

He works me in a way I never realized I needed, touching me in places I've never been touched, and as he rolls his hips and reaches that spot deep inside of me, I cry out in the sweetest pleasure, never knowing it could be this good.

"Oh fuck, Ezra," I grunt, clutching on to him with everything I have.

"That's right, baby. Just like that," he grunts, doing it again and again before dropping his thumb to my clit and rolling tight circles again, driving me to the edge of insanity. "You like that?"

"Yes! God, Yes!"

Ezra gives me everything I need and more, and as I feel my orgasm creeping up on me, I do what I can to hold on to it. "Fuck, I'm gonna come," I warn him, feeling as I'm pushed closer and closer to the edge, the intensity already driving me insane.

"Give it to me, baby," he rumbles, his fingers digging into my skin and warning me that he's right there with me. "Let me feel the way you squeeze my cock."

His words are my undoing, and I come hard, letting my orgasm explode from within. I shatter like glass, wildly convulsing around his thick cock as my high rocks through my body. My toes curl as I throw my head back, the pure satisfaction like nothing I've ever felt.

Ezra doesn't stop fucking me, letting me ride out my orgasm on his cock as his thumb continues working my clit, and fuck, it's delicious. I pant and gasp, desperately trying to catch my breath when he grabs the back of my neck and kisses me again, and as he thrusts deeply into me again, I feel as he finishes, shooting hot spurts of cum deep inside my cunt.

I feel like a goddess, my whole body trembling as we reach our high together.

He rocks back and forth, one hand on my ass, the other wrapped around my waist, holding me to him as he breaks our kiss and drops his forehead to mine, both of us slowly catching our breath. "You have no idea how long I've wondered just how tight your sweet little cunt could squeeze me."

My cheeks flame, and instead of being embarrassed, I lift my chin and own it. "Is that all you've wondered about?"

He shakes his head, his eyes dancing with the darkest desire. "You might think you know, but I promise you, Rae, you've got no fucking idea the vile things I want to do to you."

Hunger drums inside of me, and he leans back in, closing the gap as his lips brush against mine. I capture them and kiss him deeper before pulling back and locking my arms around his neck. As I hold him, the weight of our situation dawns on me, and despite how incredible this was, it can't magically erase all the pain and resentment.

He lets out a heavy sigh, holding me just as tightly as I hold him, sensing the change within me. "I don't want to walk away from this, Rae," he murmurs, his lips brushing across my neck as his fingers dance across my skin. "The second I get out of this pool, I know you're going to act like this never happened, and I can't bear to pretend like that."

"I can't just come walking straight back into your life as though everything isn't different now. Too much has happened. There's too much I have to work through first."

He nods, knowing it just as well as I do. "When you're ready—"

"I know," I whisper.

A moment of torturous silence passes between us when he pulls back and takes my chin between his thumb and finger, his dark gaze staring into mine. "Do you want me to go?"

I shake my head. "No," I say, trembling. "Can we just . . . stay like this for a little while longer?"

"Yeah, Rae," he murmurs, dropping a kiss to my temple, just like he used to when I was a teenager. "We can stay as long as you need."

CHAPTER 22

Raleigh

16 YEARS OLD

The tattoo artist grunts at me. "Hypothetically Yours?" The big gruff dude asks. "Isn't that the song by that new boy band? Devil's Obsession or something like that?"

"First off, they're not a boy band. They're a rock band. Big difference," I say. "And second, they're called Demon's—"

"Ahhhh, shit. You're a groupie, aren't you?" he accuses, almost seeming disappointed in me. "You know, I see girls like you come in here all the time thinking if they tattoo some famous dude's name on their ass, they'll get his attention, but more often than not, I end up with them right back on my table asking for a cover up."

"This is different," I say, wanting to smack him in the face, but considering his right hand is bigger than my whole body, I fight the urge to smack him around. "I'm not a groupie."

"They're all in their twenties, aren't they? Little old for you, don't you think?"

"No. They're nineteen," I say, rolling my eyes. "And I'm six—eighteen. Besides, like I said, I'm not a groupie. I'm dating the lead singer, and my brother is the guitarist. Plus, not that it's any of your business, but 'Hypothetically Yours' was written about me."

The big guy laughs so hard he almost falls off his chair. "Okay, whatever you say, princess," he says, having to wipe the tears from his eyes. "We all have to embrace the delusion every now and then, but you're paying me cash, so I'm not about to say no. Sit tight, I'll get it drawn up."

A stupid grin stretches across my face, and I suddenly feel like an idiot for not bringing Ezra with me to hold my hand, but if he knew, he would have told me to wait until I was eighteen and to think it through. Or at least be here to call me a chicken when I freak out about the needle. But the plan is to surprise him, and tonight seems like the perfect night.

He messaged me earlier wanting to take me out, and I can't help but wonder if tonight is the night . . . not just surprise him with my tattoo night, but *the* night. It's been almost six months since the big execs from Louder Records came to watch them at their gig, and Ezra unknowingly crushed my soul. They were signed within the week, and their lives have spiraled in the best way. Their first single 'Hypothetically Yours' came out a little over two months ago, and in that time, the boys have skyrocketed to international stardom. It's been incredible, a whirlwind of craziness, but it also means that finding time alone with Ezra has been impossible.

He's here all the time but somehow so far away.

I miss him like crazy.

God, I sound like such a baby. The boys are literally making all of their dreams come true, and all I can do is complain. I mean, is it that much to ask for a moment alone with my boyfriend so I can try to seduce him? My subtle hints haven't been enough. Hell, not even the glaringly obvious ones have been. Though knowing Ezra, he's probably purposefully holding off until I'm older. He's driving me insane with all this trying to be noble bullshit. I mean, fuck. Just nail me already!

Mr. Judgmental returns with a design, and as he takes his seat, he hands me the piece of paper. "What do you think?"

Turning the paper around, I take in the beautiful design—a finely lined rose with the cursive words 'Hypothetically Yours' acting as the stem. The swoops of the y's are accentuated to create leaves, and the tops of the t's become thorns. The delicate line continues up, and at the very top is the rose.

My heart starts to race. "It's perfect," I say.

"Alright," he says, taking it back and glancing over it one more time. "Where do you want it?"

I throw my hand right over the back of my head and point to the top of my spine as I awkwardly try to turn and show him. "Right here."

"Jesus Christ," he mutters under his breath, probably knowing that

I've done absolutely no research on how badly this is going to hurt. But there's not a damn thing I wouldn't do for Ezra, and if having some big dude tattoo my spine for the next thirty minutes is what I've gotta do, then count me in. Besides, I have a high pain threshold. Mostly. Well, I mean, kind of. Or maybe not. I'm a little bitch whenever I stub my toe, but period cramps don't bother me too much, and that's gotta count for something, right?

Ahhh fuck. Maybe this isn't such a great idea after all.

"Right, hop on the table," he says, glancing over my shirt. "You'll have to take that off, but keep the underwear on. I've got something I can drape you with if you're more comfortable."

"I'll be okay," I say, certain he's seen a lot worse than some random girl's bra straps. Besides, it's not as though we're alone here. At least six other people are hanging around, and despite his judgmental tendencies, he seems like somewhat of a teddy bear.

I scooch up on the table and whip my shirt off as he gets to his feet. "Relax," he says, shaking his head at my enthusiasm. "I've got a few things I need to prepare and then we'll get started. You need anything? Food? Water? A piss? I don't want you getting up during your session and screwing with my flow."

"I'm good," I say, kinda wishing I could adopt this guy. He seems like fun. Bit rough around the edges, but I like that he's straightforward, and I'm not left wondering about his intentions. It's comforting.

He takes off, and I'm left twiddling my thumbs for a few minutes, scrolling through my gallery on my phone and trying to find a picture of me with the band to prove to him that I'm not some desperate groupie like the other girls that have been hanging around a lot lately.

My tattoo artist returns a few minutes later, and after quickly getting himself set up, my face is squished against the table with his big arms positioned over my back. Then, instructing me to take a breath, he gets started.

The pain is ridiculous, so I guess I'm nothing but a wretched liar. My pain tolerance is about as low as it can get, but I breathe through it, knowing he's going as fast as he can to get it done. He tries to talk to me, but I don't listen to a damn word until he's finally pulling away and wiping the excess ink off my skin.

"There, that wasn't so bad, was it?" he mutters, looking over his handiwork.

"You might as well have been using a chainsaw. Do I even have any skin left?"

He rolls his eyes. "Quit being such a princess. You have ink now. You're a badass."

Meeting his stare, I grin wide as a wave of pride shoots through me. "Hell yeah, I am," I agree, knowing that Ezra is going to love it.

He gets me all cleaned up, and after allowing me just a moment to check it out in the mirror, he puts some kind of fancy cling wrap over the rose before giving me a whole rundown of instructions for how to keep it clean and avoid infection.

After handing over my whole life savings, I turn and walk out of the shop but stop when my phone rings. When I pull it out of my back pocket, Ezra's name and a photo of us fills the screen, and a smile pulls at my lips. I can't help but whip back around and hold out my phone for the big burly guy to see. "Ha. Told ya," I say, sounding like a whiny child. "I'm not a groupie. He's my boyfriend."

"Uh-huh," he says, taking a quick glance at the phone. "Whatever you say."

I groan, and realizing that not even screwing Ezra on his tattoo table is going to change this guy's mind, I roll my eyes and make my way out of the shop. "Hey," I say, quickly answering the call before I miss it.

"Where are you?" Ezra asks. "I'm at your place. I thought you'd be here."

"I had to duck out for a minute, but I'll be home in . . . maybe twenty," I say, trying to get a good idea of how long it'll take me to walk my ass all the way back home. "You need something?"

"Nah, not really," he says. "But I'm hungry, so I figured we could head out a bit earlier instead of waiting for tonight. If that's cool with you, of course. Just didn't wanna have something now and then spoil my appetite later."

Oooh. I'm not going to say no to spending extra hours with Ezra. He's been at some big meeting today with the whole band and the label, so I'm sure he's dying to unload everything that went down. "You know I'm always good to eat," I tell him, having a healthier appetite than Axel does. "I'm close to that diner that has the really good burgers and cheese fries if you want to meet me there. Save me having to walk all the way back."

"Consider it done," he says, his voice softening in a way that sends shivers through my whole body. He only ever talks like that with me, and I love it more than anything else in the whole world.

Ezra ends the call, and I turn on my heel to head in the other direction. The diner isn't anything special, and while I was hoping to go home and get my hair and makeup done and maybe pick out something a little risqué to wear for a special night together, this is just as good. Having extra hours alone trumps a good outfit any day.

I make it to the diner in record time and find a booth as I wait for his car to pull into the lot. It doesn't take long, and the moment I see the familiar car, a stupid grin stretches across my face.

He disappears out of sight, and I wait impatiently for him to walk through the door, only when it opens a moment later, it's Axel who strides into the diner. My brows furrow as a wave of disappointment floods me. Don't get me wrong, I love my brother, but having him crash my date with Ezra isn't exactly ideal.

Ezra strides in behind him, and as he scans the diner to find me, a guilty expression crosses his face. He knows I'm disappointed, but he also knows I'm not about to say anything.

They make their way toward me, weaving through the other tables until finally taking a seat, and I watch in suspicion as they squeeze into the same side, both of them facing me as though preparing for something. There's a grim expression on both of their faces, and just like that, the excitement about my new tattoo vanishes.

"Just tell me," I say, my heart racing a million miles an hour.

The boys look at one another as though silently arguing over who's going to break the news, and my mind races through the worst-case scenarios. Someone's dead. Maybe Dad got into a car accident and is slowly fading away. Maybe he's finally pissed off the wrong person and they've put him into the hospital. That wouldn't be such a bad thing because then I'd be able to live freely in my own home without walking on eggshells to avoid his drunk tantrums. He's never put his hands on me, but I know that has a lot to do with the way he avoids Ax and Ezra. I feel it in my bones, the way he looks at me like I'm weak and insignificant, and the sooner I get out of here, the better.

"We, uhhh . . . We had our big meeting with the label," Ezra starts as though I might have forgotten, clearly not realizing it's been on my mind all day.

"Yeah?" I say, a little confused. Judging by the looks on their faces, I was certain they were about to hit me with bad news, but nothing bad could have come from their meeting. They shot to superstardom overnight. It could only be moving forward for them. "And?"

Ezra cringes, so Axel picks up where he left off. "And," he starts, sounding just as hesitant as Ezra had. "They're so impressed with how we're doing that they want to send us on tour."

"WHAT?" I screech, flying out of my seat, my eyes widening in surprise as the overwhelming excitement claims me. "Holy shit. That's incredible."

"Yeah," Ezra says a little awkwardly, watching me far too closely. "It's great news. We're really pumped for it. They have some great ideas for how it's going to go and have already started working out which cities and countries we'll visit, but it'll be a lot of work. They want us to start rehearsals straight away."

"Well, yeah," I say, dropping back into my seat. "Seems only natural, right?"

"Definitely," Ax responds. "I don't know what kind of places we'll be performing in, but I can guarantee it'll be a shitload bigger than the bars and clubs we're used to. We're going to have to spend every waking minute perfecting our set."

I let out a heavy breath, needing just a moment for it to sink in. "You have no idea how happy I am for you guys," I say as Ezra smiles and reaches across the table to squeeze my hand. His touch is electrifying, and if my brother weren't here, I know I'd already be in his arms. Hell, with this level of excitement, I probably would have kissed him, tongue and all, and surely he would have kissed me back. "But what's the catch?"

The boys cringe and share another glance as I start to become frustrated. "Just tell me," I mutter. "You're both sitting there looking like someone just shoved a sour lemon up your asses, and the longer you don't tell me, the harder I want to smack you."

Ezra lets out a heavy breath and adjusts himself in the booth as he holds my stare with nothing but pure devastation in his dark eyes. "Because this is our first tour, they want to overlook our rehearsals, and in order to do that," he says slowly. "We have to relocate to LA."

I'm taken by surprise, and I sit up a little straighter. "Oh, umm . . . okay. That's not such a huge deal, is it?" I ask. "I mean, it'll be a lot to organize on short notice, but switching schools shouldn't be too bad. I'll get a transfer and enroll at one of the schools over there."

"Rae," Axel says, his voice softening. "It's not that easy."

"Of course it is."

"Rehearsals are only going to be a few months, and then we'll be on tour, jetting from one place to another. You won't be able to do school that way. You need stability if you plan to go to college, and following us from city to city isn't it," he says. "Plus, you're still a minor, Rae. I'd have to get Dad to sign off on everything and somehow become your guardian, and you know how Dad is. That's not going to happen."

"Wait," I say, pulling my hand back from Ezra's. "What are you saying?"

Ezra catches my stare as I feel tears already welling in my eyes. "You have to stay here, Rae," he says as I shake my head. "Your whole life is here. School, friends, home. I can't take you away from that just to follow us around. I won't do it. You have a whole life ahead of you."

"No," I breathe, pulling right back, my chest heaving with gasping breaths as the ugly realization of what a life here with Dad would mean for me when the boys are no longer here to deflect his anger. "No. You can't leave me here. I'm coming with you."

"And what about college, Rae?" Axel asks. "You'll never even see the admissions office if you don't graduate high school, and on the road with us, that's not an option."

I shoot to my feet, the tears already rolling down my cheeks as I look between the two people who mean the most to me in this cruel world, the two who are talking crazy and saying they're about to abandon me here. "You can't do this. Please. Please don't leave me behind," I cry, waiting for one of them to realize how sick this joke is and tell me they're lying. "I swear, I'll figure it out. I'll find a way to graduate. I'm sure there's online education or, or . . . I don't know.

People get their GEDs outside of school all the time. I can do that."

Axel hangs his head in his hands as Ezra gets up from the table and makes his way around to me. He grips my arms, pulling me in close before winding them around me. "I'm sorry, Rae. You have no fucking idea how sorry I am, but we're trying to think of what's best for your future," he tells me. "Believe me, I fucking hate this. The idea of being apart from you is killing me, but the life we're about to walk into, you didn't sign up for that."

I look up at him, the tears rolling faster than ever. "Don't," I say, my voice breaking over the lump in my throat. "Don't break us like this."

Devastation flashes in his dark eyes, but I see no hint of hesitation. He's made up his mind. He's leaving me here in this bullshit town, leaving me at the mercy of a hateful drunk. For just a moment, I consider telling them how much Dad scares me when they aren't around, but if they knew . . . If they heard the way he talks to me, they'd never get on that plane. They'd never accept this tour, and they'd never get the things they've worked all these years to achieve.

"It won't be that long," he promises me. "A year, maybe. Eighteen months. Then I'll be home."

I exhale, my every emotion overwhelming me in that one breath, and I pull out of his arms, shrugging him off when he reaches for me again, not knowing a single word to say.

And with that, I turn and run out of the diner as the agonizing sobs tear from the back of my throat.

CHAPTER 23

Raleigh

Night after night, city after city, the tension worsens.

It's been two weeks since being with Ezra in the pool, and when I say that there hasn't been a single moment where I haven't thought about it, I'm not exaggerating. Even in my dreams, I replay it over and over again. I've been wondering what it'd be like to be physical with him since I was fifteen years old, and it was just as incredible as I always imagined.

I had no idea it could be like that. The emotion, the pleasure, the connection . . . holy shit. I need to do it again. I need to feel him inside me. I need to feel the way he claimed me, and I don't ever want it to stop. It was such a rush. In terms of experience, I can't exactly claim to be an expert. Apart from what happened back in Michigan, my experience with sex is non-existent.

The moment Ezra pulled away from me and left me in that pool, I've never felt emptier. How can a life without him be worth living? Hell, I don't even know how I'm going to make it through the rest of this tour. Seeing him every day and not being able to touch him or fall into his arms and tell him how much I've loved him over the years is killing me, and if it weren't for my need to succeed at this job and prove myself to Lenny, I surely would have crumbled already.

I see it in Ezra's eyes every time he looks my way. This is killing him just as much as it's killing me, but I refuse to go running back to him, not while I'm holding onto so much anger and resentment. I don't want to be with him that way, and deep down, I think he understands.

So for now, I continue to watch him from the sidelines.

Night after night, as Demon's Curse performs for sold-out stadiums, I stand at the side of the stage, watching as the only man I've ever wanted pours his heart out in lyrics that I was too foolish and broken to hear.

Night one in Paris, he had turned to me and sung about one day giving me the love he always thought I deserved. And every night since, he's done the same, picking a song, turning to me, and making sure I truly hear him.

Paris, night two, he turned to me and sang about the way his heart raced the first time he ever met me, and that still to this day, it was the greatest moment of his life. And I cried.

Italy, night one, he turned to me and sang about the anger he felt when he realized he'd allowed me to slip away, and how he's never felt whole since. And my heart shattered.

Night two in Italy, he serenaded me with lyrics about how he would look up into the stars and picture wherever I was in the world, staring at the same dark sky. And the loneliness overwhelmed me.

And now tonight, as he waves his hands back and forth in sync with fifty thousand other souls, his gaze locks on mine, and I listen to the whole stadium sing about how he will love me unconditionally until his final breath. And with that, I feel the anger and resentment finally begin to fade into a distant hum.

The moment is too much, and as I hold his dark stare, my knees give out. I crumble to the ground as tears stream down my face, my heart pulling me in a million different directions, but there's only one direction that feels like home.

I can't take my eyes off him as he captivates the audience, his words speaking right to my soul, and when he makes his way toward me, my heart races for a whole new reason. He doesn't skip a beat or miss a single lyric as he strides across the massive stage, past Rock and Dylan, and right into the wings of the stage where I remain a crumpled mess out of sight from the rowdy crowd.

Ezra offers me his hand, and as he sings the deep lyrics that shatter my soul, he helps me back to my feet. I expect him to walk away, to get back to his captivated audience, but instead, he pulls me into the warmth of his loving arms, wrapping them around me as he continues to sing.

I don't say a word, simply hold him with my face pressed against his wide chest as the beat of his heart matches the bass of Rock's drums.

A moment passes, and as the lyrics fade into Jett's guitar solo, Ezra pulls back, lowers his microphone, and drops his intense stare to mine. His fingers brush beneath my chin, raising it until my lips are barely a breath from his. "Fuck, I love you," he tells me.

All I can do is swallow over the lump in my throat as I hold his piercing stare, and when I don't respond, he leans in and kisses me. It's only a brief kiss, his lips lingering on mine for only a second before he pulls back. "I'm sorry, Rae. You're too fucking beautiful to be on your knees for any man," he tells me. "I needed you to hear it. I needed you to know what it's been like all these years without you."

"I know," I murmur, clutching his strong arms. "It's been the same for me."

He nods, and as Jett's solo comes to an end, Ezra takes a step back and lifts his microphone once again. His lyrics flow out of him so beautifully, it's impossible to believe such words could have been written about me, and as he makes his way back to the center of the stage, all I can do is watch, completely mesmerized by this incredible man—a man I so desperately wish to call mine.

The rest of the show goes off without incident, and I manage to remain on my feet right until the explosive finale. Just like every night, I watch in awe as the pyrotechnics team does their thing. It's incredible. Axel would have gotten such a kick out of it.

Dylan comes off the stage first, and just like every night, he scoops me off my feet and spins me around. "Fuck, that was a good one," he says, completely pumped up. "You heard that crowd, right? Fuck. We were on fire."

"You were," I laugh as he settles me back to my feet.

He doesn't release me though, simply holds my arms as he captures my stare, a seriousness washing over him. "You're good though, right?" he murmurs, his gaze subtly flicking toward Ezra as he makes his way toward us. "That moment . . . you know, seemed a little intense."

I give him a beaming smile and push up onto my tippy toes as I brush a kiss to his cheek. "I'm good," I promise him just as Ezra comes past us, only he slows right down and takes my hand, gently squeezing it as he passes. His gaze locks onto mine, and for just a moment, my heart completely stops.

Everything that I am belongs to him.

Ezra continues, and our hands fall apart but my fingers feel as though they've been infused with electricity.

Rock crashes into me and Dylan, his arms locking around us both. "You know," he muses, his grin way too suspicious. "If Rae wasn't so head over heels in love with Ez, you two would make a cute couple."

My gaze flicks back to Dylan's, and a wave of awkwardness washes over us. "Ewwww, gross," Dylan sputters, trying to get away from me. "She's like my little sister."

My lips twist with disgust at just the thought of being anything more to Dylan. Don't get me wrong, he's amazing, and any woman— hopefully Madds—would be lucky to scoop him up. But I am certainly not that woman. Madds on the other hand hasn't been able to stop talking about him since their drunken night in my hotel room.

Rock laughs. "I know, I'm just fucking with ya," he says, pulling back and clipping Dylan across the back of the head. "I'm fucking starving though. You down to eat?"

"I'm always good to eat," Dylan says, finally able to release me properly.

"Count me in," Ezra says from somewhere deeper backstage, and I turn back, glancing over my shoulder to find him putting his favorite electric guitar into its case. As if sensing my stare, his gaze shifts to mine. "What about you, Rae? You coming out with us? Just like old times?"

I let out a heavy breath, my cheeks blowing out. "Right, because that wouldn't be a recipe for disaster?"

Ezra grins, and his whole face lights up, making my heart leap into action, racing a million miles an hour. "You're not scared, are ya?" he questions, striding toward us.

I scoff and arch my brow. This boy always knew exactly what strings to pull to get me to cave. "Of you three? You wish."

"Then it's settled," he says, his gaze darkening as it lingers on me, suggesting that after dinner, he'd like to have me for dessert.

A shiver sails down my spine, and I make a break for it, speed walking away before I accidentally jump him right here in front of Rock and Dylan. "Dinner sounds great," I call over my shoulder, refusing to meet Ezra's eyes. "Text me the details."

I storm away, listening to the sound of Ezra's laugh behind me, and the sound takes me back to a time when we were carefree and in love, a time when we didn't have pain and resentment forcing us apart. And it occurs to me that whatever anger he had, whatever had him so frustrated when he first saw me, he's let go of it. He's happy, and the thought warms me in a way I wasn't expecting. I just wish I were capable of doing the same.

After making my way back to my hotel room, I flop down on my bed, needing just a moment of peace before the rest of my night turns upside down. Don't get me wrong, dinner with the guys used to be my version of normal, and to be able to do that again is amazing, but I know I'm going to feel Axel's absence. It's almost bittersweet.

A text comes through from Dylan, letting me know which restaurant they've chosen, and when he adds that I have twenty minutes to not only get my ass ready but to be there as well, a sheer panic rolls over me.

I throw myself from my bed and kick off my shoes before digging through my luggage. I managed to find a few spare moments in Paris and Italy to start refreshing my closet, and so far, I'm in love with everything I've found, but it's always a struggle to pick out the right outfit now.

I've never had issues dressing the part before, and never really cared, but something makes me want to put in the extra effort tonight.

Picking out a black, form-fitting bandage dress, I get to work shimmying into it and doing what I can to get the zipper all the way up. I spruce my hair, wearing it down and doing what I can to accentuate and tidy my unruly loose waves.

After slipping into a pair of strappy heels and adding a little more makeup to take me from rocker-chick to evening goddess, I deem myself officially ready. I haven't got a little clutch yet, so I'm stuck using the back of my phone case as a purse and after shoving my room key and some cash into it, I make my way to the door, only as I reach for the handle, a soft knock sounds through the room.

I pause as my heart starts to race, somehow already knowing who stands on the other side of the door, and as I lean into the heavy wood and peer through the little peephole, I find Ezra in all of his rockstar glory.

He looks as though he's freshly showered, and just the memory of what that used to smell like is enough to cripple me. His hair is just as unruly as mine, almost jet black and falling into his eyes, and as my greedy gaze trails down his body, I become weak.

He wears a black button-down with the top few buttons left to their own devices, showing off his sculpted chest with those three chains hanging low around his neck.

He looks delicious, and I hate how desperately I want to take a bite.

"Rae," he says, his voice so low it awakens something deep inside of me. "Are you going to open the door or just keep staring at me through that little fucking hole?"

"I'm not staring," I throw back at him.

A stupid grin stretches across his ridiculously perfect face. "Uh-huh."

Asshole.

Letting out a breath, I relent and reach for the handle, pulling the door open until I stand directly in front of him, and as the cocky smirk on his face morphs into awe, I feel the blush creep into my cheeks.

His gaze slowly trails down my body, taking me in as though he's never seen me before. "Holy fuck, Rae," he breathes, never having seen me wear such a beautiful dress before. "You look—"

"Don't finish that sentence," I warn, stepping into him and laying my hand against his racing heart before pressing a kiss to his cheek. "You and I both know we can't handle it."

"Speak for yourself," he mutters darkly before having to clear his throat.

"What are you doing here?"

"Thought you might need some company."

I arch a brow as a stupid smirk settles across my lips. "And if I don't?"

He scoffs, but there's no mistaking the laughter shining in his eyes, and for just a moment, I could almost pretend that things were just like they used to be, that we weren't two tortured souls desperate to find their way back together. "Then it'll be a really fucking awkward walk to the restaurant."

I can't help but laugh as I roll my eyes and head off down the hall. Ezra falls in step beside me, and when he takes my hand, lacing his fingers through mine, I don't dare pull away. He loops our joined hands over my shoulder and pulls me in close beside him as we reach the elevator, only when it arrives and we're closed inside, the shift in the air makes it almost impossible to breathe.

The tension rolls off us, and just as the elevator begins its descent, Ezra shifts beside me. I keep my eyes locked on his, watching him turn to face me, stepping in so close that we breathe the same air. His dark eyes are hooded and locked on mine as his hand takes my waist, sending the sweetest shiver sailing down my spine.

His darkened gaze drops to my lips as my chest rises and falls heavily, willing him to close the gap and kiss me.

God, I need him. That night two weeks ago in the pool wasn't nearly enough. I need to feel him on me, his lips against mine, making me come alive.

The seconds tick by, and the tension grows so thick I can't handle it another moment. His eyes are telling a story, a desperate plea for me to end his agony, to come around and finally give us the chance we deserve to start fresh, to give each other the love we so desperately crave.

His hand tightens on my waist, and as my heart booms like thunder in the deadliest storm, he begins to lean in.

I suck in a breath, and my hand involuntarily slides up his chest, preparing to claim him as my own. And just as I feel the slightest brush of his lips against mine—*ding*. The elevator arrives at the ground floor, and the door opens wide into the lobby where the concierge waits. "Mr. Knight. Miss Stone," he says as I feel like a bucket of ice water has just been emptied over our heads. "Is there anything I can do for you? Reservations? A car?"

Ezra and I spring apart as though what we are doing is somehow wrong, and I watch as he offers the concierge a kind smile. "No, thank you. We're okay. We're going to walk."

"Lovely," the concierge responds. "It's a beautiful evening for a stroll. Most of the fans and paparazzi seem to have cleared out."

Ezra nods and as he glances back at me, he clears his throat before dropping his hand to my lower back. "Come on," he murmurs before leading me out of the hotel lobby.

We walk in awkward silence as we step out into the street and find a few photographers that have lingered behind, but compared to the millions that were here earlier in the night, it seems somewhat peaceful.

Two girls rush up to us, beaming smiles across their faces as they shove band merch at Ezra with a Sharpie and giggle like idiots while begging for a picture. Ezra takes the merch from them almost on autopilot, signs it, and after letting them have their photo, they scurry away, leaving us to our night.

"That must get old," I murmur as the street becomes silent.

He shrugs his shoulders. "Just part of the job, I suppose."

"A shitty part."

"Got that right," he scoffs. "Axel was always the best at dealing with it. He always had time for fans, even the ones who wouldn't get the hint to disappear."

I laugh, remembering it so clearly. The few times I got to see him were always crazy. Fans would stalk us through stores, and by the time we'd finish anywhere, paparazzi had found us and were madly snapping pictures. It was insane, but Axel always had a smile across his face.

"I miss him," I say with a heavy sigh.

Ezra's arm falls around my shoulder, pulling me in just like he'd done in the hotel. "I know," he murmurs. "Me too. Every fucking day."

Silence falls around us, but this time there's not a hint of awkwardness, just two people heavy in their own thoughts.

We make our way to the restaurant, and I'm not surprised to see Rock and Dylan already here, but when I spy Jett sitting at the table, irritation burns through me. "Really?" I mutter under my breath. "Why's the tag along here?"

"Kind of a dick move not to invite him, don't you think?" Ezra says. "Besides, it's not like we can have a band dinner without him."

"Sure. If this *was* a band dinner, but it's not," I say, hating how hostile I sound, but where Axel's replacement is concerned, I can't seem to help myself. "I thought it was just going to be us. Back at the show, you said just like old times."

He peers down at me as we weave through the tables to get to ours. "Should I tell him to go?" he questions, raising his brow in challenge as if to see just how far I'll push this.

Asshole. He knows my weaknesses.

"No," I sigh, pressing my lips into a hard line. "I just don't like being around him. It's nothing against Jett, he's an alright guy, I guess. He's just a constant reminder that Axel isn't here."

"I get it," he says. "But give him a chance. He's really not so bad. Plus, you know after getting past his tendencies to run his mouth when he shouldn't, Axel would approve."

Being too close to the table, I keep my mouth shut, and as Ezra pulls out my chair for me, I can't help but smile up at him. "Well, well," Dylan says with a cheesy grin across his loveable face. "If it isn't the world's most repressed couple."

Ezra rolls his eyes as he takes his seat, pinches a small bread roll from Rock's plate, and launches it at Dylan. "Shut up."

Dylan snickers, proud of his ability to always be the biggest moron in a room, but we all love him for it regardless.

"Nice of you to wait for us," I say, not wanting to linger on the status of my and Ezra's non-existent relationship, as I indicate toward their filled plates.

"We tried," Jett says. "But the second we sat down, they just started bringing shit to us."

"Ahhhh, lifestyles of the rich and famous," I mutter, glancing between Rock and Dylan. "You know that shit isn't normal, right? Mere mortals like me have to scavenge for our food."

Rock scoffs. "Mere mortals like you? Please. You haven't had to scavenge a day in your life."

I clench my jaw to keep from saying something I shouldn't and instead, I simply roll my eyes and laugh it off, knowing that not one of them will ever know just how hard I've truly struggled over the past two years.

"Besides," Dylan adds with a smug expression. "We're lying. There was no trying to wait. The second Ezra said he was going to get you, we figured you two would get too caught up staring at each other like love-sick puppies that you wouldn't even make it out of your hotel room, so we ordered the whole fucking menu the moment we sat down. But here you are. I suppose we're all having nice little surprises tonight."

I give him a blank stare. Had it been anyone else, the quip about me and Ezra in a hotel room might have made me blush, but not where these idiots are concerned. "What's the matter, Dylan? You sound a little off. Jealous that you didn't get some rockstar knocking on your door tonight?"

He scoffs and smirks. "Don't write it off just yet. The night is still young. There's still a chance that I could have a rockstar knocking at my back door. After all, you know I love a little sword crossing."

I groan and roll my eyes, watching Rock and Ezra laugh. "Are you three physically incapable of holding a conversation without making it about sex?"

Rock salutes me. "Affirmative."

After I put in an order for something simple, the boys rave about the show. They go on and on about how great the vibe has been here in Madrid, and they're absolutely right. It's been insane. The crowd has been incredible, along with everything else.

The waiter drops off our food quickly, and after twenty minutes of conversation, I swallow my pride and reluctantly agree that Jett isn't so bad. It doesn't make me miss Axel any less though.

Throughout dinner, I feel Ezra's gaze locked on me, and with every bite I take, that tension grows between us again. Only this time, it's not filled with the same intense sexual undertones like it was in the elevator.

This is raw. It's desperation. It's the point of no return.

I've done everything I can to avoid his stare, but when his hand slips under the table to my thigh, my gaze snaps to his. I shake my head, unable to handle his proximity a moment longer, and without warning, I push back and hastily get to my feet, my chair scraping against the floor. "I, uhhh . . . I need to pee," I tell the table before disappearing through the restaurant.

I find the ladies' room and storm through the door before bracing my hands against the marble counter, hanging my head as I focus on taking deep breaths. I stand directly in front of the mirror, but I can't bring myself to glance up and see the torment reflected in my eyes.

I take heavy, shaky breaths, willing myself not to fall apart, and I'm so lost in my head that I don't notice anyone coming in until it's already too late.

Familiar hands find my waist, and I straighten out, pressing my back flat against his wide chest as I close my eyes, finding the sweetest pleasure in his touch. Ezra's hand curls around my body, holding me to him, and when his lips drop to my neck and gently kiss me there, all I can do is breathe him in.

"I got you, Rae."

I don't dare open my eyes to meet his stare through the mirror. Instead, I turn in his arms, folding into his warmth as I take a moment to find my composure.

"It's un-fucking-bearable, Rae. Tell me what I need to do to make this right. I can't take it any longer. You belong with me, right here in my arms where we don't need to pretend," he tells me, his voice cracking in agony. "Tell me how to fix this."

"You can't," I whisper, my bottom lip quivering with the threat of tears. "It's not yours to fix."

"What are you talking about? Of course it is. I'm the one who left. I'm the one who broke your heart. I'm the reason you're in here unable to even look at me. Of course it's my problem to fix."

I shake my head, the tears flowing free. "It's not. You left, and I know you were only doing what you felt was right. You wanted me to have a normal life, go to college, and get my degree just like I always said I wanted. And despite that," I cry, barely able to hold myself together as I pull out of his arms and truly let him have it. "I have blamed you every day because it's what was easy. Because it's easy to tell myself that everything that happened was on you when it's not. It's my fault, Ezra. I knew something awful would happen if you left. I had this gut feeling, and I chose not to say anything. I chose to keep my mouth shut because I knew if I said something, you never would have gone, and I didn't want to be responsible for you and Axel not getting everything you'd worked for."

His hands run back through his long hair as he starts to pace the small bathroom. "What the fuck are you talking about, Rae? Is this about why you won't go back home?" he demands, stopping his pacing to search my eyes. "Why are you so afraid to open up? It's me, Rae. It's you and me, and despite everything, you know you can tell me anything, and I'll always be right here."

My heart shatters. It's too much, and I pull back again, the tears streaming down my cheeks. "I . . . I can't," I cry, breaking piece by piece.

"Rae—"

"No," I cut him off, starting to panic, but he steps back into me, wrapping me in his arms and holding me to his chest. "Please. Don't. It's too much. I can't . . . I . . . I can't."

"Okay," he finally says as his hand roams up and down my back, holding me as though I were the most precious crystal as he desperately tries to calm me. "It's okay. I won't push it anymore."

Relief surges through me, and I relax into his arms, knowing he'll stay true to his word and wait for me to be ready. But that doesn't change the fact that when the time comes to tell him about my horrendous past, it's not just going to cripple me, it'll cripple him too, and that's not something I could do lightly.

"Thank you," I tell him after the panic has seeped out of my bones. "I promise, when the time is right . . . When I'm ready, I'll tell you all about it. But until then . . . just know that I'm sorry. I've held on to so much anger and hurt, and I don't know how to move past it, but I'm trying. I don't want to be this way anymore. I'm done being broken, and I know that if I just allow you to, you'll make the pain go away."

"It kills me seeing you hurting like this, Rae," he tells me. "It was never supposed to be this way."

"I know," I say, snuggling into the safety of his warm chest. "But just know that being here with you and getting to see you every day, getting to touch you again . . . It's helping so much more than you could ever know."

He rests his chin against my head, and I listen as he lets out a heavy breath. "I never should have left you behind."

Pulling out of his arms, I force a smile across my face, not wanting the rest of our night to go to shit. "Let's not get caught up in the could have, would have, should haves. They're only going to make everything worse."

He nods, and just as he goes to reach for me, the door barges open and a strange woman looks at Ezra in horror, clearly not having expected to find a man in the ladies' room. "Fuck," Ezra mutters before glancing at the woman. "Sorry, I'll give you your privacy."

She narrows her gaze as though trying to figure out where she knows him from, and with that, he gives me a small smile, silently asking if I'm good now. I nod, and not a moment later, Ezra slips out of the ladies' room, leaving me to finally find my composure, and with it, the strength I need to finally start putting the past behind me.

CHAPTER 24

Raleigh

Anxiety pulses through my veins as I stand at the side of the stage, watching Rock, Dylan, and Jett get night two in Madrid underway. The intro has quickly become one of my favorite parts of the show, watching the crowd as the boys finally appear on stage, and the way Rock dominates the beat is insane. The whole stadium is already on their feet before Ezra even appears on stage.

I pull back a step, watching Ezra make his way through the backstage area, preparing for his grand entrance.

Then as if sensing my stare, his gaze sails to me, and a soft, knowing smile lights up his face. Last night was rough, and I know he's still feeling the effects of my bathroom breakdown, and honestly, so am I, but I've come to the realization that I can't go on like this. I haven't been able to heal for eight years, and keeping apart from him is only hurting us both more.

Every word I said to him last night was true.

I've spent years blaming Axel and Ezra for the hell I went through, putting my pain on their shoulders instead of where it truly belongs— my father's.

He's the one who should be punished. He should be the one to feel my wrath. And one day, I will see that it happens, but today is about Ezra.

Yes, there were some things that we could have done differently as a couple. I could have tried harder to keep in touch, to respond to his emails and texts, and try to make it work long distance. I could have listened to his lyrics and tried to see things from his point of view. He was trying to give me the life I'd always talked about, and if I had been honest back then and told him and Axel what was really going on at home, everything would have been different.

It really was my fault.

But now it's time I take back what's always been mine and finally make this right. Hence why I'm so fucking nervous. After my little panic attack in the restaurant bathroom, I spent the remainder of my night on the phone with Madds, and after working out a plan, I'm finally ready. I think . . . shit. Maybe I'm not.

Ahhhh, fuck. Fuck. Fuck.

This is absolutely ridiculous and could go wrong in a million different ways, not to mention, it could possibly get me fired, but there's no backing out now. The wheels have been set in motion, and

I'm not finishing my night without getting to call Ezra Knight mine.

I watch his every step, and as he watches me back, his brows furrow, clearly sensing something is going on with me, but he doesn't have the time to question it. He keeps going to take his position beneath the stage, preparing to catapult up through the ground.

Every night it's insane. I'd love to know what it feels like being on that catapult, but to be completely honest, I think I would shit my pants. Instead, I prefer to watch him shoot out of the top with the lights, the crowd, the music, and the vibe. It's everything.

Ezra is out here living his dream each night, and I couldn't be prouder.

The drum tempo picks up, and I shuffle back into the stage wing to get the best view in the house. A stupid smile cuts across my face, and I cheer right along with the crowd. When Ezra finally launches out of the stage, tears of absolute joy spring to my eyes.

He glances at me just as he does every night, and seeing the stupid grin across my face, his whole world lights up. I haven't seen joy like that since before he left for that very first tour.

The smile on his face is intoxicating, and as he grabs his microphone and lets loose on Madrid, I realize that as long as I have him, I won't ever have to worry about the hell back in Michigan ever again. You know, apart from when I finally find the courage to lay it all out on the table and be honest.

Just like every show, Jessica and Stacey hover in the wings during the first song, and despite their constant scowling and judgment, nothing could wipe the smile off my face, especially tonight.

Hearing their cue, they head out on stage, shaking their fake asses, and all I can do is laugh as a wicked smirk stretches across my face.

God, this is going to be fun, in both the best and worst ways.

Since I'm finally becoming familiar with the lyrics, I start singing to myself, and as the lyrics resonate with my marketing brain, I pull my phone out and jot down new ideas, never having felt so in my element.

The show goes by quickly, but with every passing minute, my nerves skyrocket until my whole body is visibly shaking.

It's not too late to pull out. Actually, it's definitely too late to pull out. It was too late to pull out the second I slipped laxatives into Stacey's and Jessica's water.

The thought makes a ridiculous witch-like cackle bubble up my throat, and as if on cue, I watch Stacey and Jessica exit the stage and give each other a strange look. Stacey scrunches her face, her hand clutching her stomach, and Jessica does what she can to maintain her composure, but in an instant, it's game over.

Horror washes over both of their faces, and I hold back a laugh as they each take off in a dead sprint toward the bathroom.

God, this is fun.

Phase one of the plan complete. Now on to phase two.

I stand in the wings as Ezra sings "One Day" to his captivated audience, and with every word that pours out of his soul, the most brilliant warmth spreads through my chest. The song comes to an end, and by the time a roadie moves the chair to the middle of the stage and Ezra lowers himself into it for the sexy part of the show, my nerves are shot.

Hoooooly fuck. What have I done?

The music shifts as the boys start the intro for the song "Scarlett Rose," and after leaving myself no choice, I let my coat fall to the ground, leaving me in nothing but a pair of heels and a black, skimpy lingerie set.

I slink out of the wings and onto the stage, the same way the dancers do. I pass Dylan, and finding the courage, I glance up at him and have to smother my grin as he gapes at me in horror. His eyes are wide with shock, and as he flicks his gaze between me and his unsuspecting lead singer, the shock morphs into silent laughter.

He shakes his head, knowing shit is about to go down, and not a moment later, he turns toward Rock and gets his attention. My gaze shifts toward the drummer, and I almost lose my composure as Rock's eyes all but fall out of his skull. His face twists with disgust, clearly not pleased with seeing someone he considers a little sister in her underwear about to seduce their friend, but just like Dylan, the laughter is there in his eyes.

I resist the urge to tell them to look away because what they're about to witness is not for the faint of heart. Jett, on the other hand, looks more than happy to watch the show.

Ezra's gaze remains glued on his captive audience. This part of the night hasn't been his favorite. He doesn't like when the dancers are all over him, but the producers insist. The first night, he played along, but since the moment he realized just how much I hated it, he's done the bare minimum during this portion of the show.

Tonight though, it's going to be different.

He doesn't bother looking my way, expecting Jessica to sneak up on his left, and as I finally reach him, my fingers dance across the back of his shoulder blades. I walk behind him, taking my time as the crowd manically cheers. Most of them know my face, and the hardcore fans know there's history here, and me being Axel's little sister, they know that whatever is happening right here is a big deal.

I watch him, up close and personal, as he lifts the microphone to his mouth, and when his deep voice fills the stadium, I lean in, letting my hand trail over his shoulder and down his chest. My lips linger by his throat and as they brush across his warm skin, his body stiffens.

A wide grin pulls at my lips, and I kiss him there, rolling my tongue over his neck. "Hey rockstar," I murmur by his ear. "You ready for a show?"

Ezra's gaze snaps to mine, shock in his dark eyes, but all I can do is smile as I slowly step around him, watching the realization dawn in his penetrating stare.

His brows arch, and as the music goes on, I turn to face the audience, dropping down right in front of Ezra as my hand disappears between my legs, just like I've watched the dancers do night after night. He has no choice but to sing, and the shift in his tone is everything.

He's in trouble, and he knows it, and if he's not careful, the headlines in the news tomorrow aren't going to be about what an incredible show it was, they'll be about how the lead singer of Demon's Curse couldn't keep his dick in his pants.

I roll my body as I turn on my strappy heels, stepping in between his spread knees. His gaze is locked on mine as he sings the sensual words that I've wanted to hear from him for so long, and as I move my body, he becomes captivated, just like his audience.

There's a strain in his tone as my fingers dance across his skin, and when I roll back against him, his hand curls around my waist, holding me there. I grind against him, feeling just how hard he is through his pants, and I grin, feeling the greatest victory.

We're halfway through the song, but he's struggling, and when I kick my leg over him and straddle him, his hand roams down my back, grabbing hold of my ass as I press into him. "Hi," I murmur, holding his stare as my body moves like a fucking demoness, grinding and taking what's mine.

He can't respond as he sings, but it doesn't matter. I can picture his responses so damn clearly.

"Just so you know," I tell him as his deep, strained words fill me with the wildest hunger I've ever felt. "The moment you step off this stage, I'm going to fuck you."

He clenches his jaw, his hand tightening on my ass as I put on the performance of a lifetime.

"It's going to be long," I breathe, leaning in and biting down on his earlobe. "Hard." He shudders beneath me as I grind against his cock, my hands slipping beneath the fabric of his shirt, my nails digging into his skin. "Wild."

His voice cracks as he sings, and as he lowers the microphone for Jett to take his solo, Ezra grasps me by the throat and pulls me in as his adoring crowd roars so loud that I feel the vibration in my chest.

He pulls me in, and without warning, his lips crush down on

mine. He kisses me deeply, and my eyes roll as the sweetest pleasure pulses through my veins. "You're in so much fucking trouble, baby," he rumbles as he breaks our kiss.

"Oh yeah?" I challenge, rolling my tongue over my lips to savor his kiss. "Whatcha gonna do about it? Fuck me right here in front of fifty thousand people?"

My body rolls as I drag my fingers across his fiery skin, feeling the way he shudders beneath me. I've never seen him so worked up, not even that night in the pool. That was a night created out of desperation and lust, but this is different. It's fire. It's greed. It's a deep-rooted hunger spanning the width of years.

Taking his shoulders, I lean away and circle my hips, arch my back, and tip my head, which pushes my tits right up. When I pull myself back up to him, he locks his strong arm around my waist.

He groans, but as the guitar solo comes to an end, he lifts the microphone to his mouth. I slide off him and lower myself to the ground. I push between his knees, and he reaches down, brushing his fingers across my jaw as I look up at him, and I know without a doubt he's wondering how it would feel to have my lips wrapped around his thick cock.

I spin around on my knees and lower my chest to the stage, leaving my ass in the air just for him, and to my surprise, he comes down behind me, grasping my hip and grinding against me as I push back, so desperate to be touched.

The hunger is like nothing I've ever felt before, and when he locks his arm around my waist and pulls me back to him, I gasp. His hand trails higher, circling my throat as the heat from the overhead spotlights bears down on my skin.

As he sings the final chorus of the song, I tilt my chin up toward him, making a show of licking my lips. "God, I'm so fucking wet for you, Ezra Knight."

He chokes on the lyrics, having to do what he can to quickly recover, and then just like the dancers do, I get back to my feet and slowly walk away, feeling his heated gaze locked on my back with every step I take.

Settling back into my position in the wing of the stage, I scoop up my coat and pull it over me, only I leave it loose in the front so every time Ezra looks at me, he's reminded of exactly what I'm wearing beneath it.

There are two songs left for the night, and he struggles the whole way through it, and with every crack and strain of his voice, my victory spurs brighter in my chest.

I've got him exactly where I want him.

Dylan and Rock laugh the whole way through the finale, knowing that whatever's about to happen between us is somehow significant, and the moment Ezra puts his electric guitar down and farewells the audience, he all but races off the stage.

The crowd is still chanting his name when he reaches me, and before I even get a chance to say a single word, he scoops me into his strong arms and crushes his lips against mine.

My legs lock around his waist as he kisses me deeply, somehow navigating through the backstage area as the crew tries to mind their business. He finds their dressing room, and the moment he barges through it, it's on.

The door slams behind us with a loud BANG and within seconds, my back is pressed up against it. He grinds against me, and when he breaks our kiss and we start pulling at our clothes, he meets my fiery stare. "Fuck, Rae. I need to be inside you."

"What the hell are you waiting for?"

Ezra groans and tears my panties clean of my body, shredding the fabric in his skilled hands as I grip the front of his pants, hating how many pieces of fucking clothing he has on.

I free his straining erection, and as my fists curl around him, he steps in closer, shuddering beneath my touch. "See what you do to me?"

A thrill booms through me, and I love every moment of it. I never got to experience him like this before, never got to see this wild desperation that he always hid, and now seeing the way I affect him . . . fuck. I crave it.

I go to kick my heels off, but he shakes his head. "Leave them on," he groans as he takes my ass and lifts me into his strong arms.

His lips crash back to mine, and in the same instant, he shoves me back against the door again. The desperation is too much, and I lock my legs around him, pulling him in. "Ezra," I pant between kisses. "Don't make me wait."

He groans, holding me tight, and after guiding himself to my entrance, he thrusts inside, taking me deep, inch by desperate inch. "Fuck," he grunts as I tip my head back against the door, feeling the way my walls stretch around his delicious intrusion.

He draws back, and I feel his pierced tip glide within me, making my walls clench around him. "Oh God," I pant, clutching his big shoulders. "More."

Ezra doesn't hesitate, thrusting inside of me again and again. I cry out in the sweetest agony as the rapid pleasure rocks through my body. I'm so fucking wet for him, so worked up. I've never needed anything more.

He takes me fast and hard as though he's just as desperate as I am, and as his fingers bite into my skin, I welcome the bruises I know he'll leave behind. "Fuck, baby. You feel so good," he rumbles before pulling me away from the door.

He quickly crosses the room to throw me down on the couch, and just when I think he's about to come down over me, he flips me onto my stomach, pulls my knees up under me, and settles in on the couch, his hand taking my hip.

Without skipping a beat, he lines himself up with my cunt and slams back inside of me, both of us shuddering with hunger. He fucks me from behind, ramming into me over and over as I push back against him, taking him deeper.

My pussy trembles, and I reach down between my legs, rolling my fingers over my clit as my hips jolt with bursts of electricity. "God, Ezra," I pant, arching my back and asking for more—which he's all too happy to give.

"That's right, Rae. Show me how you like it."

My fingers furiously work over my clit as he gives me everything I need, and when I feel that familiar pull deep in my core, my eyes flutter closed. "Fuck," I cry, burying my face into the couch cushion. "Don't stop. I'm gonna come."

I groan loudly as his fingers bite into me, and as I push back against him, he does what he can to hold me still. "Give it to me, Rae. Let me feel you come."

I feel my orgasm building inside of me like a coil getting tighter by the second, and soon enough, it's going to explode, but I need more. As if sensing that desperation within me, Ezra rolls his hips, taking me at a whole new angle, again, and again, and again.

My pussy clenches around his thick cock, and with each new thrust, I feel the sweet magic of his piercing inside me. It's too much. I can't take it anymore. My hips jolt again, and as my fingers roll over my clit, my world explodes.

"Oh, FUCK!"

I cry out as I come hard, my orgasm rocking through my body as I vividly come undone. My body spasms as my pussy wildly convulses around him, and as I start to see stars, I feel the very second he reaches his climax.

Ezra shoots hot spurts of cum deep into me, and as I crumble around him, he doesn't stop moving, letting me ride out my high.

It's everything, and as his movement finally begins to slow, he trails his fingers down my spine and watches my skin prickle with goosebumps. "Fuck, Rae. I will never tire of being inside you," he says, barely able to catch his breath.

Before I can say a word, Ezra reaches down, pulls me into his arms, crashes onto the couch, and brings me down over him. Without skipping a beat, he slides straight back inside my pussy.

I straddle his lap, and I don't hesitate to rock my hips, getting a feel for what it's like to ride him. As I move, he tips his head back against the couch, his dark, piercing eyes hooded as he watches me.

"I can't keep away from you," I tell him as my heart races, feeling the way he hardens within me. "I don't want to be someone you used to know anymore."

"I'm right here, Rae," he tells me, reaching up and cupping the side of my face before pulling me down to him. His lips brush over mine in the sweetest kiss as I continue rocking my hips. "All you've gotta do is take it."

"Oh yeah?" I ask as his cock massages me from within. "Just like that?"

"Mm-hmm," he groans, capturing my nipple in his mouth and flicking the pebbled peak with his skilled tongue. "Just like that."

He thrusts from beneath me, taking me deeper, but I capture his hands at my hips, threading my fingers through his and holding him captive. "Nuh-uh," I say, shaking my head as I pick up speed, feeling the way his cum spreads between us. "You had your fun. Now it's my turn."

"What exactly do you plan on doing?"

A wicked grin stretches across my face. "I've missed out on riding this thick cock for eight long years, Ezra," I remind him. "I have lost time to make up for, so I suggest you sit back and enjoy the ride. Perhaps strap yourself in because I anticipate this being a long, bumpy ride."

CHAPTER 25

Raleigh

16 YEARS OLD

Tears stream down my face as I race after Ezra, not able to bear the sight of him leaving, but I've known it was coming for the past two weeks. I've prepared for it and mentally scolded myself over it, but nothing could ready me for the moment he pulled away and headed through the terminal to board his flight.

"Ma'am," a woman calls after me. "You can't be here without a boarding pass. Ma'am!"

I don't stop as security sprints after me, and as Ezra hears the commotion at his back, he turns just in time for me to crash into his wide chest. His arms wrap around me, holding me so damn tight that I know nothing will ever feel like home again.

"I can't lose you," I cry into his chest, my heart shredding into a million broken pieces.

"Never," Ezra promises. "We're going to make it work, okay? I'll call every day. We're going to get through this. Day by day, and then I'll be right back here as though I were never gone. I'm not leaving you, Rae. Never."

"I can't say goodbye to you."

He buries his face into the curve of my neck, breathing me in. "Don't ever say goodbye," he tells me. "Don't ever say goodbye to me, Rae. You hear me? I fucking love you. This isn't over for us."

I lift my gaze, and as tears stream down my face like raging rivers, I crush my lips to his. He kisses me back, holding me as though I'm a figment of his imagination, but as a beefy arm locks around my waist, hauling me back, it's over before it even starts.

"Don't fucking touch her," Ezra argues, reaching for me. "Just . . . Just give her a minute."

"No," I cry, clawing at the arm around my waist, but he's too strong.

God, I was such an idiot not to come here sooner. I was too fucking stubborn, too broken to admit how much I needed this. I've spent all day at the lake with my phone off, refusing to be here, refusing to watch him go, and now it's too late to say all the things I needed to say.

Ezra comes after me, but Axel is right there, pulling him away. "Come on, man. We have to go," he says, his big brown eyes locked on mine with a heaviness I've never seen from my big brother before. "We're doing the right thing. She'll be okay. She just needs some time."

Ezra fights against him as Dylan and Rock join in, desperate to get Ezra on the plane, and as a second security guard steps in, I stand no chance.

I'm dragged away, kicking and screaming, not getting the chance to say everything I've been needing to say over the past two weeks. Hell, the past three years. And as I desperately try to look back, all I see is emptiness.

He's gone. Really gone.

The security guards take me right outside, kicking me to the curb, and as I sit in the gutter, all I can do is cry as I watch the private jet take off and disappear into the sky with the other half of my soul.

How can he be gone just like that? I didn't get to hold him, didn't get to tell him how much I'll miss him, how much I love him.

I've spent the last two weeks hating him, refusing to see him as I buried myself in the agony, but last night, he barged through my bedroom door, climbed into my bed, and as I spent the night falling to pieces and demanding he look after my brother, he held me, not daring to let go. But by morning, I was gone, and now, I feel like an idiot.

I should have stayed. I should have begged him not to go.

God, it hurts. Just like the night I lost my mother, only that night I had somebody to hold me through the pain, somebody to tell me everything was going to be okay. Not now. Not anymore. There's nobody here to hold me. Nobody to take away the pain. I've never been so alone in my life.

The agony tears through me, and as the sun begins to set on the horizon, I shakily get to my feet and start walking.

I'd taken a bus to get here and sat with a bouncing knee the whole way, willing the driver to hurry up and hoping like fuck I didn't miss him, but now . . . I almost wish I had. No goodbye was worth seeing the pain in his eyes, the desperation, and agony that I know was reflected in mine . . . It fucking gutted me.

This is his dream, he should have been riding off into the sunset with pride, not despair.

I walk for hours, and by the time I reach my home, all I can do is stare up at it with emptiness.

I've feared this place for months, never wanting to come home unless the guys were here, and now without them, I've never been more terrified.

The way my father looks at me makes my skin crawl. The way he talks to me makes me sick, and the way he touches me when I don't realize he's standing right behind me . . .

I never should have let them leave, not without being honest first.

Oh God, what am I going to do?

Slipping through the hole in the back fence, I saunter up to the back porch and steal the small throw blanket off the old swing chair before moving around the side of the house and curling up on the ground, surrounded by the remnants of Mom's dead garden.

Dad will no doubt be drunk and passed out on the couch, but at some point, he'll wake up and take himself to bed, and when that happens, I can't be in the house.

At maybe two or three in the morning, I'll be free to make my way inside and go to bed. I'll have to brace the door with my dresser, but then I need to be up and out of there before six, otherwise, he'll look for me in the morning.

My stomach clenches, and I pull my knees right up against my chest before resting my chin against them and pulling the blanket around me.

The emptiness gnaws at me, and after what feels like a lifetime, my phone dies and as my eyes grow heavier, I crave my bed like never before. Maybe tomorrow night I can stash some snacks and a pillow out here, maybe a few energy drinks to keep me going.

When the emotional exhaustion wears down on me, I force myself to get to my feet. My knees shake, and I suck in a breath as I creep around the outside of the house, peering through all the windows.

There's no sign of my father on the couch, and I let out a relieved breath, realizing he's already taken himself to bed. I should be good to sneak in. I just need to get through the back door, up the stairs, and into my bedroom. Once I'm there, I'll be free.

Fear rattles me as I make my way back around to the front door and silently slip my key into the lock. The door opens with a soft creak, and as I slip inside the old house, I hold my breath and slowly glance through the darkness.

Everything is as it should be.

I start toward the stairs, going as slowly as possible to not make a sound, and as I pass the dining room, a voice sounds through the darkness.

"Well, if it isn't my delinquent whore of a daughter," my father grumbles, slurring his words. "Where the fuck have you been?"

"No . . . Nowhere," I stutter, backing up against the wall as my heart races with terror.

He stands and slowly strides around the dining table as I awkwardly shuffle toward the stairs, keeping my eyes locked on every step he takes. "Who have you been fucking, huh? Now that your little boyfriend is gone."

"Nobody."

"LIAR!" he roars, launching toward me and grabbing my shoulders, before violently shaking me. My back slams against the railing for the stairs, but I don't say a word about it. "You're a fucking whore, and it's about time I treat you like one. You go around here in your skimpy little skirts with your tits hanging out, begging me to do something about it like a little fucking tease."

"Touch me and die," I spit, trying to get out of his hold. "You're drunk. Go to bed."

My father laughs, and the smell of whiskey assaults my nose. "Where's your little protection detail now, huh? You're all alone with nobody to save you."

"You're an asshole."

He backhands me so hard, I taste blood in my mouth, and as I cry out in pain, he reaches for his belt. "You want to get mouthy with me, you little bitch? I'll give you something to get mouthy about."

Oh fuck, no.

I shove him hard, not waiting to watch as he stumbles back, and with his body blocking the hallway to the front door, I'm left with no choice but to sprint up the stairs. I take them two at a time, not even having a moment to form a scream.

His big body crashes up the stairs after me, but if I can just get to my room and get the door shut behind me, I'll be fine. I can barricade the door and jump out the window. It'll be a big fall, but I'll take it a million times over what he has in store for me.

I'm halfway up the stairs when his hand locks around my ankle and yanks me back. I drop hard, my face slamming against the corner of the step, and I cry out as my nose crushes beneath the weight.

Blood spurts from my nose, but my father still holds me down, bracing his hand against the back of my head, and squishing my face into the stairs as I scream in agony. I try to fight him off, but as he drops his full weight over me, there's nowhere for me to go.

I scream until my throat hurts, and as he reaches between us and pulls my shorts down, all I can do is cry. "Stop acting like you haven't been beggin' for it," he grunts.

I try to fight him off, try to slam him with my elbow and wriggle free, but it's no use, I'm pinned under his weight. There's nowhere to go, nowhere to run. And when he forces my legs apart and slams viciously inside of me, tearing right through my virginity, I cry out in pain.

He presses against my head to get leverage, and not a moment later, he starts to move, painfully destroying my innocence and taking what little light I have left.

His grunts and groans fill the air as his body quickly grows clammy. I can smell the alcohol seeping from his pores, and I will him to stop, to die from alcohol poisoning, or at the very least make himself so sick that he has no choice but to pull away.

It lasts far too long, and I do what I can to focus on Ezra, to focus on the love I have for him and ignore my father's brutal torture, but it's impossible. Every deep thrust, every agonizing touch, kills me, and by the time he finally finishes emptying himself inside of me, any sense of my childhood is gone.

He pulls himself off me, using my discarded body as a crutch on his way up, and all I can do is continue staring at the carpeted stairs as blood gushes from my nose. My father gets to his feet, and I hear as he tucks his dick back inside his pants before scoffing at me on the ground. "How'd you like that, whore? Is that what you've been begging for?"

Fat tears roll down my cheeks, and I don't respond, just wishing for him to leave, but instead, he laughs. "Tight. Just like your mother."

Bile rises in my throat.

"Things are gonna be different around here now," he says, kicking me aside on the stairs before continuing his way up.

I listen to his heavy footsteps as he reaches the top and rounds the corner to his bedroom, and the moment the door closes behind him, I scramble for my shorts and phone and sprint to my bedroom.

My whole body shakes as I slam the door behind me and use every ounce of strength I have left to push my old dresser across the room and barricade myself inside. I fall to the ground, feeling my father's cum leaking from inside me, and I've never felt so dirty in my life. I need to shower, need to scrub the scent of his alcoholic sweat off me, but I won't dare leave this room until I know he's gone. Instead, I crawl across the floor and lock myself inside my closet, folding my knees to my chest as I cry, and cry, and cry.

I stay there until I see a sliver of light shining from under the closet door and only then do I risk moving out into the main part of my bedroom.

I find my phone discarded on the floor, and I plug it into the charger before making my way over to the mirror. I look like a complete stranger. Blood soaks the front of my shirt and is caked across my face and chest. There are bruises marring my skin and blood smeared between my legs.

My eyes are red and swollen from a night filled with tears, and my body is utterly destroyed.

As I stare at the stranger in my mirror, I listen as a slew of texts start coming in, and I pull myself away just long enough to scoop up my phone. I go to sit on the edge of my bed, but everything hurts, and I stay standing instead, trying to figure out how the hell I'm supposed to survive.

Swiping my thumb across my screen, I find a flood of texts from Ezra and Axel checking in on me, even a few from Dylan and Rock, and the second I open the first text from Ezra, I break.

Ezra - I'm sorry. I love you. Please tell me we're okay.

I crumble to the ground, throwing my phone aside. If only they never left. If only I had been honest with them, this never would have happened. I'd be safe in his arms, away from the monster who sleeps down the hall.

My body never would have been destroyed, my innocence never violently stolen, my world never crushed into a million shattered pieces. I would never have to fear coming home, never have to fear what might happen if I open my door, never have to fear showering. I would never have to know what it feels like to be pinned down, never have to feel the rough carpet indented on my face, never have to peel clumps of dried blood from my skin.

Never have to wipe my father's cum from between my legs.

My nose wouldn't be broken. There wouldn't be bruises covering my skin, and my throat wouldn't be raw from screaming for him to stop.

They abandoned me here and refused to listen to my cries when I begged them to take me. They thought I'd be better off, but they've never been so wrong. In what world is this better? In what universe is this where I'm supposed to be?

God, why didn't they just take me with them? Why didn't they listen to my cries?

They never should have left.

What happened tonight, it never would have happened if they were still here, if they'd taken me with them just like they always promised they would.

They lied to me. Ezra lied.

It's all their fault. Axel and Ezra, the very men who vowed to always protect me, and they let me down, and no matter how many sweet words they send to me, nothing will ever make this okay.

I hate them. God, I hate them so much.

They left me to the wolves and now . . . I don't know if I'll ever be the same.

CHAPTER 26

Raleigh

The private jet touches down in LA, and I pull myself out of the warmth of Dylan's arms. It was an awkward flight home. After spending the night riding Ezra's dick, we each went back to our respective hotel rooms and haven't spoken a word since.

Apparently we have great sexual chemistry, but when it comes to talking . . . zero.

It's almost ironic how it used to be the other way around. We used to talk until the early hours of the morning while he did everything he could to avoid getting physical with me. Now as adults with our own forms of trauma, talking is the last thing I'm prepared to do.

As I boarded the jet, I was faced with three options—Ezra, Rock, or Dylan.

Ezra looked at me with expectation, as though if I dared to sit down beside him, he was going to ask questions I wasn't prepared to answer, and in return, I would end up trying to seduce him to avoid having to talk at all. Rock already had his drumsticks in his hands, so sitting down next to him meant probably being used as a drum the whole flight—and I don't mean the good kind of drum where you're banged in the bathroom for the duration of the flight. And Dylan, sweet, loveable Dylan. He gave me a goofy smile and looked as though all he wanted to do was sleep.

BINGO!

I sat down beside him while awkwardly avoiding Ezra's stare, he looped his arm around my shoulder and pulled me into his side, and that's exactly where I stayed until now. Don't get me wrong, while I might have been physically comfortable, I was anything but.

I would have killed to spend the flight snuggling with Ezra, to feel his warmth wrap around me, but we're not there yet, and honestly, I'm not sure if we'll ever be. There's too much to unpack, too much heartache and trauma to work through.

Instead, I listened to Dylan gently snoring in my ear as I stared at the three pendants hanging around Ezra's neck. Axel's ring, the guitar he got from his mom before I even knew him, and the simple R that shows after all these years, I'm still home to him.

The boys have two weeks off to chill at home before we're due to get back on a flight and head to Portugal, and until then, I'm lost. Obviously, I'll spend some time with Madds and probably have to check in with the label, but for the most part, I don't know where to go. I don't have a home here, and I don't particularly want to go running to Lenny and ask for another fancy hotel room.

Hmmmm I wonder how Rock or Dylan would feel about me crashing at their places. Or maybe Madds. She has a small apartment, roughly the size of a shoebox, but I'm sure she'll be down with it. Just like old times. I can spend my nights choking on the overwhelming scents of her billion and three candles. It'll be perfect.

Pulling out of Dylan's hold, I shove my elbow into his side, waking him up. The idiot could sleep through a tornado. "We're here," I tell him as he scrunches his nose and drags his hand across his face, making me smile. I can't wait until he falls in love and finds that one special girl who's going to change the game for him. She doesn't know it yet, but she'll be the luckiest girl who ever lived. Dylan is a catch. He's the whole package, and if it weren't for our brother-sister relationship or the way I whole-heartedly belonged to Ezra, I'm sure as a teen, I probably would have crushed on him.

The thought sends an icy shiver down my spine. I can only imagine what my father would have had to say about that.

Getting to my feet, I grab my coat and go to make my way off the jet, only Ezra stands at the same time, and we awkwardly meet in the middle. His hand immediately comes to my waist, and I feel every eye on us, waiting to see what will happen. "Are you . . . ummmm. Do you know where you're staying for the next two weeks?"

I force a smile across my face, but it doesn't reach home, both of us knowing how fake it is. "Yeah, I'm good."

"Okay, well then, I guess I'll see you in two weeks."

Two weeks? Fuck. That suddenly seems like a lifetime, but also, fuck him for not wanting to see me before that. "Yeah," I say, my fake smile falling away as I press my lips into a hard line. I turn and start making my way off the jet, not wanting to say goodbye. After all, that's not what we do. Besides, what's two weeks away from him when I've already have eight years of practice under my belt?

My heart aches with every step I take off the jet, and as I reach the tarmac, I don't dare look back as I find my driver from that first day in LA and beeline straight for him. I feel Ezra's stare on my back as he follows me out of the jet. Even as my driver holds the door open for me, and I scoot into the back of the car, Ezra's eyes linger. The driver is quick to get into the car and pull away, and the second he does, I risk it all by glancing out the window and gazing at the other half of my heart.

Ezra stands by his car, leaning against the blacked-out SUV, his gaze locked on me, and despite the dark tint of the windows, I know he senses my stare on him. It's impossible not to.

Everything hurts, and I fall back against the seat, tipping my head right back and closing my eyes. It's barely even midday, and despite having done nothing but sit in a luxury jet all morning, I've never felt so exhausted. I need to sleep for the next twelve years.

"Where are we headed?" my driver asks, meeting my stare through the rearview mirror.

"Ummmm . . ." Shit. It would probably help if I actually knew where Madds lives. "I don't actually know. I was thinking of staying with a friend, but I kinda haven't run it past her yet and don't actually have her address, but—"

"Your brother's place?"

My brows furrow. "I'm sorry?"

"You had asked me to show you where he lived," he reminds me. "Are you no longer wanting to see his home?"

"Oh, ummm yeah, of course," I say. "But I'm not sure who owns it now, and I doubt I'll be able to go inside."

"We could always try," he suggests. "Besides, it shall give us something to pass the time while you wait to see if your friend is happy to host you for the next two weeks."

I don't bother to tell him that Madds will be a screaming yes followed by a string of suggestions on how to spend our time, but the thought of getting to see where Axel built his life here is too good of an opportunity to pass up.

"Okay, let's do it."

The driver smiles at me through the mirror, and without skipping a beat, he puts his foot on the gas, and we sail through the busy streets of LA. It's almost a thirty minute trip to the gated community the boys live in, and as the driver puts in the code for the main gates, I find myself sitting up a little straighter.

A strange wave of nervousness crashes through me, and as the gates open and he drives into the gated community, I find myself staring at every property we pass. It's only a minute before we drive past Ezra's home, and a flutter settles deep in my stomach just thinking about the life we could have had there together.

As he continues, I find myself straining to see around the coming corners, desperate to see the roads Axel would have traveled every day, the homes he would have passed, the neighbors he might have known. It's only a minute before the driver begins to slow, and he eventually pulls into a driveway that's overgrown with shrubbery.

My brows furrow. Clearly whoever lives here now hasn't been taking good care of the gardens. Axel wasn't much of a gardener, but I imagine he would have hired someone to care for his property.

My driver lets out a breath as he pulls up next to the keypad for the big gate at the top of Axel's driveway. "Any ideas?" he asks, referring to the code.

"Ummm . . . Try his birthday. June fifth. 0605."

The driver leans out the window and puts in the code before shaking his head. "Not it. Any other suggestions?"

"Uhhhh, my birthday, maybe," I suggest. "1103."

He tries again and when the little keypad beeps, the driver glances back at me. "We're in luck."

My eyes widen. "No way! It worked?"

As if on cue, the gates start to roll back and a wave of happiness rumbles through my chest. Why wouldn't the new owners change the gate code? Seems a little silly, doesn't it? I mean, the only people buying homes in this area are those searching for privacy and a great security system. Surely it's counterproductive not to change the passcodes from day one.

The driver hits the gas again, and we roll through the gate and up the long driveway as I gaze out the window, completely mesmerized. This isn't exactly the kind of property I envisioned my brother living in, but there's so much I didn't know about him in those last few years. I'd forced so much distance between us that I failed to get to know the real him.

He asked me a million times to come out here and visit him, and I hate that I never had the courage to do it.

The further up the driveway we get, I start to wonder if someone is actually tending to the property. While the shrubbery near the front gate is overgrown and a little wild, the gardens closer to the house are neat and tidy where the grass, while a little long, is manicured without a single weed to see.

The house is huge, just as big as Ezra's, and I can only wonder what life would have looked like for him here. Did he have to yell to have a conversation with someone in a different room? Did he run through the long hallway in his socks, just to see how far he could slide? Did he actually love it here or was it just a house to keep his possessions warm?

"Did you want to try the front door?" the driver asks, indicating the grand stairs that lead to the entrance of the home.

"Oh, I don't have a key."

"I could be wrong, my eyesight isn't quite what it appears to be, but it seems no key is required. It looks to be a keypad entry."

My back straightens as my gaze flicks to the door, seeing the keypad he's referring to. "Shit. Is it technically breaking and entering if you used the code? Like, this isn't a felony, right?"

The driver glances back at me and shrugs his shoulders. "To be quite honest, Miss Stone, I haven't got a clue. I'm sure this could be classified as trespassing, but I've always been an opportunistic kind of man, and when something stares you right in the face, why not grab it with both hands? If, and that's a big if, there is any fall out, we'll deal with it later. For now, why don't you go see the home your brother created for himself."

A stupid smile pulls at my lips, and I'm out the door before I even have a moment to really think about all the reasons why this is a terrible idea. As I reach the grand stairs that lead up to the front door, I glance back at the driver, who gives me an encouraging nod.

Making my way up to the top, I settle in front of the keypad and stare at it as a bundle of nervousness pulses in my stomach. "Ahhh, shit," I mutter to myself, reaching toward the keypad. My thumb hovers over the numbers, not wanting to get it wrong and set off some kind of silent alarm.

Okay, so common sense would suggest that the front gate code isn't going to be the same as the front door code, so considering Axel's birthday didn't work on the front gate, I start there, only for the keypad to flash red twice.

"Crap."

My birthday is unlikely. If this were my home, I'd probably make it Ezra's birthday, but I doubt Axel would have made the same call. Hmmmm . . . Mom.

A smile pulls at my lips as a wave of confidence crashes over me, and without hesitation, I start entering the code—0622. It flashes green, and I hear the soft click of the front door as it unlocks.

I gape at it as my heart races. Holy shit. I had not expected this to become my day, but fuck it. Nothing's stopping me from going in now.

Pushing the door open, I slip inside what was once Axel's home, and the most brilliant warmth settles inside of me. The foyer is huge, but the unmistakable scent of musky dust is thick in the air and has my brows furrowing. Maybe someone hasn't been living here. It smells like a home that's been locked up for years, with no sign of life. I make my way deeper through the halls, and as I pass what can only be the home office, I take in the floor-to-ceiling print of Demon's Curse live on stage against the back wall. Ezra and Axel grin at each other like fucking idiots as every last person in the crowd has their hands in the air. The rest of the office is basically a shrine to the band, and the untouched papers scattered across the desk suggest that the very last person to be here was Axel.

Holy shit. This couldn't be his untouched home, could it? Has someone staged this office to make it some kind of dedication to the great Axel Stone, or has this home really been sitting here empty for all this time?

The thought puts a jump in my step, and I hurry through the property, desperate to see what else is here. The kitchen and living spaces look like any other home and don't give away much except the blown-up photograph of me, Axel, and Ezra on the wall—a photo I loved with all my heart until the anger in my soul had me delete the only copy I had off my phone.

Tears well in my eyes, but I don't linger on it, instead, I head upstairs to the second floor, blown away with every new step I take. This home is incredible. And to think I'd been living out of the back of my car when I could have crashed here, especially on those nights that were below freezing.

I pass a room that looks like a home recording studio, and in the adjacent room is the extraordinary collection of guitars. Axel always considered himself a collector. He liked to have fancy things, and while I don't really understand what I'm looking at, I know every guitar in this collection would have a story behind it, with an even bigger price tag.

There are a bunch of spare rooms and balconies that look over the huge yard and entertaining area. Not to mention, the pool that's been kept perfect and looks like it was built for a god. In the summertime, I can only imagine the fun the boys would have had here.

Continuing on my journey, I come to a set of double doors at the end of a hallway, and as I grab them and peel them open, I realize this is Axel's master bedroom.

A lump instantly forms in my throat as I take in his big, oversized bed, still with the blankets pulled back as though he hadn't had a chance to make it before leaving. Tears well in my eyes, and I continue through the room, taking in the photo of me, Mom, and Ax on his bedside table. His phone charger still dangles from the outlet, and a glass of water still sits half full.

A suitcase is at the end of his bed, as though he'd just come in from his last tour and dumped his things, not bothering to take a moment to put his shit away. Typical Ax.

The tears roll down my face, and as I continue to his closet, I crumble to my knees, seeing all of his old clothes, but mixed in with the musky dust in the air, is him. I can smell him on his clothes, on the blankets stacked on the shelves, on the designer suits he absolutely hated.

My face falls into my hands, and as I sit here and cry, the grief comes up and claims me. "Oh God," I cry, clutching one of the old blankets and pulling it to my chest, holding it so damn tight, I could almost imagine it is Axel.

Heavy sobs pull from deep in my chest, and I struggle to catch my breath. "I miss you," I tell his empty closet. "You didn't deserve to go, and I hate that you did, and I didn't even get a chance to say goodbye. I needed you there, not just these past two years, but all the time. I need you now. I need you to make everything okay because I'm falling apart. I'm so broken, Axel. I don't know how to fix myself."

More tears come, and I wipe them on the blanket. "I wasn't good to you. I wasn't a good sister. I should have been better, but I blamed you and Ezra for everything. I was in so much pain, and I needed to blame you, and that wasn't fair. I put so much distance between us because I was so hurt and angry that you left me behind to endure all that hell. I was too blind to see that you thought you were doing what was best for me. You wanted me to have school, a home, and a path to my dreams, but you didn't know what was waiting for me at home, and I hated that you couldn't see everything I hid from you. I needed you to save me, but you were gone, and I was too afraid to speak. You were my protector and you left me all alone."

I swallow over the lump in my throat, needing a minute to find some composure. "It's not fair," I whimper, hoping somehow, somewhere in this universe he's listening. "It should have been me who died. You didn't deserve this. You had so much more to achieve, so many dreams and tours to conquer. It would have been easier if it were me. You were my favorite person in the whole world. I love you so much. I miss you so much it hurts. I just . . . I need one more hug. I just need to hear your voice telling me that everything is going to be okay. I need you, Axel. Please."

A moment of silence passes when a soft knock sounds at the door of the closet, and I whip my tear-stained face back to find Ezra hovering in the doorway. "Sorry," he murmurs, his heart on his sleeve as he watches me fall to pieces on the ground. "The security company called to say someone was in the house."

I nod, trying to wipe the tears off my face, and he doesn't hesitate stepping into the closet and offering me his hand. "Come here," he says as I take his hand. He pulls me to my feet and instantly wraps me in his arms, pulling me tight against his chest when I allow the tears to flow freely.

He scoops me up, bridal style, and drops down on a small bench, where he simply holds me, allowing the tears to run their course. "It wouldn't have been easier," he tells me, making me wonder just how much of my sob-fest he heard. "If it had been you . . . It wouldn't have been easier."

"It would have been for me."

"Don't. Don't say that," he says, getting upset. "You really think that? That life would have been easier if you were the one who died?"

"Yeah," I say bluntly, no hint of hesitation in my tone as I push myself out of his arms and scramble to my feet. "A million times, yes."

Ezra throws himself to his feet, shaking his head, instantly starting to pace through the closet. "Don't say shit like that, Raleigh," he says, rarely using my full name. "You're fucking lying. You did not want to die."

"Every fucking day I did," I say, stepping in too close, making sure he truly hears me as I feel every last bit of my control fall away. "You have no idea what I went through after you left, what hell you and Axel left me to endure, and believe me, had you known, you would have preferred I was dead too."

"The fuck are you talking about?" he demands, his eyes wild.

I shove my hands against his chest as the words I've kept hidden for so damn long come bursting out of me in a fit of rage. "YOU LEFT ME WITH *HIM!*"

Ezra catches my hands, holding them too tight as he captures my stare, shaking his head in confusion. "What are you talking about?" he says, refusing to let me pull my hands free. "Who's him? What happened to you, Rae?"

I shake my head, my heart breaking at the look in his eyes. "Don't," I cry, desperately trying to pull away. "Don't make me say it."

"Raleigh, please," he begs, his voice breaking as he pulls on my hands and brings me closer, his warmth swallowing me whole. "I can't take it anymore. Please, let me help you."

I sob against his chest as his thumbs brush back and forth across my knuckles. "Rae," he pleads in a soft whisper that shatters my soul, his broken heart just as torn as mine.

Lifting my gaze, I meet his haunted stare, and as tears pool in my eyes and race down my cheeks, my bottom lip quivers. It's now or never. I need to tell him, need to get it out in the open or I'll never have a chance to finally move past it. I need that chance to heal, and I won't ever do it if I don't have him.

"My father," I finally say, feeling the weight of the words crush me. "You and Axel . . . You were my protectors, and you left me to the vile hands of my father."

His hands go slack, and I instinctively pull away from him as he holds my stare, putting the rest of the pieces together himself. "No," he breathes, horror in his dark eyes. "No." But he sees the truth in my stare, sees the pain, the anguish, the fear. The nights I would scream in agony, the days I would stare at the kitchen knives and contemplate slicing the serrated blade across my wrists.

He sees it all.

He reaches for me again, but I pull away from his touch. "Rae."

"Don't," I cry. "I . . . I can't. Not yet."

"Okay," he says slowly.

"Just . . . I need to be alone."

He shakes his head, stepping toward me, but I hastily back up again, my back against the closet shelves. "Rae."

"Please, Ezra." I sob, breaking down again. "Please, just leave. I can't talk about it yet. I can't . . . breathe. I can't—"

"Okay," he finally says, crouching down. He reaches out and cups the side of my face, and I instantly lean into his touch. "I'm sorry. I never should have pushed you like that. You're safe. I got you, Rae."

I nod and he stands to his full height before finally backing out of the small room, and the moment he's gone, I allow myself to break, falling to pieces on the floor of Axel's closet.

CHAPTER 27

Raleigh

By the time I'm able to peel myself off the floor of Axel's closet, darkness is flooding the house, and I pad through the long hallways, trying to remember how to find my way back downstairs.

I need to find Ezra. It's time we talk.

I can't drop a bomb like that and expect him to be okay with it. He's probably halfway through a bottle of whiskey by now and considering washing it down with a cocktail of drugs.

I've avoided telling him for so long, not because I believe he would look at me any differently, but because I know he would shoulder the blame, just as I unfairly have done over the years, and that's not a burden I want him to bear.

Making my way downstairs, I find nothing but a sea of darkness.

Moonlight shines in through the big windows, and I search the walls for the light switches while wondering if I'm wasting my time. A home like this probably has a control pad on a device for the lights, not cheap light switches like we mere mortals are so used to.

Making my way to the kitchen, I pause when I find a familiar silhouette on the couch in the living room. He's hunched over, his elbows braced against his knees with his head hanging low between his shoulders, and the sight breaks my heart.

Moving toward the living room, I lean against the wall, gazing in at him. "I thought you'd left," I murmur, keeping my tone low.

Ezra lifts his head, his broken stare coming to mine. "I'm never leaving you again, Rae."

He holds my stare before patting the empty space on the couch beside him, and I don't hesitate to stride into the living room and curl up next to him. I pull my knees up to my chest and lean into him as he wraps me in his arms, but deciding it's not enough, he lifts me right into his lap until I'm straddled over him.

I curl into his chest, resting my head against his shoulder as I breathe him in while he simply rubs his hand up and down my back in soothing circles. "I'm sorry," I whisper.

"You don't have anything to be sorry for," he tells me. "You did nothing wrong."

"I should have told you a long time ago."

"It's your story, Rae. Your body. You didn't have to tell me anything you weren't ready to share."

I nod. "I'm ready to talk about it."

"Are you sure?"

"No. But I want to. I want you to know who I am now and why I fought so hard to push you away. You were hurting too. You deserve to know."

He drops his face into the curve of my neck and gently brushes his lips across my skin, preparing for the worst. His hand stops rubbing my back, and instead, curls right around me, holding me to his chest. "Okay, Rae. Start from the beginning."

I swallow over the lump in my chest and find his other hand, lacing it through mine and bridging it between us, needing it like a security blanket. "It started around the time of your first release."

" 'Hypothetically Yours,' " he confirms.

I nod and go on. "It was after Mom died and Dad was drunk all the time. He'd started taking notice of me. It was a lingering glance here and there, enough to make me uncomfortable but not enough to have thought anything more of it. Until the comments started. It was around the time I wanted to take our relationship a little more seriously, and so I started dressing a little more provocatively, hoping you'd notice. Shorter skirts, tighter tops, stuff like that, and he noticed, and more than that, he assumed I was doing it for him. That I was strutting around the house trying to tease him, begging him for something he couldn't give me."

Ezra takes a shaky breath, his hold tightening around me, and I try to ignore it, knowing if I linger on his brokenness, I won't be able to continue. "He would call me a whore a lot. That was his favorite. *Dirty little whore.* It was humiliating, but it would always happen in private.

In the kitchen, or when he passed me on the stairs. It was always the same, but that's as far as it went. He never did anything around you guys, never even looked at me, but I could sense he wanted to."

A shiver sails down my spine, but I keep going, knowing Ezra's got me, and I'll never have to face that bastard ever again. "The first time he touched me, I was sixteen. I'd gotten home from school and was rummaging through the fridge when he came up behind me and put his hand up my skirt. From that day, I started wearing pants. I threw out every skirt or dress I had."

"We left when you were sixteen."

I nod as my whole body shakes. "I knew it was going to happen. It wasn't a matter of if, it was when. I knew it that day in the diner when you told me that you were leaving, and I wouldn't be coming. I knew it when you got on the plane, and I knew it after I walked home and slept in the garden, too afraid to go inside."

"Rae—"

I shake my head, needing to get it out. "It was that night. He was up waiting for me. You hadn't even been gone a day," I tell him, tears rolling down my cheeks and soaking into his shirt. "I stayed outside as long as I could, and assuming he'd gone to bed, I crept in. I was dirty from spending hours in Mom's old garden bed, and I was already so broken after you left, I needed my bed. So I unlocked the front door, but I didn't even make it to the stairs before he was on me. He chased me up the stairs, laughing about how you and Axel weren't there to protect me anymore. He caught my ankle and pulled me down. I shattered my nose against the step, and as he pinned me down and crushed my head against the carpet, he stole my innocence and brutally ripped through my virginity. He took everything I'd always wanted to give you."

Ezra stays silent, but I know he's feeling it all. It's in his shallow breaths, in the way he keeps turning his face into the curve of my neck, in the way his fingers unknowingly bite into my skin.

"That night was excruciating. Afterward, I locked myself in my room while blood gushed from my broken nose. I couldn't do anything. Couldn't move, could barely breathe, and I sat in the bottom of my closet and wept until morning."

I swallow over the lump in my throat. "I refused to shower there and did what I could to wash the blood off my face and chest and took a change of clothes to school. I showered in the locker room before anyone noticed, and before school had even started, I was sent to the nurse, who called an ambulance. I begged her not to, and when my father was called to pick me up, he was furious, and that night, I was punished even worse for raising suspicions."

I drop my head back to his shoulder, needing a moment to find myself as he holds me.

"I'm so sorry, Rae. If I'd known—"

"Don't do that to yourself," I whisper, holding his hand even tighter. "There's no way you could have known, and that's on me. I should have spoken up when I had the chance, but I didn't because I knew you would either stay or kill him, and everything you'd worked for would be gone. I couldn't do that to you."

"You were mine to protect," he pushes.

"The road goes both ways," I tell him. "You were mine to protect too, and I did what I had to do to make sure you got everything you deserved."

He holds my stare, a hollowness creeping in. "I don't like that."

"You don't have to."

Ezra lets out a heavy breath. "How long did it go on for?"

"Two years. Right until I left for college," I tell him. "And by that point, I was an empty shell. All the furniture had been taken from my room so I couldn't barricade myself in. The bathroom door was gone, as was the toilet door. I wasn't allowed privacy. The lock was broken off my bedroom door handle, and after I attempted to throw myself out the window, that was boarded up too. He made sure there was no escape for me. Every night. Over and over again. He destroyed me."

I let out a shaky breath unable to meet his eye. "My first abortion was at seventeen. My second six months after that."

"Fuck."

I pause for a moment, needing a second. "There were times it got so bad that I considered running away, but I was never brave enough. I didn't want to live on the street. I didn't have a job or money. I didn't know how I was going to feed myself. So I stayed, and night after night, I thought about taking a blade and slicing it across my wrists. I wanted to die. I *needed* to die, and it made me feel weak."

Tears stream down my face at the admission. It's not something I've ever spoken of, not something I'm proud of, but I want to be honest with him. I want us to start fresh on a clean slate with no secrets between us.

"Some nights I stayed at the lake and slept in the bushes, and some nights I slipped through your old bedroom window and slept in your bed, but I was always punished worse when I refused to come home. Your parents never said anything about it, but I think they knew I was there because there were always clean sheets on your bed."

Ezra nods. "Mom told me that once, but I always assumed it was because you missed me. Not because . . ."

"It's okay," I tell him, squeezing his hand, knowing just how hard this is to hear about the hell I suffered through. "Going to school every day was my only reprieve," I continue. "It gave me something to work toward, something to keep my mind off it, but I struggled more than you'll ever know. I worked my ass off to get into college, and I applied everywhere I could that was far enough away that he couldn't find me. I made it my life's mission to get away, and the day my first acceptance letter came, I finally found that first ray of hope. I was accepted into thirty-two colleges, that's how many I applied for, and I hid every single one from him. He didn't know I was leaving until I was already gone, and I never looked back."

"What happened after college?" he asks, struggling to maintain control when I know every fiber in his body is daring him to get up, fly to Michigan, and end my father's pathetic life.

"After Ax died, I was in a really bad place," I tell him. "Axel was paying my rent, and I was already failing my classes. The dean gave me the option to pull out and try again later, but I couldn't fathom the idea. I was so broken that I just dropped out instead. I had nowhere to go, and I was drowning in grief, not thinking properly, and despite vowing to myself that I would never return there, I went back to Michigan and practically lived on the street. I needed a job, needed to save up some cash, and then I'd be able to leave and start a new life, but being there . . . It didn't feel like home, and I was petrified every time I walked into a store or turned the corner that I'd see him, and so I left, and since then—"

"Since then what?" he prompts.

Humiliation rocks through me, and I pull off his lap, curling up on the couch beside him. "I've lived out of the back of my car, moving from town to town, working shit jobs just to keep myself clothed, bathed, and fed. Right up until I received the call from Lenny offering me this job."

With me now free of his lap, Ezra flies to his feet and starts pacing, shaking his head. "That's two fucking years, Rae. You've been living out of the back of a car for two fucking years, and you didn't even try to call me?"

My gaze falls to my hands. "I'm not proud of it, Ezra. I know I should have called, but I was so beyond broken, and I was angry. I blamed you for leaving, and I didn't know how to ask for help. I didn't even know if you still loved me or even cared."

"Of course I fucking cared, Rae," he says, stepping in front of the couch and dropping to his knees before me. "I've always cared. I've never stopped."

I nod, reaching out and cupping the side of his face. "I know that now."

Ezra drops his head so that his forehead rests against my legs, and

I curl my hand around the back of his head, holding him to me. "I've got you now, Rae," he vows. "I'm never going to let you down like that again."

"You never let me down. I let you down when I failed to tell you what was going on, and I let you down when I put Axel's death on your shoulders. I never should have told you that it was your fault. That was cruel of me. I lashed out at you in the hopes it would take away just a fraction of my pain, but all it did was make it worse."

Ezra lets out a breath and gets to his feet before offering me his hand. "Come on," he says. "Let me feed you."

I take his hand and let him pull me up, and he leads me out of Axel's home, making sure to lock up behind him. He orders takeout, and we start walking, making our way back to his place. We dawdle, taking our time, walking in a comfortable silence as he holds me to his side.

By the time we reach his front door, the delivery driver is showing up, and after getting our dinner, Ezra leads me into his home. It's quiet, unlike the other times I've been here, and I like the peace. Axel's home is beautiful, but there's a loneliness to it, whereas Ezra's home is full of life.

He leads me to his living room, and I sit cross-legged on the couch as I eat.

"There's one thing I'm not understanding," Ezra murmurs, his fork hovering over his takeout container.

"What's that?" I ask around a mouthful of noodles.

"Why you've been living out of your car when you're fucking

loaded."

I arch my brow. "In what world am I loaded? Are you insane?"

His brows furrow, deep in thought. "Axel's will. He left everything to you," he tells me, looking at me as though I just need a moment to jog my memory and then it'll all come rushing back, but there's no memory to jog. I'd know for sure if Axel left me his whole estate. "His properties. Money. All the ongoing royalties from our music. It's all yours."

I shake my head. "I literally have no idea what you're talking about. After Axel died, that was it. I was never contacted about his estate, never even got to ask about it."

"No. That's not right. He specifically told me he was leaving everything to you. I was there when he signed his will."

I shrug my shoulders. "Maybe he changed his mind and wanted to leave it to someone else."

Ezra shakes his head. "No, I would have known," he tells me. "I'm gonna call my lawyers in the morning and see if I can figure this out."

I lean back on the couch. "Just so you know, if I've been living out of the back of my car and showering in shitty motel rooms for two years when I could have been living it up, I'm gonna be pissed."

Ezra laughs, but it quickly falls away, replaced by a sad smile. "He loved you, you know. He always talked about you, and he didn't give a shit if it gave me a hard time or not. Every time you passed an exam or had some kind of grand adventure, he'd boast about it to everyone for days."

I smile. "He was my best friend."

SHERIDAN ANNE

"I know," he says. "I'm sorry about how all of that went down, with the funeral and all. We should have fought harder for what Axel would have wanted. You shouldn't have found out the way you did, and I shouldn't have allowed the label to turn his funeral into a performance. He deserved better."

I nod in agreement. "He did."

"And you do too," he says, a heaviness in his eyes.

My brows furrow, and I put my noodles down as I hold his stare. "What are you talking about?"

"Axel's death. You deserve to know how it happened."

My stare hardens. "I do know how it happened," I say, so sure of myself. "It was when you were on the jet coming back from Australia, right? I was talking to him on the phone, and I'd slipped up and almost told him about Dad, and he was angry because I kept shrugging it off and wouldn't tell him what was going on. That's when he overdosed, right? He figured out what had happened to me and was trying to numb the pain. It's all because of me. It's my fault. I opened my mouth and now my brother's dead, and all this time I've blamed you, but it's me. I killed my brother."

"No," he rushes out, moving in beside me. "This is what I'm trying to tell you. It wasn't an overdose at all. The media got ahold of the toxicology report, made their own assumptions, and ran with it. Yes, Axel had taken drugs the night before, but not enough that he was struggling. He was fine on the jet."

"What are you talking about? I saw the toxicology report. He was strung out on something."

He shakes his head. "He wasn't, Rae," he says, that heaviness still right there, warning me that whatever he's about to say, I'm not going to like it. "After he spoke to you on the phone, he told me he was going to visit you. He said you were having a hard time and all you needed was to see him in person. He wanted to know what was eating you up, make you smile, and then he was going to head back in time for the European leg of the tour."

"No. He never came to see me."

"I know," he says. "We touched down in LA, and then he went home to pack some things, and on the drive back to the airport, there was an accident. His driver swerved off the road and he was killed on impact."

"What?" I breathe, shaking my head as I stare at Ezra like a complete stranger. "No. That's not it. That couldn't be it."

Killed on impact. Just like my mother.

"I'm sorry, Rae."

"He was going to see me?"

He nods.

"Holy fuck," I breathe, getting to my feet as the tears roll down my cheeks. "So either way, he died because of me? Because I almost told him about Dad? Because I opened my fucking mouth when I vowed to never tell either of you. I did this. He's dead because of me."

"No," Ezra rushes out, moving in front of me and taking my hands. "This is exactly why I didn't want to tell you. I knew that beautiful brain of yours would lead you down this path, but you can't look at it this way. You didn't kill your brother by sharing part of your life with him. It's just like saying he killed himself for caring about you. It's not true, and I don't want to hear you saying that shit. He would hate it. Axel was run off the road by an animal who darted out into the middle of the street. It was a tragic accident that has no place falling on your shoulders. You hear me, Raleigh? This is not on you."

He crushes me to his chest, holding me tight as the grief washes over me.

No matter how I look at it, animal on the road or not, I did this.

I slipped up in a moment of anger and said something I shouldn't have.

He was in that car because of me.

My brother is dead, and it's all on me.

CHAPTER 28

Raleigh

Soft strumming of an acoustic guitar fills the night, and I open my eyes to Ezra's bedroom, the clock on the wall telling me it's only three in the morning. I peer down the bed, following the soft music to find him sitting on the ground at the end of the bed, just like he always used to do.

He stops playing to jot something down in a notepad, and a smile pulls at my lips. He's writing.

Pride fills my chest. Dylan mentioned one night while on tour that Ezra hadn't written over the past two years. He couldn't find his muse, but now that I'm back in his life, the words are flowing once again.

I can't help but wonder what he's writing about. I'm sure he has a lot on his mind. It was an emotionally draining night. Telling him about my awful years without him only to flip the switch and have him tell me about Axel's death.

It was a lot to take in, but it was necessary, and now I feel like for the first time in eight long years, we're finally on the same page. Don't get me wrong, processing everything that we talked about is going to take a while. I don't think I'll ever be able to see Axel's death from Ezra's point of view. To me, I will always hold a level of responsibility, and I think it could take me years before I'm finally at a place of acceptance, but until then, I'll have Ezra by my side, guiding me through the darkness.

The weight of my father's abuse still lingers on my shoulders, but after finally letting it out, I feel lighter. I feel as though I have a new purpose. A fire has been lit inside of me, and there's no longer a cold darkness that puts it out. I'm finally able to breathe, and it has everything to do with the man at the foot of the bed.

He held me all night, right through all the pain until the exhaustion claimed me, and I slept right there in his arms, in a bed I never thought I'd find myself in. You know, apart from the day I hid out in here, but that doesn't count. He's incredible, still the amazing man I always knew him to be, and I hate that we missed all that time together.

Ezra drops his pen back to the notepad, and I push up onto my elbow, watching him strum his guitar. I've never been able to wrap my head around his level of skill with that guitar. It's amazing. Both he and Axel were given a gift that so many others could only dream of achieving. It's inspiring. I've seen random YouTube videos where people try to break down their technique in the hopes of being half as good, but the boys are on a different level. Nobody could ever touch them.

Ezra closes his eyes as he plays a beautiful melody, and I can't help but pull the blankets back and climb out of bed. My feet hit the ground, and I slowly pad around the edge of the bed, watching as he opens his eyes and lifts his gaze to me. "I didn't mean to wake you," he murmurs.

I step into him, and as he puts his guitar aside, I slowly lower myself onto his lap, my knees on either side of his strong thighs. "You good?" he questions, brushing my hair off my face as those dark, dreamy eyes linger on mine.

My fingers linger on his chest, slowly trailing down to his waist before curling around the hem of his shirt and slowly dragging it up his toned body. He allows me to pull it over his head, and I toss it aside before leaning in and capturing his warm lips in mine.

His hands fall to my waist as mine curl around the back of his head, tangling my fingers in his thick hair as he slowly kisses me back.

My heart races, and something feels so different about this. It's sensual, exactly what I've always craved from him, and I need it to last a lifetime, even if all we do is this.

His hands roam over my body before falling to the hem of the Demon's Curse shirt I wore to bed. He pulls it up over my head, tossing it aside to join his discarded shirt beside us, and as his fingers brush over my body, goosebumps appear like a map, pointing out everywhere he's touched me.

A shiver trails down my spine, and as I gaze at him, I can't wait another second to speak the words I've always needed to say. "I love you, Ezra," I whisper into the silence of the night as the moonlight dances across the room. "I think I might have yelled it at you a few times, but I mean it. I never stopped."

His hand curls around the back of my neck, his thumb stretching toward my chin. "I know, Rae. I feel it every time you look at me. Every time you're in the same room as me. Every time you say my name, it's there. You don't need to tell me, not when everything you are is so tightly bound to me. I'm not letting you go, Rae. You're home now."

Ezra pulls me back in, kissing me deeply while taking his time, every brush of his fingertips setting my skin on fire. He lowers his lips to my neck as his fingers skim across my thighs. Hunger burns through me, but I take my time, needing this to last the whole damn night.

A soft moan rumbles through my chest as his lips dance across my neck, teasing the sensitive skin below my ear, each swipe of his tongue sending an electric pulse right to my core. I tilt my head, giving him space to work as my hands roam over his strong chest.

My pussy clenches, and I reach down between us, freeing his cock from his pants and slowly wrapping my hand around his hardness. I pump my fist up and down, letting my thumb roll over his pierced tip and loving the way he shudders beneath me.

It's not rushed and desperate like in the pool or backstage in Madrid. It's just me and Ezra, the way it should have always been when we were younger. It's exactly what I've always needed from him, and he's giving it to me just right.

He reaches around me, his hand slipping down over my ass, and I groan as his muscles flinch, realizing he's just torn my panties right off my body, but I don't have a moment to linger on it when his fingers disappear between my legs.

His thumb rolls over my clit, making my hips jolt with need, and as his fingers continue south, my eyes roll languidly. He pushes one inside of me as I slowly continue pumping my fist up and down his impressive length.

"Ezra," I breathe, my chest rising and falling rapidly as his lips work across the base of my throat, the intense pleasure already too much for me to handle.

"I've got you, Rae," he vows just as he adds a second finger.

I gasp before grinding down on his hand, taking his fingers deeper, and when he curls them inside of me and slowly massages my walls, passing over my G-spot, I tremble. "Right there," I groan, tipping my head back again.

He does it again and again, and I tighten my grip on his thick, veiny cock, feeling the bead of moisture at his pierced tip. I need him inside of me, I need to feel the way he stretches me, and then just when I have him right where I want him, I'll ride him until we're both losing our minds.

"Ez—"

"Patience, my sweet girl," he rumbles as his fingers split inside of me, making my head fall back.

"Oh God."

"You like that, baby?"

"Mmmmm," I groan, riding his fingers as his thumb becomes the unofficial VIP of the party, working my clit just right.

"Tell me what you need."

"I need you inside me," I pant, almost sure I'm begging. "I need to slide down on your thick cock and ride you. I want to feel the way my pussy stretches around you, and I need your lips on mine when you do it."

His arm tightens around my waist, and without skipping a beat, he lines himself up with my entrance. As I slowly sink down over him, his lips come to mine, kissing me deeply. Tears sting my eyes as the closeness somehow sews the shattered remains of my heart back together, breathing oxygen into the dark depth of my tortured soul, and filling me with the kind of light I've been searching for since the day he left. With every kiss and caress, he makes me whole again.

"God, Rae," he groans against my lips, and as I slowly begin to rock my hips while moving up and down his impressive length, we both suck in a desperate gasp.

His fingers twine through mine, and I hold them with everything I have as he slowly puts me back together. He doesn't stop kissing me, even when I taste my tears on my tongue, even when the intensity becomes too much I can barely breathe.

My hips jolt, riding him the way I should have always been able to, and as his lips drop to my neck, I throw my head back. My orgasm crashes through me, and I come hard on his cock.

My pussy spasms around him, wildly convulsing as the pleasure rocks through my body, taking me to new heights. Ezra comes with me, holding me tight and grunting as he finishes, but I don't stop moving, slowly rocking my hips and grinding against him as I take what I need.

It's too much.

Too intense.

How did I never know it could be like this?

Ezra catches my lips in his, and as I ride out the rest of my high, he kisses me deeply until we crash against the ground, barely missing his acoustic guitar.

He holds me tight as we come down from our high, and not a moment later, he reaches up to the bed and pulls the blanket off, covering us from head to toe.

I stare up at the ceiling as I catch my breath, living in a world of pure elation, never so happy in my life. "Holy shit," I breathe as my fingers dance across his chest. I lay tucked into his side on the floor, bathing in the soft moonlight that shines through the window. "This is how it should have always been," I tell him as the raw emotions of finally getting to be close to him in this way begin to overwhelm me. "That's how I always pictured our first time."

"Yeah?" he questions, his voice like a deep rumble that speaks directly to my soul.

A stupid smile pulls across my lips. "Mm-hmm. Isn't that what you thought? That there would be some big special moment? Don't get me wrong, the pool in Paris and backstage in Madrid were amazing, but this was different."

Ezra drops a kiss to my temple as his hand snakes down my body to grab my ass. "Don't take this the wrong way, Rae, but I have gone to great lengths not to picture how good we'd be together. You were such a temptation. You have no idea how many times I almost snapped and did something you were too young to have any business doing."

I scoff and push up onto my elbow to meet those dark eyes. "And to think I was going out of my way to try and seduce you. It was driving me insane that you wouldn't make a move. I wanted it so badly. Just one touch. I would have settled for a simple boob graze by the end, but you were always so careful. I was starting to wonder if you were even sexually attracted to me at all."

His head snaps toward mine. "The fuck?"

I give him a blank stare. Surely he knows what I'm talking about. "You're kidding me, right? You didn't even notice?"

"Oh, I noticed, but I thought I was imagining it," he tells me. "When I was eighteen and nineteen, all I could think about was touching you. It drove me wild with need. The need to taste you . . . fuck, Rae. I had to pull away because I didn't want to do something you weren't ready for."

"You're an idiot. I was so ready for it. I was practically begging you for it," I tell him. "I don't know how many different ways I could say, *'Ezra, I need you to put a dick in me.'* It was getting exhausting."

He gapes at me as though suddenly going over every moment we've ever spent together, trying to see it through my eyes. "You're lying."

"Nope."

"Did you say it in those exact words? You know, sometimes men can't take hints."

"Did I scream at you to shove your giant dick in me? No," I say, rolling my eyes. "I didn't want to seem desperate. But I laid down those hints all over the place. You were just too blind to see what was right in front of your eyes. I mean, shit. How many times does a girl have to press up against you before you shove your tongue down her throat?"

"Bullshit."

I shake my head and settle back into his side, a stupid smile across my face. "You know the night that Lenny and those execs came to see you in that old bar?" He nods and I go on. "I had this grand plan. That was going to be the night we finally had sex."

"No," he says, now the one pushing up on his elbow to meet my stare. He shakes his head, clearly remembering that night very differently. "I went out to some bullshit club."

"Yeah," I scoff. "I'm more than aware, but remember before that? You and I were supposed to spend the night together? But then your stupid ass bailed and broke my horny little heart, and instead of coming to the lake with me and spending the night buried deep inside of me, you chose to fuck around with the boys."

He collapses back to the ground, his hands dragging down his face. "Fuck, Rae. I had no idea," he says. "Ax said something in the car about you looking upset, but I thought he was talking shit, and by the time we got home, you weren't there. We had to call you and then you came."

I nod. "Right before that gig, that was the night my father first tried to touch me. I'd dropped him with a knee to the balls and didn't want to go home, so I slept in your car at the lake until I knew it was safe to come home."

He lets out a heavy breath, finally understanding why I did all the things I did back then. "Fuck."

"Yeah," I say, mimicking his heavy tone. "I threw you so many curveballs, and you managed to dodge every single one of those little bastards, choosing to believe I was some innocent, naive little girl when all I wanted was to know what it was like to be yours."

"You were always mine, Rae."

"You know what I mean," I tell him. "I wanted to be with you. I wanted you to be my first."

A heaviness comes over us, and he pulls me back into his arms. "I know," he says. "I wanted that too. I wanted to be every first you ever had."

I shrug my shoulder. "I mean, I suppose there's a lot of things I'm experiencing with you for the first time," I tell him. "I've never come during sex until you. Never been able to take control. Never actually enjoyed it."

"What do you mean?" he questions. "You haven't enjoyed sex until now?"

I shake my head. "After everything my father put me through, I wasn't exactly willing to put myself out there. I've pretty much avoided men. You're the only one I've *allowed* to touch me."

Ezra rolls on top of me, bracing himself on his elbows to keep from crushing me, and I can't help but twist my legs around his. "I am?" he asks, a strange joyfulness flashing in his eyes.

"Yeah," I say with a dorky smile. "It's only ever been you."

He dips his head and kisses me before abruptly pulling back.

"Wait. In the pool—"

"I suppose, I'm kinda counting that as my first time. My first *real* time. It's the only one that counts."

"But wait," he says, rolling right off me and sitting up, horror darkening his stare. "Fuck. If I'd known, I would have done it differently. It was so rushed and desperate. I could have made it special or—"

"Stop," I laugh, reaching for him and pulling him back to me. "It was special. It was everything we both needed in that moment, and let's be honest, that night was a little . . . wild. Apart from crazy, desperate sex, we weren't going to be able to manage much else. We had to get through that to be able to get here. I wasn't in the right headspace for this."

He fixes me with a hard stare before settling back over me, his lips casually dropping to mine. "I wanna make this right, Rae. How do I fix us?"

A stupid grin pulls at my lips. "Well, for starters," I say as my fingers brush over his chest and up around the back of his neck. "You can stop writing songs like '*Cold Hearted Bitch.*'"

Guilt flashes in his eyes. "Yeah, that wasn't exactly my brightest moment," he admits. "I never should have written it."

"No, it's fine," I say, reluctantly. "You wrote what you were feeling in a dark time of your life, and I get that. There were a lot of shitty things that went through my head too. Granted, I didn't write them down and encourage the whole world to sing along."

Ezra groans and grabs me, rolling us so that I hover over him, his hands resting at my waist. "You wanna know something I've never told anyone?" My brow arches with a deep suspicion and as a wide grin stretches across his face, I feel myself growing anxious to find out whatever's on his mind. "Demon's Curse. You remember the day we came up with the band name?"

I give him a hard stare. "You mean the day my mother died?"

He cringes. "Fuck," he says, and it's not as though he'd forgotten about that time in my life, but sometimes, moments from so many years ago blend together, and it can be hard to remember the exact timing of when things went down. "Sorry. That was all on the same day, huh?"

I nod. "Same day Dad started drinking."

"Shit. I didn't mean to bring that up."

"I know," I say, dropping my hands to his chest and trailing my fingers over the lines of his tattoos before settling them over my favorite one—the one just for me. "But that doesn't mean I don't still want to know whatever you were going to say."

Ease settles into his features, and I watch as his eyes soften. "The name Demon's Curse. It's about you."

My face scrunches, and I stare at him as though he's just lost his mind. "Huh?"

Ezra laughs and reaches up, his fingers grazing over my lips as though still unable to believe I'm right here in front of him. "Back then, in those early days before anything had really started between us, I was trying to keep you at arm's length, and it was torture. Not getting to make you mine, I always likened it to some kind of curse."

My jaw drops, and I gape at him. "What? You named the band after how you felt about not being with me? There's no way Axel would have been okay with that."

He smirks back at me, his eyes dancing with silent laughter. "Axel never knew."

"Oh my god," I laugh, crashing down next to him and falling straight back into his warm arms. He holds me tight, pulling the blankets up to keep us both warm as I stare at the ceiling that somehow feels a million miles away. "You know, this house is way too big for just one person. You realize this, right? Nobody needs a house this big."

He laughs. "Oh, I'm more than aware," he tells me. "But I bought it for you."

"What?" I say, pushing up on my elbow to gape at him. "You're insane. You bought this for me?"

"Mm-hmm," he murmurs. "I always knew that at some point, we were going to find our way back together. It was inevitable, and when that happened, I wanted to be able to give you the world, Rae. We'd already lost so much time, and when I found you again, I didn't want to have to wait. That's why I bought just down the road from your brother. I thought you'd be happy to be closer to him, and I know it doesn't get to be that way now, but that's what I was thinking at the time."

My gaze lingers on his as my heart swells inside my chest. "You really did this for me?"

He nods, and I lean in, brushing my lips over his. "It's always been you, Rae. You've been my endgame from day one, and I'm done waiting for something we both know we want. I'm not waiting for a hypothetical anything anymore. I'm yours. Every fucking part of me. I've always been yours."

Tears well in my eyes, and I crash into him, my lips fusing with his like they were always meant to be. "I'm not going anywhere, Rae," he tells me between kisses, his words making every part of my being reignite with life. "It's you and me."

His arms cage around me, rolling us until he hovers over me, and as I feel him harden, I lock my legs around him, welcoming him in. He pushes inside of me, and as his lips work over mine and he brushes the tears off my face, I'm filled with the most undeniable love, and I know that from this moment on, we no longer have to fight what was always meant to be.

I'm his and he's mine. There's no more hypothetical about it.

CHAPTER 29

Raleigh

Madds loops her arm through mine as we wander down the street in LA, stopping by every store we see along the way. It's been a crazy few weeks, but now that I have a few weeks off to relax and reconnect with Ezra, I've never been so happy. Hence why it's time to go shopping. If I plan on seducing him morning, noon, and night, I'm going to need every lingerie set under the sun. Though, to be completely honest, I don't think I need anything at all. I just have to look at him, and he's ready to go. The chemistry is just there, and it's always steaming hot.

"Oooh, we have to go in here," Madds says, as we pass another store filled to the brim with designer dresses that I'm almost positive I won't be able to afford. At least, not with the money in my bank account. But if you consider my currently non-existent inheritance that I may or may not be getting, then sure, I could probably afford the whole store, and the twelve down the street. Hell, why not include the Lamborghini dealership while we're at it?

I don't exactly know how much Axel was worth at his time of death, but the boys were at the height of their career during a sold-out world tour. I'm sure there's more than I could even imagine, along with cars, properties, and royalties. It blows my mind.

I scrunch my face at Madds. "I don't know," I say, glancing through the window. "They look expensive."

"Hate to break the news to you, but *you're expensive* now," she says just as a few girls stop on the sidewalk and start gaping at me, their phones out and recording.

I let out a sigh as they squeal and bombard me. "Holy shit, are you Raleigh Stone?" one of them asks.

I give her a tight smile and nod, knowing that by the time I get three more steps down the street, my face will already be splashed over the internet. Don't get me wrong, I love being in Ezra's life again, but a part of me thought I could still fly under the radar, and for a while, it was working . . . until I decided to give him the lap dance of a lifetime. My ass was all over the internet, and it didn't take long for people to put the pieces together. They already know I'm Axel's little sister, and they already know that Ezra and I have a past. And now, the whole world knows about our flaming hot chemistry.

Just fucking great.

The girls squeal and start jumping up and down, asking random shit about Ezra, and within seconds, other people on the street have started to notice. More people flood toward me, and as it starts to overwhelm me, Madds grabs my hand and pulls me into the store.

"Holy fucking shit," she breathes, her eyes wide as she gapes at the crowd starting to gather outside. "That was ridiculous."

"You're telling me!"

"I mean, that's what you get for dating the biggest rockstar in the world."

I roll my eyes and glance around the store at the array of dresses around me. "He might be the biggest rockstar in the world to you, but he's just Ezra to me, the boy I grew up with," I say. "I mean, I've always known the screaming fans came with the territory, but I didn't think they'd care so much about me. It's him they want, but suddenly everyone wants to know every detail about my life and has an opinion about it. The lap dance was barely even forty-eight hours ago, and the whole world already knows I dropped out of college, spiraled after Axel's death, and then lived out of the back of my car. Some asshole even found my stupid abandoned car and posted it online. I can't escape it."

Madds offers me a forced smile. "Just give it time," she says. "They'll chill out soon, they just need a different story or scandal to obsess over, which is totally manageable by the way. Dig up some of Rock's or Dylan's old dirty secrets and dump them in it instead."

I give her a hard stare. "Not an option."

Madds shrugs her shoulders and laughs. "Just trying to be helpful," she sings, picking up a dress and holding it against her body. "I mean,

I could always drop mine and Dylan's accidental sex tape."

My eyes bug out of my head as I gape at my best friend. "Your what?"

"I know," she cringes. "It was an accident. We were both so drunk on your birthday, and we were taking a stupid video, and then he started kissing me, and I guess we forgot about the phone, and then the next thing I know, I'm waking up on the floor of a hotel room with a video of Dylan Pope fucking me like a god."

My jaw drops, and all I can do is stare at her.

"Say something," she says.

"I . . . you . . . SEX TAPE!"

"I know," she laughs, covering her face in embarrassment. "It just kinda happened. I've been meaning to delete it, but like . . . it's Dylan Pope. Without that video, no one would ever believe I was with him, not that I would ever show this to anyone, not even you. But also, it kinda gives me a reason to talk to him again. I'm just not sure when that happens that I particularly want to be admitting to having a sex tape of him. I don't want him to think I did it on purpose or that this is some kind of money grab because it's not. I would never do that. Plus, breaking out the phone was totally his idea. If anything, I should be the one scandalized, but like . . . I actually look kinda good in it, so, you know, I'm just keeping it for sentimental reasons."

I can't stop gaping at her. "You absolutely have to get rid of that."

"But like . . . do I?" she questions. "It would be a shame to get rid of it prematurely. What if Dylan wanted a viewing party?"

I go to tell her what a terrible idea that is, but on second thought, a viewing party of his own accidental sex tape is Dylan's idea of the best night that ever existed. "You know what," I say with a heavy sigh. "Maybe I could run the idea past him."

Madds laughs and presses her hand to my forehead. "Are you feeling alright?"

I shove her off me just as a rush of paparazzi flood the store window, their cameras flashing over and over, blinding us as they scream for my attention. "What the flying fuck?" Madds says, stepping closer to me and grabbing my arm. She pulls me away as the store attendants hurry past us to the door, quickly locking it before the paparazzi take over their store. "What's going on?"

I shake my head, not having the slightest clue, but what I do know is that this is so much more than just dating rumors. This is a scandal. I just wish I knew what.

"Raleigh. Raleigh Stone," I hear them yelling through the glass, some of them banging against it and making it rattle. "What can you tell us about your father? Are the rumors true?"

"Rumors?" Madds asks, looking back at me for confirmation, but all I can do is stand and stare at them, feeling the blood drain from my face. Please don't tell me they know about my father. "What rumors?"

"No. No. No. No. No," I start chanting.

"MISS STONE?" the paps get more insistent, their blinding flashes sending me into a spiraling panic. "MISS STONE, DID YOUR FATHER RAPE YOU AS A CHILD? MISS STONE. MISS STONE? CAN YOU COMMENT?"

Fuck.

Madds whips her head toward me, her eyes wide and filled with horror. "What are they talking about?" she questions as the store attendants start piling up clothes racks in front of the window, desperately trying to give me some privacy, but all I can do is run.

I turn on my heel and bolt, darting to the dressing rooms in the back of the store. I find the first one, diving into it and pulling the curtain closed behind me before crumbling to the ground, locking my arms around my knees.

My whole body shakes. How do they know?

The only people on the planet who know about this are me, Ezra, and . . . my father.

FUCK.

"Rae?" Madds calls, hurrying after me as I hear her searching the dressing rooms, pulling back curtain after curtain until she finally gets to mine. "Rae," she says, finding me, her tone filled with concern. She drops down in front of me, her hands clutching my knees. "What are they talking about? It's not true, is it? Why would they be asking you something like that?"

Tears well in my eyes, and as I hold her stare, she sees the truth, just as clearly as Ezra had. There's no need for me to respond, no need to delve into the horrid details, she already knows. "Oh, Rae," she cries, throwing herself at me, her arms winding around my body and holding me close. "I'm so sorry. I never knew."

I cry into her shoulder as the store attendants come to find us. "We've done what we can to barricade the door," one of them says. "But it's not looking pretty. More are showing up by the second. What do you want us to do?"

Madds looks back, trying to figure out a game plan. "I don't know. Should we call the police?"

"No. Call Ezra," I say, handing her my phone. "He'll know what to do."

Her eyes widen as she stares down at my phone, doing what she can to try and keep her composure, knowing that this is important and now is not the time to get starstruck by my boyfriend. "O . . . okay," she says, her face turning green. "I'm just going to call Ezra Knight. No big deal."

She visibly swallows before searching through my phone for his number, and as she presses call and holds the phone between us, she takes my hand, squeezing it tight. She presses the speakerphone button, and as memories of my father's assault cripple my mind, I try to focus on the sound of the call.

"Hey, baby. What's up?" Ezra's voice comes through the phone a moment later, the sound somehow starting to calm me. "We're just in rehearsal."

"Oh, ummm . . . hi," Madds says awkwardly. "This is Madds. Raleigh's friend."

"Uhh . . . okay," he says, a strange tone to his voice. "Everything good?"

"Yeah, ummm . . . no," she says, clearly frazzled, but she's doing a hell of a better job than I could right now. "We're in a store, and we got flooded by paparazzi. There are heaps of them, and they're screaming out questions about her dad and what . . . you know . . . he did to her."

"What?" he rushes out in a panic, his tone hardening. "How the fuck do they know about that? Where is she? Is she okay?"

Madds glances at me, a sadness in her eyes. "She's right here listening, but no. She's not okay. She's shaken, and there are so many paparazzi surrounding the store, I don't know what to do."

"Fuck!" He blows out a breath, probably trying to come up with a game plan. "Okay, I'm coming to get you both. Are you safe in that store?"

"Yeah. For now."

"Alright, stay put. I've got Rae's location pinned," he tells us. "We'll be there in twenty."

"Okay."

"Rae?" he asks a moment later, his voice shifting low. "You there, baby?"

I swallow over the lump in my throat, trying to sound as though I have my shit together. "Mm-hmm."

"He can't hurt you anymore. I've got you, alright?"

Tears stream down my face, and I can't manage to keep myself from shaking. "I know."

"Alright. I'll be there soon," and with that, he ends the call.

Madds lowers her hands, her eyes wide as she stares at me. "Ezra Knight is coming to get us," she says monotone, blowing her cheeks out as though that's going to help her current state of shock.

She squishes in beside me on the floor, hooking her arm around my shoulder and pulling me against her as we wait for the calvary to arrive, and as I do my best to zone out the screaming paparazzi coming from outside, Madds does her best to calm me. "Do you want to talk about it?" she asks hesitantly.

I shake my head. "Not right now."

"Okay," she says, trying to cover the hurt in her tone, probably sad that I've never opened up to her about this before when we've always strived to be honest and open with one another . . . mostly.

"I'm sorry," I whisper, not trusting my voice.

"You don't have anything to be sorry for," she tells me. "I just hate that I haven't been a good enough friend and haven't made you feel as though you could talk to me about it."

"It's not that, not even close," I tell her. "You're the best friend I've ever had, it's just not a period of my life I ever wish to relive."

"Period of your life?" she questions. "So, not just a one-off occasion?"

I shake my head, and the sadness in her eyes grows. "Tonight," I tell her, wiping at the tears on my face. "Stay with me at Ezra's place. We'll get really drunk, I'll put it all out there on the table, and then we can cry."

"Okay," she says, her voice shaking as her bottom lip starts to quiver and her eyes fill with big, fat tears. "But I think I'm already starting."

"Oh no." Seeing her tears have mine coming in faster, and as we sit on the floor of the dressing room, waiting for the love of my life, the two of us turn this shopping disaster into a messy sob-fest.

The screaming outside eventually eases, but I have no doubt they're still there, more than ready to wait me out, and after twenty minutes, when the rowdiness starts up again, I realize Ezra has arrived. The paparazzi demand comments from him, and all I can do is listen as the store attendants try to get Ezra's team through the door without causing any more issues.

"Where is she?" I hear Ezra ask a moment later.

"Back here," one of the shop attendants says.

It takes only a moment before the front of my little dressing room is crowded with people, and I glance up, expecting to see Ezra and a few of his security team, but instead, I find Ezra surrounded by no less than eight men in black suits, Dylan, Rock, and even a few of the guys from the label I've come to know over the past few weeks.

"Woah," Madds says, echoing my thoughts.

Ezra looks down at us, taking in the train wreck on the ground before pulling me to my feet. "You okay, Rae?" he asks, gently gripping me by my arms as his dark eyes bore into mine.

I shake my head, the idea of the world knowing about the abuse I suffered at my father's hand haunting me like never before. "I just . . . Take me home."

Ezra nods and pulls me in against his strong chest. "Whatever you need," he tells me, his hand roaming up and down my back. "We're going to get to the bottom of this."

I don't have the strength to tell him I've already figured it out, that it was my father. He told the world what he did to me after seeing me on stage in Madrid. Who knows, all these years he probably assumed I was dead, and while telling the world what a monster he is wouldn't be doing him any favors, I get the feeling he doesn't care. As long as I'm miserable and hurting, he's happy.

"Hey," Dylan says, stepping in beside me and Ezra, his hand lingering on my back as he steals my attention. "I'm sorry, Rae. I had no idea any of this was going on. If we knew, we would have come home. We—"

"Don't," I say, stepping out of Ezra's arms and right into Dylan's. "Don't start beating yourself up over it. I went out of my way to hide it. You couldn't have known."

Rock grabs my arm and pulls me out of Dylan's, locking me in a tight bear hug as he drops his chin to the top of my head. He's not a man of many words, but he has big feels, and they always hit the hardest. "I'm okay," I promise him, both of us knowing I'm lying right through my teeth.

I pull back, wiping the stray tears from my eyes as I look at my three boys, desperately needing the attention to be off me. I can't handle their broken hearts and helpless stares all at the same time. "Okay, so is now a good time to tell you that Dylan and Madds accidentally made a sex tape?"

Madds gasps behind me, and all eyes fly to her, including the eight security guards around us. "The fuck, Rae?" she demands. "I thought we were keeping that on the downlow."

Dylan grins and steps toward her. "No, shit. Huh? A sex tape?" he says, excitement dancing in his tone. "I suppose it was only a matter of time. Let me see. I bet I fucking rocked it."

Madds drops her face into her hands, embarrassment flooding her. "Oh, you did," she mumbles into her hands.

Dylan loops his arm over her shoulders and drags her out of the dressing room with the rest of us. "So, what's the deal? Are we doing this? Cause I need to get home. Apparently, we're having a movie night," he says, pulling Madds even closer, her cheeks flushing while looking between me, Rock, and Ezra. "You guys wanna join? We can have popcorn."

I can't help but laugh. He really does want to have a viewing party for his sex tape.

"No," Madds laughs. "Nobody but you is seeing this tape."

"Oh," Dylan says, his face falling. "Is it not good? We can make a better one if you're worried about angles."

Her brows arch. "You wanna make another one?"

"Baby, I've never come so hard in my life," he says, his voice lowering as his eyes dance with a wicked enjoyment. "I'll make one every day for the rest of my life if it means getting to eat that sweet—."

"Okay," Ezra says, cutting him off. "Let's go before we get roped into being the cast and crew for *Madison Takes My Big Square Gardens, Part Two*."

One of the security guards snickers to himself before quickly trying to wipe the grin off his face, and with that, Ezra's hand slips into mine, pulling me along. The security team crowds around us, and the moment the paparazzi see movement within the store, their blinding flashes start all over again.

There are more people crowded outside than I could have ever expected, all of them surrounding the three blacked-out SUVs that are parked outside the store. There are even more security guards outside, already working crowd control and making a path for us to get through.

"You okay?" Ezra murmurs, leaning into me as we approach the door.

I shrug my shoulders, quickly glancing back to make sure Dylan still has Madds. "Not really," I tell him. "It's not exactly a story I ever wanted to get out."

"We'll handle it. When you're ready, we can talk it through with our PR team to see what the best way to handle this would be. You can say as little or as much as you want, set the record straight with a statement, or if you're not ready, we can just lay low until it blows over."

I shake my head. "Laying low isn't an option, not with you guys heading back out on tour in two weeks. We need to handle it before we head to Portugal. We can't have this shit hanging over our heads."

"You're sure?"

"Yeah," I say, leaning into him.

His hold tightens around my waist as his security reaches for the door, pulling it open. "You ready?" he asks, looking at the mob ahead. "Just keep your head low and ignore everything they say. They'll be brutal about it in the hopes of getting a reaction out of you, so just keep your cool, and then you can fall apart once we're in the car."

Fuck.

"Okay."

With that, we make our move.

The security team falls out around us, shoving the fans and paparazzi back as they try to mob us. "MISS STONE," someone screams right near my ear. "IS IT TRUE? DID YOUR FATHER RAPE YOU?"

Another voice comes from the opposite direction. "RALEIGH, OVER HERE. OVER HERE, PLEASE!"

Fuck. Fuck. Fuck. Fuck.

"Tune them out," Ezra says, clutching my hand, squeezing it tighter than ever as the flashes from the cameras blind me. "Just focus on me. I'm right here. I've got you, Rae."

My whole attention becomes laser focused on the feel of his hand in mine, and as we slowly make our way through the mob, the noise around me turns into a distant blur.

The security guard opens the car door, and Ezra quickly ushers me in before diving in after me, and one by one, Madds, Dylan, and Rock follow. The moment the door closes behind Rock, peace washes over me. We're not out of here yet, but we're one step closer to freedom, and that's all I can hope for.

Ezra pulls me into the warmth of his body, holding me close as everyone seems to watch me, waiting for me to fall apart, but now that the guys are here and I feel safer than I ever have in my life, the need to crumble isn't as overwhelming as it's been in the past.

I'm okay. Truly okay.

The security team works on clearing the crowd, and inch by inch, the SUV begins to roll down the street. "Fuck," Dylan says. "The paps haven't been that bad since news of Axel's death broke."

"Oh sure," I mutter under my breath. "Just while my brain is reliving the hell my father put me through, let's throw in a reminder of my brother's death."

Dylan's face turns white, his eyes widening like saucers. "Shit, Rae. I didn't mean—"

"Chill. I'm screwing with you," I tease, reaching out and grabbing his hand. "I'm fine. I just wanna get back home and pretend like none of this ever happened."

"Home?" Rock asks. "Where exactly is home?"

"Uhhhhh . . ." My brows furrow. That's a damn good question. My gaze shifts to Ezra's, and he looks at me as though the answer has been staring me in the face this whole damn time, and as I pick up what he's throwing down, my eyes widen in horror. "Woah. Back up. Are you suggesting I move in with you?"

"Ummm . . . what?" Madds grunts, peering around Dylan to look between me and Ezra. "Did we just skip seasons three and four? How did we get here? I thought we were figuring out where they were going to dump us for the night."

"You've belonged right by my side since you were thirteen, Rae," Ezra says, ignoring Madds. "We've spent years apart from each other, and now I'm done waiting. I want to build a life with you, just as I should have done all those years ago. I want you with me. I want you in the home I bought for us. I want you in my bed. My life. My whole fucking world. I want to wake up every morning and the first thing I *see* is you. The first thing I *feel* is you. The first thing I hear—you. It's always been you, and unfortunately for your stubborn ass, I'm not taking no for an answer."

My bottom lip pouts out, trembling as the overwhelming happiness fills me. "Wow," I tease. "Way to get a girl when she's down."

Ezra groans and grabs me, pulling me into his arms, and before he even gets a chance to pull me right in, my lips are on his.

"Fuck yeah," Dylan cheers as the driver hits the gas, finally clearing through the mob of fans and paps and taking me back to Ezra's home where I can finally start the life I was always supposed to have.

CHAPTER 30

Raleigh

The past two weeks have been a wild ride of ups and downs. I've spent days on end in Ezra's bed filled with absolute bliss, while also doing what I can to ignore the vile paparazzi. They try with everything they can to exploit the rumors spreading like wildfire about the abuse I suffered at the hands of my father.

We had hoped that the news would eventually blow over, that some other scandal would hit the internet and I'd be free, but I've never been that lucky. Instead, I was left with no choice but to make a statement, and refusing to sugarcoat anything or allow my father to be seen in any way except for the monster he is, I laid it out for everyone. I gave specific details, times, and dates. I gave them the number of bones he'd broken over those two years, listed the different ways he had raped me, the places of my home I had to fear. I offered up every last detail until there was nothing more to give, and then turned off my phone.

It was humiliating, shameful, and made me feel weaker than ever before, but the moment it was sent out into the wild, I felt as though I suddenly had the power. I felt like a survivor, not a victim, and as the world finally knew what kind of monster my father was, I felt free.

Sadly, that little moment of power only lasted within the confines of Ezra's home—our home. The second I stepped out into the real world and was flooded by the paparazzi again, I realized nothing but time was truly going to free me. All that matters is that I've done my part. I don't have a shred of proof to back up my story, nothing I can physically use to see my father locked away, all I have is my word, and I don't know when, but someday, that'll be enough to give me the justice I deserve.

I stand in the hotel room I share with Ezra, staring out the hotel window at the beautiful view of the ocean. It's one of the most stunning sights I've ever seen, and while I love that I get to share this with Ezra, it makes me wish Ax could be here to see it.

"Did you ever come here with Axel?" I ask Ezra as he steps out of the bathroom with a towel wrapped low on his hips, making my mouth water.

Tonight is the first show in Portugal, and while I'm thrilled to be here, a part of me wants to stay right here and hide away from the onslaught of paparazzi. I'm not sure I can handle it just yet.

"Umm . . . yeah," he tells me, moving in behind me and wrapping his arms around my waist as I stare out at the ocean. "Maybe five or so years ago. It wasn't like this though. It was raining the whole time we were here. Not a hint of blue skies, and to be honest, we were still pretty young then. We didn't really take the time to appreciate where we were, not the way I do now. But he always made sure to take pictures of all the sights to send you."

"I know," I say, resting my hand over his on my waist. "I have a whole album saved in my phone of all the pictures Axel sent me from tour. I think he considered himself to be a bit of a photographer, but honestly, he sucked. They're all terrible, but that's what makes them so good."

"Really?" He laughs, pressing his lips to the side of my neck. "I always wondered if you hated getting those pictures."

"Sometimes I did," I admit. "Especially right at the start of your first tour. Every one of them was a knife straight through the heart. By the second and third tours, I started to look forward to them."

"I'm sorry, Rae," he tells me. "All those years with you not here with us. I never should have left you behind."

I turn in his arms and lift my chin to meet his haunted stare. "There are lots of things both of us should have done differently, but we were young and didn't know any better. You couldn't have known what hell I'd go through, and I should have been honest. But I'm here now, and that's what counts."

"Damn straight you are," he says as his hands drop to my ass and lift me into his strong arms. His lips come down on mine as he turns and starts walking to the bed, but I pull back, a stupid grin on my face.

"Don't even think about it," I laugh, knowing just how carried away we can get. "You know damn well that there's a full team meeting starting in . . ." I glance at the clock on the wall, my eyes widening. "Oh shit! It's already started!"

"It's fine," he murmurs, nuzzling into the side of my neck and making me groan as his lips and tongue work over my skin. I feel him harden between us, and as he grinds against me, my eyes roll in the back of my head. "They won't even know we're not there."

"You're the lead singer of the band. They'll more than notice that you're not there."

Ezra groans, and as his lips meet mine, my eyes widen in horror, and I pull back, breaking our kiss. "Oh my god," I breathe in horror. "They're going to assume we're doing it."

He arches a brow and holds my stare. "And?"

"And?" I squeak, fighting his hold until he has no choice but to put me down. "Every moment we're not there, they're already assuming you're ten inches deep. I work with these people. I need them to have some level of respect for me."

"They do."

"Yeah," I scoff. "They respect the fact I'm Axel's sister and the girl who was somehow able to reel in the spiraling rockstar. But I want them to respect me for the fact that I'm good at what I do."

Ezra holds my stare, and I watch as his begins to soften. "Don't start acting like you don't already know how much they already respect you. They know you're good at what you do. They can see it, and I wouldn't be surprised if Lenny offered you to go on tour with every fucking band he represents. I'll be fucking pissed, but not surprised."

"Pissed?"

"Mm-hmm," he murmurs, stepping into me. "You're mine, Rae. I've already let you go once before, and I'm not doing it again, and especially not for some job. Besides, once this tour wraps and your contract is up, don't be surprised if Lenny begs you on his hands and knees to represent Demon's Curse indefinitely."

My eyes widen. "You think he'd do that?"

"If the conversation I had with him last week is anything to go by, then yeah. He's already sniffing around and wanting to know what your plans are following the tour."

"And you said?"

"Nothing that we don't already know."

"Which is?"

Ezra grins and lifts his fingers to my chin, gently raising it until my eyes are locked on his. "That wherever you are, I'll be. Even if it means I've gotta chase your fine ass around the globe."

"Oooh, how the tables have turned," I tease. "How's it feel being the one who's doing all the chasing now?"

Ezra shakes his head, his eyes dancing with laughter. "Baby, I've been chasing you since the day I met you, and nothing is about to change that. I'll keep chasing you 'til the day I die."

Everything melts inside of me as a stupid smile pulls at the corners of my lips. "That was definitely the cheesiest thing you've ever said."

Ezra laughs and finally releases his hold around me before crossing the room and letting his towel drop, showing off his delicious ass. I groan. Maybe I was a fool to give up hot sex for a team meeting. "Quit staring at my ass, Raleigh Stone," he says as he continues walking away.

"Never gonna happen."

Ezra glances over his shoulder, a wicked smirk resting on his lips. "Just so you know, after the show tonight, I'm gonna bend you over that balcony, spread those pretty thighs, and just when you can't take the anticipation a moment longer, just when you're begging me to take you, I'm going to fuck you until your sweet little cunt is spasming on my cock and your knees can no longer hold you up."

Well, fuck.

All I can do is stare at him as he drags a pair of black jeans up his thighs, not bothering with underwear and leaving the button undone. He reaches for a shirt next, and as he lifts his arms over his head and his abs and pecs stretch out, I'm pretty sure I come.

"Whatcha waiting for?" he asks me when his shirt settles into place, and he reaches for the button of his jeans, acting as though I'm the one holding us up for this big team meeting.

"That wasn't fair."

He smirks at me, and my stomach releases a million fluttering butterflies. "Don't know what you're talking about."

Asshole.

Finally able to pull myself together, we make our way down to the function room on the second floor of the hotel. It's big enough to be used for weddings and special events, and while our team definitely isn't that big, I appreciate the hotel making the arrangements to accommodate us. It was either this or we overcrowd their restaurant, and honestly, I thought that was a dick move.

We walk through the door of the function room, and I let out a relieved sigh, finding everyone only just starting to take their seats, and while we were definitely late, it seems everyone else was too.

Lenny remains on his feet at the front of the room, and Ezra and I make our way past the dancers and backstage crew. Ezra's phone rings, and he pauses in the middle of the floor to pull his phone from his pocket. "I gotta take this," he says with a cringe, spinning on his heel and hightailing it straight back out the door while Lenny throws his hands up in frustration, probably annoyed that this meeting isn't already over.

I continue across the room and drop down between Rock and Dylan, smirking to myself as I find Dylan fully immersed in his phone, and judging by the look on his face, I'd dare say he's texting Madds.

The whole shopping experience in LA was a disaster, but it wasn't a complete waste. With the love of their mutual sex tape, Dylan and Madds have bonded, and while I certainly have my hangups and am nervous about two of my best friends getting close, I'm also really excited about it. Neither of them is typically the relationship type, and yet for some reason, they seem to be working. It's still new, and who knows if it'll actually go anywhere, but a part of me hopes that this can be their version of a happily ever after.

As for Rock, I think the only thing he's interested in banging is his drum set. Don't get me wrong, he's no stranger to the occasional one-night stand, but those drums will always be his one true love.

"Alright, we have a big show tonight, so let's not make this any longer than it needs to be," Lenny starts.

I sit up a little straighter, wanting to soak up every detail like a sponge. We had a huge team meeting the night before the first show in Paris, but since then, it's been crickets. On the other hand, Rock doesn't feel like listening to the boss is in his best interest. "You two were fucking, weren't you?" he murmurs, leaning toward me.

My cheeks flush, and Rock simply laughs and shakes his head. "Fucking knew it."

Dylan scoffs from beside us. "Shower sex, right?" he asks, clearly having noticed the tips of Ezra's hair were still wet from his shower when we walked in.

"Nah. They hit up the balcony for sure," Rock says.

Holy fucking shit. I'm going to kill Ezra for making us late. "Would you two shut up? I'm trying to concentrate," I say just as Ezra opens the door and shoves his head through, cutting off whatever Lenny had been saying.

"Rae," he says, his gaze searching out mine in the big function hall. "Need you for a minute."

Rock laughs beside me. "Wow. Only been separated for thirty seconds, and he's already gunning for round two."

Dylan laughs on my other side, and I smack them both at the same time before flying to my feet and turning on them both. "At least he's thoroughly getting his world rocked, over and over and over again, which is a lot more than either of you are getting right now."

Both their faces fall, and I turn before dashing past Lenny to the door. Ezra knew this meeting was a big deal for me and wouldn't have pulled me out of it unless it was important. Though, Rock might be on to something. This older version of Ezra who can't seem to keep his hands off me, he very well might pull me out of a team meeting just to drag me into the broom closet and have his wicked way with me.

"What's up?" I ask, stepping through the door and right into Ezra's side, my gaze locked on his.

"It's my lawyer," he tells me, still clutching his phone as he pulls the door closed behind me, giving us just a fraction of privacy in the middle of the hallway. "He's been looking into Axel's will and has some information."

"Oh, really?" I ask as he presses his hand to my lower back and leads me down the hall to where we can be alone from any prying eyes and ears.

"Yes, Miss Stone, I presume?" a deep voice says from the speaker of Ezra's phone.

"Yes, that's me," I say.

"My name is Martin Browne. I am Mr. Knight's lawyer. He requested I look into the handling of your brother's will."

"Oh, yeah," I say, briefly remembering how Ezra mentioned that he would ask his lawyer to look into it, but so much else was going on that I'd taken that little bit of information and stored it away for another day. "Ezra seems to think that Axel would have left everything to me, but I don't know. There might have been a time when he wanted that, but he was also a very generous man. I figured he left everything to his charities."

"You received nothing?" he clarifies.

"That's right," Ezra responds for me.

"Well, it seems this is a bigger issue than I first realized."

"I'm sorry?"

"Ezra was right in his assumptions," Martin tells me. "Your brother left his whole estate to you. Money, cars, properties, his royalties earned from the band. Everything belongs to you and was officially signed over to your name shortly after his death."

"No. That couldn't be right," I say. "I haven't got a thing."

There's silence for a moment, and I hear the soft sounds as Martin flips through some paperwork. "Okay, I have copies of the letters that were sent to your address, and documents signed by yourself."

"What? No. I didn't sign anything."

He digs a little further. "I have banking details for you for where your brother's funds were allocated, and the transfers of his assets into your name."

I shake my head, meeting Ezra's confused stare. "What address were those letters delivered to?" Ezra questions.

"I have an address in Michigan," Martin confirms as the blood drains from my face.

"My father," I breathe, my hands starting to shake as realization dawns on me. "He received the letters and signed on my behalf. He stole my inheritance, everything Axel worked for. He stole it from me."

"Fuck," Ezra grunts, reaching for my hand. "What about the assets that were transferred into her name? Does Rae still hold the titles?"

"I will have to do some title searches, which may take me a few hours," he tells us. "I'll get my associates started on this. In the meantime, I'll look into the funds transfer and find out where your inheritance is, and once we have something concrete to work with and some answers, we can start putting a case together. Don't worry, Miss Stone. We'll get to the bottom of this."

"Okay," I say, letting out a shaky breath.

Ezra wraps up the rest of the conversation as I just sit here, unable to take in another word.

My father has already stolen so much from me, and to realize he's taken everything of Axel's as well is beyond devastating. Axel would never have wanted this, and granted he didn't know just how vile our father had become, their relationship was strained since the moment he came home drunk and told us that Mom was never coming home.

He hated our father, and if he knew who he really was, I have no doubt that Ax would have ended his life.

Years later, and the asshole is still fucking with me. When is it going to end? He should be incarcerated by now. He should be locked up with the worst of the worst, spending the rest of his miserable life suffering at the hands of the men he's imprisoned with. But instead, he's out there somewhere living the high life off the money my brother left for me.

Fuck. I've never hated someone more.

Ezra's hand falls to mine, bringing me out of the torturous thoughts circling my mind. "You good?" he questions.

I let out a heavy breath and shrug my shoulders, not willing to let on just how much this has messed with me. "I'll never escape him," I admit. "Even a million miles across the globe, and he's still right there, taking anything good in my life. He's not happy unless I've been stripped of everything that's worth living for."

Ezra pulls me in closer. "He can't hurt you, Rae. You're the one who has the power here. You're not some scared sixteen-year-old girl anymore. You're a woman now, and I won't let him take your power. This is your chance to finally take him down. I know you've always hated that you've never had the evidence of what he did to you in that house, but we can get him for inheritance theft, and he'll be sent away for the rest of his pathetic life."

"I want him to suffer," I tell him.

"Don't you worry about that," he promises me. "I'll make sure of it."

Ezra swipes his thumbs across my face, wiping away tears I hadn't realized were tracking down my cheeks. "Come on," he murmurs. "Game face on. Let's get this meeting done, get to the stadium, get the show over with, and then I'll spend the rest of the night loving you."

A stupid smile pulls at my lips. "You better make it worth my while."

"Just you wait, baby."

We make our way back to the function hall, and just as the door opens, Lenny's words flow through to us. "The paps are searching for a story, and we won't be the ones to give it to them," he says. "We're here to put on a show, not to insert ourselves directly into Raleigh's story. She's been through enough to have to worry about one of us feeding the media about her past."

Ezra pauses by the door, his gaze shifting to me, his brow arching and silently asking if I'm ready to walk in there, and I let out a sigh.

"What did I tell you?" I murmur, stepping over the threshold to the function room. "I can't escape it."

Ezra's hand finds mine and gives it a firm squeeze, and as we walk across the room to where Dylan and Rock sit, Lenny goes on. "Despite this story breaking two weeks ago, it is still making headlines, and we will not be the reason for it to continue. When asked—which you will be—you are to divert your answers back to the show. We have brought a team on board who are able to give a crash course in media training if any of you would like some guidance on how to answer these questions."

A heaviness settles into my chest, somehow feeling like I'm a burden on the rest of the team, and I try to keep my expression neutral. The last thing I wanted was to be a distraction to the team or to try and take any attention off the band. This is about them. The headlines should be about how magnificent the boys are, how they're unstoppable in their prime, not about the lead singer's girlfriend who was abused.

"We are still unaware of where these stories are coming from—" Lenny continues, making me cringe. We haven't exactly told him our thoughts on that. I'm almost certain this is my father's doing. It just doesn't make enough sense for me to come forward with it. Why the fuck would he go bragging to the media about what he's done? Does he think he's untouchable? Does he think it's something to be proud of? "—and until we're able to get to the bottom of this, we all need to do our part. Raleigh is family, and we protect our own. Is that understood?"

There's a unanimous *yes* that sounds through the room, only a soft scoff has my gaze flicking to the left, and unfortunately for the dancers, I wasn't the only one who heard it. "You got a problem?" Rock asks, already on his feet.

"Come on," Jessica says, her gaze flicking toward me. "You don't think this is getting a little over-the-top? Everybody has stood by and watched Raleigh throw herself at Ezra, and that lap dance on stage? She's not even a dancer. Clearly this . . . behavior is typical of her. She's provocative. We've all seen it."

My blood runs cold as every eye in the room turns toward me, horror sweeping through my body.

"If you're trying to make a point, you better hurry up and make it," Rock grunts, shifting closer to me.

Jessica lets out a sigh before waving her hand toward me. "She's been acting like a whore since the moment she arrived," she states. "She's clearly in love with the attention she gets. Don't you all see what's happening here? She's the one who's leaking these stories. I bet they aren't even true to begin with. Nobody fucking touched her. She's just making up bullshit sob stories to keep her name in the media and have everybody feeling sorry for her. It's embarrassing, and she should be fired for bringing all this heat down over the band. It's making us all look bad."

No, she fucking didn't.

My hands ball into fists, humiliation and anger infecting my body.

Ezra doesn't move even an inch beside me, just relaxes into his chair as though he doesn't have a care in the world. "Jessica," he says, watching her gaze sweep to his. "Pack your shit. You're fired."

"What?" she demands, her eyes widening in shock. "That's bullshit. You can't fire me for expressing an opinion."

"I can do whatever the fuck I want," he says, as my knee bounces, desperately needing to rearrange her face. "Now pack your shit. You're out of here."

"But . . . no. There's a show starting in an hour. You need me." Jessica gets to her feet, looking between Lenny and the rest of the band, waiting for someone to tell Ezra he's being dramatic, but no one does, no one even breathes a word.

"We sure as fuck don't need you. Your performances are doing nothing but cheapening our show. In fact," he says, turning his gaze toward Stacey. "You might as well pack your shit too. I'm done having these two fawn all over me on stage. It's humiliating."

Stacey sucks in a breath, and I almost feel sorry for her. I don't exactly like her, but she's never been a bitch to me the way Jessica has. "But—"

"Don't worry," Ezra continues. "We'll pay out the rest of your contract, and you're more than welcome to stay here the rest of the week on us. Live it up a little. I'm just . . . The show doesn't require dancers. We never should have hired them."

Lenny cringes. "I'm sorry, girls. I'm inclined to agree with him. And of course, Stacey, we'll pay out your contract, and you can stay if you'd like. As for you, Jessica, why the fuck are you still here?"

Her eyes widen in horror as though having those words come directly from Lenny's mouth is the finality she needed, and bless her cotton socks, the bitch looks like she might cry. Only, those sad eyes quickly turn toward me, and the sadness morphs into pure, undiluted hate. "I bet you begged him for it. Quit playing the victim and realize that every lie you play up to the media only dirties your brother's legacy. You should be ashamed of yourself. Or maybe you should just go back home and beg Daddy for more, you fucking whore."

It's all I can take, and I spring from my chair, more than ready to put the bitch in the ground. Jessica screams in terror and makes a break for the door, only I don't get very far when Dylan's strong arm locks around my waist. "LET ME GO!"

Ezra murmurs beside me, his gaze shifting to Dylan's as the desperation pulses through me, knowing Jessica is getting away without the ass-whooping she deserves. "Let her go. Let's see what happens."

Mmmm. Nobody ever claimed Ezra didn't know how to please me.

Dylan's hold around my waist begins to loosen, and I see red, the rage building up behind my eyes, so potent I could explode. I can almost taste the blood.

"I swear to God, Dylan," Lenny warns. "You let go of that girl and your life won't be worth living."

"Uhhhhhhh . . ." he says, not knowing where to go from here, but realizing there's not a chance in hell that I'd catch her, the fight begins to fade from my chest, and my body relaxes in Dylan's hold. "You good now, Rae? You're not about to beat a bitch?"

I shrug my shoulders, never having felt so dejected.

How could someone just say something like that?

Ezra steps into my path, and as Dylan releases me, I fall right into Ezra's arms. "It's okay," he tells me. "You never have to see her again."

"But, she said—"

"I know. I heard her," he says. "And don't you worry. Just because you didn't get the chance to beat her ass doesn't mean I can't still ruin her. She'll never work again, Rae. I'll make sure of it, and she'll know it has everything to do with what she just said here. She's not getting away with this."

I swallow over the lump in my throat and nod as Lenny desperately tries to dissolve the meeting. "Alright, everybody. Let's have a great show tonight. You're all excused. Get a good meal in and remember to hydrate, and let's hope that tonight goes off without a hitch."

The crew begins filing out of the room until it's just me, Lenny, and the guys left behind.

"Are you okay?" Lenny asks, striding up to me and bracing his hand on my shoulder.

I give him a tight smile. "No," I tell him, deciding honesty is probably best. "I, ummm . . . If it's not a problem, I think I might skip out on the show tonight and just chill in my hotel room."

"Of course," he says. "We don't require your presence at the shows. You know that."

"Are you sure?" Ezra asks. "I don't want you being alone like that. Maybe we should cancel tonight and reschedule. I don't—"

"The fuck we will," Lenny grunts as Dylan and Rock throw in their immediate objections as well. Canceling a show isn't something they should ever do lightly, and the fact that Ezra is even willing to let down over fifty thousand fans just to be there with me means more than he could ever know.

"I'm not about to let you do that," I tell him. "I'll be okay. I'll just chill in our room, maybe take a bath with a glass of champagne and watch the live stream of the show. I'll be there in spirit, and when you get back, we can—"

"Okaaaay," Lenny says before this can get any further. "Time for me to see myself out."

Then as if on cue, Lenny, Rock, and Dylan see themselves out, leaving me wrapped tightly in Ezra's arms. "I love you, Rae," he tells me. "All you'd ever have to do is just say the word, and I burn down this whole enterprise just to be there with you."

A stupid smile pulls at my lips, and I push up to my toes and kiss him. "I would never ask that of you," I tell him. "Just getting to be the girl in your arms is more than enough for me."

Ezra grins at me. "And to think you claim that I'm the cheesy one."

I roll my eyes and shove him away, knowing he has to start making a move to the stadium soon. "Get your ass out of here and let me enjoy my night for a change," I laugh. "You stupid rockstars are far too demanding for your own good."

"Talk it up, baby. But when this rockstar is sliding into that sweet cunt tonight, I bet that smart mouth will have something different to say."

CHAPTER 31

Raleigh

The warm bath water soaks into my skin as I relax in the dimmed bathroom with a glass of champagne in my hand. The boys' show is live on Ezra's iPad as Madds oohs and ahhs over Dylan on FaceTime, watching the show along with me.

"You know," Madds says as I tip my head back against the tub and close my eyes, relaxing in the soothing bubbles. "If you're feeling up to it, you should look up some of Axel's old tour videos. There are heaps of them on YouTube. After he died, people just started posting everything they had from when they saw them on tour. There are some really great ones of his solos and stuff like that. Plus, I know it's not the same as getting to see him in the flesh, but it's brand-new footage for you, so technically, it counts as new, right?"

"Really?" I ask, putting my champagne glass down on the edge of the tub. "I've never thought to look up that stuff before."

Reaching for the iPad, I click out of the live stream and vow to come back to it later before hovering my fingers over the keyboard. "What should I search?" I ask, feeling a little overwhelmed, knowing just how much stuff could be plastered across the internet.

"Ummmmmm . . . OH! Start with his solo during 'Hypothetically Yours' from the show in Dublin from . . . uhhhh, I think it was maybe four years ago."

"Really?" I mutter as I start madly typing things into the search bar. "That song came out a little over eight years ago, would they really have been performing that on the other tours? I mean, I know it's on the current set list, but surely not for their other tours, right?"

Madds scoffs. "Clearly you don't know Ezra as well as you think you do. Now, this could all be online gossip, but apparently, Ezra makes sure that it's on the set list for every show they ever perform, even the one-off events like charity things and stuff like that."

"No shit."

"Yeah, apparently Axel said it in an interview somewhere. Actually, there's an idea. You should look up all of his old interviews. They're so funny, and sometimes he even talks about you. But the ones where they interview all four of the guys at the same time are the best. They're so funny together."

"Jesus Christ," I laugh. "I hope you tone down this crazy Demon's Curse fangirl stalker shit when you're around Dylan."

"Girl, I'm trying, like really fucking hard, but sometimes it just comes shooting out of my mouth like word vomit, and so far, he just laughs when it happens. Maybe he thinks it's cute or something, but surely he'll get sick of me at some point, right?"

"Honestly, I have no idea. This is all new for him. I've never seen him around a girl who he wants for more than a one-night stand. But clearly, whatever you're putting down, he's picking right up."

I can practically hear the way her cheeks flame through the phone. "Really? You think? Because I don't want to screw this up, and I want him to see me as so much more than just a crazy stalker fangirl."

"Of course he does," I tell her. "He sees you as the girl who accidentally recorded a sex tape."

Madds groans. "At some point, I'm going to have to scrub that little snippet of information right out of your brain."

"Not possible."

Madds laughs. "You know, he was texting me earlier and said he wanted me to fly out for one of the shows, but it was like he was making up excuses as to why he wanted me there. He said it would be good for you to have a friend, but like, he knows damn well that every spare second you have is spent either working or with Ezra."

"Just take it slow," I tell her. "He's not used to having someone who means something to him, so he's just trying to work it out. He's like a little stray puppy, and if you move too fast, you'll scare him, and he'll start running. You have to lure him in with treats."

"You mean sex?"

"No," I laugh as I finally manage to hit search and see a flood of Axel's videos popping up. "I mean with kindness and patience, but like . . . It's Dylan, so I suppose sex will also work."

I scroll through the options before finding the one Madds was talking about. Axel's face immediately fills the screen, a stupid grin resting on his lips as he glances at Ezra, the two of them feeding off each other's energy.

"Is that it?" Madds asks.

"Yeah," I breathe, relaxing into the tub as I scoop up my champagne glass and take a sip. "He's so happy."

"Just wait 'til it gets to his solo. He added bits, and with the live drums, it just hits differently."

We fall into silence, and as I watch my brother play, the sweetest joy fills my heart, a joy I haven't felt in so damn long. The whole band is incredible. Don't get me wrong, Jett is a great guitarist. He could be a star in his own right, but it's simply not the same as it was with Axel. When he and Ezra played together, the world felt their chemistry.

The camera pans to Ezra as he sings, and my heart races, loving seeing him like this, but when Axel's solo comes, I find myself sitting up, gaping at the small screen. "Holy fuck," I mutter, reaching around the iPad and turning up the volume as he hits a whole different melody while somehow keeping everything the same. I can't describe it, not having the musical ear to figure out what he's even doing differently, but when Ezra, Rock, and Dylan all grin at him, it's clear that whatever he'd just done was something special.

"Oh my god."

"Right?" Madds says, reminding me she's still there. "Oh, next, search up his performance from their first tour in Colorado. That one is insane."

Without skipping a beat, I start searching, and just like that, Madds and I fall down the rabbit hole of Axel's greatest hits, and before I know it, my bath water has run cold and I'm all out of champagne. "Shit," I say to Madds. "I better get going before more than just my fingers become pruney."

She laughs, and I have no doubt she just pictured me with a pruney vag. "Okay," she says. "Call me if you need me, but I know you won't because you'll be enjoying your wild balcony sex with your hot boyfriend while overlooking the beautiful Pacific Ocean."

I grin to myself, not having the heart to tell her it's the beautiful Atlantic Ocean I'll be looking at while getting fucked within an inch of my life on the balcony. "Kay, have a good night, and remember, be chill when you text Dylan. Don't go scaring him off."

"I know. I know," she says. "Night."

With that, she ends the call, and I pull myself out of the bath, starting to shiver as I realize just how cold I allowed the water to run. Finding my towel, I pull it around me and quickly get myself dried off. As I'm searching through my clothes for pajamas, I stop abruptly. All those videos of Ax on tour make me feel as though I've missed out, and right now, Ezra is a short car ride away, putting on a show for thousands of people while I'm sitting in the hotel room sulking.

I should be there with him. I should be watching him rock people's worlds over and over again. If roles were reversed, and I was the one on that stage, he would be there night after night, supporting me the best way he knew how. I need to be there.

Checking the time and realizing there's still a good portion of the show left, I find something nice to put on before dashing into the bathroom and letting my hair out, thanking whoever exists above that I didn't decide to wash it tonight.

After swiping mascara across my lashes, I grab my little purse and slip into a pair of heels to complete my look. Taking in my reflection, I picture the happiness on Ezra's face when he finally sees me standing in the wing, and a beaming smile settles over my lips. Not wanting to waste another second, I practically run to the door.

Gripping the handle, I yank it open, only to barge right into a solid wall. I barely get a chance to react, to even lift my head and see who it is before a hand clamps around my throat, shoving me back inside the room.

My heart races, and while I can barely see his face, I recognize that scent.

It's the smell of my past. The smell that sends me into a downward spiral. The smell that reduces me into a terror-filled child hiding in her closet hoping the monster wouldn't come for her.

My father.

Panic claims me as I clutch his hand around my throat; his tight grip makes it almost impossible to breathe. He doesn't release me, doesn't even seem to feel the pain as I claw at his skin, digging deep grooves with my nails.

No. No. No. This can't be happening. How did he find me? I thought this was in the past, and I would never have to see his face again. This can't be happening.

My father locks the door behind him as I try to scream, but with his grip around my throat, not a single sound comes out of me. As a young woman, I learned the hard way what would happen when I tried to scream. It's a lesson I took all too seriously, but I'm no longer his imprisoned toy to destroy. I set myself free and am no longer bound by his monstrous rules.

Desperate for air, my knee comes up, but he springs back, knowing my tricks all too well.

"I've been looking for you," he growls, using his grip on my throat to push me deeper into the room. He reaches the bed before throwing me down, and I desperately gasp for air as I crash against the mattress. "I'd almost given up until you decided to whore yourself out to that boy in front of thousands of people. And then it was all just a game of following the breadcrumbs. You led me here, Raleigh. And then your friend, Jessica, was all too happy to point me in the right direction."

A deep sense of betrayal hits me right in the center of my chest. I knew Jessica hated me, and after being fired today, I knew she would be feeling some kind of way, but surely he's lying. Surely she didn't tell him exactly where to find me.

"I should have known you'd be with him," he says, almost as though he can't believe he hadn't thought of it sooner. "It was always him, but that's where you're wrong, Raleigh. You're mine. You've always belonged to me, and now I have no choice but to remind you of that, and once I'm done, I will end your miserable life."

I scramble, trying to get off the bed to find something . . . anything that could be used as a weapon, but he moves like lightning, his steps surer than ever before. He's stronger, more determined, and while I can still smell the whiskey coming from his pores, there's something else there, something I don't recognize.

As I scramble away, crying out for help, he grabs my ankle and pulls me back. "No," I scream, kicking my foot back and slamming it against his chest, only he doesn't budge, he just laughs instead.

"Ahhh, it seems you've regained some of that fighting spirit your mother used to have."

The fuck? Did he used to hurt my mother like this?

There's not a moment to dwell on it before he yanks me down the bed toward him, twisting my leg so hard that I have no choice but to roll onto my stomach to avoid dislocating my hip. I try to grasp the bed sheets to find leverage, but he comes down over me, rendering my attempts at freedom useless.

"The whole world thinks you're a filthy whore," he says, reaching over me and gripping my wrist. He pins it behind my back before fighting for the other, and before I even get a chance to try and pull them free, they're bound with a rope. "Why don't we show them just how much of a whore you really are."

My father laughs as he pulls the ropes so tight the fibers dig into my skin, and I cry out, tears welling in my eyes.

This can't be happening. Not again.

I try to buck him off me, but it only spurs him on. "Calm down, my filthy little slut. I know you're fucking hungry for it, but there will be time for that. Let's wait until we have our eager audience."

The fuck is he talking about? Eager audience? It's the second time he's spoken about having an audience, and the thoughts of what he's going to do make me sick. Is he planning to record me and post it online? If he's so willing to show the world exactly what he's done to me over the years, it's confirmation that he was the one who leaked the story to the media.

His hands dig beneath me, violently searching for the button of my jeans between my body and the mattress, and I cry out again and again. "GET OFF ME, YOU PIECE OF SHIT."

My protests earn me a solid blow from his elbow, right in the center of my spine. A sharp cry slips from my lips as the pain takes me right back to those abandoned years.

"You're going down for this," I vow. "No matter where you run, you won't escape me. I'm going to make your life a living hell."

Every ounce of my soul is spoken in those words, and yet all he can do is laugh. "We'll see about that, princess," he mocks. "Once I'm through with you, there'll be nothing left worth saving."

He makes me sick.

The button on my jeans pops open, and as he pulls back off me, he viciously yanks my jeans down my thighs. I take the moment to strike, whipping myself over and kicking out, slamming my foot across his face, listening to the satisfying way his nose crunches under the impact, just like the first time he ever touched me.

"You fucking bitch," he growls, lunging for me.

I go to flee, desperately trying to scoot myself off the bed, but the glimmer of a blade catching in the light brings me up short as he presses it against the base of my throat. "That's what I thought," my father says as I come to a terrified halt, my whole body shaking in fear. "Now, here's how this is going to happen."

He moves away from me, and I scramble up the bed, putting distance between us as he reaches for my small purse that's been tossed on the ground.

"I'm going to fuck you, Raleigh. I'm going to take everything that I've deserved, and you're going to lay there and take it like the filthy little whore that you are, and if you don't," he says, his tone shifting to something more sinister and vile than I've ever heard from him. "I'll be right here waiting for your little boyfriend to return, and when he does, this blade will be plunged right through his heart. You hear me?"

Fuck.

Tears stream down my face, and all I can manage is the slightest nod as bile rises in my throat, knowing with every ounce of my being that he means every last word he says. If I don't do this, if I don't allow him to take every shred of dignity I'd painfully found over the past six years, if I don't allow him to destroy me, he will end Ezra's life.

Ezra and I would never see eye to eye on this. He would prefer I fight, prefer that I allow him to take his chances with the blade, but he doesn't know my father like I do. Whether I play along or not, he will still rape me. Whether I lay there and take it or try to fight him off, he will still brutally force himself inside of me. The sad reality is that after years of his abuse, I already know how to play the game to ensure I'm not left bleeding and broken when he's through with me.

My father grins as he pulls my phone from my small purse and strides up to me, using my face to unlock the screen. "Now," he says, searching through it before pressing a few buttons. "Smile for the camera, Raleigh. We're going to show the world just how much you like it."

CHAPTER 32

Ezra

My gaze shifts to the wing of the stage, hating that Rae isn't here, but I get why she needed the night to herself. That meeting was a shit show. Hell, the past two weeks have been a shit show, and considering everything, I think she's handling herself remarkably well. Though I won't lie, I'm annoyed with Dylan for catching her before she could get a chance to beat Jessica's ass. The bitch deserved it, and while watching Rae take her down would have been the highlight of my century, she needed it more than she could ever know. I might have to introduce her to a punching bag, or she could take her frustrations out on me in the form of wild, desperate sex. I have no issues there.

Rae and I, when we're together, it's fire. I always knew we'd be compatible in that way, but finally getting to taste her, to feel her, it's everything I thought it would be and more, and though I don't regret waiting, I wish we were able to get our shit together a long time ago.

Years were wasted between us. I can only imagine where we'd be now if we never lost those years. If I never left her behind, and she never suffered the horrendous abuse her father submitted her to. If Rae had been with me all these years, Ax never would have needed to go find her. He'd still be here. So many fucking harsh consequences for the decisions I made as a kid following his dream.

All of it rests on my shoulders, but I'm strong enough to bear the weight of the burden, especially if it means taking it from Rae. She's hurt for too long, suffered in a way no woman should ever have to suffer, and if carrying her burden makes it just a little easier for her to breathe, then fuck, it's not a burden at all. I'll take it from her willingly.

The seductive words of "Scarlett Rose" flow from me, and without Jessica and Stacey prancing around the stage and putting their hands all over me, it's fucking refreshing.

Firing them was the easiest decision I've ever made. Having their hands on me made me feel dirty, and I hated every fucking second of it. And now that they're gone, I can sing the song the way it was always intended—right to Rae. At least, when she's here tomorrow night.

I'm halfway through the song, and a wave of shock flows through the crowd, and I watch as one by one, the audience starts pulling out their phones, gasping, and looking up at me in horror. My brow furrows as I glance toward Dylan, who shrugs his shoulders, clearly seeing what I'm seeing.

Rock seems just as confused, and when the people in the front start holding out their phones toward me and screaming for my attention in a way they never have before, I have no choice but to cut the song short. "Okay, okay," I say into the microphone as the boys cut the music. "Can someone tell me what the fuck is going on?"

I glance toward the wing of the stage toward where a few of the backstage crew stand, and when one of them pulls out their phone and his face turns ghostly white, it's all I can take.

I throw myself off the stage, landing with a thud in front of the barricaded audience, and I step up to the person closest to me with a phone. "The fuck are you looking at?" I demand, never having cut a song short like that in my life, but I'm starting to get pissed that I don't have any answers. Don't get me wrong, the second I figure out what's happening, we'll be right back on stage, starting the song again.

The dude holds his phone out toward me, and I turn it to face me, expecting to see a terrible natural disaster or some kind of political announcement that will severely affect the whole globe, but instead, I'm faced with a live video of Rae on her social media account.

"The fuck?"

I take her in, finding her naked on the very hotel bed we shared last night, and my heart immediately starts to race. Something feels very off about this. I shake my head, wondering what the fuck is happening when I notice her hands aren't just behind her back, they're bound by rope.

Fear rockets through my chest when another figure steps into the camera, and horrified gasps fill the stadium. I hear cries around me, but I'm too focused to look up as the man in the room moves toward the camera and bends low to be seen. And when his face finally comes into view, the deepest rage explodes in my chest.

"She'll always be mine," he says into the camera, and somehow, I know it's a direct message to me. "You ruined my little girl, and now I'm going to ruin her for you."

He walks over to her, grabs her thigh, and yanks her down the bed, positioning her in a way that every last person watching the stream can see directly between her legs. "You see that?" Michael Stone says, glancing over his shoulder to look directly at the camera. "You'll never touch this filthy little whore again. She's all mine."

He smacks her so hard, I hear it through the phone. "SCREAM FOR ME," he roars at her, gripping her hair and yanking her back so hard it looks as though her spine could snap. "FUCKING SCREAM FOR ME, WHORE."

Horror blasts through my chest, and when he reaches for the front of his pants, I can't take it another fucking second.

I take off, launching myself back up onto the stage, passing Rock and Dylan who both look at their phones, absolutely horrified. My feet pound against the stage, and as I sprint by Lenny and the other executives, none of them have a damn clue what's going on.

"The fuck do you think you're doing?" Lenny roars at my back. "Get back out there and finish the goddamn show."

My gaze drops to the stranger's phone still in my hand at the same moment Rae's father grabs her face and shoves it into the mattress, ignoring her cries as she tries to fight him off, and not a moment later, he brutally slams inside of her.

I feel fucking sick, knowing I'm already too late, knowing that no matter how many times I vowed that he would never hurt her again, I'm reduced to nothing but a liar.

I was supposed to protect her. I was supposed to keep her safe.

Her cries and desperate pleas come through the phone, and every last one of them sends me hurtling through the backstage area faster. I leap over sound equipment and knock over the row of spare guitars waiting on standby.

Hold on, baby. I'm coming for you. And this time, I'll make sure the bastard never touches you again.

Breaking out through the back, I find three of my security guards already waiting by a car. "Get in," my head of security, Hardin, says.

I dive through the open car door, the stranger's phone clutched tightly in my hand, and as the door closes behind me and the noise of the stadium is blocked out, Rae's cries through the speakers seem so much louder.

Her father grunts while raping my woman, taking from her like he took all those years ago, night after night, as though he was entitled to her body. She cries out in pain, and as Hardin hits the gas, I can't help but scream toward him. "GO. GO. GO."

He flies through the traffic surrounding the stadium, pushing the car as fast as it'll go while expertly dodging the other cars on the road. "Your room key," Hardin says, handing me the copy of the key he has, knowing damn well I left mine back in the dressing room.

I take it from him with shaking hands, my jaw clenched. "I need to do this alone," I tell the three guards surrounding me, having been with them long enough to know they will attempt to come with me and handle this themselves.

"Ezra—" Hardin starts.

"No," I cut him off. "He's been hurting her too long. I was the one who left her to endure his abuse, and I'll be the one to make it right. I go alone."

They all look uncomfortable, but none of them try to argue. They know what I'm capable of. They're the ones who trained me to be ready for situations out of my control, the times when crazy stalkers make their way into my home or get too close on the street, but I'm sure as fuck this situation hadn't crossed their mind during that particular training. Regardless of what their intentions had been, they know that when it comes to Raleigh Stone, there's not a damn thing I wouldn't do to protect her.

My gaze remains locked on the phone, fueling my rage. If she has to endure it, then I can be man enough to take it all in. I need to know the pain he puts her through. I need to feel it right in my chest. I need to know the extent of the horror he put her through for those two years before leaving for college. I need to know exactly what it is I left her to, and seeing it like this is the most gut-wrenching agony I've ever felt. But I know that what she's going through right now is a million times worse.

I'm coming, baby. I'm coming.

"See that?" Michael Stone says, his vile tone filling the car, as he grabs her hair and forces her up to look directly into the camera. "Now the whole fucking world knows what a filthy little whore you are. Your special little guy will never touch you again, not after I'm through with you. I'm going to ruin you." He reaches down and violently shoves his dry fingers into her ass, and as she cries out in agony, my stomach coils, the rage reaching new heights.

Rae looks away, and the shame in her eyes fucking guts me.

"And when I'm done with this overused cunt," Michael continues. "I'm going to destroy this too."

How fucking dare he touch her like that.

I'm going to enjoy ending his miserable fucking life.

The live stream cuts out just as we pull up to the hotel, and I can only assume the video was mass reported, which also means it won't be long until the cops show up to handle it. "You've got 5 minutes," Hardin says, reaching back over the center console again, this time with a gun in his hand, "and then we're kicking in the fucking door. Got it?"

I nod just as the car finally comes to a screeching halt, and before he can even give me the rundown on how to best handle this, the gun is in my hand, and I'm racing out of the car and into the lobby of the hotel.

The staff try to greet me and give me their usual VIP bullshit, not having a fucking clue that they let my girl's rapist into their hotel. Bet they were responsible for giving him her floor and room number, too.

Reaching the elevator, I impatiently wait for the door to open, and the moment it does, I fly into it and slam my fist down over the button for our floor. As it closes, I watch my security team flood the lobby, their eyes wide open and hands already hovering over their guns.

The elevator moves too fucking slowly, and I consider sprinting up the stairs, but I need to preserve my energy for what I have in store for him.

Precious seconds tick by.

Level one.

Level four.

Eight.

Twelve.

Nineteen.

And then finally, the button lights up. Level twenty-two. The elevator dings, and before the doors have even opened the whole way, I'm sprinting through the long hallway, one hand clutching the gun, the other grasping the room key.

I reach room 2201 in seconds, and as I hear Rae's cries from the other side, I quickly swipe the keycard against the lock, turn the handle, and shove my shoulder into the heavy door.

Rae's piercing scream sounds through the room and I race in just in time to see Michael tear away from Rae, his eyes wide as though he hadn't anticipated anyone coming to save her.

I hold the gun up, realizing too fucking late there's a knife gripped in his hand, one I couldn't see from the angle of the video. My gaze quickly sweeps the room, noticing Rae's phone propped against the dresser in front of the bed, the screen dark. I'm sure the asshole probably thinks it's still recording.

"Get the fuck away from her," I growl as he lazily puts his dick back inside his jeans.

"Ezra," Rae panics, her eyes filled with horror, and with her father off her, she scrambles away from him, doing the best she can without the use of her hands. "I . . . I—"

"It's okay, baby. I've got you. He won't ever hurt you again."

"It's you," she cries. "He said he was going to hurt you."

Michael laughs, looking at me as though I was the sixteen-year-old kid he met eleven years ago. "Whatcha gonna do with that, tough guy?" he says, his grip tightening on the knife. "You don't have the fucking balls to shoot me."

"You don't have a fucking clue what I'm willing to do to you," I say, slowly stalking him through the room, putting myself between him and Rae. "I know it all, Michael. I know the hell you put her through, the vile things you've done to her, but your time is up. I'm going to make you regret ever touching her. It's fucking over for you."

Rae shakily gets to her feet and moves in close behind me, my body acting as a shield, and I can't help but notice the blood smeared between her thighs.

Michael scoffs and peers at Rae over my shoulder, and when his grip tightens on the knife and he lifts it behind his head, preparing to launch it across the room, I squeeze the trigger.

BANG!

Rae screams behind me as Michael goes down, roaring in agony as blood splatters against the far wall of the room from the bullet wound directly in the center of his knee. "AHHH FUCK," he growls, clenching his jaw as he tries to take the pain.

I stride toward him, rage storming through me like a fucking tornado, and as he flails on the floor, I can't help but notice how fucking pathetic he looks. My boot grinds down over his wrist, forcing him to release his hold on the knife.

"I'll fucking kill you for this," he spits, but all I can do is laugh.

"Considering you won't be leaving this room alive, I highly doubt that," I say before glancing back at Rae, and despite how much I want to end his life, I'm not the one who was forced to endure his abuse. If anyone deserves to be the one to take his life, it's Rae. "It's your call, Rae. Do you want to do this, or shall I?"

My gun remains aimed right between his eyes, and now that we've established I'm more than prepared to pull the trigger, Michael doesn't take his eyes off me as Rae rushes around behind me, keeping as close as possible. She turns and offers me her wrists, and I reach for the rope that keeps them bound with my free hand.

I quickly free her, and as she brings her hands to her chest, I can't help but notice the way the rope has cut into her beautiful skin. Anger swells in my chest, and I push harder against his wrists, feeling the bones crushing beneath my boot.

Rae grabs one of my shirts and pulls it over her head, and the moment she's clothed, I see a wave of determination flash in her eyes, and with that, I have my answer. She'll be taking control from here on out.

A grin pulls at my lips as she meets my eyes. "There's my girl," I murmur before pointing to the knife laying far too close to her father's hand. "I bet you'd have the time of your life with that."

She grins right back at me. It's nothing like the usual grin I get from her every time she looks at me; this one is different. It's broken and sad, while also filled with a wickedness that makes my gut twist. But if this is what she needs, I'm more than happy to give it to her.

Realizing there's no longer just one threat in the room, Michael glances at his daughter, and as she strides toward him and scoops the blade off the ground, his eyes widen. "Wha . . . What are you going to do to me?" he demands, suddenly no longer seeing her as the timid child he abused for years. She's a woman with a score to settle, and he can see it in her eyes, she won't stop until justice has been served. "I'll fucking kill you, girl."

Rae goes on her merry way, twisting the knife in her hand as though it's always belonged there. "Two years you violated me," she says, spitting the words like they're poison on her tongue. "I was terrified, night after night, hiding in my closet, shaking with fear. You held me down and tore through my virginity, crushed my bones, and slammed my face into the ground. You were dead to me a long time ago, father. I was more than happy to try and leave the past in the past, to move on with my life the best way I could, but you just had to try and prove some sick point, but you failed to realize that I am not the same little girl you destroyed. I'm a woman now, and I have far too much to lose to allow you to come in here and steal it like a thief in the night. Don't be fooled father, you will not leave here alive, even if it means I have to spend the rest of my life rotting behind bars."

Rae starts to circle him as he bleeds on the ground, her finger resting against the tip of the blade, trying to figure out her game plan.

"I won't miss you," she says. "I won't mourn you. I won't grieve.

I won't even care, but you can fucking bet that I'll stand right here in Ezra's arms and watch the life fade out of your eyes, and I'll be happy because, for the first time in eight years, I'll truly be free."

As if trying to catch me off guard, Michael lunges for Rae, but I squeeze the trigger again.

BANG! BANG!

One bullet through the hip, the other a direct hit through the ribs and lung.

He gasps for air, and while he's already beginning to bleed out, at least he won't be able to move when Rae takes her sweet revenge. "Go for it, baby. Make Axel proud."

A fond smile pulls at her lips, and as she looks down at her father, she flips the knife in her hand, catches the hilt in a firm grip, and with a battle cry, she slams it down with everything she has, castrating her father in one easy strike.

Michael screams as Rae tears the knife out of him and stumbles back until the backs of her knees hit the bed. "Holy fuck." She blinks in disbelief, but that determination returns, and she springs toward him again, clenching her jaw, and like the perfect little maniac I've always known she could be, she gets the justice she's owed.

The blade plunges deep into Michael's chest, over and over as she releases years of fear and finds justice for the sweet girl he destroyed night after night. She sobs as the blade comes down, letting all the rage fly free, and even after he's long gone, she keeps going, desperately needing to get it out of her system until she physically can't keep going and sags to the ground.

Rae looks up at me, and while there's a newfound freedom in her eyes, there's also a deep strain, and I don't hesitate to go to her. I toss the gun aside, ignoring every safety rule Hardin ever drilled into me in my desperation to get to my girl.

I scoop her off the ground, taking her away from her father's corpse to where she can't see it. I hold her to my chest, and we both crumble to the ground. I keep her locked in my arms as her tears run their course. "You're okay, baby," I murmur into the silence of the room. "He won't ever hurt you again. He's gone."

She sobs on my shoulder, and I gently rock her back and forth as my hand roams over her back. "He took me right back to that house. I felt like that terrified little girl again. And then . . . He recorded me like I was some kind of sideshow. I've never felt so humiliated and ashamed. Nobody will ever be able to look at me again without seeing what he did to me, without thinking I'm dirty."

"I promise you, Rae. Nobody will ever think that," I tell her, hearing the familiar sound of sirens in the distance. "They'll know you're a survivor. They'll know that you didn't allow him to destroy you, and what's more, they'll find hope in your strength. You're beautiful, Rae. You're a fighter, and he did not destroy you. He didn't ruin you, and he sure as fuck didn't make me think any less of you. You're the strongest woman I know, and thanks to your determination and strength, he will never be able to hurt you ever again."

Rae buries her face into my chest. "I thought he was going to kill you," she cries. "He said if I put up a fight, that knife was going to be for you."

"Don't worry about me, baby. As long as you're still breathing, nothing could ever take me away. Not a knife, not a bullet, not even your deadly wit. You're stuck with me, Raleigh Stone. I'm not going anywhere."

My lips press to her temple, lingering there as I hold her with everything I have, and even when my security team finally barges through the door, I refuse to let go.

Hardin takes the gun off the bed, and it doesn't go unnoticed when he wipes my fingerprints off it before doing the same with the knife. He takes one final look around the room before walking around the edge of the bed and kneeling down. "Okay," he says, his sharp gaze flicking between mine and Rae's. "This is what's going to happen . . ."

An hour later, I stand under the shower in Dylan's hotel room with Rae tucked tightly in my arms, her face pressed against my chest. We've spent the last hour giving our statements, saying exactly what Hardin told us to say to be able to claim self-defense, and with the live stream of Rae being raped, it wasn't long before the cops were satisfied with what we had to say.

"I killed him," Rae whispers into the silence of the bathroom. "I killed a man. I didn't realize I could be a monster like that. What I did—"

"You didn't kill him. I took the shot, that's on me. You don't have to bear the burden of that. The shot through his ribs is what killed him. What you did . . . That was demanding justice and taking what you were owed. You're not a monster, Rae, and what you did wasn't anything you should be ashamed or fearful of. You did what you had to do, what so many other women who've been in your position wish they got the chance to do."

"I stabbed him, Ezra. I took that knife and castrated him, and I lost control. I don't even know how many times I stabbed him."

It was twelve. I counted every last one of them, but it's not something I think she needs to be aware of, not yet anyway. I'm sure she'll eventually find out though. There'll be all sorts of documentation to go along with this, and I'm sure this is only the beginning of the investigation. We'll be questioned until we're blue in the face, but for now, I'm just glad they're happy to give Rae a moment of peace to come to terms with everything that just went down.

"It's okay. We all lose control. It doesn't make us any less human."

"How can you be okay with this? How can you stand here and hold me and tell me I'm not a monster? What if I lose control around you? What if we get into a fight one day and there's a knife on the kitchen counter? You should be terrified of me."

"Are you terrified of me?" I ask as my fingers trail up and down her spine.

"No," she says, pulling back and looking up at me with furrowed brows. "Why would you ask me that?"

"I shot your father point blank. Three times. His knee, hip, and ribs. I took the shot that ensured he bled out. Do you fear that one day I might lose control, grab a gun, and decide to shoot you?"

"No, of course not."

"Exactly. It's the same for me, Rae," I tell her. "I could never fear you for what happened here tonight in the same way you could never fear me. You took back everything he stole from you, and you did it in a way that made me so damn proud of you. He died knowing you won, and there's nothing that can take that away. You were a warrior today. You fought hard, and you won."

More tears spill from her eyes, and she squishes her face harder against my chest. "You really think so?"

"I know so," I murmur. "I love you, Rae. I would let this whole world burn just to see you smile, and today, you fucking shone as bright as the sun. You might not feel it now, and it might take a little while for you to feel okay again, but just know that I will be right here, always ready to catch you when you fall. I'm not going anywhere, Rae."

Raleigh lifts her chin, squinting as the water ricochets off my chest and against her face. "You really love me that much?"

"Do you even need to question it at this point?"

A soft smile pulls at the corners of her lips. "Not even a little bit."

CHAPTER 33

Raleigh

4 MONTHS LATER

The crowd roars as Demon's Curse makes their grand entrance for the final show of the Bleed For Me tour, and I cheer along with them, never so excited. It's almost bittersweet to see it come to an end, but I'm also pumped for everything the boys still want to achieve.

Ezra has been writing like crazy, and I know he's itching to get into the studio and finally lay down some new songs, but I have it on good authority that the eager fans won't have to wait too long. It's been far too long since they put out a new album, and sure, it has everything to do with losing Axel, so they can be forgiven, but since allowing ourselves the time to heal, the grief isn't as crippling as it once was. It'll never completely go away, and we will always ache on the inside, but now we're looking forward to all the new experiences and adventures Demon's Curse gets to have. Not to mention, it's mine and Ezra's chance to be a real couple, away from the limelight. Well, as much as Ezra can ever be, which isn't much, but it still counts. We get to experience life together like normal human beings, build a home together, and fill it with love, and nothing has ever made me so happy.

Being the last show, Madds and I stand among the crowd instead of in the wings like I usually do, wanting to experience the show the way it was meant to be, which is only made better by the fact that after being back in Ezra's life for five months, I finally know the lyrics almost better than he does.

We've been here in Switzerland for almost a week, and it's been incredible. I've always wanted to come here, and I'm so grateful to Lenny and Louder Records for bringing me along on this tour and allowing me the chance to experience the world in a way I never would have been able to from the back of my car.

Dylan, Rock, and Jett do their thing as they start the intro for the first song on the setlist, and I clutch Madds tighter, never having been so excited in my life. I know exactly how Ezra is about to shoot out of the stage. I know how he will hold himself in the air for the two seconds that he's airborne, and I know the exact stance he'll take as he lands directly in the center of the stage, yet my stomach gets butterflies every time. It's one thing getting to be with Ezra, but it's another getting to experience him as Ezra Knight, the biggest rockstar on the planet.

Dylan finds us in the crowd, and considering we're front and center, it shouldn't have been too hard for him, and when he winks at Madds, she all but combusts next to me. The two of them are doing my head in. I shouldn't have encouraged it so hard, but there's no denying how perfect they are. They're rocking the honeymoon stage, and while I love how in love they are, having to hear Madds recap their sexcapades makes me want to throw up. She's not shy about the details either. Though I have to give credit where credit is due, Dylan clearly knows his way around the female body. Maybe it's a guitarist thing. They're all good with their fingers.

Madds squeals from beside me, and as Dylan grins back at her, she grips the bottom of her shirt and rips it up, letting her tits fly free. Dylan's grin all but splits his face in half, and judging by the look on his face, he's probably wondering just how soon he can shove his face between them.

I can't help but laugh. I hope Ezra isn't hoping for the same kind of show. Though, what difference does it make? After my father decided to live stream me in that hotel room, the whole world is intimately familiar with my tits. Not to mention, the video has been uploaded across the dark web and onto random porn sites. Ezra's lawyers have been working overtime trying to scrub it from the internet, but no matter how hard they try, it seems I can't escape it.

Shit. Too soon.

The reminder has my mood plummeting. I've been struggling a lot since that night. There's no sugarcoating it; I'm a wreck, but I've been doing therapy, and so far, it seems to be working wonders. I still have a long way to go until I'm even remotely close to being okay, but just as Ezra promised, he's been at my side every step of the way. And truth be told, I feel most at ease when I'm lying in his arms at the end of a long night.

He's been my rock through everything, and I can't wait for it to be over. Even in his death, my father is still haunting me. I can't escape him. It's been one thing after another.

I've had detectives bombarding both Ezra and me about his death. I've had the media asking me to sell my story, offering me millions of dollars with the condition that I give every sordid detail about the abuse I'd suffered at my father's hand. I've been offered tell-all book deals and movie rights.

On top of all that, there's the case of the missing inheritance.

Well, it's not so missing anymore. My father was found guilty of inheritance theft, not that he's actually here to be charged with it, and considering everything, the courts were quick to rule that everything Axel left for me was returned as it should have always been. Only, over the past two years, my father did a great job at spending as much of Axel's wealth as he possibly could, drinking it away like the foul, pathetic loser he was. However, the money will soon be returned to me after the sale of the old Michigan home goes through.

As the sole living relative, the house became mine after my father's death, but I wanted nothing to do with it, and despite the good memories I had of my mother and the boys, I was all too willing to say goodbye to it and welcome a new beginning away from that part of my life.

Thank God for therapy, right? But also, thank God for the money

Axel left me because, with all these therapy bills, I'm going to be blowing through it in no time.

The tempo starts to rise, and I jump up and down like the rest of the crazed fans in the crowd, recognizing Ezra's cue, and like lightning, he shoots up into the sky with fireworks exploding around him. The label took no shortcuts tonight, wanting this show to be the best one they've ever put on, and despite Ezra only having been on stage for a mere moment, they're already exceeding all expectations.

Ezra lands in a low crouch, his gaze flicking right to mine as though the tether between us is calling him to me. He grins, and his eyes sparkle with wicked desire, warning me that the moment he's done here, he intends to take me back to the hotel suite and spend the rest of our lives making me feel alive.

He takes his microphone, and the opening lyrics of "Hypothetically Yours" fill the stadium as the beat of the drum vibrates right through the ground and into my body. It's electrifying.

Why the hell have I been wasting the past four months watching the boys from the wing when I should have been watching them from right here?

Madds loses her mind beside me, not even having spent the last few months in close proximity to the guys has done anything to dull that crazy fangirl spirit of hers, and I love that about her. And I love it even more that Dylan isn't put off by it. He embraced her crazy, just as she embraced his.

She screams the lyrics of mine and Ezra's story beside me, clutching my hand in a death grip as I watch my man perform for his loyal fans, my heart racing a million miles an hour. When he glances down at me in the crowd and sings the most adoring words about being hypothetically mine, his eyes sparkle with the most sincere kind of love, and I've never been happier in my life.

The first few songs pass in a flurry of wild emotion, and when the heat ramps up and the boys really start enjoying themselves, Madds tugs on my arm. "Check this out," she says, holding up her phone for me to see.

My brows furrow, having to grab it to see the screen properly as Madds continues jumping around beside me, and I find the text chain between Madds and Dylan, more specifically the discreet text he just sent her while on stage.

Dylan - Quick question. If I sacrifice the moon and the stars for you, then in the very least, would you sacrifice uranus for me?

"The fuck?" I laugh, glancing up at Dylan to find his eyes locked on us, laughing as he realizes I've just seen his text. But what I love most is the way he owns it, not ashamed in the least.

Madds can't help herself. She grabs her phone back, and I watch over her shoulder as she types out her response.

Madds - Abso-freakin-lutely! But give a girl some warning. You can't just go poking around her black hole without first letting her take a ride down the big dipper and into your milky way.

She hits send, and I watch the frustration on Dylan's face knowing he has a text but not being able to check it right away. Their flirty and shamefully sexual texts are their kryptonite. It's partly how their relationship began, and with each daring text, they get crazier about one another. It's the same for how Ezra writes songs about me. It's how they communicate, and I love it for them. Hell, I also love it for me, especially when their crazy texts finally gave me the courage to open my own phone and send the kind of text to Ezra that fifteen-year-old me could have only dreamed of sending. I've never been so raunchy in my life, but I liked it, and I liked it even more when he checked the text and came running.

The show goes on, and every part of it is incredible, only just as the boys are wrapping up "One Day," Ezra brings everything to a stop. "Hold up. Hold up," he says, glancing back toward Rock and Dylan, one hand pushing through his hair, and he grabs the neck of his guitar with the other, lifting the strap over his head. "I'm sorry. I just can't do this right now."

Murmurs and shocked gasps begin filling the stadium as I watch Ezra, trying to figure out what the hell is going on. If something was wrong, surely I would have sensed it, right? He's been staring at me all night, surely I would have seen it in his eyes.

He walks over to the boys, leaving his microphone behind, and he quickly says something to them before they all nod, and not a moment later, Ezra returns to the front of the stage. "I'm sorry," he calls through the microphone. "I'm sure many of you know that these past few months have been an insane roller coaster for me, and I thought I could wait until the end of the night, but I can't. I have to do this now."

Do this now? What the fuck is he talking about?

Ezra holds my stare as the stadium erupts with questions, wondering what the hell is happening, but all I can do is stare back at him, something in his eyes warning me to never look away. "Rae, baby. Get that fine ass of yours up here."

My jaw drops. "Uhh, what?" I say, knowing damn well he can't hear me.

"Don't keep these fine people waiting," he says as the crowd starts chanting my name.

Ahh fuck, fuck, fuck. Whatever this is, I'm gonna kill him.

Hardin, the head of security, shows up in front of the barricades and offers me his hand. "Sorry, Rae. I'm gonna have to lift you over," he says, reaching for me.

He doesn't hesitate to haul me over and set me back on my feet. "Do you have any idea what the hell is going on?" I question as he leads me to the side of the stage before offering me a boost up.

"No clue, ma'am, but take it from my experience, when it comes to Ezra, it's best to just roll with it."

Shit.

Shoving my foot into his hand, Hardin boosts me up onto the stage, and just as I get two feet flat on the platform, Ezra appears at my side, slipping his hand into mine. He leads me back into the center of the stage where I feel the weight of fifty thousand eyes on me.

"Switzerland," Ezra roars through the microphone, "tell my girl how fucking beautiful she is!"

The crowd blows me away, and my cheeks flame as they scream for me. "Holy shit," I laugh as Ezra pulls me into his side. "What the hell is going on?"

All he can do is grin at me as the crowd continues, and with every passing second, the most undeniable joy swells inside my chest.

"Okay, okay," Ezra says, trying to settle them down. "Now, I don't know if you guys know this, but I've been in love with this girl since I was sixteen years old. She's the muse behind all of the songs like 'Hypothetically Yours' and 'One Day.' She's been my whole fucking world since the moment I met her, and eight years ago, I made the biggest mistake of my life by leaving her behind when we went on our first tour. I wasted all those years not getting to be by her side, and I don't know about you guys, but I'm fucking sick of waiting."

The crowd roars, clearly down with anything that comes out of Ezra's mouth, and when he turns to me, the rockstar show is over, and I'm faced with the sixteen-year-old boy who walked through my door back in Michigan and couldn't take his eyes off me. Our souls connected in such a profound way that day, a connection that's now never been stronger.

"Rae," he says, taking my hands and having to awkwardly squish the microphone between our fingers. "I have loved you since the moment I met you. I've cherished you. Adored you. And at times, I have failed you. We've had more than our fair share of challenges thrown our way, some that have tested us in ways we could never have been prepared for, and with every one of those challenges, I have loved you more.

You're my soul, my world, and my heart. We have waited so long for something we always knew was written in the stars, and I don't want to wait anymore. I want to marry you, Rae. I want to build a life with you and give you everything you've ever wanted."

Tears fill my eyes, and he clutches my hands tighter as my heart races faster than it ever has before, and just when I thought my world couldn't feel more right, Ezra lowers down onto one knee, and the stadium erupts into utter chaos.

He releases my hand, and not a moment later, he produces a small velvet box from his pocket and thumbs it open, not willing to release my other hand, and despite the insane noise around us, I can't look away.

A beautiful white gold ring stares back at me with a delicate band that's decorated with a huge rock right in the middle. Smaller diamonds circle the big one in the center and as it sparkles against the crazy lighting in the stadium, I look back up to meet Ezra's stare. "I've had this ring for the better part of four years, knowing all along that we would find our way back to each other. You captured me from day one, Rae. You tethered your soul to mine the very moment I walked through that door. You became the reason I breathe, and now I don't know how to do life without you."

He pauses for just a moment as the crazed audience cheers for their leading man.

"I don't want to wake up and not see your face staring back at me. I don't want to build a life without you, and I don't want to give my heart to any other. It's always been you, Rae. I'm done waiting, and I'm done with the hypotheticals. I want to take the plunge, and I want you to jump right off the fucking edge with me. What do you say, baby? Will you do me the greatest honor of becoming my wife?"

Tears stream down my face, and I launch myself into Ezra's arms as my lips crash down over his. "I thought you'd never ask," I tell him, feeling the intense vibration of the crowd roaring with excitement.

My lips are straight back on his, and he doesn't even get the chance to put the ring on my finger before Rock and Dylan crash into us, their big arms circling us as they squeeze the living daylights out of me. "I fucking knew you two would make it," Rock says as I cry into Ezra's shirt.

I catch Madds out of the corner of my eye, scrambling over the banister with Hardin and beelining straight to the edge of the stage, and before anyone can attempt to help her, she scales the stage like Spiderman before crashing into us too, all but peeling the boys off me before yanking me into her chest. "God, I'm so happy for you," she tells me. "I think I actually peed myself a little."

The celebrations roar right through the crowd before we're reminded that the show isn't over, and as Ezra goes to lift the microphone back to his lips, I go to make a hasty exit, only he holds on to me, refusing to let me go.

"That's not the only surprise I have for tonight," he says into the microphone as Rock and Dylan make their way back to their instruments, leaving Madds to hide in the wing where I usually spend my nights. "It's been a long time coming, but what better night to tell you that our new single, *'Not Waitin' on a Hypothetical'* will be releasing at midnight tonight."

Not Waitin' on a … Holy shit. This man!

My jaw drops, and I gape at Ezra, having had no clue that the boys had recorded something new. Hell, when did they even get the time to do it?

The crowd is far beyond chaos now. They're practically on fire with their current excitement level, and despite that, Ezra still feels the weight of my stare and glances at me, and the way his eyes shine with undeniable love and happiness has me so filled with elation, I could burst.

"So, what's it going to be?" he asks his eager audience as he keeps his eyes locked on me. "Do you wanna be the first to hear it, or what?"

They roar their excitement, and not a moment later, he pops his microphone back into the stand and pulls me into his side. Rock comes in on the drums, giving us the most captivating beat I've ever heard, but nothing, and I mean nothing, prepares me for when the lyrics begin pouring out of Ezra. They're the perfect ode to us, capturing our love in the most spectacular way possible, doing us justice in a way I could only ever dream of.

CHAPTER 34

Raleigh

Crashing through the door of the hotel room, Ezra's lips come down on mine with a hunger that sets my body alight. "God, I fucking love you," he says, as we struggle to get the door closed behind us, too impatient to have one another.

I can't help but laugh as our bodies become entwined in a frenzy of limbs as we try to tear each other's clothes off our bodies. His shirt is first to go, followed by mine, and as he pops the button on his black jeans, I reach behind me, frantically trying to unclasp my bra. Our lips are permanently fused together, his moving over mine with the kind of skill that brings me to life.

Liquid fire pulses through my veins when he reaches around me and grabs my ass, hauling me into his strong, tattooed arms. My chest crashes against his as the three pendants hanging low around his neck squish between us.

"So, you're not waiting on a hypothetical, huh?" I question, my words muffled between our lips.

I have so many questions about this. Like when did he write it? What was happening when he wrote it? Were we on good terms at that point, or were we still screaming at each other in restaurant bathrooms? Was he sitting on the floor, gently strumming his guitar while I slept? And more importantly, when the hell did he and the whole fucking band find time to record it, let alone polish it off for a surprise release at midnight?

The whole night has been a whirlwind.

It's barely been an hour since the end of the show, and the news of our engagement has already made its way across the globe. I suppose that happens when there are fifty thousand people watching and recording on their smartphones.

"Not Waitin' on a Hypothetical" is also making a splash. Though all their songs always have, but being the first release since Axel's death and having everyone use the sound when they post about our engagement, it's already soaring, and I couldn't be prouder.

The guys are killing it, but so are we.

After the show, Lenny insisted that we have a whole team celebration and party the night away, and while Ezra and I were more than on board to celebrate, we could barely make it two seconds before rushing back to the hotel to spend the night wrapped in each other's arms. But I've gotta give it to them, tonight has been an incredible night, and it's definitely worth celebrating. We wrapped the tour, got engaged mid-show, announced the surprise midnight release of a new single, and gave at least fifty thousand people an early performance of the song.

Tonight hasn't just been incredible, it's been fucking wild. Though something tells me the wild nature of the night is only just beginning.

"Mmmm, you liked that little surprise, did you?" Ezra murmurs against my lips as he strides toward the bed, my legs locked around his waist.

"That was more than just a surprise," I say. "You bamboozled me."

"Bamboozled?"

"Uh-huh," I laugh.

His lips pull into a wicked grin against mine. "I've not even begun to bamboozle you yet, Rae," he tells me, grabbing my hips and throwing me down on the bed. I crash against the mattress, looking up at him as he grabs my thighs and drags me to the edge of the bed, a thrill racing through my veins.

His jeans are still on but unbuttoned, and I see just how much his cock is straining to be released, but he ignores it as his fingers brush down my waist, sending a wave of goosebumps soaring across my skin. "You're mine, Rae," he murmurs as his fingers lower to my jeans.

The excitement is too much, and I can't figure out how to form a sentence as he pops the button of my jeans and slowly drags the denim down my thighs, taking my thong along with it. When the material hits the ground, he drags his gaze over my body before stopping at the apex of my thighs and rolling his tongue over his bottom lip, a deep hunger flashing in his eyes.

"Open for me, Rae," he rumbles through the darkened hotel room. "Let me see how ready you are."

My heart races as I bite down on my bottom lip, propping myself on my elbows as I slowly begin to spread my thighs, feeling like a fucking goddess with the kind of power that could bring a man to his knees.

"Mmmm," he groans, dropping his fingers to my knee and slowly trailing them higher and higher until there's nowhere further for them to go. I gasp as they brush against my clit, my hips jolting with wild anticipation. "You like that, baby?"

I nod, swallowing hard as I watch his every movement.

He touches me again, this time a little harder, and when a deep groan rumbles through my chest, his lips kick up into a seductive grin. "Oh yes, you do like that." His fingers remain at my core, and when they lower and brush over my opening, my walls clench with desperation. "Look how hungry you are for me."

I tilt my head back, needing to glance away for just a moment to regain just a fraction of control, but when he pushes two thick fingers inside of me, every shred of that control vanishes into thin air. "Oh fuck," I groan as he takes it slowly, rotating his fingers deep inside of me and massaging my walls from within.

It's like a fucking waterfall. I've never been so ready.

In. Out. In. Out.

He fucks me with his fingers, and with each skillful thrust, my body trembles with need. I'm already falling apart, already a fucking mess for this man. "God, Ezra. Take me," I beg.

"Patience, my sweet Rae," he murmurs. "I'll take you in good time, but not before I've had my fill of you."

He keeps tormenting me with his fingers, and as he reaches his thumb to my clit and rolls it in tight, perfect circles, I shatter like glass beneath him. My hips frantically jolt with elation as my walls spasm around his fingers, coming hard and fast as Ezra watches me through a hungry, hooded stare.

"That's my girl," he rumbles, keeping his fingers moving. "Come undone for me."

My moans fill the room, and I reach down between my legs, feeling him as his fingers slowly work my pussy, moving in and out of me, turning and twisting with skilled perfection. I'm fucking soaked for him, and the scent of my arousal is thick in the air. When I come down from my high, and he slowly pulls his fingers free, I watch as he lifts them to his mouth and sucks them clean.

"Hmmmmm," he groans as I sit up, and before I even know what's happening, his lips are on mine, his tongue sweeping into my mouth and letting me taste my arousal. "See how fucking sweet you are, baby? How could I ever resist you?"

I sit balanced on the very edge of the mattress, and when he drops to his knees before me and holds my stare, my excitement becomes too much.

Ezra pushes my thighs wider, and as his gaze sails down my body and lands directly at my core, he looks as though all his Christmases have come at once. My hand knots into the back of his hair as he lifts my thighs over his shoulders, and the movement sends me crashing back to the mattress.

"Oh God," I groan, and then his mouth is there, closing over my pussy. His tongue flicks past my sensitive clit, and my body trembles, still so worked up from my earlier orgasm. He focuses there, his tongue working me like a god as my whole body becomes his to command.

He sucks, nips, and licks, giving me pressure right where I need it, and my back arches off the bed, the intense pleasure overwhelming my system.

He reaches beneath his chin, pushing his fingers inside of me and working me harder than before as my walls clench around him. It's more than I can bear, and as my body thrashes, his other hand moves to my stomach and holds me still.

"Holy fuck," I groan, reaching down and knotting my fingers into his hair again, holding him so damn tight as his tongue rolls over my clit again and again. I gasp and rock my hips, grinding against his expert tongue, and when he curls his fingers inside of me, I cry out, my whole body jolting with raw pleasure.

"EZRA!"

He groans against my pussy, and the vibrations from his mouth do wicked things to me.

"Holy fuck," I gasp.

His fingers dive deeper, hitting that spot over and over as I start to see stars dancing in my vision. My back arches off the mattress again, this time not capable of being contained by Ezra's hold over my stomach.

That familiar coil builds inside, rapidly demanding release, and as it gets tighter and tighter, my body squirms faster. "Oh God," I pant, my fingers tightening in his hair. "Please."

I can't hold on to it a moment longer, and as he sucks my clit into his mouth and plunges his fingers deep inside of me, I come again, the intensity rocking through me like a million fireworks exploding over and over.

It pulses through my body, and I throw my head back as I cry out his name. "OH FUCK, EZRA!"

My back arches, and as the intensity grows, his hand shoots up my body, cupping my tit before slowly rolling my nipple between his skilled fingers. His tongue doesn't stop moving, doesn't stop teasing and filling me with the sweetest satisfaction.

My thighs try to close around him, but he doesn't dare move, more than willing to be suffocated between my legs rather than risking pulling away. He elicits more from me as his fingers curl and massage against my G-spot, knowing exactly how to find it, and good God, does he work me just right.

My walls shatter, wildly convulsing around his thick fingers as my hips frantically jolt. I clench my eyes, and my fingers and toes begin to curl until I can't take it anymore. It's too much. Too intense.

He keeps driving me crazy, until finally, I reach my climax, and I start coming back down. My chest heaves with each new breath, and when Ezra eases up on my clit, my whole body goes limp around him.

"That . . ." I breathe, not being able to string a full sentence together. "So good."

Ezra grins as he gets back to his feet, but the way he looks at me warns me that he's not nearly through with me yet.

His knee presses against the mattress beside my thigh as his opposite hand comes down beside my shoulder, and not a moment later, his other arm is locked around my waist, dragging me back up the mattress until my head is against the pillow. "Do you have any fucking idea how sweet you taste?" he murmurs, hovering over me.

I shake my head. "You'll have to show me."

With that, Ezra drops his lips to mine, kissing me deeply, and while any lingering taste of my arousal is long gone, I still appreciate the sentiment.

I groan into his mouth before hooking my leg over his hip, using it to roll us over, and giving me control. "You know," I murmur, hovering over him. "I bet I don't taste nearly half as good as you do."

His brow arches, and as a wicked grin stretches across my lips, I crawl down his sculpted body, the anticipation of taking him in my mouth giving me all the energy in the world.

Reaching his waist, I shimmy his jeans down just enough to release his straining cock, and the moment I curl my hand around his thick base and take in the piercing at his tip and those angry veins, my mouth starts to water.

Glancing up, I meet Ezra's stare, and I love how focused he is. His gaze is hooded, and as I lean closer toward his tip and my tongue darts out over my bottom lip, his breath catches in his throat.

God, I love that I have this effect on him.

A thrill shoots through me, and I put on my best performance, letting my tongue do the work just as his did. Starting from the tip, I roll my tongue over his piercing before slowly trailing it down the length of his huge cock and back up, then as I reach the top, I close my mouth over him and get to work.

Balancing on my knees, I use both hands, working him the way I know he likes it—one hand moving up and down, following the movements of my mouth, and the other squeezing at his base. My tongue doesn't stop roaming, exploring every inch of him, and as I feel him right at the back of my throat, his deep groan rumbles through the room.

I take him further, pushing myself to my limits and testing my gag reflexes, and when his hand knots into my hair, and his hips jolt with need, I know I've got him right where I want him. "Fuck, baby. Just like that."

I don't dare stop, feeling as my pussy throbs with need, desperate to ride him and feel the way my walls stretch around him. God, I need to take him deep, hard, fast, and wild.

My cheeks hollow out as I suck, and when I roll my tongue over his piercing again, his grip tightens in my hair, pulling me back. "Fuck, Rae. If you keep going like that, this'll end right here, and I'm not nearly through with you."

I wipe my thumb across my bottom lip, never so crazed in my life, and as I sit up, I keep my other hand moving, slowly taking him up and down as my thumb rolls over his tip. "Oh really?" I ask, slightly disappointed that I didn't get to finish him off, but we have our whole lives for that.

Ezra reaches for me again, and I shake my head. "Uh-uh," I say, crawling back up his body and straddling his waist. "You had your turn to make me come, and now it's my turn, and I intend to take my time."

His brows arch, and I don't hesitate, gripping that thick cock before rising up on my knees and guiding him to my entrance. Then as I feel him right where I want him, I grasp the headboard and slowly lower myself down.

My body trembles as I take him inch by inch, feeling the way my walls stretch around his impressive size. I've never felt so full. "Baby," he groans, grasping my hips, and at the sound of his strained voice, everything clenches. He sucks in a short breath. "You're fucking killing me."

A wicked grin stretches across my face as I drop the rest of the way, bottoming out and taking all he has to offer, I circle my hips and watch as he falls apart.

"Rae," he warns, having to grip my hips tighter and hold me still. "If you're not going to play fair, I'll have no choice but to flip you over and take that pretty ass."

I circle my hips again. "You wouldn't dare," I challenge, knowing damn well he would.

His cock flinches within me, and seeing he's at the end of his patience, I give him what he needs, rising to my knees until I feel his tip right at my entrance before dropping back down. My pussy clenches around him as my eyes roll with pure satisfaction, and I can't help but do it again.

"Oh God," I groan, dropping one of my hands to his strong chest. "That's right, baby. Take it all."

I pick up my pace, riding him like a fucking cowgirl, and just because I can't help myself, I circle my hips at the same time, grinding against his pelvis while bouncing up and down his cock. I take him all, and as he thrusts his hips, I cry out with intense pleasure.

"Fuck," I pant, my pussy already trembling. "I can't. I'm going to—"

He doesn't even wait for me to finish my sentence before grabbing me and shoving me down on the mattress, my knees up under me with my ass high in the air. Ezra quickly positions himself behind me, and without skipping a beat, he slams into my needy cunt from behind, his hand still gripping my hip.

I push back against him, taking him so much deeper as I arch my back, offering him all of me. "Show me how you play with that sweet little clit, Rae," he grunts between thrusts.

I don't hesitate, shooting my hand between my spread thighs and rolling my fingers over my sensitive clit, and the moment I do, my hips jolt with intense satisfaction.

Ezra's fingers drop to my cunt, mixing with my arousal before trailing them to my ass, and as he fucks me like a god, he presses his fingers against my hole, giving just enough pressure to drive me wild. "Oh God," I groan, pushing back against him, letting him take me however he wants as long as it always feels this good.

"Take it, Rae," he grits through a clenched jaw. "Let me feel you take it."

My body trembles, and as I push back further and that thick cock pushes me to my absolute limits, I can't hold on to it a second longer.

I come hard, my walls shattering as my third orgasm for the night tears through me, sending me on a blinding high as I cry out in elation. "Oh God, YES!" I struggle to catch my breath, but I don't even care. All that matters is the way he takes me higher, forcing my orgasm to reach a new level of intensity as he fucks me from behind and presses against my ass.

My walls erratically convulse around him, and as he groans, I know he feels just how tight I squeeze him. "Come for me, Ezra," I breathe as my fingers bunch into the sheets. "I need to feel the way you fill me."

His fingers tighten on my hips in a bruising hold, and I fucking love it, and as he rolls his hips and takes long, deep thrusts, he comes undone, shooting his hot cum deep inside my needy cunt. He's fucking everything, and as he groans with his release, I've never felt so fucking beautiful.

"Fuuuuck, baby," he groans low, easing up on me and slowing his movements as I begin to come down from my high.

My body relaxes, and my pussy eases up on the death grip it has around his thick cock, and as he hovers behind me, he releases my hip and trails his fingers up and down my spine, neither one of us willing to move quite so soon.

"If we never leave this hotel room, and I die living inside your sweet little cunt, I'll be the happiest man who ever lived."

I can't help but laugh as my face is squished into the mattress, but

I don't have the energy to do anything about it. "You should be the happiest man, regardless," I tease. "You're marrying me, aren't you?"

Ezra laughs, and within an instant, his arms are locked around my waist, and he crashes down to the bed before pulling me on top of him. "Yes, Rae," he tells me a moment later. "I am marrying you, and you bet that sweet ass of yours that it will make me the happiest man who ever lived. Being with you again . . . fuck, baby. I'm never going to let you get away again. Even if it means permanently attaching that sweet little cunt to my cock."

"Permanently attaching, huh?" My brow arches. "Who would have known you had such a kinky side?"

"Raleigh Stone," he rumbles, his gaze darkening with a wicked desire that has my heart starting to race all over again. "You've got no fucking idea."

"Is that so?" I question, rolling my tongue over my bottom lip as he holds my stare.

"Mm-hmm."

"Then what are you waiting for?" I challenge, hooking my thigh back over his hip to straddle him. "Give me your worst."

EPILOGUE

Raleigh

2 YEARS LATER

There's no doubt about it, getting to be the woman Ezra comes home to every single night is the greatest feeling in the world, but second to that, is this right here. Getting to stand in the wing of the stage, holding our daughter as Demon's Curse prepares to take the stage for their biggest tour yet.

It's opening night, and it's the wildest feeling in the world. The whole atmosphere is vibing tonight. I thought the Bleed For Me tour was insane, but turns out, I didn't even understand the meaning of insane.

The last tour was made up of songs that came from a place of brokenness and despair. They were about regrets and needing to make things right. But this tour, the songs are about raw, unadulterated passion. They're about love, family, and commitment. And of course, it wouldn't be Ezra if there wasn't a song about getting head under the table at his wedding reception . . . Which may or may not have an element of truth to it.

It took all of two weeks after returning from Switzerland for Ezra to officially make me his wife. And a little over a month later, our sweet little girl was on the way.

Alexia Rose Knight came bursting into the world three weeks early after putting me through my paces with an emergency c-section, and from the moment she opened her big blue eyes, she was wrapped around her daddy's little finger.

Ezra has millions of crazy fans across the globe, but not one of them adores him as much as this sweet baby girl does. I swear, the two of them are like two peas in a pod. She'll be able to play guitar before she can even talk. Actually, she reminds me a lot of Axel in that way. Ezra always jokes that she's Axel reincarnated. Everything she does has his mannerisms mixed in with a bunch of Ezra's, and every day that she looks up at me and gives me that big toothy grin, it makes me miss my brother more.

He never got the chance to meet her, and I always find myself wondering if the boys had never left me behind, would Ezra and I have started having children sooner? Would there have been a chance that Axel could have met my little girl? Could she have had the chance to know how incredible her uncle was?

All these questions have dwelled in my mind, and they're generally a guaranteed way for my mood to plummet to ground zero. But not tonight. Tonight is too big to allow my mind to take a deep dive into the *what ifs* and *should have beens*.

As the crowd cheers for the upcoming show, I fix Alexia's noise-canceling headphones over her ears. These things are a gift from the heavens, but not even they are capable of completely blocking out the insanity that surrounds us.

The lights begin to darken, and Alexia squeals with excitement. We've been preparing her for tonight for the past few weeks, warning her just how loud and big it's going to be, but this kid isn't afraid of anything. She couldn't be more excited.

Madds steps in from behind me, making sure to make a big deal about Alexia before cradling her swollen stomach. It won't be long, and Alexia's new favorite person will be here. I can just see them now, best friends until the end of time. Just like me and the candle-obsessed sideshow beside me.

Dylan and Madds have been going strong since the day of the accidental sex tape discovery, and when Dylan came to me last night and let me know he was planning to propose after the opening show, I couldn't be more excited. Until he had to ruin it by telling me how he plans on doing it, and apparently, no amount of arguing will get him to change his mind about tying the ring to a piece of string, and then tying the other end of said string to his dick. So when she goes down on him after the show, he can pop the question, while also popping a stiffy in true Dylan Pope style. Though to be honest, I think Madds wouldn't have it any other way, but the day their grandchildren come asking about how Poppa asked Nana to marry him, I'd kill to be a fly on the wall.

The lights fade until it's almost pitch black in the massive stadium, and with almost ninety thousand people cheering for the boys, the atmosphere is simply wild. Then, like a flash of lightning, Rock slams down on the drums and my eyes widen, having no idea how the fuck he just appeared on stage.

A spotlight shines over him as he gives the best damn intro I've ever heard, his drums working overtime tonight, and then a second spotlight illuminates Dylan closest to us, and Madds screams along with the other ninety thousand people. "I LOVE YOU, YOU HORNY RAT BASTARD!"

As if hearing her, which is impossible in this stadium, Dylan looks at Madds, and his already beaming smile lights up like Christmas morning.

Next up is Jett, and just like Dylan, the spotlight beams over him, once again blowing me away. I mean, shit. How the hell are they appearing like this? Maybe I should have paid closer attention during rehearsals. Jett launches into an incredible riff, and as I feel his chords vibrate through my chest, I know Axel would be proud. It took me a minute, but I've finally decided that Jett has more than earned his position in the band, but I hold my stance that he's not a replacement for Axel; he's just another member.

Their intro is already crazy when everything goes silent.

The crowd stops screaming, wondering what the hell is going on, when Ezra's hypnotic voice sounds through the massive speakers, singing the first line of "Not Waitin' on a Hypothetical."

"Eight years runnin', baby. I'm coming home to you."

The crowd loses their shit as the stadium falls into silence again, and Alexia almost loses her tiny mind, recognizing her daddy's voice anywhere.

People frantically search the massive stadium, trying to figure out where Ezra's hiding, but the drums start again, this time picking up the tempo and making everyone go crazy. Then just like before, it falls to silence, and Ezra sings another line.

"Take my cold dead heart, baby. Make it something new."

Rock hits the drums with such force, I feel his intoxicating beat rattle through my chest, and this time, he doesn't let up when Ezra repeats the lyrics, a deep passion in his tone.

"Eight years runnin', baby. I'm coming home to you."

"Take my cold dead heart, baby. Make it something new."

As the heat kicks up and the tempo rises, everyone knows it's coming and can hardly contain themselves. And then finally, the crowd goes wild as the border of the stage lights up with fire, and right there in the center, with lights beaming up around him, is my man gripping the neck of Axel's favorite electric guitar.

Everyone loses their shit, screaming for the man that rocks my world every single day, and I couldn't be prouder.

He doesn't move an inch, just stands with a wide stance, one hand on the guitar, the other simply dangling by his side, clutching his microphone, and it's more than enough to make at least five girls in the front row collapse.

Alexia goes apeshit in my arms until I'm forced to put her down, and with her tiny little feet planted on the ground, she jumps up and down and tests her limits when she tries to make her debut appearance on the stage. Though while the label probably won't be too thrilled about it, I know Ezra will love it.

Then ever so slowly, he lifts the microphone—moving his arm out wide in the process—and tilts his chin to the sky as the anticipation rocks through the crowd. Then as if on cue, all of the guys start playing, and the show starts with a bang.

"Holy fucking shit," a voice calls from beside Madds. "This is insane."

I glance around her, not realizing anyone was there, and find Rock's girlfriend, Tiffany, with a wide grin stretched across her face.

"Oh, you've got no idea," Madds tells her, knowing all too well that this is her first Demon's Curse concert.

Rock and Tiffany haven't been together long, a few months perhaps, and so far, it seems to be going great. She's not a fangirl, which is exactly what he needs. She's more of a shy, country-music type, but when Carrie Underwood comes on with that "Before He Cheats" banger, she breaks right out of her shell. It's amazing. I have a good feeling about them, and I hope for Rock's sake, that she makes him just as happy as Ezra makes me.

I'm completely mesmerized by the show, and despite it being a little over two and a half hours, the seconds tick by all too soon. Before I know it, the boys are wrapping up their opening night, and Ezra crashes into me backstage, his arms scooping right around both me and our sleeping daughter.

His lips come down on mine before I even have a chance to tell him how incredible he was. I feel the adrenaline radiating off him, and it's like a drug, infecting the very souls of everyone within his reach. The rush is intoxicating, and I need so much more of it. I'm completely and utterly addicted.

"Fuck, baby," he groans against my lips. "That was incredible."

"You were incredible," I tell him.

His face drops to the curve of my neck, breathing me in as his hands tighten on my waist. "I've gotta have you."

"What the hell are you waiting for?"

His head snaps up, his gaze locking onto mine as if wondering just how serious I am, but he should know better. When it comes to being with him, I'm always serious. His gaze flicks to Alexia in my arms, hesitation flashing in his eyes, and I see the exact moment he figures out his plan.

He scoops her out of my arms before passing her sleeping form right to Madds. "Hey, what gives?" Madds questions as Ezra lunges for me, pulling me into him before hauling me into his strong arms.

"You're the one who keeps telling us we need to make Lexi a big sister. We're just following orders."

"But—"

"Following orders," he repeats as a laugh tears from the back of my throat, but he swallows the sound with his desperate kiss before plunging us into the darkness of one of the massive stage curtains, not having the time to search for a private room.

His hands are frantic, tearing at my pants as I do the same. Neither of us has the time to get completely naked, but before I know it, my back is against a wall as my husband plunges deep inside of me, both of us groaning with instant satisfaction.

"Holy fuck," I pant as he thrusts into me over and over, both of us chasing the high of the show. My body trembles in his strong arms as my walls shudder around his thick cock.

"That's right, baby. Take it all."

I clutch onto his big shoulders, my head tipping back in ecstasy. "Oh, God. I'm gonna come."

"I'm right there with you."

My eyes widen as if realizing too late what that means. "Wait, no," I say, barely able to catch my breath. "You can't. You have to pull out."

"What? Fuck no," he says. "Besides, I'm not sure if you recall how we made Lexi, but me not pulling out is kinda an important step."

"We're going to be out all night celebrating how amazing that show was," I remind him, choosing not to comment on his *important step*. "I can't be getting around all night with your cum spreading between my thighs."

"Why the fuck not? It'll be hot," he grunts as he rolls his hips, taking me at a whole new angle and making me cry out with desperation, no longer caring if the whole crew can hear me come. "Plus, you know every time I see you squirming, I'll know it's because of me, and you know I can't resist that."

"Ezra," I groan.

He shakes his head. "I'm not pulling out, Rae. I'm going to come hard and fast in this tight little cunt, and you're going to take it all."

Goddamn. This man.

"Don't even pretend you don't want it," he continues. "You fucking hate it when I pull out. You always tighten your legs around me and pull me straight back in. You've always been so greedy for my cock."

"You're killing me," I groan, feeling myself teetering on the very edge.

"What's it gonna be, baby?" he demands through gritted teeth. "Am I pulling out or are you going to feel me between your thighs all fucking night and know that every step you take, I'll be thinking about doing it all over again?"

Fuck.

How could I ever deny this wicked man?

"I want you to come in me," I tell him as my walls begin to tremble, and my vision blurs with the intense need pulsing through me. "Oh God! Don't you dare pull out."

I throw my head back, and his lips come down on my neck, his tongue swiping over my sensitive skin. "Never," he murmurs against my skin. "Now give me what I want."

And with that, I explode in a rush of beaming color, my orgasm blasting through me like a rocket, sailing through my veins and traveling right into my fingertips. My skin is on fire as my walls wildly spasm around his thick cock. It's more than I can take, and just when I thought it couldn't get better, Ezra comes hard and fast, deep in my pussy, just like he said he would.

"Holy shit," I pant, clutching him tighter as the sweetest satisfaction pulses through my body.

Ezra slows his movement, both of us exhausted as we struggle to catch our breath. "Baby, the way your sweet pussy clenches around me . . . fuck. I'll never get enough of you."

"I don't want you to ever have enough of me," I tell him as his forehead drops to mine, breathing me in. "I want you always coming back for more."

"As long as you're breathing, Rae, I'll be right here, on my knees, begging for more," he tells me. "You're the sun in my fucking sky. I don't know how to be without you. Every fucking day is an adventure with you, a journey I can't wait to take, and every morning when I wake up and look into those big blue eyes, I fall even more in love with you. I don't know what I would have done if it had been some other guy who walked into your home all those years ago and stole you away."

I lift my chin and brush my lips across his as he holds me to his chest. "All those words just to say you love me," I whisper, closing my eyes and enjoying this moment of peace within his arms. "Who would have known you were such a softie?"

A grin pulls at my lips, and as I feel Ezra pull back, I open my eyes and can't help but laugh at the bland expression on his face. "Shut the fuck up and tell me you love me."

My eyes crinkle from the way my smile lifts my cheeks, and I lock my arms around his neck, pulling him back in. "I love you, Ezra Knight," I tell him, my lips barely a breath away from his. "I've loved you as a thirteen-year-old girl who didn't know what the hell she was getting herself into. I loved you as an obsessed teen, jealous of all the other girls who wanted you too. I loved you when I hated you. I loved you when I stood by and watched you eulogize my brother. And I've never loved you more than when you taught me how to heal. You're my world, Ezra, and no matter how many times the words I love you come out of my mouth, they can't possibly do justice for the all-consuming way I feel for you. I will love you for the rest of my life, every day more than the last, but it will never be enough. I will never get enough. A million lifetimes with you isn't even enough."

"A million lifetimes, huh?"

"A million," I confirm.

"Well shit, Raleigh Knight," he murmurs as a slow grin stretches across his lips. "Who would have known you were such a softie?"

I let out a breath and give him a hard stare. I should have known better.

"Asshole."

"Right back at ya, baby," he says, setting me back on my feet and bracing a hand against my waist until I'm balanced.

He picks up my pants, separating my thong from my jeans, and as he hands me my jeans, I watch with a slack jaw as he slips my thong into his pocket. "You know what?" he says as a mischievous grin pulls at his stupidly gorgeous face. "I don't think you'll be needing these."

The fucker slips away, and as the sound of his wicked laugh fills the backstage area, I hastily pull my jeans up my thighs. Right away, I can feel his cum spreading between my thighs, and I vow that if Ezra Knight wants to play dirty, then I will be more than happy to rise to the occasion.

And if a war of stolen thongs is what he wants, then a war is what he'll get. But he better be prepared because I plan to play dirty, and I have it on good authority that the one thing he can't resist is when I've been a bad, bad girl.

MIDNIGHT STAGE

.

THANKS FOR READING

If you enjoyed reading this book as much as I enjoyed writing it, please consider leaving an Amazon review to let me know.

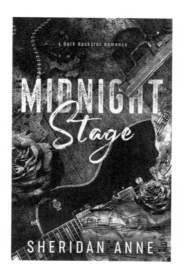

For more information on Haunted Love
find me on Facebook —

www.facebook.com/sheridansbookishbabes

SHERIDAN ANNE

STALK ME

Join me online with the rest of the stalkers!!
I swear, I don't bite. Not unless you say please!

Facebook Reader Group
www.facebook.com/SheridansBookishBabes

Facebook Page
www.facebook.com/sheridan.anne.author1

Instagram
www.instagram.com/Sheridan.Anne.Author

TikTok
www.tiktok.com/@Sheridan.Anne.Author

Subscribe to my Newsletter
https://landing.mailerlite.com/webforms/landing/a8q0y0

MORE BY SHERIDAN ANNE

www.amazon.com/Sheridan-Anne/e/B079TLXN6K

DARK ROMANCE STANDALONES

Pretty Monster (Stalker Romance) | Haunted Love (Brother's Best Friend) | Darkest Sin (Mafia) | Midnight Stage (Rockstar Romance)

DARK CONTEMPORARY ROMANCE SERIES - M/F

Broken Hill High | Haven Falls | Broken Hill Boys
Aston Creek High | Rejects Paradise | Bradford Bastard

DARK CONTEMPORARY ROMANCE - RH

Boys of Winter | Depraved Sinners | Empire

NEW ADULT SPORTS ROMANCE

Kings of Denver | Denver Royalty | Rebels Advocate

CONTEMPORARY ROMANCE

Play With Fire | Until Autumn (Happily Eva Alpha World)
The Naughty List (Christmas Standalone)

PARANORMAL ROMANCE

Slayer Academy [Pen name - Cassidy Summers]